FIRE ON THE LAKE

WILLIAM KRITLOW

THOMAS NELSON PUBLISHERS
Nashville • Atlanta • London • Vancouver

Published in Nashville, Tennessee, by Thomas Nelson, Inc., Publishers, and distributed in Canada by Word Communications, Ltd., Richmond, British Columbia, and in the United Kingdom by Word (UK), Ltd., Milton Keynes, England.

Scripture quotations are taken from the HOLY BIBLE, NEW INTERNATIONAL VERSION ®. Copyright © 1973, 1978, 1984 by International Bible Society. Used by permission of Zondervan Bible Publishing House. All rights reserved.

The "NIV" and "New International Version" trademarks are registered in the United States Patent and Trademark Office by International Bible Society. Use of either trademark requires the permission of International Bible Society.

Library of Congress Cataloging-in-Publication Data

Kritlow, William.
    Fire on the lake : a novel / Bill Kritlow.
      p. cm. — (The Lake Champlain mysteries ; bk. 2)
    ISBN 0-7852-8099-5
    I. Title. II. Series: Kritlow, William. Lake Champlain Mysteries ; bk. 2.
PS3561.R567F57   1996
813'.554—dc20
                                          95-25036
                                             CIP

Printed in the United States of America

1 2 3 4 5 6 7 - 02 01 00 99 98 97 96

To my lovely wife who's
stuck with me at great sacrifice.

PROLOGUE

From *Crimson Snow*, the previous book in the Lake Champlain Mysteries Series:

In the shadows, lighted partially by sun streaming through the back windows, stood Ginger and Mike Grogan, she in her patrolman blues, he in Joe-Friday slacks and sport coat. They were embracing, but more than that, they were kissing—hungrily and passionately.

Win would never be able to explain completely why he did what he did. Even years later when things were much clearer. He acted because the turmoil inside demanded that he act—a pressure valve, long shut tight, was being released.

Watching the two of them, his breathing became deeply erratic, the rush of oxygen pumped energy into his veins. He grabbed the back door handle, wrenched it open, and in a single stride confronted them in the kitchen.

Their embrace interrupted, they faced him, still arm in arm. At first both registered surprise, but Grogan's face quickly flushed with rage.

Ginger never got beyond shock. "Win?! Why . . . ?"

"You did it now," Grogan growled with a sound bigger than his five foot, seven inch frame.

"It's time you left," Win told him, his arm up, a finger pointing toward the front door.

A cocky smile spread across Grogan's face as he released Ginger and took a threatening step toward Win. "There are so few things I really enjoy." He smiled like a shark. "Thanks for providing one."

Win felt an immense charge surge through him. He was about to be attacked. He'd never been physically attacked before—except when his father was punishing him. He should have shrunk from it. Grogan was smaller, but he was a pro—confident, capable. But Win stood his ground, just as confident though not quite so capable. When Grogan threw a jab at Win's chin, Win caught the fist like a fastball, and held it, then squeezed it.

It was a curious feeling. Adrenaline ricocheted off his inside walls, channeling all his strength to his right hand. Not only did Win sense the bones in Grogan's fist fuse as Win squeezed powerfully, he also felt his iron fingertips fold Grogan's hand backward. The pain must have been excruciating, for Grogan's face knotted, then his knees buckled as he began to melt like hot wax. Win squeezed even harder.

But Grogan was a pro. He had his own adrenaline, and he called upon it now. He overcame the fire in his hand, and threw a desperate jab to Win's solar plexus with the other hand.

Win took the first punch, but the second and third took a heavy toll. With lungs void of air, his insides bruised, Win couldn't help but let go of Grogan's hand. When he did he received two more quick jabs, one to his chin driving his head back and one to his throat. Knowing summary execution was only a heartbeat away, but unable to prevent it, Win fell back. Now on the floor, he finally managed a breath, but his eyes opened to a black, steel hole only inches from his right eye. Grogan stood over his gun with a gleeful, nearly maniacal grin.

"Mike," Ginger cried. "No. Please, no!"

As if he'd suddenly become aware that he and Win were not the only ones in the room, Grogan glanced toward Ginger. He finally slipped the gun inside his jacket. "What's going down is too big," he mused darkly. He took a step toward Ginger, rubbing the hand Win had mashed. "It might've been fun," he said and headed for the front door.

Ginger's jaw dropped. "It might've been fun! What's that mean? It might've been . . . come back here. Come back here!" She stamped an angry foot. "What's that mean?"

Grogan didn't come back.

Betty Harmon hated her name—had always hated it. What thirty-year-old woman was named Betty nowadays? But it was the only one she'd ever had—until now. Now she seemed to be choosing a new one every few hours. But she didn't like that any better. She was on the run—for two days now, catching meals and rides by her wits, missing more than she got, watching her back all the time. She'd made it through the desert from L.A. to Phoenix, the sun hotter with each hour, the road a furnace. In a diner in Chandler, a few miles south of Phoenix on Highway 10, she contemplated suicide. She'd fall in front of an eighteen-wheeler or grab a cop's gun. It'd be easy, and her escape would be complete.

But then something happened. Something she couldn't explain. Could never explain. At two in the afternoon, the sun blisteringly hot and oppressive, she stepped from the diner and heard thip! then a thwunk! Before her, its heavy marble base buried in the hot asphalt only inches from her toes, was something she could never have expected. She looked up and saw nothing but empty blue. She looked all around—no one—parked cars and disinterested shoppers. Fallen from the sky like a stunned bird was a small statuette—an expensively crafted clown, its reds, yellows, greens, and blacks brightly enameled and accentuated by glistening gold. Its arms were outstretched, and it smiled sheepishly through its detailed makeup. Etched in red along the base were the words, "I love you this much."

As if handed a gift from God, she lifted the statuette, cradled and studied it in appreciative hands for a long moment, then slipped it into her Barbie knapsack, and decided to keep on going.

Chapter 1

Wait," came an anxious voice through Bray Sanderson's headphones. "This could be it."

A summer night on Lake Champlain, Vermont—nothing blacker. He sat in the vinyl seat of a powerboat, its expansive nose like a javelin, looking out on black water and black sky above even blacker trees. There was a moon, but its ghostly light only accentuated the black.

Bray's headgear was like a motorcycle helmet with speakers in each earpiece and a thin wire mike reaching to a point before his lips. The setup was awkward, maybe dangerous in a high-speed, bone-jarring chase. He hated it, but he knew he'd need the radio when the shooting started. That and the bulletproof vest beneath his jacket—a new, lightweight model—a bullet slamming into it would feel like being hit by a baseball bat—probably knock him down, but only just. Unless it was an armor-piercing round—or if it hit him where the vest wasn't. The danger excited him—it was like being young.

But Bray swallowed his excitement. He always swallowed it. Throughout his forty-five years he'd taught himself that excitement could be an expensive luxury. It clouded the focus and numbed the judgment. So even though adrenaline surged inside, his chiseled features were placid, his smoky eyes calm, his lips knife-edged—no matter how intense the anticipation or charged the moment.

Like now.

He grabbed a roasted peanut from his black windbreaker pocket, popped it in his mouth, and dropped the shells at his feet—then he popped another. Peanuts were an essential during a stakeout and this was a stakeout, of sorts. He sat in a Johnston Interceptor, one of seven, contained like thoroughbreds in a small, tree-protected cove on Vermont's Grand Isles, the volcanic engine, capable of propelling the sleek craft at eighty miles per hour across the water, throbbing below. The pile of Bray's spent peanut shells trembled and scattered across the wet fiberglass, eventually piling up against the rear hull. After watching them for a long while flutter and slap into one another like drunken football players, he'd finally lost interest. Now, as he waited for the signal to attack, he studied the thin strand of lights that defined the edge of the Vermont mainland. One light in particular, an oval neon beer sign, periodically balanced itself on one of the two Colt Commando submachine guns lashed side by side to the boat's amber lighted control panel. A stack of loaded magazines, each crammed with thirty rounds, was in a specially designed compartment between them. He'd spent only a few hours on the range with the M-16-like weapon that morning, and although it had its purpose, he liked his .357 Magnum better. Of course, when the shooting started, he might change his mind.

Bray looked up to see the captain on the pier. He paced like an anxious bear.

Lake Champlain dropped like a ninety-mile dagger down from Canada. Wedged between New York and Vermont, the lake was home to a series of islands. Most prominent were the Grand Isles that hung like a strand of pearls from near the Canadian border and swung east at their end to nearly touch the Vermont shore just north of Burlington. The cove that protected Bray's boat was a notch on the edge of North Hero, one of the islands. The day had been a typical Vermont mix of intermittent rain, wind, and intense sun that left the lake choppy. Now, even in this protected inlet, the boats bobbed impatiently, their dark hulls and white numbers pale in the moonlight—their sharp noses aligned like horses in a starting gate.

Bray glanced up at the clearing midnight sky. Awash with stars, it provided a smoky backdrop for the rumpled Champlain islands that appeared blacker on the horizon.

The smell of newly mown grass hung in the air. It mingled sweetly with the lush smell of the water. A squadron of fireflies dipped and weaved by a bush not far away. A typical July night on the lake. He and his late wife, Diane, had enjoyed many nights like this—before she died three years ago. Except for the guttural throb of the boat's engines, this was as peaceful as any of those nights with her. But he didn't feel peaceful.

Why'd he have to think of Diane? It made him think of Pamela. When was the last time he'd seen Pamela? Two months ago, maybe. She had looked wonderful. He leaned back against the squeaky vinyl but didn't hear it.

And how long since he'd seen Win Brady? He normally hated youth, but he'd broken his own rule and allowed himself to like Win, with his energy, his naive courage. But no more. Win was lousy with religion, something Bray detested. Although Bray had ignored Win's affliction at first, he had to face it when Pamela came down with it and broke it off with him.

Bray hurt. Twice now. Diane for twenty years, then she died. There had been three years with no one, then a few precious days with Pamela—and now no one again.

Maybe I'll just die out here tonight and all this nonsense will end.

He might. It wouldn't be hard. Out there somewhere was a dangerous enemy. It was on its way, plowing remorselessly through the darkness. For it was a dark trade, commanding a silent flotilla that smuggled cocaine down the lake from Canada. Although there'd always been the occasional shipment from the north, those more organized and measured by the ton had only started recently. L.A. and Miami were getting too hot, so the shipper and receiver both were looking for a new entry point. The vast Canadian border, largely unattended, was worth trying. With information from a New York-based Corelli crime family informant, the DEA planned to do something about it tonight. Bray, though part of the Burlington Police Department, had been asked by his old friend John Phillips, of the DEA, to attend the party.

"You ready for this?" John Phillips asked, stepping from the floating pier into Bray's boat. Like the others, the athletically built, raven-headed DEA agent wore a black turtleneck sweater, jeans, and sneakers. Taking his seat behind the controls, Phillips pushed his head into his helmet and settled in, resting a hand on the T-bar throttle between the seats.

"Used to chase chicks on Friday nights," Bray said. "Wish I had one of these boats then. I might have caught one or two of 'em."

"Chicks? Brave talk."

Actually Bray had never chased chicks on Friday nights—or girls, ladies, or women, either. Not even in high school. He'd find one girl and stay with her until he couldn't stand the sight of her. He never did get to that point with Diane. He had hoped to at least take a shot at it with Pam. "Does the communications guy hear anything yet?"

Eyes widening, John straightened. "It looks like the captain has."

Bray turned toward Captain March and brought his lip mike into position.

Captain March spoke into his mike. "Four marks are coming this way. As planned, Harper's three interceptors will emerge as they pass. They'll give chase to us, then we'll spring the trap. Be quick—surprise 'em. If they're working the boats they can't be pulling triggers. Make 'em work the boats." Captain March hesitated for an instant, then said, "There's a complication. There's a party boat on the lake that could get in the way—make sure it doesn't." March eyed his commanders with a predator's intensity. "Questions?"

Not one.

"Prepare to move out. Ten minutes. Tops."

Bray's lips tightened, his emotional controls on high. Second thoughts—that guard job at the Florida old folks' home was looking better all the time.

Sensing Bray's reluctance, John said, "You'll be great out there."

Bray only nodded. "I thought the *Saint Albans* was moth-balled."

"Huh?"

"The party boat—the *Saint Albans*—a side-wheeler. I thought they'd retired it."

"Apparently not."

Bray popped another peanut. "They'll use it as a shield."

"Not if we move fast enough. Just part of the challenge."

March's voice scratched in their ears. "Harper is about to launch," he said, his eyes distracted by what was coming over his headset.

Bray grabbed the Colt Commando. Cold, wet from the night air and the occasional splash. A little shorter and more compact than the M-16, it had a familiar feel. He'd been an MP in Saigon and had used the M-16 now and again. He slapped a magazine home, seeded a round, and pushed the weapon back on the dash. He wasn't sure where the next thought came from. It just seemed to be there and yet after he thought it, he knew. *A man should be around friends when he's about to die.* It was something he'd thought a lot about in Vietnam. The word *friend* brought Win Brady to mind. "He's probably safe at home right now," Bray muttered to the rifle. "On second thought, he's probably snuggled up with Glasgow. Preachers have all the luck."

Thwonk!

Win Brady, tall, muscular, with thinning sandy hair, had gone back to his '54 Chevy to get Ginger a blanket. They were sitting outside, overlooking the lake, and it was getting chilly. Though they'd usually head home about now, Ginger had more she wanted to talk about. Win also grabbed his "tosser thing" from the backseat. He'd discovered it that afternoon while finally unpacking the last of his moving boxes. He'd packed it away months ago when he left seminary and began a journey that changed his life's direction. The toy was an ornately painted barrel that was about two inches long with a hole in the bottom and a foot-long string stapled to the top. The string, in turn, was connected to a stick. The object of the game was to toss the barrel into the air and catch it with the stick in the hole. Before he left seminary, he'd gotten good at it.

"Look what I found," he announced to Ginger when he brought her the blanket. As tall as Win, beautiful even in midnight shadows, with gracefully high cheekbones, blonde hair, and haunting blue eyes, she sat near the edge of the tall cliff, leaning against a moss-padded shale bench, the restless lake sprawled below. Win swung the small barrel into the air. It slapped and bounded off the edge of the stick. "Don't worry, I'll get it."

"I have every confidence," Ginger said, taking the blanket and wrapping it around her legs. "That's better. The lake sure cools things off at night." She knew there was one more thing she wanted to talk about with Win, but for now she gave a sigh of deep contentment and peered out over the black water, putting her cop's eyes on hold for a moment and just enjoying the mysterious beauty. "Look, out there." She pointed off toward a distant glacier of sparkling lights. "It's a party boat. Can you hear that music? I wonder if that's the *St. Albans* back in service again." Glancing up, she saw Win toss the toy again. "You've got a real talent there."

Win sat beside her and kissed her lightly. "Recognized in my own time," he whispered. "Imagine." He flipped the barrel again. It clapped wide of the mark. "I thought the kids at church would like it."

As assistant pastor at Grand Isles Community Church, Win's job was to make sure kids attended in increasingly greater numbers. The perfect job for him. There were five new kids coming now. Chad, Ginger's ten-year-old, made six.

"Chad got this hard-core kid to come last Sunday. No idea where he found him—Todd something—his parents work at the apple orchard north of the church. He'd love this thing."

"Hard-core? What's that mean?"

"Means you don't want to know what it means. But he'd love this. It'd be in his pocket in a second."

He flipped it again, but before the barrel hit the stick, Ginger grabbed it. She let it fall. "The kids aren't the only reason you brought that out now, are they, Win Brady?"

He tossed it again. "If I get some more of these we could have a contest. All I need is a spiritual dimension. How can I relate this to salvation?"

Ginger eyed the barrel. It swung on the end of the string like a head at the end of a rope. "I'm sure you'll come up with something."

"I'll see what Chad thinks," Win said.

"Win," Ginger continued their earlier conversation, her voice frustrated, "I can't let you get away with this. You have to deal with it sooner or later."

"Later's good. Much later's better." He tossed the "thing" again and speared the barrel on the stick. "Great!"

"Win, there is no later. We're getting married on October eighth—just three short months. We have to talk about this."

"I'll send a telegram from the honeymoon—that's the ticket."

"You have to invite your father to the wedding, sweetie."

Win kissed her blonde hair. It smelled wonderfully of lilac shampoo, and she'd been letting it grow, making her even more luscious to him. "It's my wedding, too, and I prefer he learn about it at the last possible moment—if at all. When he gets the bank statement is soon enough."

Ginger cocked a disapproving brow. "Your magic checkbook? You said you weren't going to use that anymore."

Win's magic checkbook never ran out, no matter how big the checks, no matter how often he wrote them. His father, a sporting goods manufacturer, always kept the balance well above zero. The magic checkbook had seen Win through seminary, all six years of it, and had kept him going for the few months since then. To Win's credit, he'd never abused the checkbook, his only lavish expenditure being his boat.

Win's expression went sheepish. "On what the church pays me I can't even afford flowers, let alone a ring."

"We can use flowers from my garden. The reception will be a potluck. You like potlucks. Then, when it's over, I can write a book on putting on cheap weddings and clean up."

"What about the ring?"

"An old copper wire'll do."

"Copper! Dream on. With just one more check that copper wire'll be yours. Then I'll put the checkbook away forever."

Ginger wrapped an arm around Win's. "Get me a ring when you're installed at some big church somewhere." She stopped cold. "You did it again. You got me to change the subject."

"Ginger, facing things later is always best."

"Even if later makes things worse?"

"Sure."

Ginger laughed softly and shook her head.

He kissed her hair again, and she placed a warm hand on his leg. "He can't hurt you. You're six feet tall, built like a tree—even more so since you've started working out again." She rubbed his leg with a certain urgency. "Do we really have to wait another three months?"

"Then we'll have known each other six. Your family was so desperate I didn't want to put it off any longer. But it shouldn't be any sooner."

"Desperate? My family? Encouraging, maybe." She shook her head. "Not desperate."

"When you told them we were engaged, Mom burst into an elated scream and your dad cried, 'Finally.' That's desperate."

The party boat continued to approach. To the north, outlined by white lights, the box-shaped side-wheeler glided down the lake, the music and laughing voices shimmering off the lake like strands of jewels.

"Look, Sorrell's place." Win pointed south along the island coast. Martin Sorrell's Inn, a white, two-story cluster of buildings, was silhouetted darkly, only a few of its lights still on. Sorrell was a multimillionaire, a slight, timid fellow whom Win had met only a couple of times. They'd attended the same church when Win first arrived at Grand Isles. Sorrell had done some things he should have gone to jail for—but his money served him well, and he had escaped justice. Even God's justice seemed to have been thwarted. "At first I thought he was going to turn that place into a hermitage," Win reminded Ginger. "The scuttlebutt said he'd fired all his staff, hired a once-a-week groundskeeper, and wouldn't accept any more reservations. I was thinking he'd made a jail for himself. Now the place seems busier than ever. I went to visit him once, but I couldn't get by that guard shack he built near the highway. Can't get in unless you have a reservation. Mel said he tried to get one and couldn't. But Sorrell does seem to be doing quite well for himself."

"I wouldn't mind being in a jail like that with *you*. Three months more, eh?"

What Ginger said didn't register. "And he's just down the street from the tent," Win continued. The tent was what he and Mel Flowers, the pastor, called their church—it was a real tent—a remnant from Mel's traveling evangelism days. "Maybe God just wants to remind us we can't win 'em all."

"Well," said Ginger, "you've done it again. I can't believe how easily you distract me. We have to invite your dad. We just have to," she continued. "God doesn't want families split apart like this. Whatever your dad does, we'll deal with it at the time."

In the light thrown by the *St. Albans,* Win saw something else reflected in the water. "Look! There are speedboats around it."

Ginger's cop-sense caused her brows to narrow, and she pulled herself up to a sitting position. "A funny time for that."

Win also sat up. With steady hands on Ginger's shoulders, he watched the scene below them. Suddenly the action broadened. Three other speedboats, bright lights flooding the lake before them, sprang from the mainland to intercept the first set of boats. "Are they racing?" he asked doubtfully.

"It's no race—not at midnight."

The three new boats were leaner, more muscular than the others, their growl more insistent. They appeared in a sudden rush, their white wakes peeling away, their searchlights bright. They injected themselves between the smaller boats and the *St. Albans*. "They're herding the other boats south," Ginger said.

"Something's going on," Win said, his voice apprehensive.

"Do you think . . . ?"

Win eased himself to his feet and stepped to the edge of the bluff. "Look. Rifle flashes." Then they heard the rattle of gunfire. "They're firing at one another!"

Ginger sprang to her feet. "This is big!"

"Check in," March ordered.

John spoke into the lip mike, "Boat One ready."

"Two ready," another voice scratched, then another and another until all seven DEA boats had reported in. Bray didn't know who manned which—and he didn't care.

While the others were reporting in, Bray slipped his .357 Magnum from its holster, checked the load, then returned it to his holster. He adjusted the bulletproof vest, hoping it would work, then planted himself in the seat. He checked his seat belt and left it unhitched.

"Harper's launched!" March announced.

Suddenly Bray heard a distant burst of machine-gun fire followed by three crisp shotgun reports.

John and Bray eyed each other. All the talk was over, all the peanuts eaten, out there bullets gnawed the darkness.

More machine-gun fire—still distant—staccato reports more like spitting than death. Suddenly an explosion, a loud, angry roar, then another—still distant—still subdued—and yet there was no mistaking it—then the flash of light. It reached up over the hedge of trees that stood between them and the lake, pushed through the tangle of limbs and leaves—then it went black. *Someone's dead—maybe two or three someones. Whose side?* The thoughts flashed quickly through Bray's head.

"Okay," March said, his voice resolute, grim. "Saddle up, and move 'em out."

John wasted no time. Deftly working the wheel and the throttle, he adjusted the boat's position so it pointed down the cove toward the opening to the lake. Then he punched it. The surge of power lifted the nose out of the water and eased them forward.

"Time's come," a voice scratched.

"Maybe yours, not mine."

"Quiet—only talk when it matters," March growled.

"Yeah, right!"

"Shut up!"

The earpiece went silent as each boat fell in line in back of John and Bray and followed them around the tree-studded point onto the lake.

"Holy hoptoads . . ."

"Woo wee! The demolition derby . . ."

The description was perfect. As the trees parted like a curtain, Bray was suddenly on the lake—dark, choppy, the sky as black as the water. The light thrown by the party boat showed a gilt-edged chaos everywhere—a deadly chaos of boats, bullets, and white, swirling wakes—and Bray was now a part of it.

Chapter 2

The four drug boats, aware of the ambush, veered—two hooked right, two hooked left. Two of the original three DEA pursuers peeled off after them. The third boat, north of the action, was burning like a torch. Not far from shore, it bobbed dead in the surf, the flames reaching up as if from a hole in the water. The seven interceptors exploded from the cove. Hoping to catch their prey in a vise, they instead found themselves joining the chase as the four drug boats tried desperately to avoid capture. Gunfire, some single shot, most rapid bursts, erupted from everywhere like deadly firecrackers on the 4th of July—the muzzle flashes like ignited hornets, and below it all, the thunder of the engines—enraged beasts.

Voices over the headphones:

"We'll take the black one."

"They're all black!"

"Look at 'em go—"

"Wow! Nothin' moves that fast."

John injected, "Shut up. Just choose one and get after it."

"Right, Bwana."

Harper's two remaining boats sent up a sheet of water as they spun around in pursuit. The flaming third boat provided a grotesque entertainment for the pleasure boat that churned a little farther north. Its lights blazed, its passengers crowded to the stern watching the flames while the boat attempted a slow turn out of harm's way. Some passengers cheered, some screamed; to Bray it was just noise, muffled at that. He could only hear the thunder of his own boat.

Like the interceptors, each drug boat had two men aboard, one pilot, one riding shotgun. The shotguns began doing their job.

"Hey, man, real bullets."

Bray heard the horrific spitting of Uzis off somewhere. The sound woke his sense of reality. Forsaking his Magnum, he tore one of the Commandos off the dash and laid it across his lap.

"We need more speed out of this thing," he heard someone say through his helmet.

"Surely you jest . . ."

"Don't call me Shirley."

Exasperation. "Where'd they go?"

"Is there a fog bank out there or something?"

"Just night."

"Shut up and find 'em," John growled, his own pursuit becoming futile as the running lights slipped off into the black.

"The *St. Albans* is in trouble," Bray cried.

Bray was right. Although several hundred yards away, the party boat had two drug boats heading directly at it.

"Who's near the party boat?" John cried into the mike as he brought his boat around and punched it. No one replied. As the boat jarred him, Bray struggled to keep his balance while slamming a loaded magazine into place. Then he leaned back in his seat to take a breath.

The drug boats were setting a blistering pace, one that John couldn't match. Nor could Bray have fired at them; a stray bullet might reach the party boat. All they could do was watch the drug boats approach the light-ringed side-wheeler. As they did, the crowd pushed to the side rails. Some pointed, some laughed, some shouted, some were confused, some panicked, some froze; both drug boats heading straight for them. In the blazing lights, it looked to Bray like both would go right through it. Then, when collision seemed inevitable, both drug boats deftly pulled apart, made a wide circle in opposite directions, then disappeared behind it.

The crowd split and followed the boats along the rails.

"What's back there?" John asked.

"More lake—an island or two."

The crowd returned as the boats did. One on the left, one on the right—as if they'd just continued on around—now both roared toward Bray and John. The displaced water that geysered up on either side gave each approaching craft an insolent grin.

"One's bad enough. Now we got two."

Bray stood, as before, throwing arms over the windshield, aiming over the barrel. "The more the merrier."

Suddenly what motivated the drug boats to continue on around emerged. Bathed in light, Boat Six exploded from behind the party boat in pursuit.

"It'll be a minute before we're in range, John," the voice scratched in Bray's ear.

"We don't have a minute," John muttered.

John was right. Seconds later, Bray could make out the four men's faces and could see their weaponry—all of it aimed in his direction.

Bray popped off two quick bursts. Then two more. The second took a bite out of a windshield. Sensing that it would be best to separate, the boat that Bray hit abruptly pulled left toward the open lake. Without missing a beat, Boat Six took off in pursuit. An automatic weapon spit from the escaping drug boat, sending a spray of lead at its pursuer.

Bray couldn't afford to take his eyes from the boat blasting at him, but over the roar of his engine he heard Boat Six return the fire—it sounded like a small cannon—loud shocks and geysers of water sprang up in the druggie's wake.

"We need one of those," Bray called out.

"More than one," John said.

Their drug boat kept coming—suddenly a micro-Uzi opened up on them. The 9mm rounds came in a great hail. The windshield shattered; the deck before the windshield splintered. John unlashed the seat belt and dove as a wash of bullets walked across the back of his seat. As he struggled back to his seat, the boat suddenly bucked, and John tumbled into the black water.

Bray set himself to return fire. Suddenly a searing pain exploded in his upper arm, and a warm river of blood poured into the elbow of his jacket. *No time for pain—no time for blood.* The drug boat was only seconds from ramming them— he fired four quick rounds. All missed. The drug boat flashed by them, its wake tearing against their side. Hitting the wake, their boat jarred violently—

After Bray recovered he turned to his left. *John—where's John?*

Bray's arm burned, but there was still no time for pain. He grabbed the wheel and steadied the craft just in time to see the drug boat pull around for another pass. The guy with the Uzi was standing, calm, confident that he would be soon delivering a death blow. The guy behind the wheel had a predator's look, eyes and jaw set, shoulders rigid. Bray worked the wheel with his weak hand, felt a stab of pain reach deep into his heart, then lifted the now heavy submachine gun and rested it on the control panel where the windshield used to be.

The Uzi spit angrily at him—but for only a second. Bray fired four quick blasts—no time to aim—just fire. The first missed altogether, but the second blew a hole in the nose of the other boat, the third took out the guy with the Uzi, and the fourth shattered the windshield to the right of the pilot. Shocked, the pilot spun the wheel to the right, sending a sheet of water onto Bray. The drug boat seemed to rise up on its tail, turn completely around, slap the water as it came down, and head toward the party boat.

Bray felt like he'd dipped his arm in lava. The pain was hot, the blood loss persistent. "I hate this," he groaned. With the danger lessened, he turned and looked for John. He saw nothing but black water.

Martin Sorrell's Inn sat in a low clearing, its gardens and boathouse hugging the lake on one side, a broad expanse of empty grass lapping against Highway 2 on the other. A massive, white, two-story structure, it had been a landmark for years. No more. Now its owner often hid himself in the basement, its single window his only opening to the world. Little more than a slit of glass, eighteen inches tall and three feet wide, it looked out across a fifty-foot strip of grass to the lake. But Sorrell rarely looked out through that window. When secluded in his basement he was too busy.

With the long, cold Vermont winters, Sorrell had some time ago converted his basement into an artificial greenhouse. With the use of expensive "grow" lights, he'd perfected the art of growing flowers indoors. Now that *they* had taken over his inn, he kept busier than ever. With the "grow" lights on sixteen hours a day and the dim night-lights on when he worked late, he could pretend the basement was his entire universe—and more than anything he wanted to be alone in the universe. So far he'd never quite managed it, but he got close when he concentrated on his roses.

Sorrell loved his roses. He loved nurturing them into bloom, fighting off the pests and disease. He loved hybridizing new roses, shaping them, bringing them forth like a father brings forth his child. In his basement workroom he had everything he needed, except for food for himself, and sometimes that didn't seem too important. There were days when he didn't eat at all, days when he remained in the basement just so he didn't have to go back upstairs and be reminded that he'd mortgaged his soul—such that his soul was.

He'd been in the basement most of the day and, now, into the night. In all that time he'd been alone—buried.

But no longer.

She was with him—Gatlin-something. She stood on a chair peering out the window—age ten, walnut eyes, long unkempt hair, willowy as only a ten-year-old girl can be. She belonged to one of them upstairs, and she came down to bother him more often than he wanted her to. Sometimes he enjoyed her company, but those times were few. Mostly she reminded him of a pesky fly.

He turned and found her standing on a short stepladder staring out the window. "What's out there?" he asked.

She didn't answer but continued to stare out the window, shuffling to this position and that, trying to see what she obviously couldn't see.

"My dad. But I can't see."

"You'd get a better look upstairs." Then he said under his breath, "Please go upstairs."

"I can be anywhere I want."

"But I'm working. Don't you have bugs to squash or higher forms of life to torture?"

"There are no higher forms of life in this house—except for

my dad. And he's out there getting shot at. Or that's what he said."

"I repeat, you can get a better view upstairs. Your room looks out over the lake, as I recall."

"And *I* repeat, I can be anywhere I want." Then she said in a low, offhanded voice, "Who wants to be alone while watching your dad get shot up?" She stepped down from the ladder. "You playing with your roses again?"

"Always." He held an X-acto knife and pointed toward a vase of unarranged pink roses that sat on the corner of his workbench.

What are they?" she asked, moving closer to the workbench.

"The Mary Rose."

"Is there a Gatlin rose?"

"Not with your disposition."

"I'm just me."

"A cross no one should be forced to bear."

"What do you do with them?"

"See these?" He pointed to two thorny stems. At the top was a spent flower and a bulb beneath it about the size of a cherry. He pointed at the bulb. "Rose hips. The seeds are in there."

He noticed her glancing toward the window. "I thought I heard something," she said. "Gunshots—like a machine gun—or like something blew up."

"I really don't want to know anything about what your father does. Ignorance is my only consolation."

"My dad says only wimps play with roses."

"Wimps live longer—and often achieve more. This particular wimp is trying to hybridize a black rose," he said.

"For funerals?"

"The rosarian who actually creates it—well, he'll be quite famous."

"Hmmm—a famous wimp."

Ignoring the little viper, he peered off into the night. "At least then my life will have some meaning. Maybe these seeds will get me closer. After removing them I put them in the refrigerator for several months, then plant them."

Sorrell heard the door to the basement squeal open. A gravelly voice, "You down there, Sorrell?"

The girl grunted. "It's Wacko."

"Waco," Sorrell corrected softly. "Close enough," she muttered.

"I'm working," he called to the intruder.

Waco was a Neanderthal—a thickly built Italian with tightly groomed black hair and narrow, foreboding eyes. He was Sorrell's guard—always near, never trusting. Now he stood at the bottom of the stairs. "It's after midnight—ain't you supposed to be in bed, kid?" He stepped to the window. After taking a quick peek he pulled back. "I thought you'd be watchin' the fun. You can see it from your room if you get on your tiptoes." He snorted a laugh. "You know, the next time you see your dad he'll be in a body bag."

"He'll want to know you said that."

"There you go scaring me again."

"Then they'll put *you* in a body bag—if they can fit it over your belly."

Waco groaned. "Get upstairs," he ordered Gatlin. "You sleepin' down here again, Sorrell?"

"I'm working."

"Go on, kid, upstairs to bed."

Gatlin turned to Sorrell as if to ask for assistance—but Sorrell had no intention of interceding. Rather, he said nothing as Waco prodded the little girl step by step to the top of the stairs where both disappeared behind the door.

He glanced at the window but remained where he was. "I don't want to know," he said to the room. "Whatever it is, I just don't want to know. I'll live longer."

He returned to his workbench, and with grave concentration, cut into the rose hip, exposing the seeds.

Bray trolled several minutes in a wide circle looking for any sign of John, then finally gave up. Other things demanded his attention. The drug boat, now with only a pilot, was heading for the party boat again and for the vast, black water beyond.

Bray didn't like any bad guys escaping. Not at all. Especially when they'd left a calling card buried in his arm.

Suddenly a flash of flame. Boat Six had nailed its prey. Still hurtling away from them, bounding over the chop, the drug boat was now a flaming missile—slowing, but only gradually. Silhouetted in the flames were two men struggling to get into the water. One dove, then the other. Boat Six eased up beside one of them, the whole scene illuminated by the blaze. A curious, violent abstract . . .

But Bray's drug boat was getting away. And he couldn't allow that.

He slammed the Commando into its latch and shoved the throttle forward. The Interceptor leaped forward, banging and clipping the top of the chop. He regretted his action instantly. Jolt after jolt, the searing pain was so intense it took his mind from the pursuit—more than once he reawakened to reality—to the drug boat pulling farther and farther away—to the conviction that catching the guy was the only reason he had for living. And the guy was getting away. Already a crowd on the side-wheeler was forming at the rail; already the arms were pointing, the beers being downed, the shouts and screams rising. Soon the guy would pull around back and disappear into the darkness.

The drug boat's engine coughed—then sputtered—then purred again and gained speed, but then it sputtered and slowed, then went slower still. A permanent condition.

"Maybe there *is* a God," Bray groaned to the dark. Gaining now, he grabbed the Commando and rested it on the dash. It bounced nervously there.

And that's when something very unexpected happened. Great spires of flame erupted from the drug boat's engine compartment—then spread. Seconds later the boat became the very definition of flame. Maybe a fuel line, maybe an explosive. It didn't matter. The crimson tongues leaped from black smoke—and the pilot dove into the lake. But the boat kept moving—toward the party boat. Although much slower, it slapped along fast enough. A blazing torpedo.

"Is anyone near the party boat?" Bray cried into the mike.

"We're too far—"

Bray was closest. A hundred yards from the drug boat which was another hundred yards from burying itself into the side of the *St. Albans*. The partyers saw their problem. Bray heard their screams over the roar of his engine, over the pain that dulled his senses. Knowing he was their only chance, he kept the throttle wide open—the Interceptor slammed ahead, gaining. But would he be fast enough?

The revelers knotted at the rail, pointing, animated, beginning to panic.

Half the distance had evaporated. Bray heaved a sigh of great resolve. He knew what he had to do. Easing up on the throttle, he pulled the wheel to his right and forced the Interceptor into a wide arch. The drug boat was completely engulfed in flames—it had slowed a bit, and Bray was traveling a good deal faster now. It could explode any second, or it could explode when it slammed into the side-wheeler—how many would die?

Bray pulled parallel to the *St. Albans*—only yards from the blur of lights, only yards from the screams on a course to intercept the flaming boat. He was going to make it—he knew it now—a cakewalk. To assure victory, he opened the throttle all the way. The lake slapped at the fiberglass bottom, and volcanic pain erupted in his arm again. But it would be over soon—he knew that—all the pain would be over soon. A strange euphoria.

"Don't do it!" a woman's voice pierced the thunder. "You'll die—don't die!"

He looked up, searching the sea of panic. A face—young, hair whipping in the wind . . . Diane's face . . . Diane?

He threw his eyes back toward his objective. And that's when he realized how much he hated the idea of dying in flames. He'd always wanted to die in his bed, asleep. Just check the alarm for the morning, drift off to sleep, and never wake up. That would be a good death. Not this way, slamming into a flaming boat just to save a bunch of drunks.

More screams from the boat—words—

". . . faster . . ."

"Don't miss . . ."

"He's gonna die . . ."

The flames were only yards away now, only a heartbeat, less than a heartbeat . . .

Wham!! The drug boat became a flaming vapor. The blast nuclear—the crimson fireball was instantaneous—a mushroom of red and orange and heat. The party boat was scorched—then a shower of molten fragments—fiberglass, chrome, glass—then the water enveloped it all—a rush of steam—more flames down by the waterline and then cheers from the party boat—cheers and crying and then an avalanche of wild, loud words. Finally silence.

After the first blast, Bray saw and heard none of it.

Chapter 3

Ginger leaped to her feet when she knew the boats would collide. She gasped when the flaming boat exploded. It was so real. So very real. Someone had to have died. Right before her eyes. She'd been a cop for six years. She'd seen the aftermath of auto accidents that made her stomach turn, but never had she seen a person die. And certainly never like this—in an act of incredible heroism. It took a long moment, long enough for the sound to reach her, long enough for the flash to die to flames and flames to die to a hiss of steam before she realized her heart was beating again. Trying to force air into her lungs, she turned to Win. He, too, stood at the cliff's edge, his eyes glued on the still chaotic scene below.

"I saw him get blown from the boat," she said.

Win didn't answer her.

"Did you see that? It's like a war—the guy was a hero. My dad was in Vietnam—it looks like Vietnam. Win? You there?" She was looking at him again and was taken aback at his expression. He stared at the lake, eyes fixed where the boat had exploded. He blinked, but that was all.

"Win? You okay?"

She had to ask him again before his rigidity lessened and he finally turned toward her. "I'm sorry," he said, his voice weak, preoccupied, but more than preoccupied—concerned.

"What's the matter?"

He managed a wan little smile. "I don't know. I felt something."

"What? You mean shock. I bet you never saw anything like that at the seminary."

"No. But it wasn't that." He looked out over the lake again. The party boat was continuing on as if nothing had happened.

But the voices seemed more animated—energy popping like firecrackers from the group who remained at the rail.

But Win's attention was drawn somewhere else.

A half-moon of light glistening off a ball floating on the surface of the lake about two-thirds of the way to shore from the explosion. It bobbed there for a while—a head. It watched the boats converge as a search began for the man who'd become a hero moments before. After a minute or two, the head turned and became a man swimming.

"What did you feel?" Ginger asked.

"Not now. One of them's escaping," Win said, his adrenaline surging. "He's swimming toward land down there. It's probably the pilot of the boat that exploded." Win was already drifting toward the swimmer. "Is your gun in the car?"

"In my purse."

"Get it and follow me."

"Win. You can't. This is for the police."

"You're the police."

"Oh, right—sure." Upset at her lack of instincts, Ginger spun and ran to the '54 Chevy parked ten yards away. When she returned with her Glock firmly in hand, she saw Win charging down the hill toward the water's edge. She tried to make out the swimmer in the darkness but couldn't. Either he'd landed or he was hidden in shadows somewhere. She wanted to call out to Win to wait for her, but she didn't dare—the swimmer would hear. So she simply charged after Win.

By the time Win reached the bottom of the hill, he was already questioning his actions. He had no weapon, and he wasn't a fighter. His only fight had been a dismal failure. It had started out okay, but the guy quickly got the better of him, and Win ended up looking down the barrel of a very large gun. But somehow all that didn't matter right now. There was not only a steady pulse of high-grade endorphins pumping through him, but they were propelled by a strong sense of justice and duty. After all, he was a member of God's army, and this guy had just been responsible for someone's death.

The coastline was very rugged here—huge boulders and tricky inlets shrouded in bushy shadows. Plenty of places to fall and even more ways to make noise, the last thing he wanted to do. By Win's figuring, if the guy had continued straight to shore, he'd be about a hundred yards ahead of him.

As it turned out, his figuring was less than perfect.

Before he'd gone fifty yards on a nearby dirt road, Win caught sight of a small flame sparking through the trees. A lighter. It glowed for only a moment then died. But that light was replaced by a steady glow, a cigar, one that pulsed more brightly with each drag. After a while Win saw him return a metal cigar holder to his jacket pocket.

Win watched the guy so intently that he nearly leaped out of his skin when hands grabbed his shoulder.

"You see something?" Ginger whispered.

Win caught his breath and pointed. "He's taking a break. What kind of escape is that?"

But then she brought the Glock up. "I'll tell you what kind of escape it is," she whispered. "Short-lived. Come on, Winsome Brady. Let's kick fanny."

To their surprise and delight, they quickly found a path through the small grove of maples. It allowed them to creep silently through the brush until they stood at the edge of a clearing that hugged the water's edge.

The guy hadn't moved. He sat on a tangle of tree roots still breathing heavily, the cigar planted between his thumb and forefinger and occasionally between his lips.

Win eyed Ginger. She glanced at him.

Each taking a deep breath, they charged to within a few feet of the guy.

"Police. Move and you're dead," Ginger spoke fiercely, the Glock leveled at the guy's head.

Ginger couldn't believe the reaction. There was none. "Did you hear me?" she cried again.

"I'm not moving," he said, the cigar smoke acrid.

"Hands behind your back. Win, I've got some restraints in my—"

That's as far as she got.

Like the strike of a snake, the guy came around with the end of his cigar and drove the lighted end into the back of Ginger's gun hand. A volcano of sparks erupted from her skin. She screamed. In what seemed like the same movement, the man came up with what looked like a bat-sized root. He struck the same hand. As the branch hit her burn, she emitted another painful scream. The gun flew from her hand, and it catapulted into the darkness.

"Ginger!" Win gasped, seeing her hand twist as she tried to shake the pain away. As he did, Win caught the glint of the gun's trajectory out of the corner of his eye. But there was no time to go after it. The guy suddenly leaped to his feet. Maybe because she was the one with the gun, the guy turned on Ginger. Before Win could react, the guy took a swing at her.

Grabbing anything he could, Win found the "tosser-thing" in his hand. The instant the guy's fist blasted past Ginger's nose, Win swung the small barrel and caught him on the temple, just above the eye. He saw the skin break.

Shocked by the sudden impact, the man straightened, but only for a moment. Before Win could swing again, Ginger's assailant spun and headed for the water. Ginger, having dodged back to avoid being hit, fell, tripped over a root, and sat hard on the rocky beach.

Seeing the woman he loved injured, Win's adrenaline went volcanic. He dove at the dark figure and managed to clamp his arms around one leg.

One leg was enough. The guy went down.

Ginger, seeing Win struggling, could see no solution but to find her gun. Forgetting her painful hand, she went after it. She'd seen it fly off toward the trees, but when the guy swung at her, she'd missed where it landed. But it had to be out there someplace.

Win couldn't wait for the gun. With his arms wrapped around one leg, he did his best to hold the guy to the land. But their suspect had no intention of staying put. The instant he hit the ground he began kicking at Win with his free leg. He kicked at Win's arms, trying to force them open. He kicked at Win's head and face in an attempt to brain him. He kicked anything available.

And it took its toll.

Win's arms were quickly bruised, his cheek scraped and bleeding.

But Win held on.

"Find the gun," he cried out to Ginger in desperation, knowing he couldn't hold on much longer.

"I can't," she cried back.

"Then beat him with that club."

The man didn't like that idea at all. The kicking became more emphatic, the blows more debilitating. Win could take it no longer. His grasp broke, and the leg tore away from him. For a moment he thought about giving up. But he couldn't. What would he tell Ginger?

And there'd been that feeling on the cliff.

But more than anything he wasn't alone in this—or any—fight. What would he tell Jesus?

His strength renewed, he struggled to his feet. By the time he did, the guy was in the water, his knees kicking up a frothy wake. Win dove at him again. This time his knee nailed the man hard in the middle of the back. Win heard a *Whoof!* as the wind left him. The guy was driven forward into deeper water. Now both he and Win disappeared beneath the surface.

No air in his lungs, unable to replenish it, the man fought furiously for the surface. For Win, victory lay in keeping him down.

Victory might lie there, but the probability of it didn't. Where Win was fighting for honor, his opponent, every bit as strong and agile as Win, was fighting for his life. He became an unstoppable force. Thrashing like a frenzied shark, his feet suddenly found the lake bottom. Crouching, he propelled himself up.

Both men broke the surface. When the guy filled his lungs, he became more than he'd ever been before. He spun out of Win's arms like a serpent. Facing Win, now in shallower water, the guy brought both fists down. One slammed the side of Win's face; the other pummeled the base of his neck. Trying to mount a defense, Win threw a couple of quick punches, but his face was aflame, and his shoulder felt shattered. His punches were worthless. The man struck him again, this time on the other cheek; then he planted another quick, power-driving punch to Win's chest.

Staggered, Win fell back. But before he fell, he heard Ginger shouting "I found it," from the beach. "Get away from him."

As Win's head splashed below the surface and the world became cold and wet, he heard shots explode, then the concussion of the bullets hitting the water. Afraid to come up for a moment, Win spun, trying to find the guy's legs, but his chest felt like it had been in a cave-in, and his face was molten. He moved sluggishly, and by the time he'd made it around, there was no one to find.

He push himself to the surface and found Ginger standing at the water's edge. "He got away. He dove under and went somewhere. I can't see him anywhere," she shouted.

Broken and defeated, Win waded to shore and was embraced immediately. "You okay, sweetie?" she kept saying. "Your face. He was a pro. Come on, let's sit for a minute."

"I'm okay," he said, his lungs still straining for air. "What about your hand?"

"Burned—but it'll heal."

He took her hand and examined the back of it. Though he could hardly see in the darkness, the blistered discoloration was hard to miss. He winced then planted himself beside her on the tree roots.

Kissing her wound lightly, Win sighed and painfully stretched sore muscles. "If I'm going to keep doing this, I need some lessons."

Almost as an absent gesture, Ginger reached down and, with her good hand, picked up Win's "tosser-thing" and handed it to him. "You dropped this."

"Don't ever tell the kids I used it that way. They'd kill each other."

"You okay? Your cheek's raw."

"I hurt. But it won't last. I guess we both hurt. Maybe we ought to go get fixed."

They became aware of a roar on the lake. Turning, they saw a powerboat growl into the cove. "We heard shots," called the young pilot.

"I'm a cop," Ginger called back. "The guy who piloted the boat that exploded was here. He escaped."

"Here?" Impressed, the pilot grabbed the radio. After talking on it a moment he told them, "We'll start a search. You okay?"

"Sort of," Win called back.

"You need a doctor?"

"The lady does," Win said.

"I'll be all right," she told him. "What's going on?"

"We're DEA. Just having a little fun on the job. Come by the police station in the morning, and we'll take a statement."

The boat pulled away and soon disappeared.

"Can you make it now?" Ginger asked.

"I'm okay," he said. Then, with some effort, Win stood.

Ginger stood beside him and examined her hand. "I gotta ask you something. On the cliff you said you had a feeling when you saw the explosion. What was it?"

Win took a deep breath and winced. Grabbing his side to contain the stab of pain, he said, "I had the feeling that it was going to have something to do with me."

"I'd call that prophetic." She laughed softly. "God spoke to you?"

"Just a feeling," he said, moving cautiously toward the dirt road beyond the trees. "Like God giving me a heads-up. Instead, I should have kept my head down."

"A heads-up about this little war here?"

"About what the DEA is doing. That's sort of the sense of it."

"So we need to find out what's going on," Ginger stated.

"Bray would know," Win said with a somber air of discovery.

"Bray? We don't dare ask him. He's so mad at you right now, he might try to finish what that bad guy started." Ginger laughed and wrapped a supportive arm around his waist. Stuffing her Glock in her belt, she kept her injured hand raised across her chest.

About thirty yards offshore, nestled in the crease of a rocky outcropping, waves churning around and sometimes over him, Ram Lucha watched Win and Ginger leave the beach. His temple stung where he'd been struck. The skin had split, and the cold water irritated it.

That those two were still alive was not to his credit. Worse, though, it was a problem. They'd seen him. Though only in shadows and only fleeting glimpses, and though they'd probably miss him in a lineup if it ever came to that, they might identify him somewhere else accidentally. That was too much of a chance for him to take. He'd have to remedy the situation. Soon. Who were they? She'd called him Win; he called her—something—what? She'd identified herself as a cop—and she was beautiful.

Even without her name, finding them would be easy. And the lake was big and deep. *It's a pity sharks only live in salt water,* he thought.

The fifty-year-old owner of a diner in Bushkill, Pennsylvania, glanced at the woman again. She wore jeans, a blue sweatshirt, and a blue and green windbreaker. She wasn't bad looking—if she'd clean herself up, fix her hair a little—short blonde, the roots blatant—maybe brush on a little makeup. Of course makeup couldn't help her eyes—moss green, they looked tired, hollow. She had draped an uncharacteristically heavy kid's knapsack, with a Barbie on it, over the chair next to her.

She'd been sitting there nursing a glass of water for a half hour now. It was time to do something.

"You can't just sit here, lady," he said, walking toward her.

"I'm not just sitting," the woman said. "I'm drinking this water you brought me. It really is great water. You guys up here in the mountains always have such wonderful water. I'm just sitting here drinking it."

"But you have to order something." The owner always felt uncomfortable at times like these. She was obviously down on her luck. Even though it was summer, it looked like rain any minute, and he didn't like the idea of throwing someone out in the rain—even if she wasn't a paying customer.

"I'm a little embarrassed." Although her lips were thin and drawn, she managed a coquettish smile. "I don't have any money. I've sort of run out. I've been on the road for almost a week. I knew I would run out before I started, but I just had to go. Just had to. I couldn't let my baby die without seeing her."

"But you have to order something," the owner said. Then it registered. "Baby?"

"I have to keep going."

"What baby?"

"My baby. Oh, she isn't a baby anymore. She's nearly ten. She's got leukemia—cancer."

"But if she's yours why are you—?"

"You don't really want to know. I mean you're being polite and all. I'll just leave. I don't have money to buy anything, so I better leave. I'll find some way to get some money tomorrow. It's just that I didn't want to take the time. I could waitress or something. I was a waitress for a while when I was a teen. I could have done that to earn money. But it would have taken time. She doesn't have that much longer to live."

"She don't?"

The woman shook her head pitifully. "I wasn't a good person when I was younger—maybe I'm still not. I got pregnant—"

"People do."

"I adopted her out. I just found out a couple of weeks ago she's dying. I want to see her before she dies. I'd better go."

"What's your name?"

"Mona Simpson," she said. "It isn't raining yet. If I get going now, maybe I can make it to someplace I can spend the night."

"You pro'bly want her to know you, too, before she—uh—dies."

"Yeah, I guess. Could I have another drink of water before I go?"

"Sit. You like stew? It's a special. I got more back there than I'll ever sell tonight. I'll warm up some biscuits."

"You sure? You really don't—"

"I got lots of stew."

"I probably ought to be going," she said. "I've got a long way to go. This is Pennsylvania, right?"

"Sit."

She ate the stew quickly, dipping the biscuits in it as she went. It was okay stew. But okay was good enough—wonderful really.

A few minutes later she thanked the guy profusely, grabbed her knapsack, felt the unusual weight, and stepped outside. She didn't like being in any one place for very long. It was drizzling now, a cool, steady cloud of drizzle that enveloped her the instant the front door closed behind her.

There'd been a trucker in the diner. She'd watched him out of the corner of her eye. He ordered a steak, asked for Lea & Perrins but settled for A-1, and ate slowly. He was in his mid-thirties—a year or two older than she—and wore a wedding ring.

The diner sat on a two-lane country road just off the turnpike. After leaving the diner, she stood by the road not far from the truck. It wasn't one of those big eighteen-wheelers—more of a moving van—but it was plenty big to take her someplace.

"You okay, miss?"

She'd been thinking about the truck and hadn't heard the trucker leave the diner and approach her from behind. She knew she looked like a drowned rat, or at least a very damp one. Good. "I'm okay," she said. "I'll catch a ride soon."

"Where you going?" he asked.

"Where *you* going?" she asked back.

"I'm not allowed to pick people up. I just wanted to know if you were okay."

"I'm a little wet. But it's only water. I'll pretend I'm in a shower with my clothes on." She smiled warmly.

The trucker, a nice-looking guy, smiled. "Well, you take care."

"Could you do me a favor?" she asked hurriedly.

"What kind of favor?"

"My name's Mary Singleton."

"Billy Tonto," he introduced.

"I'm on my way to see my daughter—she's got severe pneumonia. I left her with my mom and went west to—well—earn my fortune. I earned somewhere in the neighborhood of thirty dollars. I was trying to be a model. The thirty dollars was from cleaning up my agent's office. Now I'm broke. That guy in there was kind enough to give me some food. I'm pro'bly going to be stuck here for a while. Maybe all night. If I gave you the phone number, could you call and let them know I'm still on my way?"

"Call? Why can't you call collect?"

"She won't accept. My mom doesn't like me much. I just want to get home before my daughter—no. She won't die. I won't even think that. I try never to think of horrible things like that. There's got to be a God up there taking care of girls like me who are a little dumb at times."

"Get in the cab. I'm heading through Albany to Vermont."

"Vermont?"

"Green Mountain state. The hot green mountain state."

After the first hour, her senses reacted to the nervous strain of the engine against the truck's load, and she fell asleep. Some time later, though, she woke to the sound of the radio. News. An anxious broadcaster picking up reports as the action occurred. "It's a report of a gun battle on Lake Champlain in Vermont. Local authorities are saying that the DEA is conducting a drug raid . . ." Used to just reading the day's news, the fellow was stumbling all over himself to keep on top of the story as it unfolded. "It appears that one of the DEA agents is a genuine hero." He then described how one of the agents saved a crammed party boat from being struck by a flaming powerboat.

"Wow. Something else!" Billy exclaimed. "Sometimes I wonder if I could do something like that."

"Sure you could," she said, but her mind was still on the location of the news story.

Lake Champlain.

Vermont. *Someone could get lost in Vermont,* she thought. *Easily, I bet.*

"You got a map?" she asked Billy.

"Sure." He handed her a road atlas, and she quickly opened it to Vermont. She studied the dagger-like contours of the lake for a long moment then set the map on her lap. She hadn't considered Vermont before. Hers had always been a flight to the farthest possible point from Los Angeles. But she'd heard a lot about Vermont, particularly about its autumns—she'd seen pictures of its fiery red rural countryside. Nothing but trees and cows and battered farm buildings. *A person could hide in such a place, hide for a long time. Maybe forever.*

Concerned about Ginger's hand, his face and chest recovering quickly, Win decided to take a detour to his cottage before continuing on to Bray's.

"Why are we here?" Ginger asked.

"Let's take care of your hand before—"

"I'll be okay. I want to find out what's happening."

"It'll only take a minute."

In the deepest corners of her heart, she was glad they stopped. Win couldn't have been gentler or more attentive than he was as he did what he could to ease the sting of her burn. Of course, there wasn't much he could do. Since the blister had been broken in all the excitement, he washed it in cool water, then dried it with one of his softer towels. With deft fingers he applied some Neosporin, found a large bandage, and covered it loosely. "My mom always said burns need to stay clean and get air. Is that what your mom always said?"

"My mom always said, 'Don't get pregnant, and eat your green beans.' We talked very little about burns." Though Ginger kept her tone light, her heart was soaring. No man had ever been so caring as Win was at that moment.

"I hurt you," he gasped, looking up from the bandaged hand. "You're crying."

She shook her head and kissed him on his raw cheek. "Let me help you," she said.

He submitted to her as she, too, cleansed his abrasion and applied a layer of disinfectant and a strip bandage. It didn't quite cover the wound, but it would provide some protection. "Thank you," he said.

She said nothing but kissed him again, this time allowing her lips to caress him for a long, wonderful moment. "I love you, Win Brady," she whispered.

"I love you too."

"Who'd a thunk it?" She smiled. "Now, let's find out what's going on out there."

Fifteen minutes later they pulled up in front of Bray's

cottage. After knocking tentatively on the door, they heard the sound of fumbling from inside and the door opened. Larin Breed stood there. Breed was commander of the Burlington PD's detective division and was Bray Sanderson's boss. Win had seen him only a few times, but his was a face that could never be forgotten—thin, predatory, with swarms of wrinkles all over it. His expression was uncharacteristically soft, a little lost.

Ginger had seen him often—too often.

"Where is Bray?" Ginger asked, trying to peer around the skinny man to see inside the house.

"What are you doing here?" Breed demanded. Then a bony finger came up. "You're Brady—the guy—well, sure you are. What happened to you? She nail you with that hand or something? Doesn't matter. I don't want to know. Bray's not here." He took a deep breath as if building enough pressure to force the words out. "He's been hurt. Bad—a DEA thing. He's a hero though. Saved about a hundred people on a party boat."

"That was him?" Ginger gasped.

"We saw it," Win exclaimed, shocked, then arrested by a sudden realization. "I should have known," he said, the feeling back on the cliff taking on a greater shape and substance. Now it reached beyond the fight in the cove—it touched someone he cared about—deeply.

Breed continued, "He's at Fletcher Allen Med Center, and he's going to be there for a while. I felt useless, so I thought I'd get him some things."

Win looked down to see an old tin coffeepot in Breed's hand, the cord trailing behind.

"He doesn't read," Breed explained.

Since being ushered upstairs, Gatlin had tried to get a look at the battle out on the lake. She actually hoped to see her father. She had seen a little of the fight. Or at least she thought she had. A distant burst of light, maybe flames, then a drumroll of machine-gun fire. She only saw her father in her anxious imagination—the bullets tearing into his boat, him fighting to maintain control of it, it bursting into flames.

But then everything, real and imagined, died away.

No more flashing lights, no more gunfire—only silence, the wash of crickets.

Was her father still alive? Fear suddenly drove a spike into her heart.

But she couldn't dwell on it.

Waco came up and forced her to turn off all the lights in her room. Now she was left alone in the dark with just the glow from those heavy metal posters her dad thought she liked. Metallica, Guns N' Roses, The Cure—they hovered on the walls—slime green, grotesque apparitions.

Waco's visit emphasized what the loss of her father would really mean. He had to come back. If he didn't, life would become something unimaginable—unbearable.

What if her dad were lying out there wounded? Or lying in the water somewhere, swimming to her with injured arms. With the lights off, he wouldn't be able to find her.

She flipped on the lamp in the corner again. Then she posted herself by the window and peered into the darkness, hoping she and the light would be a beacon her father couldn't miss.

But after only a couple of minutes, the door to her room sprang open. The man standing there didn't enter but remained in the hall shadows. She knew who it was—the boss. She heard others call him Bones, but he'd never spoken to her. She'd seen him only occasionally, but when she had it had been like watching a walking grave. Now his eyes blazed in his skinny head on his skinny body. "Shut the light off."

"But my dad won't be able to find us."

"Neither will the Feds. Shut it off, or I'll shut you off."

Reluctantly, Gatlin did as she was told. Now they were both in the dark. The boss disappeared from the doorway, leaving her alone again.

If her father were alive, he'd be coming home soon. He'd come in and kiss her on her ear. She liked his warm breath just before his lips touched her. What if she'd experienced his warmth for the last time when he left that morning?

She plopped desperately down on her bed. He couldn't die. What would become of her if he did? The boss would think of something and whatever that something was, it frightened her.

More than frightened—terrified her. Although she didn't know exactly what these men did, she knew they meant her no good. She'd asked her father a hundred times to leave these people. She'd loved reruns of *Fantasy Island* and knew that somewhere was a Fantasy Island they could hide on. But he never listened to her He seemed to like these people. How could he like them and her both?

Her heart began to pound.

So hard that it was difficult for her to breathe.

She stood and stared at the door. If there were no Fantasy Island, at least she had a fantasy room. She crossed to her dresser, pulled out the second drawer, and rummaged among her underwear and socks until she found a key—a heavy brass one with a round end and an ornately etched number—a large 208—room eight.

Without hesitation she poked her head out into the hall, found it clear, and quietly crossed the hallway to room eight. She slipped the key in the lock, silently turned the knob, then pushed the door open. She stepped quickly inside and closed the door behind her. Leaning against the door, she became aware of the door's texture against her back, and the anxiety drained away.

The dim light from the world beyond the lacy white curtains delicately caressed the interior of room eight. And in the mystic shades of gray the room revealed itself magically—it was filled with dolls. Sitting on the bed pillows, standing in glass cases on the dresser and on shelves, resting on other shelves and acting as bookends. Cloth dolls, plastic dolls, porcelain dolls, apple-faced and wonderfully painted dolls—elegant dolls in long evening and wedding dresses, teenager and farmer dolls. A wonderfully fanciful world, and Gatlin became a part of it when she lifted a fleshy baby doll in her arms and cuddled it.

"I've missed you, Melissa—did you miss Mommy? I'll never leave you, you know."

Muscles rigid as stone, Mike Grogan stood on the bridge of his twenty-four-foot power cruiser. Running a relieved hand through coal black hair, he watched the lake return to normal, his dark, Irish eyes showing just a hint of a smile. This marked the end of a year's work. All of this was his idea, the whole enchilada, all the scaffolding that now supported the biggest deal the Corelli family had ever put together. Mike Grogan, grandson of an Irish immigrant, had made it happen. And so far, at least, it was all working according to plan.

The cocaine railroad coming through Miami up the coast was under increasing pressure. L.A. too. There was some talk about widening the Texas and Arizona pipelines. That possibility only intensified the problem—quick DEA response, committed border patrols, well-trained and sensitive American law enforcement, local Mexican officials eager to take money from both sides.

In the shadows of his own mind, Grogan had put it all together then approached the Corellis. "Canada? Yer kiddin', right?"

Since the coke was transported as tightly packed one-hundred-pound bales that were heat-wrapped in several layers of plastic, the shipments could be loaded into the oil tankers through the large pipes carried along by the river of black crude, then unloaded after the tankers were emptied. Not only would the stuff be undetectable, but they could transport tens of tons—like in the old days before the war on drugs began, and these large shipments were common. Now twelve hundred pounds was huge. The drug could come up from Colombia, meet the tankers at Valenzuela, bypass the eastern U.S., then come down the St. Lawrence Seaway to Montreal.

The Corellis liked the idea and picked up the ball by finding some guy named Perez—the Colombian connection—who wanted to establish himself in Canada. He set up a "pipeline" that took the coke from Montreal to just over the Canadian border to an ancient, unoccupied house on the lake they'd found—a termination point.

But they still needed a distribution center. When Sorrell called the family asking for a favor, that final link in the chain fell into place.

Martin Sorrell had gone to college with one of the Corelli sons. Sorrell and the son had been reasonably close, although they'd drifted in different directions after graduation. Sorrell had a problem and knew that his friend's "family" had ways of solving problems.

It was a joke to father Corelli—Sorrell wanted to scare some high-strung husband into driving his wife away so that he could step in and sweep her off her feet. *Why doesn't he just waste the guy? It's clean, neat, and no one comes back to blow the whole deal a year from now.* Father Corelli gave the scare job to Grogan. And then the Corellis moved in for the payback.

After the deal with Sorrell was established—one that essentially made him a prisoner in his own home—Sorrell's Inn became the distribution point, the end of the line from which the huge shipments would be divided and distributed.

But then the Corellis got cold feet. Anything this big would be impossible to keep under wraps. The DEA would get wind of it.

Grogan had even worked this one out. A brilliant plan—at least he thought so.

"First," Grogan explained to the Corellis, "we let them know we're opening the Canadian route."

"What? Send 'em a telegram?"

"Tell an informant. Someone we've used before. He'll inform. We'll let them nail our first big shipment and think they've closed us down. Then we ice the informant. We can even send them the body—do something dramatic to tell them they won. Then we go underground. The route will be ours. We'll be permanent guests at Sorrell's Inn. We can come and go as we want—anytime, day or night. It's a hotel, isn't it? It'll be our own personal hotel."

The only part of the plan the Corellis didn't like was turning over the first shipment of coke. "They can attack us, they can think they shut us down, but if five bucks worth of that coke is lost, you're history," the boss told Grogan.

Grogan modified the plan.

Satisfied, the Corellis acted.

The known informant was a small-time thief, Bic Doyle. An average-looking guy who usually needed a shave and let his hair grow several months between haircuts, he fed a deep thirst for Jack Daniels and did what he needed to do to keep a few bucks in his pocket. He was easily set up.

Bic was having a drink one Tuesday morning at his favorite haunt when he overheard two Corelli capos talking. Less than five minutes later, after being promised a C-note for the information, he told the DEA.

The Corelli capos watched all of it.

Grogan had seen to the last major step—the battle. Tonight it had all gone down. There'd been casualties, but a ton of coke—a street value of eighty million dollars—was worth a few. And there'd be a hundred and sixty mil more soon, and more after that.

The route was open and healthy.

Mike Grogan was that much closer to becoming a "made man," a wise guy, a member of the family. Not easy for an Irishman. For all he knew, he'd be the first. The Corellis would know that this mick was as good as any of those dagos kissing his ring—any of them.

Of course, that would be his second job. His first was as a detective with the Burlington Police Department working alongside Bray Sanderson. He laughed to himself. If those cops only knew who their next commander would be.

He'd waited about an hour after the final shots were fired to make sure he wasn't seen, then he slid behind the wheel of his power cruiser and eased it out onto the lake.

On the way to the hospital Win's mind raced; thoughts and feelings rushed at him like the oncoming wind. Fear, rage, anxiety, sadness, excitement, and, strangely, a sense of promise—none of them pure, each tainted by the others. Each tainted by his recent battle at the cove. He could have been killed. Fortunately his opponent had had no weapons or chose not to use them. Win knew he'd be going to heaven, but he didn't want to go just yet. But enough about him. He turned his attention to Bray again. "He's got no business doing heroic stuff. Doesn't he know he's not saved?"

"He hardly knows what it means. But he did *save* a boatload of people," Ginger answered.

"He could be on the way to hell right now."

"That heads-up you got on the cliff was right," Ginger said, her eyes on him. Win was so many things, and now he seemed to have a pipeline to things she truly didn't understand. "What do you think it was?" she asked.

"Just an impression. Maybe like a whisper you don't quite hear but understand anyway."

"What did it say?"

"That what I was seeing mattered to me."

"You could have been killed—that would have mattered."

"He knew I wouldn't be," he said.

"I just wish God would have told *me* you were going to live. I was beside myself looking for that gun. I knew he was a pro, and the longer I took, the more opportunity he had to prove it. My claw marks are all over that beach."

"Well, except that my neck and side hurt, I'm okay."

Ginger fell back into the seat. "Death is scary—it takes people away. Now you're here—then you're not. My first husband—and nearly you. He wasn't much, but you're the best thing that ever happened to me—and Chad. I don't want you doing things like that again. I'm the cop. Let me take care of it."

"I'm also a man—men react to other men swinging at their—well—women."

"Oh," she said, smiling. "Yeah—well—I can understand that. But I still couldn't bear to lose you. To go through all these wedding details . . . the invitations, the flowers, the dress—which reminds me. I need someone to help me choose a dress. I want to look so beautiful for you. Anyway, I couldn't go through all these preparations and not have this marriage last at least fifty years. Or sixty. Think sixty."

"At least," Win added. Then his expression chilled. "I haven't seen Bray in a couple of months," he said. "And when I did see him last, he stared daggers at me."

"Daggers?"

"At least darts. I was with Pam at Judy's Restaurant for a cup of coffee. We were discussing Pam making a larger porcelain cross for the church. She really does good work. Her dolls are finally starting to sell. Anyway, Bray walked in and sat down at a nearby table. Pam was up like a shot. She sat with him for a few minutes until Bray saw me. He looked like he'd bitten into an apple and found half a worm. Less than a minute later he was out the door."

"Bray doesn't understand—Christianity's a myth to him—a bunch of silly stories."

"And I haven't—" Win stopped. He *had* tried to share the gospel. Every chance he'd gotten. But Bray was not one to be browbeaten. *Maybe I should have pushed a little harder. But salvation is from the Lord, not from me.* It was easy to say. He'd said it a hundred times in the seminary. But everyone in the seminary was saved. No one close to him had ever been unsaved. What was that like? What would it be like to have an unsaved child? Would it be as easy to say that he'd done everything he could—that salvation was the Lord's responsibility—that his hands were clean? Especially if the child lay dying? But all his grim thoughts were countered by a growing hope. One he dare not even express for fear it would evaporate.

Ginger expressed it for him. "Maybe the Lord's going to use this to bring Bray in."

"Maybe the feeling was God's way of assuring me that all of this was going to work out. That he's in on it all. That I'm not to worry."

"Romans 8:28 says that," Ginger reminded him. "But tell me the truth, now. Not to second-guess God, you understand, but wouldn't it be easier if God just phoned? 'Hi, this is God. Don't worry about that plague. When you get it, it'll just be a bad cold. That flood won't get too high, and that hurricane'll just be a breeze by the time you feel it. That guy with a cigar on the beach, he'll try to kill Win, but he won't succeed. Everything'll just be fine.'"

"Or a telegram." Win suggested, "WIN—ALL'S WELL—STOP—GOD. It'd work for me."

"This belief stuff's really draining." Ginger slipped a hand around Win's neck and kissed his ear. "To see that big ape come out of the water like Shamu and come down on your neck—I needed some assurance right then and there. Romans 8:28 in big lights. Really big." She watched the road unfold before her for a moment. "But, if you believe that verse . . . I've been around Bray Sanderson for many, many years. For him to look for Jesus, he'd have to be at the bottom—really at the bottom. Maybe God's putting him there."

Win took a breath. I hope you're right. But the only thing we know for sure is the plan—whatever it is—is unfolding.

She pressed a gentle finger against the abrasion on his cheek. "I guess those plans can hurt sometimes."

"No more than your hand."

"It'll be fine—now." For an instant she relived his satisfying touch.

"And they can scare the devil out of you, literally."

"Then cheer up. This could be the answer to prayer."

Win nodded, but for all his hope, for all his belief, for all the hours and hours he'd spent buried in the Word—there was still a part of him that doubted that God—his Father—would ever do anything that good for him—would ever save his best friend.

Win didn't like hospitals—their alcoholic smell, the antiseptic cleanliness, the purity he was undoubtedly contaminating. He didn't belong. He was a hopeless outsider. "It's so quiet. I hate it," he muttered as they stepped up to the main entrance. "It's like if I cough or accidentally kick a door, somebody dies."

As it was just after two in the morning, the hospital was dimly lit, the corridors like lifeless caverns. Win and Ginger stopped at a directory. "Emergency will know where he is," Ginger said.

The emergency receptionist, a woman who probably looked pretty on a date but not now, sat in a cubicle behind a counter. "He's still in surgery—a couple of hours now," she replied to their question after consulting a computer. Then she eyed their bandages. "You want us to look at those?"

"I'm okay," Win said.

"Me too. How bad is Sanderson?"

"Bad," she said. "We just kept him alive and sent him upstairs."

"Can we wait someplace?" Win asked.

"You can wait with me," a man's voice came from behind.

They turned. The man standing before them looked more tired than the receptionist. His eyes were dark holes, his black hair disheveled. He wore a black turtleneck, black jeans, and black shoes—all of which looked slightly wet. His face had been quickly washed and still had a ring of black around it, particularly on the ears.

"You are?" Win asked.

They drifted away from the emergency desk toward the elevators. "John Phillips—DEA. Sanderson was working for me tonight. I was going down for coffee when I overheard you."

"Win Brady, and this is my fiancée, Ginger Glasgow." All shook hands, Ginger with her left. "Bray and I worked together on a case a few months ago," Win explained.

"I'm an officer for the BPD," Ginger told him. "I've heard of you."

"I was with Burlington PD for a while." John noticed their wounds. "A fight? Each other?"

"The guy piloting the boat that blew up in Bray's face—we found him on a beach."

"You got him?"

"No," Win said. "He nearly beat me senseless. Ginger got the drop on him, but he managed to get away."

"Could you recognize him if you saw him again?"

"It was dark and things happened pretty fast."

Ginger nodded. "If the lighting was just right. Maybe then."

"I'll send a unit over to investigate the area. We'll get him. We'll get all of 'em."

"You know any more about Bray?" Win asked, concerned.

"I know he's a hero. Something the DEA needs these days."

"Is he going to be a *live* hero?"

John Phillips's eyes darkened. "He's been shot, but the thing that concerns them most is his ruptured spleen and the pulmonary edema—like a blister on the inside of the lung. The explosion was hot—lots of sudden pressure. I spent some time with the doctors. And there's probably a bunch of things broken and bleeding inside. He's been on the table for two hours now."

"Where do we go to wait?"

"Third floor."

The waiting room was little more than a bench in an indentation in the wall. But at least it was a place to sit. A single nurse worked at a station not too far away, and she assured them she'd let them know the moment Bray was in the recovery room.

So Win and John sat. Ginger remained standing. "I saw a pay phone by the elevator. I need to call Mrs. Sherman—she's been so good to watch Chad. She's got to be worried. And I think Pam would want to know."

"At two-thirty?" Win was incredulous.

"Women want to know," Ginger told him. She turned and stepped toward the elevator, leaving Win with John.

After a long silence, Win finally asked, "You always dress like that?"

"When I'm working. Beats a suit and tie."

"Find anything out there?"

"Can't say."

"Ah," Win replied.

"You know Bray long?" John asked.

"Few months."

"He must have made an impression—for you to be here at two in the morning."

"Making impressions is what he does best."

John laughed softly. "Like an anvil on the toe. He was my anvil for three years. Taught me a lot. Mostly about focus. He never lost sight of the problem. Like a dog with a bone. Like tonight. There was a problem, and there was one solution. It didn't matter that it almost cost him his life."

"I saw the boat blow up and Bray thrown into the water."

"He's a hero—a real hero." John was shaking his head, deeply affected. "And we're going to let the world know."

"Did you get all of 'em? Besides the one we let get away?"

"Assuming two per boat, the others are all accounted for. And we've got a net all around the lake. We'll pick your guy up."

Ginger walked up. "Pam's coming."

"Pam?" John asked.

"Bray's—uh—friend," Ginger explained.

Win's brows knit as he looked up and down the floor. "Isn't Bray a little vulnerable here?" he asked John. After all, if Pam could just show up—or he and Ginger for that matter—so could someone with a score to settle.

"We'll put someone in the hall. He'll be okay," John said.

Win felt a warm hand on his shoulder. "Sweetie," Ginger said as if waking him up from a troubled sleep. "There's a little chapel around the corner. Let's go pray."

Win looked up.

Prayer. He had personal knowledge of the bad guy's commitment. These guys the DEA was after meant serious business. If someone wanted to serve Bray up on the altar of revenge, Win doubted they would be stopped by a single cop in the hall.

He stared at the elevator for a long moment and pictured the DEA agent sitting there, a .357 Magnum in his lap, then the elevator opening and a guy with a ski mask and Uzi stepping out, the weapon spitting death everywhere.

But God had visited Win out there on the cliff. It had just been a hint of a meeting, but it was real. Just as God had been with Win at the cove, God was at work in his friend's life, and he surely wouldn't let such an attack take place. Why would God snatch him from a fiery death one minute and kill him in the hospital the next? No matter who might be out to get Bray, he was safe here in the hospital.

Yet for all the consoling thoughts, Win felt a nagging sense of foreboding. God was a planning God, one who worked out everything in accordance with that plan—but he was also a complex God. Deep inside Win knew there was more to this than what he was now seeing. That this was only the beginning.

What lay ahead?

He stood and placed a firm hand on Ginger's back. "You're right. Prayer's our only hope here. If there's ever been a job for God, this is it."

Chapter 4

The chapel was a small room paneled in oak with oak pews and a long glass inlaid mural that had all the appearance of a stained glass window—a dove descending with an olive branch. Win and Ginger sat in the front pew. Their prayer had been disjointed. Other than praying for Bray's salvation and well-being, they said little else, yet there seemed to be so much more to bring before the Lord. Those spiritual packages seemed wrapped and tied rather than open and laid bare, however.

There were no more words.

Win's head came up. "Could you catch a ride home with Pam?"

"Why? What are you going to do?"

"I want to take a look around that cove."

"You're kidding, right?"

"No." Win was clearly serious.

"Let the cops do their job. They said they'd investigate."

"Two heads are better than one," he argued.

"You nearly had yours knocked off. Please, Win."

"I'll be fine. I just want to feel useful. I'll see you in the morning."

"Win. There's nothing you can do. Really."

"I just need to feel like I'm contributing."

"I'm the cop. Why don't you stay here and I'll—"

"I'll call you in the morning." He smiled.

Without giving her a chance to renew her protest, he left.

Ginger watched him go, feeling as helpless as he probably did. Although Win's life had all the earmarks of someone who enjoyed just sitting around thinking—six years in seminary attested to that—but in the few months they'd known each other she'd seen just the opposite. Sitting made him antsy;

sitting when his best friend was near death was probably intolerable.

"Just stay out of trouble," she called out after him.

There was usually nothing blacker and quieter than the lake at three in the morning. Normally the only light came from whatever moon there happened to be. Not this morning. There were two salvage operations going on. One near shore, the other where Bray had been caught in the explosion. In each place floodlights lit the area like mini-suns. Several boats were stationed nose to nose for divers who rose and dove with rapid frequency. On the surface was a steady grind of voices and equipment. Win stopped his car at the crest of one of the island-connecting bridges and watched for a moment. Although muffled by distance, he could make out a little of what the voices were saying.

"Anything?" someone called to a surfacing diver.

"A couple of pieces. Nothing you want to find, though."

Someone screamed from a house on shore, "How long you gonna do that? This country was built on work, and I gotta get up early and build some country."

"Won't be long now," someone called back.

To add to this early morning odyssey, there was traffic at three in the morning. One news van growled by Win's car, then another. In the distance, on the roads that hugged the lake, he saw the occasional police car, their red and blue bubbles erupting like fireflies. *Maybe they found something*, Win thought. *They're nowhere near the cove.*

Win drove farther up Highway 2. When he neared the turnoff for the dirt road that would eventually take him to the cove, he slowed, then pulled over. He wasn't ready yet. There was something to think about.

Had he really felt something on the cliff? He wanted to say no. He wanted more than anything to think that he'd just imagined it, that there was nothing extraordinary going on. He'd had a strong dose of the extraordinary a few months before when he'd been up in the Sugar Steeple Church bell tower. When he'd felt the presence. The oppressive, evil presence that chilled his blood and caused him to run down the stairs as if Satan himself were on his heels.

Maybe he was. Or if not him, certainly one of his buddies.

Win had no desire to plug into that side of things again. He wanted to live his life like everyone else—just reading about things like that and seeing them on television's *Unsolved Mysteries.* But the sensation out on the cliff had been too close to that plug—even if it were God.

Anyway, God wasn't supposed to nudge him like that. He was supposed to communicate by responding to prayer or highlighting scriptural text or working through circumstance.

Not tap him on the shoulder and say, "Watch out."

But God had. The sensation had been very real.

The encounter in the cove was real too. And it was time to take another look at it. The guy had been sitting there a while before they'd arrived. Maybe he'd left a clue to his identity somewhere. Or, more likely, maybe he'd dropped something during the struggle. In either case, whatever it was now lay there waiting for Win to find it.

Aiming his Chevy along the road, Win soon found the right place. Killing the engine, he grabbed a flashlight from the glove box, then pushed the thick door open. He locked it, closed it silently, and after igniting the flashlight, he took his first cautious steps toward the cove.

The sound of crickets met and washed over him. Somewhere out on the lake a fish leaped from the surface and splashed. Waves pearled against the shore, and leaves and branches rustled hauntingly.

With no time to enjoy the scenery, Win focused the cone of light ahead of him. Stepping along the little path through the brush and the maples, he soon stood on the beach. It certainly hadn't changed, but then he'd not had time to study it before. Like most of these little inlets, there was really no beach to speak of. Rather, it was an irregular half circle of shale shelves, steps deeply covered in loam and leaves. The lake lapped at the shale as if caressing a friend.

Sweeping the light across the area in front of him, he saw evidence of their struggle. The ground cover was violently disturbed, the battleground a wide splash of scraped and twisted piles of leaves, twigs, and earth.

For an instant he relived the struggle—his desperation. The sense of win or die—he hated sensations like that.

At least he hadn't shrunk from the battle. He'd actually charged in without regard for his safety. His father would undoubtedly find some way to impugn his manhood by what he'd done, but he knew there was nothing to impugn. He could look himself in the eye in the morning knowing he'd risen to the challenge. Of course, he'd gotten himself beaten up for his trouble. But that was okay.

Before making a detailed search, he stepped inches from the water and peered out over the lake. Maybe a couple of hundred yards offshore directly in front of him, the brilliant lights illuminated the salvage operation—the one looking for Bray's and the other boat. He'd first seen the guy swimming somewhere between the cove and those lights. He'd reached this cove, pulled himself up, took the cigar from its case, lit it, then waited. After the fight, he'd struck out again. The way he was panting when Win and Ginger found him, Win doubted he'd made it very far after the fight, but the guy was probably long gone by now. Which meant that somewhere out there in the night, maybe miles away, was the guy who'd put his best friend, the one not speaking to him anymore, in the hospital.

Win glanced at his watch.

By now Bray was probably out of the operating room. Win should be there. But why? Bray wouldn't be able to talk to him anyway—even if he were willing to. Maybe he could do more good here. Especially if he were able to give the police information to help ID the guy. Maybe Bray would talk to him then.

Win's search began. As an analytic, he worked methodically. He started from the farthest point south and slowly moved north, his search radiating out from the water's edge then back again. He only stepped where he'd already looked and was careful to look under everything that could be overturned—leaves, rocks, twigs. When he got to the battleground, he took special care to sift through the piles of leaves and dirt. He'd take a handful and let it run through his fingers. Bray would have been proud of him. He found nothing—until he got to the roots where the escaped pilot had been sitting. There at Win's feet was the cigar. The lighted end was crushed and ragged where it had struck Ginger. The other end was bitten and soggy.

Why in heaven's name would a guy escaping from the DEA finally get to land and, instead of running as far and as fast as he could, stop for a smoke?

Win had an envelope in the car, and after returning with it, he stabbed the burned end of the cigar with a sharp stick, placed the butt in the envelope, and sealed it. He felt so official in doing so. Envelope in hand, he stood for a moment and scanned the water again. Their fiercest battle had taken place out there. The guy could have dropped just about anything out there—keys, wallet, anything. And out there, buried in the murkiness, it would probably stay.

While Win stood on the shore, something happened. He began to feel uneasy, as if he were being watched—like ants were crawling along his nerves.

He spun and swept the light around. Just rocks, water, bushes.

No one.

The feeling persisted—intensified. The ants joined and tightened around his heart then gnawed at the muscles in his neck. Spilling over in great armies, they attacked the nerves in his arms and hands. Again they joined and clamped onto his muscles—he shuddered, actually shivered as if he'd been suddenly thrown into a deep freeze—but there was no chill, only rock-hard, quivering sinews. His breathing became rapid even before he realized it.

Fear. Panic. Both. One climbing upon the other.

He spun again, sweeping the area with light, scraping it with his eyes. This time all the way around. More rocks, more water, more brush. He lifted the light to the trees half expecting to see snakes slithering there, positioned to dive on him.

"Hey, kid," came a voice. "What're you doing?"

Slapped by the sound, Win stopped cold—dead. "What? Oh. Just looking around."

"Who are you?" the voice came again as a uniformed police officer emerged from the oak grove, his flashlight ablaze and his Smith and Wesson out of its holster but pointing down and away from Win.

"Win Brady," Win told him, his eyes fixed on the gun. The feeling of fear was subsiding. "I'm a pastor at the Grand Isles Community Church—the tent church."

"You got some ID?"

"A wallet."

"Move slowly, and take out the driver's license."

Win did.

Placing the flashlight under his arm, the officer eyed it quickly, saw that Win was telling the truth, and handed it back. "What are you doing out here?"

"This is my second time, really." Win told him everything about his previous visit, and when he finished, he proffered the envelope. "There's a cigar butt in here. The guy was smoking when we surprised him. The DEA said they'd investigate the area, but they haven't had time yet."

The officer hesitated for a moment as if deciding whether Win was telling the truth or not. Coming to a conclusion, he used a handheld radio to call for an investigator. Then he turned to Win. "You'll have to stay here 'til the detective arrives. He'll probably have a few questions."

Win nodded his compliance and sat on the gnarled root. He noticed that he was still breathing hard as if he'd been running. Slowly, over the next few minutes, as the officer tried to engage him in conversation, Win's breathing returned to normal.

He had experienced it again. That same feeling of dread, of hovering, expectant doom he'd felt in the bell tower those months before. He shuddered, and a part of him wanted to run away as he had after the bell tower encounter. But he couldn't. Not only did he have a police officer babbling at him, but he'd grown since then—running was no longer something he did.

"You okay?" the officer asked.

"A chill I guess," Win lied. He looked down at the ground then casually up at the trees, the twisted shadows the result of both flashlights.

What was it going to mean this time?

Ginger didn't like just sitting there in the chapel, but it was more comfortable than the waiting room, and she did have a sense of calm. Even though the wall was a fake stained glass window, God seemed present and able to keep the tension to a manageable level.

After about fifteen minutes Pam Wisdom stepped in, her salty dark hair pulled hurriedly back, her usually bright expression a disheveled mixture of anxiety and relief. "Good. You're here," she said plopping herself beside Ginger. "I don't think there's another prayer in me. What happened to your hand?"

"Cigar burn."

"Nasty things. You should give 'em up."

"You okay?" Ginger asked.

"Me, sure. But poor Bray." Pam sighed. "He's so vital. So alive."

"He's a hero."

"Do you think the Lord will ever change that heart of his?"

"I hope that's what this is all about," Ginger said.

"Do you really think so? I sure hope you're right. He looks so terrible, though."

"You've seen him?"

"They were wheeling him into ICU as I left the elevator."

"I've been waiting to see how he fared in the operating room."

"They won't know for a while—these are the critical twenty-four hours. I hope they got the guys who did this to him."

"I'm sure we'll see them all sent up. You don't declare war on the DEA and get away with it."

"I wish I could believe that. Seems the more evidence we have against someone these days, the more likely they'll get off. A videotape of the crime is the criminal's ticket to freedom."

"No. These guys will be put away forever."

John Phillips poked his head into the chapel. "I was hoping I'd catch you still here."

After introducing Pam to John, Ginger asked, "Is there news about Bray?"

"He's critical. They'll know more in a day or so. But right

now I have to leave. I've got to come up with a way of keeping the guys who did this to Bray behind bars. Their lawyer seems to be working magic."

"Told you," Pam muttered as John left.

"I can't sit here any longer," Ginger said, getting to her feet. "Let's go see him."

They couldn't see him, but they could see glimpses of the machinery keeping Bray alive—monitors with their spiking green lines, tubes hanging like garland.

Pam sighed. "This is cruel. God lets me fall in love, then makes it so I can't even date the guy. Now he may take his life. God's not a cruel God, is he?"

"It can look that way sometimes." Ginger's mind flashed to the night she learned her husband was dead—when she was left alone with a four-year-old and a new job that would take her out of the home, sometimes at night. It certainly seemed cruel at the time. "But when you look back on what he's done," Ginger said, "his mercy shines through."

A nurse, Doris, her name tag proclaimed, stepped from Bray's cubicle.

"How is he?" Ginger asked.

"You from the media?" she asked.

Pam said, "I used to be his girlfriend. He means an awful lot to me."

"I'm a cop," Ginger said, pulling her badge from her back pocket.

At that instant, the elevator door opened, and Larin Breed stepped from it. Weary eyes proclaimed a tough night, one that could easily get tougher.

Breed greeted Ginger warmly and introduced himself to Pam. "I've seen you with Bray," he told her.

"Maybe you'll see me with him again."

Turning his attention to Doris, he introduced himself and told her, "I want everything you know on Bray Sanderson."

"You got ID?"

Breed had more than she needed. After she scanned it, he went on, "There's a storm of news media downstairs. I've got some officers keeping them at bay, but I won't be able to do that for long. I want to know how he is. He's my man—and I want to know it all."

Doris hesitated but gave in. "They performed a splenectomy and tried to stop all the internal bleeding. They treated the pulmonary edema and have him on a ventilator. He's suffering from a severe concussion, blunt trauma to the chest, bullet wound in the upper arm, and a broken right arm and left leg. Broken ribs too. There are a number of complications that could materialize, so we've got him on a raft of monitors—we're even checking the blood pressure at the heart. If things start to deteriorate, we'll know quickly."

"Well," said Breed, not sure how much of his considerable concern he should show, "he's tough—he'll do fine. I'll check back with you later." Then he turned to the others. "Get some sleep. I'll station one of my men here as a guard. The DEA wanted to do it, but he's my guy. I'll do it."

"Make sure he's got a cannon with him," Ginger said.

Their attention was instantly drawn to a beeping monitor in Bray's cubicle. "Doctor," Doris cried as she ran back to Bray's cubicle, "his heart. VTAC—252—hurry, it's up to 276."

Two white smocks burst from the back and converged on Bray. One of them grabbed the curtain and pulled it around him.

Breed, Ginger, and Pam spun as a single person. They heard orders being barked.

"Come on, Bray," Breed muttered.

They heard someone say it was up to 302. They heard a call for the shock paddles, then another cry: "Clear." There was a dull slapping sound. Then silence. "Again—clear." Another slapping sound.

"He's flopping like a fish," Breed whispered, hardly daring to make a sound.

"Okay," they heard, "he's stable. Wheel him back to OR, and we'll see what damage we did." Seconds later, Bray appeared on a gurney, the IV rattling along beside him.

"Well," Ginger said. "If the Lord's going to work, at least he's got Bray's attention."

Billy dropped Betty Harmon, now Mary Singleton, off on the Troy, New York, side of the bridge across from Albany, his plans to go all the way to Vermont having changed. It was well after midnight, and Billy was getting tired. Mary chose to be left on the Vermont side of the little village of Troy in front of a nondescript motel.

"You gonna be all right?"

"I'm gettin' closer all the time," she said.

"I'm sorry about this, but my eyelids are at ten pounds each. I got a couple of fives here to help. I was gonna stop on the way back for steak and eggs. I love steak and eggs on a trip. But you take one of 'em, and I'll have me one of them Denny's Grand Slams or something."

"No, I couldn't. You've been kind enough already." She meant it. He had been kind. He'd been pleasant company, and driving her at least twenty miles out of his way was even more reason why she owed him that steak and eggs. "Consider the steak and eggs my treat."

Reluctantly he nodded. "Okay, I will."

"What time is it?"

"Near one. I'm going to sleep until six." The engine throbbed while he searched for the right words. He'd never left such a pathetic woman in such a pathetic situation before. "I hope all works out for you and your daughter."

"She's so fragile," she said. "Like me in a way."

"You fragile? Hardly."

She smiled, patted him lovingly on the hand, and slid out of the cab. A few minutes later, the cab's red taillights faded as it headed back to Albany.

The drizzle had stopped an hour before. Now there was just the persistent wet made brittle by a cool night breeze. When she'd started out a little more than a week ago she never thought she'd end up this far north or east. Now it didn't feel far enough.

A leathery hand came from behind and grabbed her shoulder and spun her around roughly. Her heart stopped as she stared into hideous, drunken eyes, a scar cutting the unshaven skin from the edge of the left eye down the cheek. For an instant another face, another scar, exploded in her brain. She screamed, her throat raw with it.

The drunk straightened. "I didn't mean nothin'. You all right?"

"Get away from me," she cried, pulling the heavy knapsack back like a weapon. "Get away."

"Aw right. No probl'm." The drunk waved partially controlled hands and stumbled off toward a car parked at the motel. He turned and peered at her one more time before opening the door, sliding behind the wheel, and driving off unsteadily.

Knowing she needed rest, she made it to the motel lobby. Without acknowledging the puffy-eyed night clerk, she sat with dramatic weariness in a chair against the wall opposite the counter.

Betty Harmon, now Muriel Sweet, propped her head up on her hand, her eyes nearly closed. At least in the motel lobby she was reasonably warm. But it wasn't the cold—it was the scar. It jolted her. A scar nearly like it had branded her dreams for over a week now.

Feeling he had to say something, the night clerk asked, "Are you okay?"

"I'm just tired," she said. "I've been on the road all day and most of the night. Can I just sit here for a while? Maybe I'll get lucky and sleep a little."

"Where are you going?"

"To Maine. Portland. My mom lives there. You and your folks get along?"

"Mostly." He shrugged.

"My mom is a wonderful mom. My dad died when I was twelve, and it set me off. I hated everybody and everything and ran away to the West Coast. I heard just a week ago that my mom was dying. Breast cancer. It's in those node-things. All her money's gone on medicines and things, and I don't have any money, so I'm heading home any way I can. I'm close now."

"The owner won't let anyone just sit in the lobby. Maybe you can go to a church or shelter or something."

"Churches want to infect you with God, and shelters have

a bunch of drunks. I was nearly raped in a shelter when I first started off. No. No churches or shelters."

"But you can't stay here."

"Then I'll go. Hopefully it won't start raining again. I spent the last three nights in barns—well, there was an old shack thrown in there a couple of nights ago. Drafty. Really damp. I think I picked up the cold there—in the barns, I mean. I wrapped up in the burlap bags, but they weren't as warm as getting under the hay. Of course, I didn't sleep well under the hay—allergies. Nose closed like a bent straw. But I'm sure I'll be fine. I think I passed a barn not far back."

"There's no barns around here. Toolsheds. But they'll be locked."

"I'll find something. Don't you worry about me. I wish I had time to work and earn money, but I'm afraid Mom'll be dead by the time I get there if I keep stopping. Can you imagine wronging your mom like that and never having the chance to say you're sorry?"

The motel clerk dipped his head in recognition of the feeling and glanced behind him to the row of cubbyholes and the several with keys. "You'll have to leave before seven, and you'll have to change your own sheets. I'll wake you up at six-thirty."

He handed her the key to the last room in the row, the one nearest the railroad tracks. In the room she placed her clown statuette on the nightstand, its outstretched arms welcoming her home, and she climbed beneath clean sheets. Lying there, she found herself shuddering at the memory of the face and the grisly scar. Was he gaining on her? Would she wake with that face of doom staring down on her? She reached over and caressed the statuette. It calmed her somehow, and she slept.

Through a foggy, disturbing sleep, Gatlin sensed she wasn't alone. There were smells—musky, wet smells and the odor of tobacco. For an instant it blended into a sudden dream . . .

She was on the lake, the boat bounding, slapping against the waves. Gunfire, bullets chewing away at the boat. Geysers of exploding water drenching her, the boat twisting and turning in a wild slalom between explosions. She screamed. Out of con-

trol. A cigar smell. She looked to the pilot's chair. Her father sat there, a cigar planted firmly between his teeth, a smile on his lips. "Hang on. Yer gonna love this."

"Mom—where are you?"

"Gatlin, wake up. Yer gonna hurt yourself."

"Huh?" Her eyes remained closed.

Ram Lucha took the cigar from his lips and laid it on the edge of his daughter's nightstand. Taking her shoulders in both hands he gave her a quick shake. "Come on, Gat, yer havin' a dream."

"Dad? Oh, Dad." Both arms shot up and wrapped around his neck. She pulled him to her but actually lifted herself from her bed, burying her chin under his.

Taken aback by her fervor, he wrapped his arms around her and held her there for a moment. "You okay?" he asked gently.

"You're back. You're alive. You're wet—yuck!" She released her arms and fell back onto the bed.

"I took a swim."

"With your clothes on?"

"I had to."

"Did your boat sink or something?"

"Exploded."

"Oh, no. You were almost killed," she gasped. "Oh, no, you were hurt." Her hand reached up to touch the cut on his left temple. Blood had seeped from it and was now crusting.

"I'm okay. I got back as quickly as I could to kiss you good night."

"Daddy, don't do this again. Please."

Ram smiled down at her. "It's the job."

"Then get another job."

"It's not that simple." He kissed her lightly on the nose. "You'd better get some sleep. It's late."

"I was having this bad dream. I don't remember it, but I know it was bad."

"Then it's good you don't remember it."

"You love me, don't you?"

"I love you very much. Everything I do is for you."

"Will Mommy ever come back?"

Ram's eyes narrowed, "I told you never to ask."

"But why?"

"Because knowing would only hurt."

Gatlin hesitated but then said, "You get shot at, huh?"

"But never hit. That's the important part. I'm never hit." He got to his feet and peered down on his daughter. She looked so fragile lying there. Ten years old. He was running numbers at ten years old. If he'd been a girl, he'd have been walking the streets. That would never happen to her. "Well, you get some sleep. It'll be dawn soon. Maybe we can go out on the lake tomorrow—or rather, today."

"On the boat?"

"We can explore some of the islands around here."

"That'd be fun."

"Good. See you when you wake up." He took the cigar he'd placed on her nightstand and replanted it between his teeth. He casually put a hand in his pocket, then, concerned, searched his other pockets. "I must have left my key. I'll get one from downstairs. Good night, sweetie."

A few seconds later Gatlin was alone again, but the smell of cigar still lingered. It was her father's one vice, smoking those "stogies," as he called them. Actually, it was her father's second vice. The first one was that he killed people. But he was her father, and she had to overlook these things.

Win waited for the detective about a half hour, and when he arrived, Win cringed a little inside. "Well, Win Brady," Mike Grogan greeted. He wore a tan sports coat and shoulder holster. "How's Ginger? I haven't had the chance to talk to her in a while."

"She's fine," Win said, his voice tense. Grogan had made a hard play for Ginger a while back. Somehow Win had beaten him out.

The police officer handed Grogan the envelope. Grogan opened it and peered at the cigar. "So you saw the guy swim in here? You actually fought with him?" Studying Win's bandage, he said, "I suppose asking how you did wouldn't serve any purpose."

"I survived. Ginger was injured slightly."

"She was here too?"

"She got a drop on him, but he managed to knock the gun from her hand and that's when the fight occurred."

"Did you get a good look at him?"

"No."

"Could you pick him out of a mug book—maybe a lineup?"

"The DEA already asked me that. I don't know."

"Describe him."

"My size, my age, black hair—but everything was black. He was very strong."

"But you didn't get a good look at his face?"

"Things happened fast."

"He was smoking this?" Grogan pushed the cigar toward him.

"There." Win pointed his light at the gnarled roots. "He was just resting and smoking as we came upon him."

"Guy's pretty stupid. How did he keep the cigar dry if he swam in here?"

Win shrugged. "A cigar case."

"Could he have been sitting here watching things on the lake and you just happened upon him? You know these hicks up here. Anybody pull a gun on them and they'll fight."

"I saw him swimming away from the explosion. That's why we came down here."

"What if the guy you saw swimming also saw this guy here and swam somewhere else?"

Win thought. "I suppose that could be. But Ginger identified herself as police—at least I think she did. Yes. She did. If he were just some innocent bystander, you'd think he'd just submit."

"Sometimes they don't."

"The more logical conclusion is that he was the pilot of the boat that exploded. Swam in here and was discovered. He did what he had to do—fight his way out."

"Would it be logical for him to swim in here having escaped from the DEA, then stop, and while taking the chance of being seen from all the way across the lake—just the glow of this thing would draw attention—light up a smoke?" Grogan spoke calmly, logically.

"I'm supposed to know this? You're the detective," Win said, feeling his original hostility toward the detective begin to surface.

"I think you *want* to be a detective, Win Brady. That pulpit getting a little boring?"

"There's nothing more exciting than preaching God's Word," Win stated as strongly as he could—feeling duty bound to do so.

"Well, I'll take this in, but I think your guy was just some local boy watching the fireworks. I wouldn't be surprised if you don't end up getting sued over this for harassment—maybe for millions. Your dad's rich, isn't he?"

"I don't think my dad has anything to do with it." Feeling the anger grow, Win decided it was better to leave. "I really want to get back to the hospital and see how Bray Sanderson's doing."

"He's in the ICU," Grogan reported. "He's beat up but alive."

"That's a relief."

"It *is* a relief," Grogan said, managing to sound sincere. "Well, thanks for your interest here, but you really should have called us first. If there was a suspect here, you've probably messed things up so badly we'll never find anything useful."

"I didn't think of that."

"Hopefully you will next time."

"Frankly, I hope there never will be a next time."

"Amen to that, eh?" Grogan laughed softly.

More drained than tired, Win said good-bye and slid behind the wheel. Before he cranked the Chevy over, he sat there for a moment. Grogan had been easy on him. Having worked with Bray once on a murder case, Win had assumed he was justified in continuing the search tonight. But Grogan was right. He wasn't a detective. He was a preacher, and he could have destroyed a lot of evidence. Grogan should have nailed him, but he hadn't.

And maybe the guy *was* just a bystander enjoying the fireworks with a good cigar. Maybe he hadn't heard Ginger tell him she was a cop. Who knew? Well, God did. As did the presence he'd felt there on the beach.

The presence. There was no mistaking it. But why there? Why after he'd been in that very spot at least a couple of times before? And where did it go when the officer came up?

Knowing that there was a spiritual warfare raging all around and actually catching a glimpse of it were two different things. But more important than the glimpse was why he had been given it—again. He once more asked himself the question: What did it mean this time?

Chapter 5

Win Brady had spent his boyhood in a bedroom with soothing wood hues, with a bed that was too large and too sturdy for a boy. So when he and his magic checkbook furnished his room back at the seminary, he had found a bed he really liked, a '57 Corvette bed, one with a headboard that looked like a convertible top at half-mast. His phone sat on the fender, and now, with morning light breaking in hot streams through his uncurtained window, it rang.

"Hi, it's me," Ginger said. "How's your head?"

"Too early to tell. How's your hand?"

"Hurts a little less—you did a good job dressing it."

"Will it bother you on duty?"

"I'll have it checked sometime today. Burns can get infected easily. And there's a lot in that lake that infects. Hey, you ought to see the papers this morning. They're painting Bray as a mix of Mother Teresa and Schwarzenegger."

"He deserves it."

"I thought maybe you'd come back to the hospital last night."

"Did you get a ride home with Pam?"

"About four. Needless to say my eyes are red hot this morning."

"Mine too." He told her what he'd done after leaving her at the hospital.

"Grogan's investigating? After he pushed that gun in your face a few months ago, I can't warm up to him."

"You did the same thing to me, about five minutes after he did, as I recall."

"Yeah, but we're going to get married. There's a difference."

Win laughed.

"I called the hospital before I left this morning," Ginger

continued. "There's no reason for you to go there today. He's still unconscious. They're keeping everyone away. Thought we were going to lose him last night. His heart went nuts, and they had to use those shock paddles. Then I guess they examined him pretty closely and found some bleeding in a sac around his heart."

"Is Mrs. Sherman watching Chad?"

"When he wakes up. You going to the tent?"

"For a little while. Mel likes to go over plans for Sunday. After last night, the Sunday message ought to be a pip."

"When Chad gets there, be prepared; he'll want to go fishing."

"Fishing."

"You want to barbecue tonight?" she asked. "I'll pick up some chicken on the way home. What about corn on the cob? You can soak 'em and do them in the husks."

"What about the fish Chad and I are going to catch?"

"Like I said, I'll pick up chicken."

"Ye of little faith."

"Me of great knowledge." She laughed. "I'll be a little late. Pam and I are going out to look for a wedding dress."

"So you still want to marry me?"

"If I find a dress."

"Then I'll sew you one myself. You want the sleeves the same length?"

"Ahh, a special order." She paused. "So Grogan blew you off."

"Took the cigar and suggested the guy was just a bystander—a lookie-loo."

"A bystander? He didn't act like one after we arrived."

"At least Grogan didn't haul me in for destroying potential evidence."

"That's not the Grogan I know." She hesitated, then said, "Actually I liked it last night. The two of us working together— acting like detectives."

"I can only survive fun like that occasionally."

"No, seriously. We make a good team."

"Think so?" Now it was Win's turn to pause. "You want to become a detective?"

"Work with Bray? Now, there's a challenge."

"Well, I'll support you whatever you decide. But it is more dangerous."

"I already work in traffic—everything else is a piece of cake."

Win laughed. "Well, I'm sure you can be whatever you want to be."

"You really believe that?"

"Sure." He could actually hear her smile of satisfaction over the phone.

"Well, have a good day, and I'll see you with that chicken this afternoon."

The battering he had taken just a few hours before made Win's shoulders feel like they were carrying around an anvil. Moving slowly, he showered, dressed in shorts and T-shirt and tennies and headed for the tent.

The tent was located along Highway 2, a two-lane road that strung the Grand Isles together, across the road and a little north of Martin Sorrell's Inn. A hundred feet long and forty wide, the tent's canvas was a worn white with pronounced red and white rippling stripes along the side and a patch of blue with white stars on the left. The door was a wide flap that Win tied up when he arrived at about seven-thirty. Walking over the wood chip flooring, tossing the barrel of his "tosser-thing" as he went, he crossed to the office area behind the altar's "wall." He tied that flap up as well. Although there was little stopping anyone from crawling beneath the tent wall and stealing everything, if someone tried, he'd find little worth stealing. There were two desks, each with a folding chair, two phones, and assorted files stacked on the corner of each desk. There was running water at a tap in the back.

Win laid his "tosser-thing" on his desk, filled the coffeepot at the tap and got the coffee going, then took his seat at the desk. For just an instant, after reading a couple of chapters of Scripture, his eyes burning from lack of sleep, he placed his head down on his desk.

"Win," he heard through the veil. He felt a hand on his shoulder.

"Huh?" His eyes fluttered, and he became aware of the world again.

Mel Flowers, a pastor in his mid-forties with an expansive warm face, stood over him. "Rough night? What happened to your face?"

Win didn't answer right away. He straightened and leaned back in the chair. "You ready?" Win warned.

Mel sat, head cocked, ready to hear it all. Win told him the condensed version. Because Win was still very confused about the "presence" he'd felt—still wondering what it could possibly mean, still wondering if he'd truly felt it—he left it out.

"I slept all the way through it." Mel tossed a newspaper on the desk in front of him. "I must have been the only one not on the lake." Win studied the front page. Ginger had been right—Bray Sanderson was spread all over it. Several of the people on the party boat had taken pictures, and though the lighting was poor, a number of them had been enhanced and showed Bray's boat on the intercept trajectory. One showed the explosion. Though blurred, there was no suppressing the drama of the moment—and the incredibly dramatic result.

"What do you think God's up to with him?" Mel asked, clearly leading Win.

"Wouldn't it be nice to know what God's up to? Whatever it is, it doesn't seem to be going according to my plan."

"Your plan."

"Sure. I mean, God started out okay. He brought Bray face-to-face with his own mortality, then showed him he was a heartbeat from eternity. But he hasn't confronted him with his need for a Savior—Bray has to be conscious for that, which he's not. My plan would be to start Bray on a slow recovery, which would give me a chance to work him to salvation. He'd be so grateful to God that he'd reach out for Jesus and— *wham!*—we'd have another convert on our hands. And I'd have my buddy back. We wouldn't even care what a crusty critter ol' Bray is."

"And it's not going that way?"

"God not only brought him to the brink of eternity, but then shoved him even closer by letting his heart go berserk. The guy was unconscious. God didn't need to do that."

"He's overdoing it a little in your mind."

"Really overdoing it. Now Bray's lying there unconscious.

May even be in a coma. None of this is going to matter to Bray. When he comes to, he won't know any of it happened."

Mel was sitting on his assistant's desk, and while Win spoke, he picked up Win's "tosser-thing" and flipped the barrel casually. Mel was very good at many things. He was lousy at this. "The only way I've ever been able to figure out what God is really doing is to wait until it's over and look back. Then his footprints stand out pretty clearly."

"What do you think of those strange, kind of supernatural feelings—like sensing a presence?"

"Like in the bell tower."

"I told you about that?"

"A couple of times." Mel dropped into his folding chair. "We've got to get more comfortable chairs." He screwed himself around to position the metal crosspiece in his back. "I know you're a little more rigid in your feelings about such things than I am . . ."

"God closed the Bible. The last paragraphs of Revelation do that. No one's to add or take away from his Word. And yet—"

Mel nodded and scratched the side of his nose. "I think God limits himself. He can obviously do anything, but he limits himself. He keeps his word though he could easily break it. He works his plan when he could probably get things accomplished quicker by edict—he did make the heavens, the earth, and all the creepy crawly things in six days. But he's got his reasons—I think mostly it has to do with the battle with Satan."

"Do you think I could be sensing Satan or his minions?"

"Jesus talks about binding the strong man then letting him loose at the end. That's probably why we don't see the demon possessions that Jesus seemed to encounter all over the place. But God can, if he wishes, use evil for good—Joseph shows us that. Now, what's all this about?"

"I've been thinking about it lately."

"This is me here, Win. When did it happen?"

Win took a deep breath. "Twice last night. Once when that boat blew up—and once in the cove when I returned to look around." Win then told Mel the details.

"You're sure? Our emotions can do strange things under stress."

"I've gone through all those arguments—every pro and con I can think of. In the end I come up short. I just don't know."

Mel cocked a brow. "Then probably God's not through with you yet."

"Or I'm just dumb."

"We're all dumber than he is. If the Lord wants you to turn right, he'll put a sign in front of you that says 'Turn Right' with a big arrow. If you don't know how he's directing you—"

"There'll be something more."

"And if there's not—" Mel prodded.

"Then I've dreamed the whole thing."

Mel neither nodded nor shook his head. "Maybe it means you're supposed to be a little confused for a while. I don't know."

"At least I'm in good company."

"Christians always are." Mel paused and looked at Win's "tosser-thing." He tossed the barrel in a wide arc. It hit the stick and bounced off. "What're you going to use this for?"

"The kids. I still need a spiritual tie-in."

"Spiritual tie-in—my specialty. Uh, how about 'before Christ, life is hit and miss. After Christ, the miss is taken out of it—all things work together for good.' Just think. What if life became a sure thing—five for five?"

Win laughed softly in frustration. "In seminary I was hitting five for five. Not here."

"You're hitting five for five, but you just don't know it."

"When that guy last night used my head as a tetherball, he was the one hitting five for five."

Mel smiled. "I met a guy the other day who goes to one of the churches downtown. His hobby's woodworking. I'll see if he can make up some more of these. Leave it on your desk, and I'll take care of it." Mel flipped open his Bible in preparation to start working on his message. "I wish getting us through the winter were that easy. Being an itinerant preacher, I used to just take the ol' tent to Florida. But not this winter, and when it's fifty degrees below zero, this tent won't attract a huge congregation."

"Only the really sturdy ones."

"A congregation of crash dummies." Mel laughed. "I've

actually been in churches like that. Anyway, by Thanksgiving we'd better be in a new place. With walls and a very large heater. I'm rather delicate where cold is concerned."

Win took a deep breath. "I'm not helping much. Chad brought someone last week. . . ."

"Todd Breckenridge—his folks work in the apple orchard north of here. No excess stocks and bonds there."

The phone rang and Win grabbed it. Ginger was on the other end. "You listening to the radio?"

"No. Why?"

"They've let all the guys the DEA captured last night go."

"You're kidding."

"They found no drugs in any of the boats they were piloting, and their attorney is threatening some kind of humongous lawsuit saying the DEA overreacted. They were just having a friendly boat race."

"With an Uzi for a starting gun?"

"Start a lot of races really quick."

"Well," Win said, not sure what else to say, "I'm glad Bray doesn't know. It'd kill him."

"It's killing me. Even if we'd caught that guy last night, he'd be on the street this morning. Well, enough bad news. Chad'll be there in a few minutes. I just talked to him. He'll be with that new boy, Todd. He's still talking about fishing."

After a word of good-bye, Win hung up. "They let all the bad guys go."

"It wouldn't happen that way at the seminary, would it?" Mel asked sympathetically.

"Things were a lot easier," Win said, grabbing his "tosser-thing" and nailing it the first time.

Mike Grogan, his coal black hair slicked down, his coal black eyes sparkling like obsidian, stepped into his office. Saturday was unusual. It wasn't considered a workday, but usually Grogan came in just in case there was something to learn. He'd putter around until he was satisfied that he'd discovered all there was. This Saturday was different. There was a purpose to it. He'd been working all night with the DEA, keeping his ears open and gumming up the works as best he could. As it turned out, he didn't have to do much. There wasn't much to find.

Brady and Glasgow's encounter—and that cigar—posed a problem.

If those two half-wits happened to identify Ram Lucha as the guy—Ram was the only one at Sorrell's who smoked cigars—that cigar would nail down the guy's coffin. If they did DNA tests on the saliva, they'd match it to Ram Lucha. If they studied the tobacco, they'd find it was Ram Lucha's favorite—whatever that was. If they ever had to prove Lucha was the guy, the cigar would do the trick. So Mike Grogan ground it with his heel before returning it to the envelope. His report just said that it had been found in a cove and a thorough search had turned up nothing else. Of course there was no search. The last thing he needed was more evidence.

What if Brady went back to the cove? What if he found more evidence?

Grogan wanted to ride Ram anyway. He made sure the surrounding offices were empty and punched in Sorrell's number. He asked for Ram when Waco picked up the phone.

When Ram answered, Grogan spoke quickly. "It's Grogan. You got a problem."

"What kind?"

"That woman cop might be able to identify you. And her boyfriend brought in your cigar."

"Getting rid of it is your job. Getting rid of them is mine."

"If bodies start floating to the surface—particularly ones associated with last night, the DEA won't believe we've left."

There was silence on the other end of the phone.

"Listen, Ram. It was dark—even the DEA said things moved pretty fast. Just stay low for a while. As time goes on, the memory will fade."

Ram knew what Grogan was saying was true. He'd wait. Bide his time. Strike only if necessary. "I'll do what I have to do," said Ram. "But I will do what I have to do. Understood?"

"You keep an eye on the cove," Grogan retorted. "They might just go back looking for more. There's no telling what you left behind."

Ram remembered the key . . . but he'd probably dropped it in the lake. No one would find it there.

"And if they find something, you'd better hope they bring it to me," Grogan warned.

"Your job is to make sure that doesn't matter." Ram hung up.

Wondering if he'd gone too far, Grogan also hung up—just in time to overhear Commander Breed talking to one of the other guys. What Grogan overheard worried him.

Back at the inn, a lookout was posted in an upper room, one with a panoramic view of the lake. The instant Ram hung up, he made his way to that room. By the time he left, the lookout knew that if he saw any activity—people searching, police boats patrolling—in a particular cove just north of the inn, the lookout was to tell Ram—only Ram.

Ram then left the lookout and returned downstairs where he'd been playing pool.

At the police station, Grogan waited a few minutes for Breed to go back to his office before knocking lightly on Breed's door. After Breed acknowledged him, he entered. "Looks like Sanderson did some good last night," Grogan began amiably. "The papers are full of it."

"It's getting national coverage. I have messages here from all the networks."

"What are his chances?"

"He's still critical." While Breed spoke, he didn't look up but shuffled paper on his desk.

Grogan found Breed's distraction disconcerting. As Breed's fair-haired boy, Grogan usually commanded all of Breed's attention when in his office.

"I'm going to send a guard over there," Breed said. "I owe him. He and I used to be friends, and I've let him down." Now Breed's eyes came up. "If he gets through this, I'm going to get him back here."

Grogan knew exactly what that meant. If Sanderson came

back, Breed would recommend him for commander, the slot Breed would vacate when he retired in six months.

That was Grogan's slot. He'd not only worked to get it, but he'd been *ordered* to get it. He couldn't *not* get it. "It'll be good to have him back," Grogan said, the strain in his voice evident. "Well," he said. "I've got some things to clear up."

Back in his cubicle, Grogan planted himself on his chair and rubbed his chin feverishly. After five minutes of thought, he came to the same conclusion he'd come to after only a few seconds of thought. Sanderson was a dead man.

Like every other cop on the face of the earth, Mike Grogan had started out clean. That lasted about a year. Then a friend on the force was killed execution style. The police knew who did it but couldn't prove anything.

Grogan planted the evidence that sent the murderer up. It felt good.

That anti-criminal act somehow made it easier when he had the opportunity to join them. He was aiding a drug bust. Six officers lay in wait for a courier. The plan was simple. Wait for the buy, when the money changed hands, jump out and make arrests.

Plans changed when someone pulled a machine pistol. Suddenly bullets were everywhere. Two officers went down, one of the druggies bit it. Grogan saw one druggie take off. He peeled off in pursuit, caught up with the guy in an alley, wrestled him to the ground, and was about to slap the cuffs on when the guy pulled out a thick envelope. "Take it. Let me go and take it."

Grogan had never seen so many hundred-dollar bills. He'd heard of piles of drug money confiscated in raids but had never seen it. Now he held a good deal of it in his hand.

It took a second to decide.

Money stuffed down his pants, he got off the guy, and let him escape. About a month later, he was on a stakeout for a different drug buy. He and another cop were trading four-hour shifts. Just as Grogan began, he got a phone call over the closed wire. Expecting one of his own, Grogan answered it, "Yeah."

A hoarse whisper. "How much did you get when you let the Hammer go?"

"Who is this?"

"We're going to be making the buy in about ten minutes. You don't see nothin'. It'll be worth something to you. If you see something, we tell your boss about the Hammer's miraculous escape. Understood?"

"When do I get the money?"

"You'll get it."

Grogan hung up.

He witnessed the buy ten minutes later, and when his partner came on duty, he told him nothing had happened. He found five thousand in used twenties in his locked mailbox that night.

The payoffs became more frequent, and as he climbed in the department over the years, his involvement in the crime family also grew. It didn't take long before everything he did had one objective—to become a "made man," a member of the family.

When they wanted somebody for their inside guy in Vermont, he jumped at the chance.

"You're to become the top detective," ordered the family boss. "The guy there will be retiring in a year or two. I want you in that slot."

Since he'd arrived a year before, he'd wormed his way into Larin Breed's heart. Breed wanted a young man to replace him, a go-getter who'd go after criminals like a dog after a bone. Grogan filled that bill. As insurance, he'd discredited Sanderson, the next one in line, by making him look like a chump in his last investigation—that murder in the church. Not only had Grogan made Sanderson look incompetent, but he caused, well, almost caused, that wimp Sorrell to be caught—which created Sorrell's debt to the family and, thereby, the family's occupation of Sorrell's Inn.

Now things were changing. But he couldn't let Sanderson get that job. He'd have to keep an eye on things—a close eye.

Chad Glasgow and Todd Breckenridge arrived at the tent a few minutes after Ginger had called Win, and Mel had already buried himself in preparation for Sunday's sermon. Standing before Win's desk, the two boys couldn't have looked more different. Chad was a towheaded kid with a roundness to him, a shape something like a pear; he possessed a round middle and a round, cheerful face. Todd, on the other hand, was lean and hard, with a longish, nearly gaunt face below a shock of matted black hair. He wore a denim shirt with the arms torn off and denim shorts, his pockets always bulging. There was nothing cheerful about him.

"We want to go out and teach those fish a lesson," Chad said first thing.

"You, too, Todd? I'm not much of a fisherman," Win answered cheerfully.

"Maybe we could toss a cherry bomb at 'em," Todd suggested, reaching into his pocket. Win raised a restraining hand, sure that the kid probably had a cherry bomb in there.

"Speaking of tossing things . . ." Win began, grabbing his "tosser-thing."

"What's that?" Chad asked.

"It's my 'tosser-thing.' Works like this." Win tossed the little barrel up, did a quick whip of the wrist to turn the barrel, and deftly caught it on the stick. "Pretty neat, huh?"

"Let me try it," Chad asked, grabbing for it. He tossed the barrel twice and missed wide both times.

"You wanna try, Todd?"

With a who-cares sweep of his eyes, Todd took the handle and tossed the little barrel into the air. It fell farther away from the stick than Chad's had.

"This is stupid," Todd spat.

"Actually, it's a kick. You just have to practice," Win said.

Chad tried it a couple more times, one was a near miss.

But Todd refused to so much as touch it again.

"I was thinking I could get a bunch of these made up, and the kids in Sunday school could have some fun with them," Win explained.

"Sounds good. But you have to let me practice so that when they get 'em, I'll be the best right off."

Win laughed. "You little fraud. You wouldn't even tell them you had the extra practice, would you?"

"It's none of their business." Chad smiled slyly.

"No one would want to play with that," Todd said contemptuously.

"Well, some might," Win said with a note of finality. He placed the "tosser-thing" on his desk and asked Chad, "Did your mom tell you about Detective Sanderson?"

"What about him?"

Win told Chad everything, showing him the pictures from Mel's newspaper. When Chad saw the one of Bray saving the party boat, his mouth dropped a foot.

"Let's go visit him," Chad said. It was no surprise to Win that Bray was one of Chad's favorite people. Bray had helped Win save Chad's life one very stormy night on the lake.

"He's a cop?" asked Todd. "Who cares about a cop?"

"He saved my life," Chad told him. Then as if realizing, "And my mom's a cop."

"Lucky you," Todd said. "Nobody saves me but me. Wanna see my knife?" The hand went to the pocket again.

"We can't visit him now, anyway," Win injected, trying to get things back on track. "He's still unconscious. But we'll keep him in prayer, though."

"Maybe we could pray right now?" asked Chad.

While Todd dipped into his pocket and grabbed a miniature yo-yo, Win and Chad bowed their heads, and Win said a quick but heartfelt prayer.

"That's weird," Todd groaned, stuffing the yo-yo back.

"I used to think so too," Chad replied. But then he turned to Win with a huge, excited grin. "Okay, let's fish!"

Win eyed Mel for his approval to leave, who, with a concerned eye on Todd, gave it with a nod.

A half hour later, the fishing tackle gleaned from Win's boathouse wall—worms procured from a local bait shop—they were trolling out in the middle of the lake in Win's sixteen-foot Bayliner. The spot they found was not far from the church and also not far from Martin Sorrell's Inn. It was also not far from the cove where Win had fought the cigar-guy and experienced the ominous sensation. He found himself staring at the cove and only stopped when he heard the boys telling him he was nearing a small island. The island was little more than a bushy outcropping. Win decided to remain there because the channel was wider there, and he thought the island might attract fish. Win had heard that somewhere. When they arrived, though, two other fishermen were trolling, or drifting, in the deeper places.

"Uncle Joel's a little nervous about us using his tackle." Win cautioned. "So be careful."

Chad hurrumphed. "Like I'll throw it in the lake or something."

"You ever fish before, Todd?" Win asked.

"Some," said the boy, his eyes scanning the pole as if trying to figure out which end to grab. "Perch," he added.

"You're gonna pull an old perch you caught out of those pockets of yours, aren't you?" Win laughed.

"Not so old," Todd shot back.

"My barber fishes all the time. Says there's lake perch in here."

"That's why I'm here," Todd professed. "Lake perch. Have you ever fished before?" he asked Win.

"Never in my life," Win said, exuding confidence from every pore. "But that doesn't matter. I'm the grown-up. And as you know, grown-ups never make mistakes."

"Good," Chad piped. "Bait my hook."

"Mine too," added Todd. "I'm really not a wormy kind of guy. And if there's one thing I told Chad right off—Pastor Win's wormy. Didn't I, Chad?"

"His very words." Chad laughed, but Todd kept the needle in with sarcastic, penetrating eyes. He was schooled in the use of sarcasm, and he seemed to like using it.

Win took at least a couple of minutes to bait Chad's hook with the slimiest worm he'd ever handled. Then he gave the youngster the pole and gingerly let out the line for him.

"Yer not going to cast it?" Todd jabbed.

"Worms first—casting comes when you hit high school." While Chad began fishing, Win pinched a particularly long worm between thumb and forefinger and held it up. Then he ran his hand along Todd's line until his finger was jabbed by the hook.

"Good way to find it," Todd said.

"Works every time," Win replied, eyeing the hook and the worm and wondering if tying it on using a simple granny knot might work just as well.

"You waiting for it to die of natural causes?" Todd asked.

Win said nothing and took a deep, resolute breath. "Sorry, skinny," he said to the worm and jabbed it unmercifully with the hook. To his surprise it went on with reasonable ease. Even Todd seemed impressed. A moment later, with his line tossed a few feet from the edge of the boat, Todd leaned on the railing and studied the floating bobber.

As Win chose his own worm, a short fat one, he heard Todd's voice. "I got a question."

"Shoot."

"You guys like this cop-guy who's in the hospital, right?"

"Right."

"And you believe there's a God."

"And we find him through our belief in Jesus Christ."

"Whatever. And he's a good God, right?"

"The best."

"Then why does this good God let your cop friend get hurt—maybe killed?" Todd asked, his eyes still fixed on the bobber floating a few feet from the boat.

Now baiting his own hook, Win tried to split his attention between the third slimiest worm in the world, the barbed hook very near his finger, and the answer to the king of all theological questions.

"It's part of the plan," he said—rather flippantly, he thought. But the worm wasn't cooperating, and he was squishing it between his fingers.

"What plan?"

Win stopped mid-worm. "God plans everything. In the Bible—Acts, actually—God says he sets our boundaries, where we live, what we do, and what happens to us, so that we'll seek him. And then he carries his plan out. I'm hoping that Bray's being hurt will lead him to seek the Lord." Win looked at the boy, his worn jeans, his hair in need of a comb, his fingernails still dirty from yesterday's play. "If you have things you don't like about your life, then seek God—call upon Jesus—place him in your heart. You'll be surprised what changes."

To let his words sink in, Win continued with the worm and immediately drove the hook into his finger. "Argh!" he groaned.

"That's quite a plan God's got for you," Todd pointed out.

After easing the barb out, Win's first instinct was to suck the blood off the tip of his finger, but part of a worm was there. He wiped it on his once white T-shirt, leaving a red-brown, gut-smeared streak. He laughed in frustration. Here he was trying to explain deep spiritual things while toying with worm guts. *Einstein and Goofy.* Dean Joel Watkins, the owner of the house he rented and the tackle they were using, had said that Win had two emotional settings—Einstein and Goofy. Not much had changed in the past few months.

Chad joined the conversation, "But Bray being hurt was a bad thing—God doesn't do bad things."

"Right," Win said, still wanting to suck the blood off his finger but unable to. He returned to the worm's agony. He was about to answer Chad when, to his surprise, the answer came from Todd.

"He's saying if it helps the cop, then no matter how much it hurts, it's a good thing. My mom uses that argument when she comes after me with a wooden spoon. 'You'll thank me for this later.' Not hardly."

"But what if he dies?" Chad continued, genuinely concerned.

"Unsaved people die. I won't like it in Bray's case, but they do."

"But he'll go to hell."

"I already been to hell," Todd said, hardly loud enough to be heard. "My dad calls hell my mom's cookin'." There should have been a laugh there but there wasn't.

Win ignored Todd and addressed Chad's concern. "God saves his people, Chad. We need to pray that Bray's one of them. I know it's hard. Believe me, I know. But God tells us to spread the gospel and make sure he's at work in *our own* lives. He takes care of everything else."

Saying it was so easy, yet as Win spoke the words, he wasn't even sure he believed them. His heart seemed so disconnected from them, like they were being said by someone else. Why wasn't life simpler? Why didn't it unfold like he wanted, or at least as he expected it to? Why wasn't his mother still alive?

Why wasn't his friend getting better by now? Calling for him? Why could he do nothing about it?

"There's no God," Todd said with conviction. "There's only this pole and a bunch of fish down there thumbing their noses at us." For emphasis, Todd angrily tossed the pole, and reasonably expensive reel, out into the water.

Shocked and not sure what to do, Win watched as the pole and reel hit the water and quickly began to sink. "What'd you do that for?" he asked. But there was no time to wait for an answer. He dropped his own pole on the deck and leaped over the side.

"Hand it up to me, Win, when you get it," he heard Chad call as he dropped below the surface. To his surprise, he kept dropping. Although near the little island, there was no shallow bottom. Realizing he needed to breathe soon, he fought his way back to the surface and spun around looking for the rod and reel. It was long gone. He dove under again, but the water was murky and cold.

Giving up, he broke the surface again.

"If you could afford this boat, you can buy another fishing rod," Todd called down to him coldly.

"Maybe you've got a replacement in your pocket," Win fired back. He felt angrier than he thought possible. He reached up, grabbed the boat's railing, threw a leg up—and fell back into the water. He tried again, and this time, with Chad's help, pulled himself aboard.

"Reel the line in, Chad. Fishing's over for today."

But Chad wasn't listening. While Win was struggling on board, Chad had heard something else. Laughter. High-pitched bells of laughter coming from somewhere toward shore. Then he saw her—in a boat something like theirs. Her father or someone was driving, and she was at the back of the craft, her hand on the railing for balance while she watched and laughed at Win's antics. Leaving Win in his final moments of sliding back in to the boat, Chad went to the bow of the boat, the point closest to the girl as the guy piloting her boat sped away. Staring at her for a moment, her muted laughter still ringing over the lake, Chad waved. To his surprise, she waved back. But then, as if catching herself, she turned and ran to the bow and stared off somewhere, her back to Chad.

Betty Harmon, now Marion Sylvan, waded through a day that moved with agonizing slowness. The rain-threatening cloud cover brought an unusual humidity. It made everyone grumpy. Getting rides was difficult. No one cared that she had an ailing son or daughter, or that her mother was about to die alone. No one cared that she had no money or had somewhere important to go

But for all that, by evening she'd crossed the Vermont border and was in Bennington, not far from the Grandma Moses Museum, as a sign announced. But there were few prospects of getting any farther. Tired, hot, feeling an overwhelming sense of defeat, she collapsed on a parking lot railing and thought seriously about crying.

But after only a few minutes, she heard a woman's voice. "You okay?"

She turned to see a woman behind the wheel of a new model Cadillac. Clearly used to finer things, she wore a tailored gray suit, and her soft blonde hair was delicately molded.

"I am now," she said.

"Need a ride?"

"I'm going north."

"Canada?"

"Lake Champlain. I have friends there."

"I can take you partway," the woman said. "I've a meeting in Rutland in the morning."

"Thank you," she said.

The Cadillac rode like a dream. All great cars did. She always wanted a great car but had to settle for a Hyundai Accent back in L.A.

"What's your name?" the woman asked.

"Marion Sylvan," she said.

"Doris Willem," she told her. "I'm in sales."

"I used to go to sales—at the malls," Marion added as if she had to explain her joke. "Thanks for coming along. I need to stop worrying for a few minutes. I'm escaping—my husband beats me up. Well, actually he's not my husband, but he acts like he is. I just got the nerve to leave him this morning—while he was in the shower. I just grabbed some essentials, stuffed them in this bag, and took off."

As her new story rolled off her tongue, she realized its genius. Every woman would empathize and want to help, and no woman would ever betray her to her pursuer—if they did, they'd be betraying their very womanhood. In a very real sense, she was building an impenetrable wall behind which she could hide forever.

The help was also more substantial. Not only did this woman take her half the way to Lake Champlain, but she put her up for the night in a Rutland Motel Six and even left the tab open so she could have another night there if she wished.

Not only a good Samaritan—a great Samaritan.

This was Marion's first night in Vermont, and even though there was nothing warm and fuzzy about Rutland, it was a small city in every sense of the expression; she felt curiously at home there. So at home that the first thing she did when she unlocked the motel door was to place her loving little clown on the dresser, then on her end table when she moved to the bed. She even placed it on the sink when she took a warm shower and prepared to go to bed. Those outstretched arms were beckoning her home, and she felt like she had arrived.

With dinner over, Ginger and Win sat on the end of her dock while Chad played with his soldier figures near the water's edge—an amphibious landing.

"I forgot to ask. How's the search for your wedding dress coming?" Win asked.

"Didn't go. Pam had a rush job she needed to get done. We might go tomorrow after church."

Win took her right hand and looked at the oval burn on the skin. "How's it feel?"

"Hardly notice it." She then took his hand and kissed it lightly. "Have you called Uncle Joel about the fishing rod?"

"You should have seen him, Mom," Chad called up. "He was like a hero diving in after a drowning kid."

"I know I'm supposed to love all kids—everybody, actually. But loving Todd's really tough."

"He's a kid. Chad says he's got a rough home life. Always moving around. Probably built some high fences."

"He told me he lived four places last year," Chad said. "He has trouble making friends."

"He moves his life with him," Win said. "It's all in his pockets. Every time we needed anything, his hands went to his pockets." But even as Win spoke he realized how hard he sounded. "Okay, you win. I guess I feel sorry for him. But he fights me every chance he gets."

Ginger hugged his arm. "I'm sure seminary never taught you that ministry was going to be easy."

"They did say it was hard. Why do you think I stayed there six years? It was safer, and while I was there I could put that goat in Professor Winters's bathtub. It was just my little way of dealing with the hard facts."

"Did you call the hospital about Bray?" she asked him, her head permanently on his shoulder now. A warm breeze with a cool, lake-sharpened edge slipped by.

"They didn't have much to add," Win said. "It *was* a lot easier at the seminary," he added, continuing his previous thought. "You know how much I dislike someone disliking me. It's bad enough when it's someone on a bus I might accidentally offend—someone you only meet once—but when it's my best friend who can't stand me—that's a real bummer."

"When he comes to," Ginger said, "he'll see you. He'll probably realize, since he almost died, just how important a friend you are."

"I still think if I showed up there, a few minutes later he'd order a paddy wagon to drive me to the county line."

"He'll call," she said with assurance. "I bet you."

"You'll bet what?"

"A pizza—shrimp, artichoke and—what else—Canadian bacon."

"I don't think Willie's Pizza Shack has shrimp, artichoke, and Canadian bacon. They have pepperoni. Lots of pepperoni."

"You'll have to buy the ingredients at the market, take them to the pizza parlor, then watch those guys to make sure they don't burn it."

"You've got it all figured out."

"Because I know he'll call."

As if on cue the phone rang inside. Ginger was about to tell Chad to get it but didn't have to. He was up like a shot and in the house before she could form the words.

A few moments later Chad appeared at the door. "That was the hospital. A nurse or something. Bray wants to see you, Win."

"Is it too late to add brussels sprouts?" Ginger grinned.

Chapter 6

Ginger and Chad waited for Win as he was taken by the nurse into Bray's cubicle.

Win wasn't sure what to expect. The nurse had cautioned him before taking him back. The only reason they were allowing this visit was because Bray was getting agitated, and satisfying his request to see Win seemed the only way to calm him down. And above all, Bray needed calm. "We don't want to use heavy sedatives if we don't have to. Be quick. He's still incredibly weak."

He was.

Mummified in a white sheet, tubes and wires falling off of him like garland, Bray lay still, his face ashen, his eyes little more than slits. Win now felt guilty for even *wanting* to bother Bray.

"Win? That you?" The voice rose like steam from the ghostly face. His lips, only thin reminders of what they ought to be, barely moved as he spoke.

"Right here." Win laid a warm hand on Bray's. He felt it move as if Bray were trying to grip his in return.

"You're the only one who'll tell me the truth," Bray said, his voice reflecting pain. "Am I going to die?"

"You're close. But you're stabilizing."

"I don't want to die—hate the thought of it." Then, after a shallow attempt at a deep breath, he asked, "What happened?"

"You're a hero," Win told him. "The boat blew up in your face."

"I don't remember," Bray whispered hoarsely, his breathing suddenly labored, every movement of his chest excruciating.

"I saw the guy in the boat swim away. But Grogan didn't think much of what I told him." Win couldn't help giving Bray the few facts he knew.

The instant Win mentioned the name, Bray tightened noticeably. For an instant he stopped breathing, and his eyes actually opened to half-mast. "Grogan? Why Grogan?"

"He's investigating what happened on the lake. But they didn't find any drugs. They've let them all go."

"Grogan's investigating what happened to me?"

"Partly, I guess."

"I bet he's loving that," Bray groaned.

The nurse was suddenly there again. She eyed the monitors with grave concern.

"But he can't beat me again," Bray said; even his thin voice registered desperation.

"Relax, good buddy," Win said soothingly.

"I can't," Bray said, his hands beginning to shake. "What didn't Grogan like?"

"I fought with the guy who piloted the boat that blew up on you," Win told Bray. "Then I gave Grogan some physical evidence. He didn't think it was very important."

"You fought? Where?" he managed.

"In a small cove. The guy swam there."

"Can you recognize the guy?"

"Don't think so. Things were happening pretty fast."

"What did you find?"

The nurse intervened. "I'm sorry. You need to let Mr. Sanderson rest."

"Search that cove again," Bray continued. "Go over it again—comb it."

"Bray, that's the police's job."

"I'm the police." Bray coughed, then shuddered painfully. "Bring what you find to me."

"I'm sorry, Mr. Brady," the nurse said. "You must leave."

"Bring what you find to me." Bray coughed again, and the nurse gave Win a gentle shove and turned back to her patient.

Win scooped up Ginger and Chad on the way past the nurse's station. They didn't speak until they were at Win's car. Before he got in, Win fell against the edge of the car roof. It dug into his back. "The guy's a breath away from death, and he's still trying to compete with Grogan."

Ginger leaned against his shoulder, her back against the car. "How? What did he say?"

"He wants me to search the cove again—then bring what I find to him. He's competing with Grogan. Looking like someone whose bungee cord was cut at the critical moment—and he's competing with Grogan. He wants to find out who did this to him before Grogan does. Bray's nuts."

"And if you ever want to see him again, you'll have to do it."

Win only nodded. "Well, it won't be tonight. I'll wander over there after church tomorrow."

"I'll go with you. We can cover more ground together."

Win smiled, then said sarcastically, "Well, we found the guy and the cigar last time. Maybe this time we'll find the match. That ought to set the DEA on its ear."

"Is all this part of God's plan, Win?" Chad asked, his voice also betraying a certain sarcasm.

Win dipped a brow at him. "Right," he said.

Gatlin lay on her bed watching *Saturday Night Live*. She didn't like it. Never had, but there was nothing else on. Her father was downstairs playing poker with the others. They were celebrating. They were always celebrating something. A Knicks game or somebody winning in court. And there were always new people coming for a few days then leaving. All knew her dad, but none had time for her.

This time they were celebrating having gotten out of jail. A celebration that made sense.

"Bic Doyle's gonna be delivered Monday morning," the boss said.

"C.O.D.?" one of the guys joked.

"Yeah, Cut-up on Delivery." More laughing.

"After that, more than ever, us stayin' gotta look like tourists. Those goin' will go a few at a time throughout the day. We don't want to raise no suspicion." Then Gatlin heard her dad's name. "Ram, take the kid out durin' the day. Make her visible."

She didn't like being called a kid, but she liked being outside a lot. Being visible meant she could do a lot of swimming and boating, and since they'd arrived at the lake a couple of months ago, she had fallen in love with the place. It was a lot better than Delaney Street where she had lived before. Summers were hot, and the other kids were hard as nails. She didn't like it. Her father was gone most of the time, sometimes day and night. When he was gone there were baby-sitters, and though her dad spent as much time with her as he could, she was mostly with baby-sitters.

He wasn't all that particular about them and rarely listened to Gatlin when she complained. All he cared about was that someone was around to get her out of a burning building or a gas main explosion. All the other stuff like having fun or talking or playing with her or even cleaning her up when she was young always came second. Here at the inn, though, everything was different. Out here, canyons of cement and the hordes that lived in the canyons didn't exist.

"What do you want her to do when I'm away?" her father asked.

"She stays in."

Gatlin was about to remind the boss that her father was away a lot but didn't. She'd just have to spend all that time indoors. But why? She was responsible. She knew where she could go and where she couldn't. She knew what to say and what not to. She'd been a prisoner of sorts all her life. Her father was always telling her she had a big mouth. The last thing she wanted was to get her dad in trouble. She'd never say anything. Never. They could pull her toes off one by one, and she wouldn't tell. Of course, she didn't know what she could tell anyway. He went out and came back. He had guns, and sometimes she'd overhear him and one of the others talking— maybe she did have something she could tell. But she never would—not even if she ended up with no toes at all.

He was her dad. She could never tell on her dad.

But why couldn't she go outside when he was away? She didn't like being a prisoner. She liked it outside. The lake was great. She loved the boat. Loved her father speeding around. Loved the fresh air and the splash of cold water on her.

She found herself laughing. A TV commercial came on—a

guy fishing in a stream losing his footing—a Jeep ad or something. She remembered the guy jumping out of the boat that morning and the two kids trying to help him back in. The one who waved was a little chubby, but from a distance, cute—cute in a fun sense. But he was out there somewhere, and she was stuck here. She wondered what he was doing.

She got to her feet and went to the window. Opening it, she craned her top half out the window and looked around. There had to be a way to get out of this place without them seeing her. There'd be only five or six of 'em for a while. And she was small and could move like a lightning bug through the shadows. And even when the rest returned, she could get lost in the crowd.

She'd think about it. If there was one thing she could do, it was think, figure things out. There had to be a way, and if she thought about it enough, she'd find it.

Martin Sorrell listened to the celebrating upstairs and hated every laugh, every verbal jab. This was his inn. Although many years ago it had started out as his prison, his place of exile, it had quickly become his home. And now these barbarians had taken it over. They didn't have the right to enjoy it. Not a second of it.

But there was nothing he could do.

Nothing.

But work with his roses . . . were these seeds his black rose?

Another burst of laughter. Now music. Sinatra.

Up 'til now he liked Sinatra. Now all the rumors about him being connected in some way with the Mafia circled around him, and he hated Sinatra just like he hated all those guys upstairs.

How could Sorrell possibly be so alone?

He had fifty million dollars sitting in all sorts of investments in all sorts of places. He could buy a dozen hit men to clean them out. He could buy a whole army.

But he couldn't do anything like that. Ever again. It was that kind of reckless behavior that got him into this mess. No. He'd just wait it out. One day he'd wake up and find them gone.

That's how it would be. His life had always worked itself out. Even when he was fouling things up for his father, things always worked out. They'd work out this time too.

All he had to do was wait.

Oh, how he hated Sinatra and the whole lot of 'em.

Could one of these seeds really be the black rose? Would it ever really matter?

Todd Breckenridge sat on a wooden lounge chair outside his folks' shack beneath an ancient, gnarled apple tree. It was rumored to be a Johnny Appleseed apple tree. Grown-ups were idiots. Not only were they idiots for believing that that tree had anything to do with Johnny Appleseed, but Johnny Appleseed was an idiot for scattering seeds everywhere and letting everybody else eat his apples. He should have built a fence around 'em all and stockpiled the profits.

But who cared about apple trees anyway? Todd's folks picked and managed a crew, but they didn't care about apples. They cared about making money. They also cared about television, which his father watched. And beer, which his father, Frank, and mother, Lois, drank while his father watched television. And canasta, which his mother played every night with two of the picker-women while she drank the beer. They didn't care about him at all. They sent him to bed about ten every night—when he was home—and he promptly climbed out the window and sat in the lounge chair for a while daring them to find him. But they never found him. They never looked for him. He hated television and canasta, though he had nothing against beer.

Now his folks were in bed. The canasta game broke up about eleven which was about the time the news was over, so they both stumbled off to bed and snored—his father like a freight train, his mother like a cat being shoved into a water barrel. Todd wasn't tired at all and felt restless.

He stuffed a hand in his pocket and pulled out the miniature yo-yo. He played with that for a minute or two then stuffed it back in his pocket. The night was growing cool, and as the temperature dropped, his restlessness grew.

He pulled out his knife. He'd won it from one of the pickers about a month ago pitching pennies. It had a bone handle, and the blade was four inches of sharp steel. He loved that knife. It threw really well. To prove it to himself, he flipped it at the old apple tree. He was surprised when it stuck. He retrieved it and threw it again, and it bounced off into the tall grass.

He retrieved it, folded it up, and stuffed it back into his pocket.

Time to go exploring.

He went down to the lake and sat on a large boulder. There was nothing going on. The lake was like black glass, and what few lights there were along its edge shimmered in long white spikes. Someone other than Todd would have found it beautiful. Todd found it boring.

Then he thought of something that sounded like fun—well, not so much fun as a challenge—well, not so much a challenge as a way of showing that stupid pastor how really good he could be. That thing you toss in the air and catch on a stick. He'd get that thing and get good at it—then he'd show that stupid pastor guy. And Chad. Fat little know-it-all.

It took him fifteen minutes to get to the tent-church. The place was dark, the flaps pulled down and tied. Getting in would be too easy. A car rambled by. Todd walked around to the back. It seemed darker back there. Just him and the weeds, the lake lapping at the shore about twenty yards away.

He thought about crawling beneath the canvas for a moment. But that didn't seem like what a man would do. He could untie the knots on the flaps, but canvas knots wet with dew were hard.

He took out his knife, unfolded it, and neatly stabbed the canvas. The blade punched through it easily, then he pulled it down, slicing as he went. When he'd cut a three-foot opening, he stepped through it.

The smell was musky and airless, the darkness complete. He fell over a chair. Realizing he'd nearly stabbed himself, he folded the knife and returned it to his pocket. Standing again, he reached out to feel his way. *How do blind people do this, anyway?* Glancing off a typewriter, he found the pastor guy's desk. Still feeling around, he knocked over a pencil holder, spilling pencils and pens everywhere. He found a stapler, then a rock, then the string that tied the stick and the barrel together. He grabbed it, stuffed it in his pocket, and stumbled back to the slit he'd made.

For the next hour he sat on the lounge chair flipping the barrel onto the stick. He was determined to master the thing.

"Todd!" came the rasp of his father's voice. "You gonna do that all night? Go to bed. Lois, it's after one. He's out after one. What kind of a son you got?"

"Stuff a sock in it," groaned his mother.

Todd flipped it one more time. The barrel landed on the stick. "Yeah!"

Gatlin lay on her bed. She didn't know how to live near a television if it were off, so it was still on. Some old black and white movie. She felt terribly disconnected from it—from everything. She wanted to talk to someone.

Not her father. He'd only tell her to get back to bed. Who else? Sorrell? She was surprised when she realized she actually wanted to talk to him.

She peeked out of her bedroom. The hallway empty, she crept stealthily to the stairs. The party was still going on below, louder than before. The boss must have been losing his grip because he'd ordered them to be quiet when they were much quieter than they were now. The party was in the game room, which lay between her and the basement and Martin Sorrell.

As it turned out, the partyers were too drunk to notice her as she crept by the game room and on toward the door to the basement. When she got to the bottom of the basement stairs, she saw Martin Sorrell illuminated by a small night-light on his workbench, his head down on folded arms, sleeping. She'd never found Martin Sorrell very endearing, but now, as he snored softly, with a gentle rattle, Gatlin found herself smiling. But she hadn't braved death to listen to him snore.

Forming a hard fist, she slammed it into Martin's shoulder.

"Huh, what? Huh," he babbled as he sprang zombielike to a sitting position, rubbing dead eyes, gasping unintelligible words.

"Good, you're awake," said Gatlin, dragging a chair over. She sat staring at him.

"My shoulder hurts. Why does my shoulder hurt?" Martin groaned. "And what are you doing down here?"

"Couldn't sleep."

Martin rubbed his eyes. "I must have been. I was working—" He stretched. "So, tormenting me during the day's not enough now?"

"I just wanted to talk."

"You're ten. Don't you have guns to play with?" He yawned.

"You can hear the party from down here," she said, ignoring Sorrell's question.

"Heating ducts," he said. Then he looked up to the ceiling. "A bunch of animals."

"Not my father."

Sorrell only looked at her.

"If not guns," he asked, "what about dolls?"

"There's a whole roomful upstairs."

"Room eight."

"It's neat."

"I put it together in an afternoon," Martin said. "Just went out and bought dolls. I thought someone would like it. I guess that's you."

"I guess."

"I saw you on the boat this morning."

"You saw me?"

"I always wonder who's using my boat."

"It's neat."

"Maybe I'll get to use it someday."

"I like the boat a lot," she said, feeling excited at the very thought of it.

"What else do you like?"

"Swimming. I like swimming. Lying in the sun."

"How about boys?" he asked. There was a time in his youth when he actually expected to be married one day. During those flights of fancy, he imagined having a talk like this with his daughter. He'd asked that question several times before—in his head.

"Most are real goons."

"Most."

"Some are okay. There was one I saw this morning. Kinda cute."

"Kinda?"

"Yeah. Kinda." She blushed. She couldn't remember when she'd last blushed. She hadn't felt comfortable enough to blush for a long time.

"I never thought about girls much."

"I can't imagine you as a kid. Like ten years old or anything. You got a Coke down here?"

"It's got caffeine. It'll keep you awake."

"I'm awake already." Now she yawned. "I'm tired." She glanced at the cot. "You sleep there?"

"Sometimes. Most of the time."

Gatlin moved toward the stairs. "I'll see you tomorrow."

Martin eyed his watch. "It's already tomorrow."

"See ya."

She bounded up the stairs and was gone.

"Win." Sitting next to him on the sofa, Ginger nudged his shoulder. "It's late. You need to get home. You've got kids at church who are counting on your having your eyes open in the morning."

"Kids are always optimists." Win's eyes fluttered, the jazz Ginger loved still seeping from the stereo. "What time is it?"

"Nearly two. I fell asleep too."

"Do you think we'll still like each other when all we have to do is stumble down the hall together when it's time to sleep?"

Ginger laughed. Then she struck a resolute pose. "I've decided something."

"While you were asleep?"

"I want to be a detective."

"What's that mean?"

"I don't know. I'll find out Monday. You think Breed likes me, don't you?"

"Why wouldn't he? After church we'll take a look around the cove, and when we come in with the guy's wallet and the drug operation books—which I'm sure I inadvertently knocked out of his hands—he'll promote you on the spot."

"Think so?"

"No doubt."

Chapter 7

Mel and Win normally arrived at the tent about an hour before the service to pray with the three elders. Mel always arrived a few minutes early, Win a few minutes late. When Win got there Mel was standing perplexed before the slit in the outside wall of the tent.

"You're kidding!" Win exclaimed when he saw the hole.

"A good wind will take the whole side out now," Mel said. "I can't find anything missing."

"Why didn't they just untie the knots?"

"Remind me to ask."

Win set his notebook on his desk while continuing to study the vandalism. "I guess we sew it up."

"Real tight."

Sitting at his desk, he grabbed for his "tosser-thing." He planned to show it to the rest of the kids in Sunday school. It remained just a plan. "Did you take that thing to the woodworker?" he asked Mel when he couldn't find it.

"Couldn't get ahold of him."

"Then it's gone."

"They stole *that*? There a treasure map in the handle or diamonds maybe?"

"Or maybe a kid with a knife in his pocket just—" Win stopped as Mel bent over and picked up a small, white yo-yo. "Todd must have dropped it," Win said.

"You recognize it?"

"I'll talk to him. He should be here this morning."

"Just ask him to sew it up—you can help him. One of those Kodak witnessing opportunities."

"I'll take care of it. Kids are my job."

Mel nodded but remained by the wall, his eyes on the invasive hole.

"What's wrong?"

"Looks like we've got two things to pray for now," he mused. "A winter replacement for this tent—and no high winds."

"We're always leaning on God for something," Win added, thinking about how he was going to broach the subject with Todd. "Always something," he whispered.

While Mel's sermon unfolded inside, Win worked with Chad, Todd, and the other five regulars. They gathered on a flat area in a crescent of rocks not far from the lake. Sitting around a couple of card tables, Win taught the lesson, then got them to participate in a fun game. When church ended and the parents came to collect their kids, he told Ginger to take Chad and then pulled Todd aside.

"Got a minute?" he asked, placing a firm hand on the youngster's shoulder.

"Why?"

"Need to talk to you."

"Then talk."

Win could easily see the defensiveness in Todd's stance. It was rigid, ready to bob and weave—thwart and challenge.

"You dropped this when you visited us last night." Win presented the yo-yo.

"What do you mean, last night?"

"Or early this morning. When you came and borrowed my barrel-toss thing."

"Borrow? What's that?"

"All we're asking you to do is help sew the tear in the tent. I'll work with you, but we really want you to at least do that."

"I didn't do nothing. I probably dropped that some other time."

"Todd," Win said, searching for words. "We're not mad at you. We're all sinners saved by grace. All of us have at one time or another done something like this. But it's important to turn away—"

"I didn't do nothing," Todd retorted.

"You're sticking to that."

"I'm no thief."

"Okay."

"I won't stay where people think I'm a thief."

"Todd, we want you to stay."

"So you can accuse me of stealing something else."

"So you can learn about Jesus."

"I didn't steal nothing. And you can teach someone else about your precious Jesus. Who wants to know about him, anyway? Not me. He's just a dead guy. Who cares about dead guys?"

"Todd, please—"

But Todd was gone. He spun and ran north along the shoreline and disappeared among the trees.

The instant he was gone, Chad reappeared from somewhere. "Is this another part of the plan?" he asked.

"Now, Chad—" Win's voice was on the verge of harsh.

"Don't worry," Chad said quickly. "He'll be back. Did he really steal something?"

"Only God knows for sure."

"It's always that way."

"There's truth to that. Come on. Let's find your mother."

"She's talking wedding dresses with Miss Wisdom."

Chad was right. Pam and Ginger stood out in the sunlight in front of the tent. Ginger leaned against Win's Chevy while Pam stood in front of her. Ginger straightened and slipped an arm in Win's as he walked up. "Hi," she greeted, giving him a light kiss.

"Hi, yourself."

Pam chimed in, "Ginger said you saw Bray yesterday. Did he ask about me?"

"He wasn't in his right mind," Win said.

"Then he didn't."

"He would have, but his competition with Grogan took center stage."

Pam looked instantly down. In an attempt to pump some life into her, Ginger chirped up, "After we search the cove, Pam's going to help me choose my wedding dress."

"That'll be fun for you," Win said, not sure whether it would be or not—he was having trouble being enthusiastic after his encounter with Todd.

"Then I go on duty about six—keep them cars moving and give out those tickets." Ginger noticed Win's worried expression. "You okay?"

"Not really," Win said hesitantly. "We think Todd stole something from the office, and when I confronted him, he bolted."

"What did he steal?"

"My 'tosser-thing.'"

"Now there's a capital crime."

Win sighed. He was feeling the same thing about now. But theft was theft. He knew that people, no matter how young, needed to be confronted with their sin so they would know they needed a Savior. He just wished the confrontation had gone differently. Just as he hoped Bray's recovery was going differently today. He'd much rather be telling Bray about the Lord than sifting through meaningless dirt and probably killing him with excitement if they found something or killing him with disappointment if they didn't.

"But Win says," Chad began, his eyes twinkling with sarcasm, "that it's all going according to God's plan, and he's not worried."

"Chad, the Bible also says that God appoints us only once to die. Any day might be your—" Win continued.

"Okay, you two," Ginger injected. "Let's go scrape rock and sift dirt."

"Boy," said Chad, "you guys have all the fun."

The lookout on Sorrell's second floor knew exactly what Ram meant when he ordered him to tell only Ram about any activity in the cove. It meant just that. No one but Ram must know. So when he saw two people show up in the early afternoon and begin poking around, the lookout quickly slipped downstairs, and found Ram playing a solo game of pool. A moment later, Ram was peering through binoculars studying the two people. "It's them all right," Ram muttered.

The pair drifted in and out of view as they appeared to be

engaged in a serious, methodical search. The woman worked on the far end of the cove, the guy on the near side.

"Check out the chick," the lookout said.

Ram said nothing.

"Nice, huh?"

Ram didn't react.

Again Ram said nothing as he continued peering through the binoculars. After what seemed like forever, he handed the glasses back to the lookout. Without another word, he went downstairs.

"Where you going?" came the dark voice from a dark figure standing in the game room doorway.

"There's something I've got to do," Ram answered briefly.

The boss leaned on his pool cue. "Whatever it is, don't mess it up."

Ram only nodded and stepped out the back door.

The crystalline sunlight felt uncomfortable. It was bright, the colors invigorated by it blared at him. The green of the grass and the trees, swaths of yellow dandelions or vermilion wild roses, the deep blue lake—all too harsh for him. He preferred the shadows, the dying sun, or no sun at all.

He ignored all things that had no immediate impact as he made his way to the boathouse, grabbed some fishing gear from a hook, and climbed into Sorrell's powerboat. He untied it, fired it up, and pulled onto the lake.

Keeping his eyes on the cove, he growled toward them at half speed. When he was close enough to see both of them, he throttled back, grabbed a fishing pole, and began trolling in a wide arc, his eyes never leaving the two of them.

Win had searched, as he had before, every inch of his half of the cove. This time, though, it was daylight, and he could see every speck of debris—every pop-top, every old candy wrapper, every sliver of glass from every beer bottle ever broken in that cove. But nothing more.

Ginger found the same thing. Plus the ancient remains of a campfire with burned doll parts. When she first came upon it her heart lodged in her throat and she gagged. But then the body parts began to bear a remarkable resemblance to Barbie, Ken, and GI Joe. She'd never been so relieved. But relief turned to deep disapointment when their search ended, and they'd turned up nothing.

"How about underwater?" Ginger asked.

"You really think we'll find anything?"

"After that battle you had with him out there," she told him, "he must have dropped something."

Win stared at the water for a long moment. "Where do we start?"

"With all the currents, one place is as good as another. Let's just wade out there and get to work."

"But the bottom's so slimy."

Ginger groaned a laugh, "Oh, be quiet and come on. Let's pretend we're partners here. Out there is something of his, and if we look long and hard enough, we'll find it."

Ram heard the thread of voices over the steady grumble of the engine. He was trolling his closest as he watched the two of them toss their tennies to the side and step into the lake. He watched as the woman coordinated the search, the guy on the left, she on the right. They waded out to their waists and began.

Each disappeared beneath the surface for a while, then reappeared. It became obvious that the girl was a little more committed. She stayed under longer, and she brought up more for study in the sunlight. The guy on the other hand, stayed under half as long, stayed above the surface longer before going back down, and never came up with anything.

"Are we done yet?" Win called to her when she surfaced for the umpteenth time.

"You're not into this are you?"

"I just think it's hopeless," he said.

"It becomes hopeless when we give up."

"It's so slimy."

Without reply she dove beneath the surface again. This time she extended her stay. So long that even Ram became concerned.

But then she exploded to the surface, her excitement splashing all around her. "I found it. It's got to be his." She held up something. "It's a key." She studied it while Win splashed toward her.

On the boat, Ram pushed his hand in his pocket and pulled

out the key he'd gotten to replace the one he'd lost. Was there anything on it that identified the inn? No. But it was a distinctive key as were the numbers. He stuffed it back in his pocket. He was in trouble.

"Key to what?"

"There's a num—"

Ram watched as the two converged. When they got within a couple of feet of each other, things went haywire. All the guy's splashing caused the chick to lose her balance. She grabbed at the guy but missed. Looking like the fourth stooge, her hands and legs went into the air as she fell backward. Then, after the water churned frantically over her for several seconds, she exploded through the surface screaming, "I slipped! I lost it! It fell out of my hand. I lost the key. It was so slimy."

She spun and dove back underwater. This time the guy became more animated and joined her.

Ram could hardly keep from crying his relief.

They were under for a while then sprang to the surface again. Ginger was beside herself. "I don't see it. Did you see it?"

"I'd have it if I saw it."

"I'm going under again."

She did and he followed. Their feet kicked the surface frantically. After another long disappearance, they bobbed to the surface.

"I can't believe it," Ginger cried.

"There's a ledge—a drop-off. If it went down there, it's gone."

Ginger stumbled backward in frustration. "I just can't believe it."

"You saw it. What was it a key to?"

"A motel room or somewhere. It was a heavy key—like it might be a classy place."

"A name or number?"

Ginger just stood waist deep in water and shook her head. "I can't believe it. What a klutz I am. What a klutz. My husband was right. My dad was right. I'm a klutz. How could I have lost that key?"

Win splashed toward her. "Now, wait a minute. We'll just

get keys from everywhere, and you can ID the right one. What was the number?"

"Two something. But it was a heavy key, and the numbers were stylized. Like italics."

"See."

"But I don't have anything to show Breed."

Ram leaned back in his seat. She didn't have the key, but she had the memory. That was enough.

Win wrapped a consoling arm around her as they trudged, hair dripping, clothes clinging, to shore. "You go look for your wedding dress with Pam—and have a good time. I'll run around the islands and pick up some hotel keys—at least the classy, heavy ones. Then you can take a look at them when you get back. And you're not a klutz—this lake's just slimy."

The fishing pole still firmly in hand, Ram watched as they left the water. He'd have to do something. And he knew of only one thing to do. With her clothes wet, even Ram found it hard not to notice. The woman was beautiful. It always hurt when he had to kill someone beautiful. His wife was beautiful—he had hated killing her. But both women knew something they shouldn't, and they were both about to tell.

Unlike his very ex-wife's death, this would look like an accident.

And it would happen quickly before his key could be identified. It was time to find out who this beautiful cop was.

Using his cellular phone he made a couple of quick phone calls. Within a few minutes he knew her name, address, and that she was going on duty at six that night. He'd just keep an eye on her until then. When she was driving alone somewhere after dark, he'd strike.

The sun suddenly seemed brighter. He shaded his eyes. He hated all this light. Things could be seen in the light.

"Most wedding dresses," said a saleswoman in the boutique, "have no room for a gun—I suppose we could do something in pearls—"

Pam just shook her head. This was the fourth dress Ginger had tried on. They were all glistening white, one garlanded with delicate lace, one only accented with it, one rolling in pearls, this one only accentuated by them. They all looked beautiful on her—mainly because *she* was beautiful. Pam wished she looked half as good. "What kind of a question was that?" she asked Ginger.

"I don't know," Ginger said, peering at herself critically in the full-length, double-wide mirror. "I'm a cop. I'm supposed to carry my weapon everywhere I go. Which one do you like best?"

"You could wear a flour sack and look good."

"That's no answer."

"The second one is my favorite so far."

"I don't like any of them," Ginger said very softly, still studying herself in the mirror. Then, overcome by something inexplicable, she began to cry. Her mouth contorted behind her hands. Her tear-filled eyes never left the mirror.

"We have others—a whole bunch in the back. I'm sure we'll find what you want," said Madge, eager but confused. "The traditional look really does look wonderful on you."

Pam was standing next to Ginger now, both hands on her shoulders. "You okay?" she asked.

Trying to fight back the tears, clearing a rasping throat, Ginger managed, "Which do you think Win would like best?"

"What's wrong?" Pam asked, beginning to massage her back through the lace. "We don't have to do this today."

Madge produced a box of Kleenex. Ginger grabbed a wad and blew her nose and wiped her eyes. "But I want to do this today. I have to find a dress." Again as she studied herself in the mirror, she began to cry.

Pam took charge. She turned to Madge who stood a few uninvolved paces away. "Your dresses are great. But my friend and I have to talk."

Madge nodded. "It's not that holster thing, is it? We could put it under the train. I did a biker wedding once and they wanted places for knives and tire irons."

Pam smiled stiffly at her. Then she spoke to Ginger. "Get dressed, and let's go have coffee."

Not much later they found a table at Judy's Restaurant, a converted Victorian near the boutique. Ginger's eyes still red, they ordered iced teas. Then Pam asked, "What's going on?"

"It's my wedding. I'm allowed to cry."

"You're allowed to cry even if it isn't your wedding," Pam said. "But this isn't about weddings. And that question about the gun. That came from the cosmos somewhere. Now take a sip of tea, and tell me about it. Are you having second thoughts?"

"Oh, no." Ginger shook her head emphatically. "Not a one. Win's so good to me and Chad, and I really do love him. No. No second thoughts."

"Then what is it?"

"It's the dresses."

"What about them?"

"It's how they look on me."

"They look beautiful. I mean really beautiful. I hope there's a wedding waiting for me out there sometime, and I hope I look half as beautiful."

"Oh, you will," Ginger said fervently, reaching both hands across the table and taking Pam's hands. "You will."

"What about the dresses?"

"They're so feminine. The lace, the beads. So white. So pure and feminine. Too feminine for me."

"What's that mean? You're the most feminine woman I know. You're Grace Kelly feminine."

"No," Ginger said, taking a long drink of tea. "No. It's not me in those dresses. I'm not like that."

"Like what?"

"A woman like that."

"What's that mean?"

"I wear uniforms. I carry a gun. I drive a big police car—I hunt around in a slimy lake for clues. I handcuff people. And the person in those beautiful white dresses was a woman. A woman who goes to teas and drinks coffee from fine china—I drink it from a mug."

"Women do all sorts of things. That's the great thing about the nineties. Not only are we free to do all sorts of things, but if we don't, people think there's something weird about us."

"It's not that I can do all sorts of things, it's that I don't belong in that dress. The sort of woman I look like in those dresses, I'm not. Win deserves that kind of woman."

Pam heaved a great sigh. "You're a woman who, for six years has been both mother and father to her son—"

"I like wearing a uniform and carrying a gun," Ginger said, cutting Pam short. "I *like* it. I like fumbling around in a lake for clues. I also should like being the kind of woman I look like in those dresses."

"You're a woman who's doing what traditionally has been a man's job. You wouldn't do it unless you liked it. But that doesn't mean you're less of a woman. There are differences between men and women—but they're fundamental—praise God for those fundamental differences. What you make of yourself on top of those fundamentals is just what you are."

"I want to be a detective. I want to be even more of a cop."

"Then do it. But don't think you're less of a woman if you do."

"I just looked at myself in that dress. I wanted to be what I saw there, and yet I knew I never could."

"What you saw there was you. All you. That's what I thought when I saw you in it."

"Do you think the Lord wants me to be more—delicate—feminine?"

"You've been at this faith thing longer than I have, but I think the Lord wants you to be all you can be. Live life to the fullest. Now you've got a little boy, and you're about to have a husband. Whatever you do, you're going to have to balance it with your responsibility to them. But God has given you talent and desire. You'd be shortchanging him if you didn't take them as far as you can."

"You think so?"

"I know so. I work in porcelain. I've struggled a lot with the ideas of growth."

"You know I can't even make tea," Ginger confided.

"Boiling the water a challenge?"

"No. The loose tea. Once I was making it for my husband's mom. She was in her seventies, and I boiled the water in this teapot and put the loose tea in. I let it brew for about five minutes. All the caffeine got her shaking so bad she spilled the tea. I don't think she slept for two days. Lay there in her bed with her eyes wide open—like saucers—all whites."

While Pam laughed, outside the restaurant a Chevy station wagon pulled up across the street. The Chevy was supposed to look like a family was traveling in it. The inside was strewn with stuff—various toys, magazines, even a couple of bags of refuse. A family had never been in it. Ram Lucha eased the car to the side of the road, relieved that he'd found them again. He'd been following the cop and her friend for over an hour now. Figuring they'd be in the wedding shop most of the afternoon, he decided to visit the bathroom in a nearby service station. When he'd come back, they were gone.

Now he'd found them again. Things were back on track.

That morning Martin Sorrell had opened his long, thin basement window for air and to his delight, heard, though faintly, the music from the tent-church not far away.

It must have been some trick of sound because his window faced the lake, and there was a lot of wood—both lumber and growing trees—between the church and him. He longed to go to church again. But after what he'd done to that lovely woman's life the last time, he certainly could never go back to Sugar Steeple. When the tent-church sprang up, he thought about going there, but he'd left Sugar Steeple not only because of what he'd done, but because he was now a prisoner.

The tent-church was out.

But the music had found him this morning, and for about an hour, he enjoyed listening to it. Like his roses, the music was beautiful, fragile, easily obliterated by a passing boat or a child's crying. But when the rest of the world was silent, it blossomed in brilliant summer colors.

The music was gone now.

There was nothing to do but work on his roses and hope his visitors would leave today. Of course, they wouldn't. So there were only his roses, and somehow after hearing the music, even though it was only piano background and a few strong voices, the roses didn't seem like enough.

So Gatlin's voice was actually welcome. He'd not heard her descend the stairs, so buried was he in his thoughts.

"It's hot down here," she complained, her tone bored.

"It's summer," said Martin Sorrell.

"I know it's summer," Gatlin informed him.

"So," Martin began, "what are you up to?"

"Nothing. My dad said we'd go for a boat ride, but he seems to be gone. I just thought I'd come down and find out what you're doing."

"What I'm always doing."

"Have you always been alone?" Gatlin asked, the question just coming out.

Martin was a little taken aback by it. It seemed a little personal—the implication of it. "Yes," he said, not happy about the admission.

"Why? You're not bad looking."

"Are you sure you're only ten?"

"I see things," she said as if she actually had. "Were you ever married?"

"No."

"How come?"

To avoid the question, Martin studied a rose he'd studied many times before. "Oh. I suppose I could tell you I just haven't met the right girl. But that's not exactly true. I've met lots of right girls. I've just never acted on any of them."

"Why not? You're a nice guy."

"Really? Well, I'm just not very good with women."

"You're good with me."

"I get tongue-tied around them. Can't talk, somehow. I'm not captivating enough. I'm really rather dull."

"But you're nice. Sometimes nice makes up for it. Hey, do you got any games stacked in the corner someplace?" Gatlin said, already looking.

Martin shook his head. "I don't know. Over the years—"

"Monopoly!" she exclaimed like a forty-niner finding a rich vein.

Martin groaned. He immediately remembered why the Monopoly game was down there. "I hate Monopoly."

"Who hates Monopoly? I used to play it all the time back in New York. I'd play it by myself even. Never lost."

"Really, I'd rather not."

"Why don't you like Monopoly?"

Martin's attention was drawn to the heating vents. From them came the squeals and laughter of several women. The way "the Boss" was talking at the party last night, Martin had not expected new guests. But here they were—the fifty-year-old guys and their twenty-year-old girls using his inn as a playground. He hated that more than Monopoly.

"Please answer me," Gatlin said, her voice begging. "No one ever listens to me."

"Oh. I'm sorry. I just heard voices from upstairs. I—well, I don't like Monopoly because one of the businesses that went broke while I was running it for my father was a chain of nurseries named 'Marvin's Gardens.' Every time I play, I'm reminded of what a failure I am."

"A failure?" Gatlin's eyes became immensely understanding. But then they brightened. "Just the kind of guy I want to play. Come on. We'll have a blast!"

Even before Marvin's Gardens, Monopoly never seemed like a blast.

But at that moment it seemed like an okay thing to try. They set it up on the workbench, each of them on a stool.

An hour later, his first houses built on Marvin Gardens, he gave an excited whoop and nearly fell off the stool.

"But I got the green ones," Gatlin protested with an evil laugh. "You just think you're winning."

"Did you find a dress?" Win asked when Ginger stepped through her door. He'd been busily preparing dinner, hoping she'd return before he had to head for church and the evening service.

"Yes—a couple I'm thinking about."

"I've got chicken barbecuing in the back. Some Noodle-roni on the stove—cheese and broccoli—and corn on the cob boiling. Everything should be done soon." He kissed her. "After church, Chad wants to do some night fishing. Someone told him that was a good thing."

"Just so he doesn't fall in. Did you get the keys?"

"I went to all the motels and hotels on the island. Nothing. Sorrell's Inn was the only place I couldn't get in to. The guy at the guard shack wouldn't let me through. It could be there, but an old inn like that would probably just have plain old latch keys. I'll try the mainland tomorrow. It might not even be from around here."

"Well, you tried. I was sure hoping to have something for Breed."

"And Bray. He got so worked up when I saw him yesterday, I was afraid to tell him anything today. I'll go by there in the morning and let him know we tried."

"Maybe I'll go to the cove again tomorrow. I don't go to work until three—maybe I can find it again. Is there a diet Coke in the fridge? Looking for wedding dresses is grueling. Oh, I stopped by the stationers. The invitations are in the car. Fill one out for your father, and get it in the mail."

"Are we back to that again?"

"Fill it out. Or that wedding dress will be permanently on hold." She emphasized her point with a finger jabbed to his chest. "Now, where's my baby?" she asked, peering out the back window and seeing him playing in the back. "Chad," she called, "come to Mommy."

The Chevy wagon was parked at the crest of the hill where Ram could keep watch. His plan was simple. Traffic cops have beats. He'd follow her through a couple of repetitions of hers, choose his spot, and nail her.

Betty Harmon, who went to bed the night before not sure who she'd be in the morning, slept until the sun rose and seared the morning with a sultry, New England heat. A mosquito whined in her ear. She brushed it away and tried to sink back into sleep. It was the first morning since her escape from L.A.

that she didn't want to rise and get going. Being in Vermont, having left behind a trail of women eager to tell anyone who might ask that she was heading for Maine, she felt a certain security.

Acting on it, she didn't rise until the maid knocked on the door. But then a sense of alarm overtook her. The guy with the scar, the guy she was eluding, was probably looking at the map and figuring out where she would go. Her only hope was to get moving again.

Lake Champlain had to be close. She could picture herself on the shores of it, maybe on one of the islands. Free from worry. Safe. Burlington. Then maybe up those islands that hung down from Canada. Yes. The lake held the answer—a permanent one.

What day was it? she asked herself. Sunday. Yes. She'd left on a Wednesday. Ten, eleven days on the road. Maybe another day and she'd reach the lake and then another one or two to get settled—whatever that meant. She didn't actually know if she was being hounded. But she couldn't imagine, with what she knew, that she wouldn't be. There was at least one person, a sociopath with a scar, who wanted her dead more than anything else in the world. Assuming he'd find those people who'd helped her, she'd been careful to tell everyone she was heading for Portland, Maine. Hopefully he'd head there when he hit the wall she'd built—her identity as a battered woman running from her violent husband.

Although it was only a three-hour drive from Rutland to Burlington, it took her all day. She walked much of it, rode on the back of a motorcycle for some of it, and was finally deposited at the lake about sunset. She'd worked her plan. She'd accepted rides only from women and told them her story as they rode. It was the perfect story—one woman to another. Everyone believed it, even though she had no scars or bruises. Women tended to distrust men, and helping a battered woman trying to escape seemed to be a way of getting just a little even.

When sunset finally came, she saw it red and radiant reflected on the coal black surface of Lake Champlain from the Burlington to New York Ferry dock. It was gorgeous. But more than gorgeous, it was wonderfully refreshing with the breezes wafting off the water neutralizing the summer heat, the squeak of gulls hovering freely above.

Everything was better than the beaches of southern California, smaller, more intimate as if the breezes were blowing just for her. So when she breathed it in and let the air fill her lungs, she felt a wholeness of being, as if its freshness were proclaiming a welcome.

She'd made it. She was here, and she felt uncharacteristically free and safe. Had her little clown been able to float, she would have placed it on the water.

Looking north, beyond the city, now a dark silhouette, was a ragged shoreline while toward the center of the lake were islands, at times sparkling with evening lights. All were ignited by the sunset, their edges burning orange, gilded as if her invitation were gold embossed.

If there was a God, he'd brought her here and meant her to be safe.

But this was a small city teaming with people. Though the chance was remote, it was large enough that someone might recognize her and put a call in to L.A.

She had to leave—go farther north. Somewhere up there was a hole she could burrow into. But not just this moment—after the sunset. It was too rejuvenating to leave.

A college girl gave her a ride, but it ended quickly when the girl had to return for a book she'd forgotten.

She deposited her along Highway 7 not far from its junction with Highway 2.

Night seemed even darker here. It was about eight-thirty, and even though there was a slight moon, the blackness seemed oppressively thick, the highway frightening. Only a few cars screamed by, certainly not enough to light her path. She couldn't help thinking that any minute now she'd stumble and fall in front of a semi thundering by. A part of her laughed at the irony of such a fate—now that she'd found a place she thought safe.

A swirling red light danced behind her as a patrol car pulled up. She turned, expecting the worst. The police had never been a friend.

Ginger stepped from the car, the red bubble pulsing on both

of them now. "You okay?" she called to the woman who turned toward her.

"Not really," she replied.

Training about Vermont's concealed weapons law told Ginger to stay a good distance away and keep this woman's every move under cautious surveillance. But there was something about her look of vulnerability that set Ginger's mind at ease.

"You know you can't stroll along the highway. Where's your car?"

"I was given a ride then dropped here."

"Where are you going?"

"Up those islands."

"Hands against the car and spread 'em."

Obediently, she did as she was told.

Ginger locked a foot around the woman's and patted her down, then she asked her to empty the knapsack. "Funny thing to be carrying around with you," Ginger commented when the clown with the welcoming arms came out.

"He's been my only friend on this trip."

Satisfied she had no weapons, Ginger said gently, "In the car." Ginger headed up Highway 2.

"What's your name?" Ginger asked.

The woman hesitated. She was where she ultimately wanted to go. It was time to settle on a name, one she would be willing to live with for a while. "Mary Seymour," she said.

"I'm Ginger Glasgow."

"Hi," Mary said with a self-conscious laugh.

"Why no car?"

"Uh—I'm escaping," Mary said as if revealing more than she wanted.

Ginger's brows knit. "What?"

"Not jail," Mary said. "No."

"What then?"

The story came out as it had all that day, and when it was finished Ginger only nodded.

"Getting out's good. How about a shelter? Then we can make a police report and put this guy away."

"No," Mary protested, shaking her head. The excuses came next. She was afraid of shelters, had had a bad experience in one, and they'd never put him away; he'd kill her before any trial. "I just need to hide. Somewhere up here."

"Then Mary's not your real name."

"As real as any."

There was a silence for a while.

"My husband was a drinker," said Ginger. "He never hit me, but he was no fun to be around."

"It's hard, huh?"

"Very. But the Lord's been faithful. In your case he says to flee from danger. In my case, I'm going to be married again."

"You left your first husband?"

"He died."

"I wish mine had," Mary said. "What's your new guy like?"

Ginger smiled. "He's the greatest guy—sometimes he's like a kid—but he loves me and my boy. And I don't think I've ever loved anyone so much in my life. I was looking for a wedding dress today."

"I looked really beautiful in mine," Mary lied.

"Well," Ginger said, drifting away from that subject, "he's a pastor—assistant pastor—and part-time detective." She laughed.

"Sometimes I think God brought me here," Mary said slowly.

"Are you a Christian?"

"I don't think I'm anything. But I'm here after ten days on the road. I couldn't have done it on my own."

At that moment Ginger saw the small market not far from Sugar Steeple. Usually closed by now, there were still lights on inside. Without a word, Ginger pulled into the gravel parking area.

"What are you doing?"

"Come with me," Ginger said. "I can't leave you unattended in the car."

"But what—"

"Just come."

With Mary beside her, Ginger banged authoritatively on the front door.

There was some shuffling in the back, then an irritated voice, "We're closed."

"Police," Ginger called back.

There was a groan and the door opened. The chubby woman who owned the market stood there. "There a problem?"

"I've got a woman here who's escaping a battering situation. She's running out of toiletries."

Five minutes later the door to the market was closed and locked again behind them and Mary had refreshed her supplies—toothbrush, paste, soap, brush and added hair spray, and makeup. Nearly twenty dollars' worth.

Mary was overwhelmed. "I don't know what to say."

Nor did she know what to say when Ginger thought of something else and returned to the cash register with a rolled sleeping bag. "It's not the best, but it'll keep you warm tonight—until you can find a bed."

Beside the register was a display of decorative disposable lighters. Ginger included one with a single rose on it. "You might need a fire," she said.

"Hard to believe in this heat," she said. "But thank you for everything."

Back in the car, Mary thanked Ginger profusely.

"There is a God, Mary, and he's given you these things. They're from Jesus. What do you think about Jesus?"

"I don't, I guess. I will, though."

"Good. He'll like that. What now?"

"Find a place to spend the night. Then get a job—I used to waitress—find a place to live."

"Maybe I could find you someplace."

"No," Mary said firmly. "No. You've done too much. More than I deserve. I just want to disappear. The fewer the people who know about me the better."

"Can I find you a place to stay tonight? There are mostly small cottages up here, but there are a lot of boathouses."

"No. You've been too kind already. I'll be fine. I saw a sign for a state campground. I'll use the sleeping bag there."

"Well," said Ginger. "This is about as far north as I go. I usually turn around in this parking lot."

"Then I'll say good-bye."

"Maybe I'll see you again. This is a pretty small place."

"Maybe."

A few minutes later Ginger watched her disappear into the darkness. She felt a tinge of guilt telling her about the boat-houses—a suggestion, really, but there were a lot of them, and there was little harm the woman could do by spending the night in one of them. She might even find a comfortable boat. Who'd really care? And if she were safe and dry, maybe she'd think a little bit about Jesus. Ginger felt invigorated as she returned to her car and reported back in. Then, after a quick U-turn, she proceeded back.

She'd been along her route twice now, a fifteen-mile stretch from where Highway 2 began at the junction with 7, then up the isles. After a quick cup of coffee at Judy's, she'd do it again. It was getting boring. If she were a detective, she'd be either home right now or she'd be doing something infinitely more interesting.

Maybe that's all she wanted. A little excitement.

Less than fifty yards away, the Chevy, its lights extinguished, waited in a turnout to give her some.

Chapter 8

Gatlin's Monopoly game with Martin had evolved into a standoff. Neither ended up with all the money, they were making and losing about the same amount of money with each turn, and neither had a property that could wound the other mortally. It had become endless volley. They had decided to continue it some other time.

So Gatlin was at loose ends.

She walked past several giggling old men and young women toward the stairs to her room. But the last thing she wanted to do was confine herself there. Especially when there was a whole world outside to explore. If caught, what would they do to her anyway?

Halfway to the stairs she drifted toward the large French doors in the back, one side of which was open. The outside wall light by the door was host to a million bugs flitting around. Out toward the gardener's shed, fireflies bobbed and weaved, leaving their lit memory trails. So peaceful—fairylike. And if she got out there, it would be all hers—at least for a little while.

She stood still for a few minutes, just long enough for the people in the sitting area to get used to her. Then she slipped outside to the right, putting the inn wall between her and everything else. When she'd gone about halfway down the wall, she stopped, determined a path through the yard not touched by lights, and quickly traversed it to the trees by the lake.

Had the second-floor lookout been scanning her direction, he would have seen her. But he wasn't. He was asleep.

At the trees she stopped. After making sure her escape had so far gone undetected, she flipped her room key because she had no coin, and chose to go south.

"You okay up there?" Win asked Chad, who sat at the top of a large boulder, fishing pole in hand, his fishing line tossed about ten yards from the shore—everything so dark he couldn't see it anyway.

"I'm going to catch a big one," Chad said. "I feel it."

"That's good," Win said, looking up at where he was perched. "You certainly won't be able to see it if it isn't huge. Well, I'll be sitting on the dock thinking deep spiritual thoughts."

"Like that plan you're always talking about."

"That's about as deep as they come." Win laughed and wandered over to the dock and took his place on the lounge chair at the end of it.

Win had been gone about five minutes when Chad heard a whispered call, "Chad? What you doing up there?"

It was Todd. He stood in the shadows at the base of the rock.

"What are *you* doing?" Chad returned.

"Messin' around. You wanna come?"

"I'm fishin'."

"You can fish anytime," Todd said impatiently.

"I can mess around anytime. Hey, why'd you take that thing?"

"What thing?"

"Win's thing. I heard him talking to my mom about it. Why'd you take it?"

"I didn't, man. I'm always being accused of stuff."

"Wanna fish?" Chad tried to be conciliatory.

"Naw. I'm headin' out. Gonna mess around the lake some."

"Okay, but you're missing out."

"Sitting on a rock? A real blast. See ya."

Todd was gone.

Chad went back to studying the water's tug on his pole. Had he felt something grab at the worm? No. Not yet.

Ram Lucha had studied the terrain as he'd followed the police car in its rounds. The first time through he saw something that looked promising; the second time through he confirmed it.

There was a spot where the road crawled along the crest of a reasonably tall cliff, a field on the driver's left. The field didn't hug the cliff, but it was within thirty yards of it. On the driver's right was another, taller ridge with a couple of roads, each about a mile apart, spilling down from it. If he timed it right, as she came along the highway at a pretty good clip, which was the way she drove, he could explode from one of those feeder roads, cut her off, and drive her over that cliff. Below was probably nothing but boulders. It would be over in seconds.

He hadn't seen another car in more than half an hour, so he was confident that there'd be no witnesses. It was perfect.

His plan firm, he made the U-turn ahead of hers and sped away. He only had a few minutes to set it all up.

"How come you're sitting up there?"

Chad heard a girl's voice from about the same spot Todd's had come from minutes before. He turned. Even in the shadows he recognized her. "You're the girl on the boat."

"Boat? Oh—you were with that guy who jumped overboard. That was funny."

Fishing forgotten, Chad set the pole aside and slid from his perch, jumping the final bit to the ground. "Where you from?" he asked.

Having heard voices, Win called, "Chad, who's there?"

"Just a friend," he called back.

Win returned to stargazing.

"Your name's Chad?"

"What's yours?"

"Gatlin."

"Where you live?"

"That way." She pointed up the coast.

"How come you're out so late?"

"Just wanted to take a walk. I'm glad I saw you. What were you doing up there?"

"Fishing. Some guy told me fish were easier to catch at night. I thought I'd try."

"Are they?"

"Don't know. Don't think so." Chad fumbled for more to say. "Do you live somewhere where I can see you during the day? I've got this little boat—an aluminum thing. Wanna go out in it sometime?"

"Not during the day."

"I can't take it out at night."

"Well, maybe we can do something else."

"Maybe I could teach you to fish."

"You ever touch a fish?" she asked.

"None I've caught."

"They're yucky. And the worms. You use worms?"

"Big ones."

"Double yuck."

"My mom doesn't like the lake at all. She gets scared in the boat."

"That your dad?" she asked.

"Soon. He and my mom are getting married."

Gatlin looked off toward Win. He was fully reclined on the aluminum lounge chair staring at the stars. "What's he do?" she asked, taking a few steps back toward the way she came. Chad took them with her.

"He's a pastor. At the tent-church."

"I've seen that. Well," she said, "I guess I'd better go back."

"Really? I could walk you."

"Just a little ways."

They walked slowly, their steps casual.

"Is your mom inside?"

"She's working. She's a cop."

Gatlin tightened perceptibly and stopped. They had gone about ten yards. "Where is she?"

"I don't know. But she mostly works traffic. Gives out tickets and stuff. She gets bored."

"There's not much traffic around here."

"Sometimes, when she's on the night shift like now, she'll go all night without seein' a car."

"Not a bad job, I guess. Well, I'll see you."

"You have to go?" Then he spotted something. Near his feet was a pile of debris, a torn white bag and burger wrappings.

Someone had had a picnic and left the trash. But in the midst of it, its shiny surface reflecting what little moon there was, was a scratcher game card. "Hey, look! I love these things," he said, picking it up.

"What is it?"

"A scratcher—you win something if you get two that match. Wanna do it? Hey, there's two cards—look, three! It's a gold mine." He scooped up the cards and presented them to her.

"They're with other people's old food. Yuck!"

"Just paper. Here, I'll scratch 'em then." Using his thumbnail Chad slowly worked the gray substance from the card.

Now that she didn't have to touch them, Gatlin became enthusiastic and instantly impatient. "Here, use my key," she said, handing him her room key, a heavy, brass thing which Chad eagerly accepted.

With his new weapon he dispatched the first card quickly. "Nothing," he groaned. The next one was a winner—a free Quarter Pounder. The last one was even bigger. A free breakfast.

"Those people didn't know what they had," Chad exclaimed happily. Then he became slightly official and handed her the two winners. "You take 'em," he said.

"But what about you?"

"Maybe you can keep 'em until we can get together and share 'em. What about that?"

Gatlin smiled. She received very few gifts from people other than her father, and though she knew she'd never be allowed to use the cards, that didn't matter. "Okay," she said, accepting the cards and slipping them into her pocket. "We'll share them sometime."

"Good," Chad said, pleased.

"I have to go now. But I hope I see you again."

"I'll be out here tomorrow probably."

"See you, then." Clutching her two cards, she turned reluctantly and slipped off into the shadows.

He watched her disappear, then, feeling a sense of restlessness he didn't completely understand, he walked over to the dock. "You asleep?" he asked Win.

"Just thinking."

"What about?"

"Sometimes I wonder why God gives me things to do without preparing me for them."

"You mean like a surprise that sort of walks up on you?"

"Something like that."

"Been there," said Chad, staring off in the direction Gatlin had gone. "When you get married, are you going to tell Mom to stop working nights? I miss her at night."

"I'll talk to her."

"I mean, she never does anything at night. There's nothing going on out there. Nothing." Without thinking about what he was doing, Chad slipped Gatlin's key into his pants pocket. After a few minutes, he and Win went inside, and Chad went to bed. He changed his clothes sleepily and absently kicked his pants under the bed.

Ram positioned the Chevy on the access road with his lights off. Perched above the highway, he had an unobstructed view of the road, and he didn't have to wait long. Because of the darkness, the patrol car's lights were visible from a distance as they approached.

Ginger listened to the cross chatter on the radio and considered all the ramifications of being a detective. She thought about solving puzzles, like Bray always talked about. She thought about being at the forefront of investigations and being respected. That was paramount. Being respected for her mind and her abilities.

Of course, she did lose the key.

If it were that guy's key, she'd actually lost the one piece of evidence that would have helped find the guy responsible for putting Bray in ICU. Maybe she could find it again. This was the age of technology, right? Maybe there were high-powered metal detectors they could use. Maybe there were vacuums that could suck the slime right off the lake floor and push it through sieves. But to even find out if those things existed, she would have to tell someone what a klutz she'd been.

Her attempt to impress Breed would become his evening's entertainment.

Good grief! What's this!

Suddenly time became measured in gasps, in fragments, in glimpses—glued together by a blaze of terror. A car appeared. Its lights like suns, the sudden explosion from the blackness blinding her for a moment. Her lights igniting its panel—tan— it blasted from the side road, slid onto the highway toward her passenger-side bumper. She pulled left—narrowly avoiding collision. Then slowed slightly to let the guy get in front of her. But he didn't get in front of her. He continued to press her right corner. She turned harder left, her car still moving well over fifty miles per hour. What was he doing? Didn't he know she was here?

She left the road. The patrol car's heavy suspension bounced over and dug into the field—but hardly slowed at all.

Lord, what's happening?

She slammed on her brakes, but she was on soft dirt now. The wheels locked—slid over the slick weeds.

"Oh, God—God—God."

Each word higher pitched. Each closer to a scream.

Her car slowed but not enough. She grabbed for the handle, but her door was locked. The handle rattled—useless.

The car that had forced her off the road abruptly spun away. Grabbing for the lock, she pumped the breaks, but the car refused to slow. Out of control. Ground devoured in split seconds. She careened forward. The door was unlocked but too late.

"Oh, no!" she cried—the cliff.

She was airborne.

Her scream erupted from her very center as she felt the car drop, then nose forward, the world before her became a sea of twisted shadows.

She landed—hard. Was she at the bottom already? It didn't feel like she'd fallen far enough. Slowly Ginger opened her eyes.

The windshield was shattered—the air bag billowed, pinning her against the seat, then exploded and deflated. A sharp limb, skinned by metal and glass had plunged into it. She'd landed on a tree! The car rocked, then she heard the sound of splitting wood and the car lurched. The nose fell again, and more twisted, tortured limbs pushed through the shattered windshield. Any one of them could have nailed her. She screamed as they dug into the passenger seat, tore at the dash, missing her by inches. The car stabilized for a moment. She ducked beneath the dash. But her sharp movement caused the car to rock, then to list to the driver's side. Limbs scraped and cracked. One of them snapped by her ear; a sliver slapped at her cheek. The side of her face stung, blood seeped from the wound.

Would the car roll off the tree?

She wished it would. Maybe she wasn't that far off the ground. But it didn't roll. It must have been caught in the crotch of an oak—one of the large, ancient gnarled ones. But how could even the largest of the oaks hold a ton of metal?

Suddenly, as if on a pivot, the car listed, driver's side down. The door suddenly became the floor and fell open; when it did, the floor dropped out from under her. Ginger struggled for footing on the edge of the floorboards and instinctively grabbed the steering column and hung on.

Unfathomable blackness everywhere. If there had been a moon, clouds had erased it. Hanging there, still struggling to find a foothold, she tried to see what lay below her.

The car settled; the tree strained.

Her heart caught.

She screamed.

But now there was a clearer view of what lay below.

She could hardly breathe. She dared not. Now she knew exactly where she was. Lone Oak.

Older than time itself, its root system held fast to the top of a pile of boulders. At one time it had stood at the crest of a tall cliff overlooking the lake. Over eons, the lake had worn away the cliff. Everywhere but where the oak stood. Now the oak and her car stood thirty feet from a rocky floor—three stories below.

Lord, Jesus my Savior, let's talk salvation one more time.

Metal groaned, and the limbs began popping. If the car dropped, she was dead. "Please, Lord," she whispered.

What was she going to do? There was no climbing up and out—too many limbs snarled above her.

She'd have to drop down and find a foothold somehow—before the car dropped on top of her. Bleeding, suddenly aware that her hands and arms stung from repeated tree limb assaults, her thighs bruised from the impact, and her cheek still stinging from being cut, she prepared to ease herself down from the car.

If she dropped, she'd fall about ten feet to a boulder below, then probably another twenty feet to the rocks below that. Not a good prospect.

Catching her breath, she noticed the seat belt hanging beside her. Grabbing it, she walked her hands along it until all but her chest was below the car. Filling her lungs with air, afraid that any radical movement might send the car spinning to earth, she finally decided to take the chance. Swinging her legs in smooth, measured arcs, she tried to find a foothold. Nothing. She walked farther down the seat belt until she was hanging near the end of it, her head below the car. Although every neuron wanted to panic, there was no time for that. She had to put away everything put purpose. Although it was black as coal below her, she did her best to evaluate the situation. The car, severely battered by its battle with the tree, rested on two thick limbs. Both were cracked, the white meat of interior wood glowing like jaws. Crossing below and between those two limbs was another branch. If she could get to that one, she'd be okay. Her plan was simple: get her ankle on the cross limb and use the protruding limbs to support her while she worked herself to safety.

She had to move quickly. One of the major support limbs creaked, the tear opening another couple of inches. The car rocked, then dropped. If it dropped another foot or if the limbs gave way altogether while she was under it, she'd be crushed.

She looked around for another possibility.

There wasn't one.

"Lord, you know what we have to do here."

She swung under the car and caught the underlying branch with her ankle, bringing her other ankle up beside it. The bark cut at her skin, but she put the pain away and pulled herself by the ankles so that she could grab another branch. She now lay face up beneath the car, her head and chest facing the open interior, her legs beneath the chassis—if it fell now, the chassis would act like a thick cleaver.

Working hands and legs, she managed to get her knees over the cross limb. But there was no time for triumph. The car heaved and dropped another inch, the tear in one of the limbs opening wider. With renewed vigor, she took another hand-hold and worked her legs another couple of inches. Suddenly a limb just below her snapped. Sounding like a rifle shot, it slammed into her back. The broken smaller limbs, ripped and honed by the car's action to short spikes, tore through her uniform and stabbed her back while the greater limb jarred her backbone. The pain radiated from her back to every part of her. Tears broke free, and she fought to keep them in check. But pain or no pain, she had to get out from under that ton of steel.

The car shuddered again.

She pulled her head through the opening just as both limbs supporting the car gave way simultaneously. The car spun off the tree, crashed against the rocks ten feet below, rolled away from the boulders, then bounded to the lake's edge twenty feet below that. When it hit, the front doors flew open, the bubble top popped and exploded. Finally the gas tank ruptured, the gas flooding over the rocks into the water.

But all that didn't matter.

She'd made it. She was hurt severely, but she was alive. Breathing like every breath was brand-new, she fell back on the cross limb, winced as the bark dug into her new wounds, then eased herself to a new, less painful position. She needed a moment to rest. She stretched out as best she could and laid her head back, allowing the aches, the pain, the terror to drain away. It wasn't sleep, but it was as close as she could possibly come. Abruptly she opened her eyes again.

Had she heard a gunshot?

If she had, it came just before the car exploded.

An intense fist of flames reached up at least twenty feet, scarring the rocks all around it, including the ones on which her now tortured oak stood. The gasoline on the lake also ignited, sending a fiery tongue far offshore. Even though the car was off to the side, the instant it went up, a geyser of furnace hot air enveloped her. Now, actually sensing a nurturing warmth from the flames, Ginger allowed herself to give way to exhaustion. She closed her eyes. "Lord, you pulled me through again," she whispered.

Above her, hidden by brush, Ram Lucha watched the whole thing. He'd seen her go over the cliff, miraculously end up in the ancient oak, seen the tree envelop the inside of the car, seen the car fall from the tree, and when it hadn't exploded on its own, he'd helped it out with a single, well-placed shot. Then he'd seen the car aflame.

He had not seen her escape.

She had to be dead. Or if she weren't, she soon would be. He'd succeeded.

Knowing the flames would quickly attract a crowd, he got into the Chevy wagon and pulled back on the highway. In case he was being watched, when he reached a roadside phone a few miles away, he called 911. After giving the operator a fake name, he reported the explosion. They already knew.

Satisfied with the night's work, he got back in the car and drove to the inn.

While a throbbing MedAlert helicopter lifted Ginger from the tree, a patrol car ground over the gravel in front of Ginger's cottage. The officer woke Win from his sleep on the couch with the news. Win, his heart racing, woke Chad. On the way to Fletcher Allen Med Center, the officer briefed them completely on what had happened.

Everyone, Ginger included, converged at the hospital at about the same time.

The instant Win saw her being wheeled in on the gurney, a bloody sheet draped over her, he pushed through the attendants to her side.

"I'm okay," she assured him before his worried lips could speak. "Just scratched and banged up a little. It's a lot better than it could be."

Win was left behind as Ginger was wheeled into the emergency room.

Relieved, but having reached a new level of emotional

exhaustion, Win found Chad beside him and wrapped a reassuring arm around him. "She'll be all right," he said to the boy.

"This time," Chad replied, his eyes red from frightened tears.

It was a little after ten when the guard at the front entrance to the inn waved Ram Lucha by. As a precaution, Ram parked the car behind a tall stand of bushes so that it wasn't visible from the road. His intent was first to make sure Gatlin was okay, then see what else was going on.

But the boss, his eyes little more than questioning slits, greeted him as he was about to go up the stairs. "We gotta talk," the boss said.

In the game room, the boss said, "There was a guy here today—out at the guard shack—said he was a collector of motel keys. Waco then tells me that you needed a replacement."

"I lost it escaping from the Feds Friday night."

"When I asked Grogan if there's cops out there looking for room keys, he tells me you had a run-in with a couple of locals—one of 'em a cop—a woman but a cop anyway. You didn't tell us."

"They couldn't recognize me. It didn't matter."

"What about the key?"

"That's been taken care of."

"You sure?"

"You'll read about it in the papers."

"It had better look like an accident."

"It did—will."

"A lot depends on what we're doin' here, Lucha. It won't go well for anyone who messes it up."

"Right."

Ginger's wounds, though not severe, required a lot of treatment, from special bandages to several stitches. To her surprise, she did have a broken finger and a sprained ankle. She was nearly an hour in the emergency room. After hearing the extent of her injuries, Win left Chad in the waiting room and took the opportunity to visit Bray.

"Don't upset him like you did before," Bray's nurse said. She sounded weary. "He's a handful. He's getting no better. He uses all his strength doing other things. He needs to rest."

Feeling like he was contributing to his friend's demise, Win stepped cautiously past the nurses' station to Bray's cube. The nurse was right. Things hadn't changed. His face was still a ghostly mask, his hands still lay stiffly at his side, the machines and monitors were still fed by knots of tubes and wires. An intravenous setup was dripping at his right side.

"What did you find?" Bray groaned the words through frozen, bloodless lips.

"Bray, you've got to rest. The nurse says you're not getting better."

"I'll get better. I always get better. What did you find?"

Win gave up and decided to play Bray's game. "Ginger found a motel key offshore. It could be to the guy's room."

"What motel?"

"Don't know," Win told him. "I've been looking for a match but haven't found one."

"Let me see it."

"Can't. Before we could get it to shore, Ginger fell and lost it. We looked everywhere but couldn't find it again."

"Lost it?" Although Bray's face was already ashen, it seemed to lose even more color.

"The fact that she found it in the first place was a miracle."

"The miracle is that she's in uniform at all."

"Now hold on," Win said, feeling his blood surge.

"Oh. I forgot. She's your girlfriend. I had a girlfriend once, but then you and your foolishness came along."

"You can say what you want about me. But they brought Ginger into the emergency room an hour ago. She was on duty and got run off the road. She was close to being killed."

"Run off the road?" Bray sounded thoughtful.

"God was with her. She landed in a tree and got out of the car before it fell."

"How was she run off the road?"

The nurse was suddenly there again. "Mr. Brady, he's beginning to boil over again."

"Oh, shut up," Bray managed. His lips moved. "Answer me."

"A car shot out from a side road, had a hard time making the turn, and forced her off the road. She couldn't stop before going over the cliff."

"They get the guy?"

"No. Must have been drunk or something. Probably didn't think anyone would be on the roads. There seldom is on the isles at night."

"When you searched that cove, was it daylight?"

"Sure. Couldn't find anything at night."

"She make a big deal about finding the key?"

"She was excited."

"Did you see the key?"

"She described it to me. But no. I didn't see it."

"You don't see a coincidence here?"

"Mr. Brady, if you don't leave soon I'll have to call security," the nurse interrupted.

Win ignored her. "You think someone was trying to kill her?" he asked Bray.

"Please, Mr. Brady."

Win glanced at the nurse but then stared at Bray. Bray's twenty years in law enforcement had given him impeccable instincts, although it was Win's instinct that had shone in their last case together. Win found himself trusting Bray's judgment immediately. "I'll keep my eyes open."

"Keep hers open too," Bray whispered.

A few minutes later downstairs in the emergency room, Ginger laid her new set of crutches aside and wrapped grateful but aching arms around Win's neck.

"You okay?" he asked, not sure where to touch her or how enthusiastically.

Unencumbered by any of those worries, Chad ran up and wrapped relieved arms around her waist.

She winced but didn't push him away. "Oh, sweetie," she exclaimed, hugging him gingerly. "This is so good. Really good." Turning her attention back to Win, she answered his question. "Better than I ever thought possible," she said, her voice elated. "I thought I'd be flat enough to put syrup on, so a few stitches, a splint on my finger, and a sprained ankle are nothing." She reset herself on the crutches and hobbled between her two men.

"Let's get you home," Win said gently.

"My sergeant came in while they were sewing me up," she told them. "I told him about the key we found. He was a little concerned that we were taking things upon ourselves. But when I told him I wanted to talk to Breed about becoming a detective, he said he'd put in a word for me."

Mike Grogan parked his car just where the tire marks indicated two cars had left the road. Walking through the police yellow ribbons, he saw clear evidence that Ginger had locked her wheels in a vain attempt to stop the car. He could also see that the other car had spun away when he was sure Ginger's path would intersect with the cliff.

Ram's plan should have worked.

It was just bad luck that it hadn't.

"Grogan, that you?" one of the officers called.

"None other."

"There's a good set of tracks over here." The officer pointed to the ground with his flashlight.

Grogan had to admit, the cop was right. Lucha had left a very clear calling card.

"Is there anything on the car down there?"

"Just charcoal."

"I'll make a cast of the tracks and look around, then you can release the area."

Grogan got a plaster kit from the car, mixed up the stuff, and poured it into the impression. He laughed to himself as he did it. He was pouring it into one of Ginger's tracks. After spending about an hour looking around, he retrieved the plaster cast, placed it carefully in the trunk of his car, and drove off.

As he drove, another plan formed. Reaching Sorrell's Inn, Grogan turned into the main drive and rolled to a stop at the guard shack. A few moments later, he backed up and pulled onto the highway, the guard's room key in his pocket.

He continued on to the station where he prepared for a little exercise in deception. As he prepared it, though, another plan began to take shape—a bigger, deadlier plan. As it solidified, he began working with a greater resolve. Not only was he going to save Ram, but he would also save himself.

By the time Win pulled up to Ginger's cottage, the euphoria had worn off, and both Ginger and Chad sat heavy-eyed. As for Ginger, the painkillers were beginning to wear off. Not only did the myriad new wounds sting excruciatingly, but the burn on the back of her hand was throbbing again.

It was all she could do to kiss Chad good night before leaning the crutches against the wall and falling into her own bed. After she was safely under the covers, Win stepped in and sat on the edge of her bed. "They said you had to be stitched up in several places."

"I was a pin cushion," she told him. Rising up she turned her back to him and lifted the back of her pajama top.

Win groaned as he saw the horrible track of wounds. Some were neat holes, others were savage tears. All were either butterfly bandaged or sutured, the threads ugly. "Oh, Ginger. Sweet, sweet Ginger. What happened?" And he gently kissed each one of her wounds—softly, tenderly, kissing the pain and trauma away. "Oh, I wish I'd taken the hit instead of you."

She slowly dropped her shirt and turned back to him. Her eyes moist with tears. "You mean that, too, don't you?"

"With all my heart."

She fell against him. Ignoring the pain, she wrapped her arms around his neck. They kissed. "You do love me, don't you?" she said, sniffling away the tears.

"I can't imagine you facing that alone. I hope you never have to face anything like that again."

"I guess it goes with the territory," she said, feeling a certain power as she did.

Win only nodded. "I'll be on the couch out there if you need me."

"Thank you," she said, pulling her arms away and falling back on the bed, wincing when she did.

"I'm your nurse tonight."

"One thing to remember, then. A good nurse lets the patient sleep as late as she wants."

"Can't," Win jabbed good-naturedly. "We start therapy in the morning. Early."

She cooed, "The real therapy starts in three months."

They both laughed softly.

But when the laughter died, Ginger said, "I nearly died tonight."

Eyes grave, Win nodded. "I know. Just the thought of it makes my heart numb."

"But I came through it."

"I've never been so glad about anything."

"I didn't panic, Win. I kept my head. I did what I had to do."

"I'm proud of you."

"Any second those limbs could have cracked and that car could have gone down, but I ignored all that and shimmied under it."

Win placed a hand on hers and squeezed it encouragingly. "I'm sorry you went through that."

"I'm not." Her eyes lit. "I felt like I was being tested out there. And I passed. I kept my head, I got through the gauntlet, and I passed."

"And I've never been so glad someone else got a good grade in all my life. You grew out there," Win said. He was about to tell her what Bray had speculated but decided not to. She needed her sleep, and that news wouldn't help her get it.

Chapter 9

Betty Harmon, now Mary Seymour, woke to a stream of light coming through the dirty boathouse window, she felt reasonably refreshed and ready to head even farther north. Sleeping bag slung over her shoulder, she began her journey. At a nearby gas station, a wooden structure that looked like it had just barely weathered its last winter, she told the "escaping from a violent husband" story to the attendant. She made sure she was loud enough to be heard by a woman pumping her own gas at the only set of pumps. The woman heard and, with bubbling sweetness, volunteered a ride.

After forty-five minutes, Mary's eyes ever peeled for just the right place, she saw a small meadow reaching out from Highway 2 and touching a stand of trees—maples surrounded by tall brush, the morning blue of the lake peeking through. It looked wonderfully inviting.

She asked the woman to let her off. Perplexed, but understanding Mary's delicate situation, the woman complied.

The meadow was lush, deep with green grasses, and painted with yellow dandelions. But it wasn't the meadow that caught her eye. Perhaps there'd been a house in the meadow at one time, but now, just peeking through the trees, was a boathouse—this one deserted and in need of repair. But it was shelter. Pushing the brush aside, she stepped through the trees to the house, the lake lapping below it. The door stood slightly ajar, and there was a dilapidated dock leading to it. Although there were boards broken and missing, it was enough.

Inside the boathouse was the walkway around the berth, and light streamed in through a couple of windows. The lakeside entrance, a garage door, was closed; a lever to open it was on the wall. As if claiming the boathouse for her own, she marched to the lever and pulled it down. The door opened onto a wonderfully clear panorama—a magnificent picture window.

There was no telling when the boathouse had actually been built, but it was sturdy enough to use for a little while, until she found a job and got herself settled.

And the scar-man, the one searching for her, would never find her here. Never.

Feeling a renewed sense of freedom, she took her tennis shoes and socks off and sat on the edge of the berth, dipping her feet in the cool water.

It felt so good.

She kicked her feet a little, actually making some noise. After splashing them playfully for a moment, she scooped up a handful of the cool liquid and dipped her face in it, allowing the water to drizzle down her neck and chest. The refreshing trails excited her skin and made her feel alive—but there was more. She became aware that she was experiencing something she hadn't experienced since being a child—maybe she'd never experienced it. But she knew what it was. She felt like she was placing down roots—anchoring herself like the trees and the grass. She'd come home.

An enormous calm settled over her as she grabbed her knapsack, removed her beloved clown and set it on the boards beside her. Her little friend appeared more in charge than ever. He, too, looked at home.

"Me too," she said to the clown, throwing her hands wide apart. "I love this place this much!"

Win was surprised when he found Grogan at Ginger's door. Grogan carried a briefcase and gave Win a Cheshire smile.

"How's Ginger?" he asked, his tone a symphony of concern.

"I'm fine," she called from the front room sofa. She sat there draped in a lush terry cloth robe, her injured ankle propped up on a pillow on the coffee table.

"Word has it you guys found a key."

Win straightened. "How'd you know that?"

"It's my job. Also you've been trying to gather keys from the island motels, probably to find a match."

"We don't have a match," Ginger said, eyes down. "I lost the key."

"But you know what it looks like, or you wouldn't have been gathering them." Grogan placed the briefcase on the unoccupied portion of the table. "In this case I've got motel keys from most of the places in the surrounding area, on and off the islands." After a dramatic pause, he opened the briefcase.

He was right, the case was filled with keys—all kinds of keys—each with a string and a tag. "Do you see it?" Grogan asked Ginger.

Ginger just stared at the pile and then eyed Win. "Maybe I don't want to be a detective."

Grogan laughed. "Get at it."

With a sigh, and with movements consistent with frequent stabs of pain from her ordeal the previous night, she began first by fingering the pile. Then she took the keys out two or three at a time and placed the discards into a pile on the table. There was nothing particularly arduous about the search, it just took a while. The Grand Isles and the surrounding area was a magnet for vacationers, and there were a lot of motels and hotels to accommodate them. The sea of keys proved that.

About ten minutes into it, Ginger found it. It and two other keys hung at the end of three strings, each attached to a tag. She'd become bored and wasn't paying as much attention as when she started. But there was something so unique about the key that even though her brain was numbing, she perked right up when she saw it.

"This is it," she announced, handing the key to Grogan. "Look at the numbers."

"Great—I can see how you'd remember this. Heavy—brass. Unusual." He took the key back and looked at the tag. "Bremerton Inn," he read. "I know that name. Well, I'll check it out. I'll call you back with what I find."

Less than a half hour later Grogan kept his word.

"Dead end," Grogan said. "Burned down about three months ago. That key's probably been in the water for six."

"So the key's meaningless?"

"Looks that way. But that's the way detective work is. Most of what you find out is useless."

"I'll tell Ginger. She's sleeping now."

"Well, keep at it. The more people we have working on this, the better the chance we'll bring 'em in."

"Right," Win said and hung up. Pouring himself a decaf, he sat at the counter. *If the key is meaningless,* he thought, *so is Bray's theory. Why do I still think Ginger's accident wasn't?*

Grogan got to the nearest pay phone and called Sorrell's. He asked Waco to put the boss on. Waco laughed and told him to call back just before noon. "Then get Ram," Grogan ordered.

"What? Are you two joined at the hip or something?"

"Just get him," Grogan repeated.

Ram answered in his room. "Yeah."

"The girl survived."

"You're kidding."

"But you have nothing to worry about. I've taken care of everything. Just lie low for a while. The only thing I ask is that you remember this, please."

"I'll remember," Ram said. Had he been capable of appreciation he would have given it.

"Meaningless. The key's meaningless?" Ginger asked incredulously.

"I gotta ask you something," Win said, sitting on the edge of her bed while she ate the breakfast he'd prepared.

"Sure. What?"

"Were you forced off the road on purpose?"

Ginger's fork stopped at the midpoint between the plate and her lips. "You think someone was trying to kill me?"

"Were you?"

"I don't know. I could have been. But it just seemed like the guy came barreling out of the side road without looking, and I ended up over the cliff trying to avoid hitting him—or her. I never saw."

Win nodded. "Okay," he said haltingly. "Did anything else happen that might lead you to believe it was an attack?"

Ginger set the fork down. "Who's suggesting this? You or someone else?"

"Bray was the one who first said it. I told him what happened while you were in the ER—about you finding the key and then getting hit. He said it was too unlikely a coincidence—well, words to that effect."

"But the key didn't mean anything."

"I know," Win said. "But it still seems like weird timing. Can you think of anything?"

Ginger thought—hard. "There is something."

Win's ears perked.

"The car fell from the tree, and when it hit it didn't explode right away. Just before it did, I think I heard a gunshot. I can't swear to it. I was so relieved at having made it, and the tree limbs were popping and banging together all around . . . but it could have been a shot—then the car exploded."

"Like someone was trying to finish the job by frying you to a crisp."

"Do you suppose? Being involved in an accident is one thing. Being the target of a killer is something far different."

"Tell me about it," Win said, having been in a similar situation only a few months before. "But you're not sure about the shot."

"I could have heard it. Should we tell Grogan?" Ginger asked.

He wasn't sure exactly why, but Win shook his head. "John Phillips. This is all tied to his operation last Friday night. I'll tell him." Win got to his feet. "How are you feeling?"

"I hurt. My ankle's a little better, and the finger's just a bother. But all the wounds—I feel like that guy on the Orient Express—the one everybody took turns stabbing."

"Nice image. You take it easy. Before I leave, I'll get Chad working. I won't be long. I'll just let John know the facts—just the facts—and then I'll head back here."

"I was just wondering if you'd like to kiss my back again. I kinda liked it."

John Phillips's office was a few blocks up Winooski from the police station. It was a standard office building—one of the newer ones in town. From the fifth floor he had a view of the other buildings around it. *A shame,* John thought. *Working in*

Vermont, I should have views of cows or the lake. Or Ben and Jerry's Ice Cream Factory.

His secretary, Mrs. Warner, now spoke over the intercom. "Mr. Phillips. A Win Brady here to see you."

Another civilian. Now that's all he needed. But he pressed the button anyway. "Send him in."

Win stepped into the office. Richly paneled, with a broad sweep of bookshelves, it was an office that seemed as much for show as for business. Win planted himself in one of the two leather chairs that sat before John's cherry wood desk. "Nice office."

"A lot more than I need now."

"My office is in a tent. Sometimes I think that's more than *I* need," Win said. "Have you seen Bray lately?"

"I've been keeping up with news bulletins."

"The police have a guard posted at the elevator."

"That's why I didn't post one of my own."

"Sorry you weren't able to keep the guys you caught behind bars."

"No sorrier than I am, and I'm sorrier than you'll ever know."

Win's brows furled. A few things Phillips had said were joining up in his mind. "What's going on?"

"The Miami office won. Friday's was a costly operation for the DEA—in more ways than one. With nothing to show for it, Miami took the initiative. We'll keep a couple of guys around to chase the students, but I'm to be on a plane to Tampa tomorrow morning."

"So they think the flow's dried up?"

"They think we were lied to to divert our attention from the south. Now—what did you want of the DEA?" John asked, his patience wearing very thin.

"I wanted to tell you something and get your opinion."

"Well, I got 'til tomorrow morning. Shoot."

Win told him about his and Ginger's fight in the cove, about the key, about Grogan's information about the key, about Ginger's "accident," and about what she thought might have been a shot fired to cause the car to explode. "If there was a shot, that means we're getting close. If there wasn't, then nothing matters," he concluded.

"True."

"Ginger's sharp. Sometimes sharper than others, and if she heard something that sounded like a shot—"

"A lot of things sound like shots. And if Grogan found that the key didn't mean anything, there's no reason for Ginger's accident to have been anything else but an accident."

"It just seems too coincidental."

"No. Accidents happen. I had a beef-dip sandwich before a truck hit me. I'll never have a beef-dip again. Is that logical?"

"But a beef-dip sandwich doesn't have anything to do with a thwarted drug raid."

"And probably the key doesn't either. Have you looked through a mug book yet?"

Win shook his head.

Phillips turned and grabbed a thick binder from his credenza. "Try this. It's the Corelli family. They're the ones involved in this."

Win eyed the binder for a moment, then opened it to the first page. It was laid out in logical fashion—one picture after another, a yearbook. But the faces weren't innocent high schoolers. Each face had the stamp of evil on it—a stern indifference to morality—a hostility to it.

He'd gotten to the second page, the last of the "A's" when both he and John heard a shrill voice calling them from the outer office.

"Mr. Phillips, you'd better come out here. A crate's just been delivered—there's blood."

John moved quickly out the door with Win right behind him.

In the center of the waiting room was a crate. Three foot on a side, it was an old-fashioned wooden crate with "Fragile" stenciled on all sides. From the bottom of it seeped something that had the unmistakable appearance and quality of blood.

"Mrs. Warner, I think you might want to go for coffee," John said.

"No way," she said. "I've dreamed of this moment. What do you think I took the job for?" By the time she finished her sentence she'd produced a hammer and screwdriver. "Want me to open it?"

"Call 911. I'll do the honors," John answered.

Win stood back while Mrs. Warner punched in the three numbers and John poised the hammer above the well-placed screwdriver and gave it a couple of quick slaps.

After a few more the cover lifted off.

Win had never seen anything like it.

Larin Breed called the hospital and was told that Bray was resting comfortably. "First time ever," the commander grunted. But he was pleased. He called the chief of police and briefed him on Bray's condition. Before he hung up he said, "And when he's back, I'll be recommending him as my replacement."

"You sure you want to do that? I thought you were grooming Grogan. You wanted youth—*vitality* I think was the word you used," the chief replied.

"I've made my decision. If Bray gets back here able to do the job, I'm recommending him. Youth has its place, but people will follow a guy who has proved that he'll lay his life down for others. That impressed me."

"Well," the chief said, "remember, it's only a recommendation. I'm the final word."

"And you'd go against me?"

"It'll be my decision. But I've never gone against you before—well, that's not entirely true, but true enough."

Breed hung up and to his surprise saw Grogan standing at the door. "Yes?"

"I wanted to brief you on Glasgow's accident last night," Grogan said. "I got tire marks, and they're running them down right now. Looks like a hit and run. There's nothing left of Glasgow's car to search so the tire marks are all we have. I think we'll have to chalk this one up. Unless someone gets drunk and starts babbling."

"I'll see about getting the car replaced. Is there evidence of any negligence on Glasgow's part?"

"None that I can see. Her story checks out. She probably

would have been better off to ram the guy instead of trying to avoid the accident, but there's no faulting that choice."

Breed nodded. "Her sergeant says she's asking to come to work for us. What do you think about that?"

Grogan considered. "She's a little spacey at times."

"But easy to look at."

"If the National Organization of Women could hear us now," Grogan chuckled.

"If my wife could. Well, I'll think about it."

"I heard you talking on the phone about Bray Sanderson. How's he doing?"

"Okay. Finally resting. He's a tough character. He'll do fine."

"I heard you were going to recommend him for your job."

"I know you and I had talked about it, but circumstances have changed. Promotional opportunities come along all the time. You'll be all right."

"I'm sure I will be," said Grogan and left.

Betty Harmon, who was beginning to think of herself more and more as Mary Seymour, decided to spend the day relaxing. And an essential part of relaxing was to take a bath. After picking and eating a few apples from some wild apple trees nearby, she eyed the boathouse. Sure. Why not? She could put the door down and splash around in there all she wanted.

After all, she had to be clean to look for a job.

For added comfort, she scanned the area. Finding it deserted, she returned to the boathouse and levered down the garage door. Opening the side door to gather in more light than the two windows allowed, she climbed out of her clothes. There was something risqué about being naked in a boathouse—it was probably the big door and the world so close beyond—or maybe she just didn't like the idea of being so vulnerable. But none of that deterred her. Grabbing a bar of soap and a bottle of shampoo from her knapsack, she jumped into the cool glassy water.

In seconds any discomfort vanished. The water came up to her chest and though the rocks were irregular and caused her to stumble now and then, the bath was wonderfully invigorating. She quickly lathered up and rinsed off, then lathered up again. After rinsing again, she leaned back to wet her hair. Oh, her hair felt good as she shampooed it. She couldn't believe how soothing it felt. She shampooed a second time, then slowly, experiencing the luxury, she rinsed it. Maybe camping wasn't all that bad. When clean, she found herself treating the enclosed area like a pool. She floated and kicked and swam laps for exercise.

She enjoyed herself. At one point she even barked like a seal.

If there was a God of girls on the run, he had smiled on her. What a wonderful day this was. She knew they all couldn't be like this. There would be rain on her parade one day. But somehow she thought the rain wouldn't last. Things would now be better. So much better than L.A. So very much better than the rage of death she was escaping from.

When done, she lifted herself from the water, dried off, climbed back into her now dirty-feeling clothes, and stepped outside. The air was heavy with humidity, but there was something comforting about it; it seemed just part of things—the glassy blue lake gently kissing the land, the emerald trees, sometimes bucking in the breezes.

After another hour, though, the sun was high, and she began to feel restless. Like she was wasting time—time she didn't have to waste. After she had a job and a permanent place to live there would be time for resting.

She did the best she could to freshen up her clothes, then put on some makeup and went out to find a job.

Chad was growling around the lake on his aluminum twelve-footer when Win drove up. Still aching with what he'd seen, he fought the need to share it with Ginger. It was so gruesome, hauntingly so. The images seared his brain—an emotional branding iron.

"Win, is that you?" she called from the bedroom.

"You need more painkillers yet?" he asked.

"Not yet. Stay out there, I'm getting dressed."

A few minutes later Ginger appeared, balanced on her crutches.

"You look like you've seen a ghost," she said. "Compared to you, Bray's a rainbow."

Win looked up. "You sure you want to be—well—"

"What?"

"You know I love you."

"Sure. I wouldn't let you see me without makeup if I didn't." She cocked her head. "What's wrong? Did Phillips say something? He thinks I'm stupid for losing the key. But the bottom of the lake was slimy. You said it first."

"Nothing like that. But I'm not so sure I like you being in such danger all the time. And now you want to be a detective. That's even more dangerous."

"Traffic's got them both beat. I'm a walking example. You don't see Grogan on crutches."

"These people you cops are fighting against mean real business."

"So do we."

"Yeah. But they have a different rule book. You have to read them their rights—while they're cutting you to pieces with a chain saw."

Ginger grimaced. "Yuck!" she said. She eased herself down on the arm of the sofa. "Okay, come clean. What's this about?"

"Well, let's count the ways—first you're burned on the back of the hand by a cigar when we try to apprehend some guy. Then two days later you're perched with the birds in a police car a million feet above a pile of rocks; you're poked full of holes and miss being roasted by inches."

"So?"

"Now what could happen? I just came back from John Phillips's office. A little package was delivered to him. In it was the informant who told John and his people that drugs were coming down the lake last Friday night. He was sawed in little pieces, and nailed to his forehead was a note. I mean nailed there."

"What did it say?"

"Does it matter? Even if your aerial experience was an accident, the guy with the cigar was with the same kind of people who did this. What if they just decided to clean house? You might be part of the cleaning process. We both might. We saw him. Sort of."

"What did the note say?"

Win shrugged. "Something about the drug guys being beat. That the DEA had won. And, so that they didn't think it was a total victory, here's one of the DEA's people back."

"The DEA won?"

"That's what it said. Phillips wasn't convinced. You see the people that wrote the note lacked credibility in his mind." Win looked up at her with pleading eyes. "But John Phillips doesn't care much about any of it anymore."

"He doesn't? Why not?"

"His office is being closed down. People are mad at him because nothing came of the raid, and I guess the Miami DEA people were able to convince the budget people that a full-scale war up here wouldn't matter much anyway. You're on your own up here, Ginger—love of my life."

Ginger knew exactly what Win was saying. By nature she wasn't a brave person. When she did something unusually brave, something of greater courage than getting up in the morning and facing the day as a single mom, it was because she had to. She didn't look for ways of becoming a hero. But maybe that was changing—something was hardening inside of her.

"The Lord will take care of us," she said. She took a deep breath. There were times when she could be quite forceful. There were other times, particularly when she was stating a position that was important only to her, personally, that it took some doing. "Now I've been giving this a lot of thought lying in that bed in there—between stabs of pain. My first responsibility is to Chad and, when we're married, to you and Chad both. Whatever I do, it has to fit in that context. But I feel like I have to grow this way. If there's anyone who should know what 'being called' is all about, it's you. And with those encounters you seem to have with God and the other guy—you should believe there's a God who loves and watches out for us."

"I should," Win said, almost as if he didn't.

"Jesus is calling me to do this. Again, within the confines of my responsibilities. I know that."

"If you'd only seen what I saw."

"Maybe there's a reason I didn't. Maybe if you'd seen missionaries burned at the stake, you wouldn't have gone into the ministry."

"Maybe—certainly not if I'd seen them torn apart by a chain saw."

Ginger swallowed hard. "I don't know why I feel this way. I'm still a klutz at times. But at others I know I can be good—really good."

Win sighed. "I'm just afraid for you—and for me. I don't want to lose you."

"And I don't want to lose you." Looking toward the kitchen she asked, "Could you toast me up a bagel or something? I'm famished."

Win nodded. "I don't think I'll be eating for a week. And for the rest of my life, lasagna is out."

The instant the bagel popped out of the toaster, the phone rang.

"This is Dr. Forest. I'm one of Bray Sanderson's attending physicians."

"What's happened?"

"He's asking for you again. Please come. There are large blood vessels at risk here."

Hanging up, Win told Ginger about the call. Then, quickly spreading the cream cheese and pouring the coffee, Win set up a tray and took it over to her as she reclined on the couch. "I could get used to this. I'm not sure I'd want to repeat what got me here, but the result is good," she said, smiling.

"I saw Chad out on the lake in his boat when I drove up," Win said as he got ready to go to the hospital.

"I'll go out in a sec and check on him."

"I'll be back as soon as I can. Call Mel and tell him what's going on, okay?"

When Win got to Bray's room, Bray was awake. Eyes wide, the top of the bed cranked up a little this time so he didn't look quite so much like a mummy. He still looked like a very sick guy, however.

"Brief me," Bray demanded.

"The key turns out to be from a place that burned down several months ago."

"How do you know that?"

"Grogan's handling it. He told us."

Win should have never mentioned the name. Bray stiffened and shaped his thin lips into a frown.

"He came to us," Win explained. "Anyway, he's doing a good job. He's checking on some tire tread marks at the scene of Ginger's accident."

"It wasn't an accident."

"I'm actually leaning your way. But there's no proof. Just hunches."

"What else?"

"A major else."

"What?"

"The DEA's pulling out. Phillips is being reassigned. Washington's mad at him for Friday night, and the Miami people have stripped his budget."

"I usually like Florida."

"I gotta hand it to you guys in law enforcement, though. How you can come to work every day and see some of the things you do."

"What did you see?"

"The DEA's informant was shipped to Phillips's office in a crate. He was sawed to pieces. Blood everywhere. Just thinking about it makes me want to toss my cookies."

"Toss 'em somewhere else."

"There was a note too."

"They wrote the DEA a note? Why does that sound so weird?"

"It said that the DEA had won and they were sending their guy back to just let them know they hadn't won it all—or something like that."

"The DEA won?"

"The implication was that no more drugs would be coming down the lake."

Bray managed a grimace. "It's all a lie."

"A lie. They nail a note to a guy's forehead, and it's a lie? Phillips thought so too."

"It's a trick."

"But it doesn't matter," Win said.

"Doesn't matter? Why?"

"The DEA's gone. Except for the local police and a couple of DEA guys left to chase students, there's no presence here. No one to fight 'em."

Bray's head moved to an incredulous posture. "There's us."

"Us? Have you seen *us* lately? You look like a failed Frankenstein experiment, Ginger looks like a cross between a pin cushion and an ad for MedicAlert, and I'm just not sure I'm up to this. I get queasy when I see a contortionist screw his body parts all around. At least with the contortionist they're all still connected."

"Well, get sure. I'll die before I let Grogan beat me again."

"That may be true."

"Where's that God of yours? Why aren't you relying on him?"

Win just shook his head. "I don't know. Why aren't I?"

"There are kids dying because of that stuff, Win."

"I know. Listen, you get some rest. You need rest. And there is no *us* right now. We're all currently casualties. All of us."

Chapter 10

Standing in the hallway on the second floor, Martin Sorrell heard the voices downstairs and heard even more coming from outside. Older men and their younger women. The men all had wedding rings, few of the girls did. A year before he would have taken great interest in his guests. He'd taken great pride in the hospitality his inn showed its visitors. Being an innkeeper had been the first job he'd ever done well, and he was jealous of his reputation. But not now. Though the deed still proclaimed him the owner, the inn was no longer his.

What made all this an even greater tragedy was that the inn was all he owned. The only thing, except for some expensive shirts, that had his name on it.

His father was a multibillionaire. He'd made his money in banks, real estate, the financial markets and, later, a number of business enterprises. He was a ruthless man, as Martin saw him, wielding power like a sledgehammer. The hammer came down on his only son when the fifth business in a row that he'd been put in charge of lost money—actually lost everything. His father took action much like Hitler attacking Poland.

Carl Sorrell placed fifty million dollars in trust for Martin, bought the inn, and planted his son in the middle of it. The inn became Martin's only success, the thing that gave his life value, and now it too was gone, taken from him again every time one of the mobsters showed up.

He'd lovingly decorated all the rooms himself. He had a flair for it and had given each a unique personality. One was dedicated to George Washington. The painting of him crossing the Delaware hung over the bed, and a first edition biography graced the nightstand. Another told how maple syrup was made. The room was splashed with autumn colors as a mural explained the step-by-step process. Room eight was his dollhouse. It was such a sweet little room. He enjoyed putting young starry-eyed couples in it—stars he used to hope he'd see in someone's eyes looking back at his. But he never had. Not only did the dolls provide magic, but the four-poster bed with its lacy white bedding bathed the room in a cherished purity, a purity antithetical to what was happening at his inn.

As he stepped from his upstairs room where he'd gone for a shower, he saw Gatlin step into his doll room, and the door close gently. She was stealing away to another world, and he wished her well.

On his way past the room, though, he heard sounds that indicated all was not well in room eight—an "Oh, no," and "How can I ever get that back together?"

He opened the door and found Gatlin at the foot of the bed, holding in her hand a doll whose head was cocked very far to one side, its neck much longer than it should have been.

"I think I broke it," she said to Martin.

He crossed to her and reached out a hand. She placed the doll in it.

She was right. The cup that held the head in place was damaged. Probably the years had weakened it. "I'll see what I can do," he said.

But at that moment another figure appeared in the doorway. It was Gatlin's father. Clad in a green jacket and jeans, he looked like he was on his way out. But he stopped when he spotted them. His expression was disapproving.

"What are you doing in here?" he asked Gatlin.

"It's the doll room," she replied.

"It's all right," Martin said, not even sure of the guy's name. He never wanted to know any of their names. Knowing Gatlin's was a compromise he feared he'd someday regret.

"You've got your own room. Play in there. And dolls are for other kids. Not for you. Life's not about dolls."

Martin hated that. Life may not be all for dolls, but some part of it certainly was. And if more of it was, life would be far more liveable. Of course, he remained silent.

"I'm going out for a while. Stay in your room while I'm gone," Ram commanded Gatlin.

"May I make a suggestion?" Martin said, fearfully.

"What?"

"I'll be working on my roses. She can stay with me while you're gone. That way she'll be watched."

"Can I, Dad? Mr. Sorrell and I have a Monopoly game going."

"What's wrong with the video games? I just got you *Annihilator*."

"Monopoly's fun."

Ram's brows knit. "Okay. But stay there."

"Okay, Dad."

Ram Lucha left his daughter in Martin's hands. Although Ram couldn't admit it, he liked the idea of someone taking care of her. It relieved his mind. But his mind was relieved for only the time it took him to go downstairs. The boss, who had summoned him, stood at the game room door; as always, he leaned on the pool stick.

When Ram stood beside the boss, he handed Ram a fax. It was from the family underboss and said that there was a special job for Ram.

"That's the Halfway House," Ram said as he read the fax's contents. The Halfway House was about a mile down from the Canadian border. Now deserted, at one time it had been an ornately built Victorian summer home. It now served as the drop-off point between the Canadian connection, which was largely Colombian, and the family in the U.S. There was only one resident there on a permanent basis; he was the subject of the fax.

"This takes your special talents."

"Says here I'm just supposed to lean on him."

"We've got a shipment coming through tonight, and there's evidence that guy's tampering with them."

"Those bales? How?"

"Punctures, knife marks—he's taking some for his own use. He's the Colombians' man so we don't want to come down too hard until we know for sure. But we want him to get the message to lay off tonight. There's eighty million dollars worth—a spoonful gets lost and the profits go down. The Corellis like profits."

Fearing the car might be recognized, Ram said, "I'll take the boat. It'll be faster in the long run."

"Whatever."

"I told Gatlin she could stay with Sorrell. That'll keep her out of your hair."

"Sorrell's got something else to do. She stays in her room for now."

Reluctantly Ram nodded. He returned upstairs and broke the news to Gatlin, who was as reluctant to spend the day in her room as she was to see her father leave again. "Be careful—please," she pleaded as he left.

While Gatlin and her father were talking, Waco summoned Martin Sorrell. At the game room door, Sorrell stood while the boss made a tough pool shot. Then the boss straightened. "Our guests are complaining about the food. Too much chicken and fish and not enough red meat. Plus we're getting low on booze. Waco, get your uniform on and drive the good innkeeper here to town." Then he pointed a pool cue at Sorrell. "You'll sign for everything. Maybe that's how we'll get all your money. We'll eat it up."

"I'm telling you, the accountants will get suspicious. I'm sure they're already worried about the lack of income," Martin said.

"If they do, we can always find another place. But they'll never find you."

"I understand," said Sorrell, his tone short.

Mel Flowers eyed his assistant as he stepped through the tent doorway. "You see Bray?"

"He's getting crazier and crazier. But that's improvement, right?" Win fumbled with the Sunday attendance cards sitting on his desk. It was Monday's ritual to go through them, find the new people, and call for a visit. Win hadn't done any of it yet.

"I talked with Pam," Mel said. "She saw him early this morning and had nothing but good things to say."

"Well, I saw him about a half hour ago, and he wants to make his room drug-bust central with him astride the white horse. He can't even feed himself, and he's trying to act like General Schwarzkopf."

Mel smiled. "He's feeling useless. The young guys are taking over, and he doesn't want to relinquish the lead."

"Well, there's more."

Win told him about the DEA pulling out and finally about the body he'd seen. "I'm afraid Ginger's going to end up in a crate like that. What's really scary is that she's got more faith than I do right now."

"Why is that?"

"Because I'm losing it. I see my best friend an inch from death, and God seems to be doing nothing about it—neither curing him nor bringing him into the fold. I see kids who ought to be responding to the gospel rejecting it and even stealing from this very church."

"Have you seen Todd?"

"For all I know, he was the one who forced Ginger off the road."

"Anything else?"

Win nodded. "God and I used to have this special relationship at the seminary," Win continued. "We used to commune for hours. Praying, reading, learning. Now I feel like I'm a stranger."

"Or like he is."

"Right. Ginger trusts him. She's all set to get those wounds healed and get back into the saddle—heading up the posse."

"And you're sitting here bemoaning the loss of a friend."

"Well, Bray's not lost yet—"

"I was talking about Jesus."

Win's eyes came up and he studied Mel's empathetic face. "Yeah. I guess I am."

"When I feel like that—and believe me I have—I find that the best thing is to just get busy. So, get busy." Mel indicated the stack of cards in Win's hand. "Start calling and setting up appointments. We're not going to get out of this tent by winter if we don't have enough summer people to pay for it."

Win stacked the cards in his hand. Five. They were averaging a couple of new families a month. Five was good.

"This being in the real world is hard. When I was an itinerant evangelist, I could run away from the real pastoral problems. Tell myself they were someone else's. Not now. I'm in this with you. Remember that."

The hand Mel put on his shoulder felt good. But in the final analysis, he still felt very much alone.

His eyes caught the invitation Ginger wanted him to send to his father. It lay just as the stationer had printed it, on his desk. Maybe he'd send it tomorrow. Not today.

On the way to the boathouse, Ram had difficulty washing Gatlin's pleading face from his mind. In the last few days he'd been skirting death. On the beach when those two found him, then with the key, and finally with the car. Had any one of those incidents exploded in his face, Gatlin would have been left alone.

That wouldn't be disastrous. People grow up. They get by, with or without parents. But she was the only one in the world he actually felt a little responsibility for, and the idea of shirking it by getting himself killed, hit, or sent up preyed on what little conscience he had.

But there was a job to do, and Ram Lucha did his job.

A few minutes later, with Gatlin's worried face tucked away, Ram climbed into the seventeen-foot inboard, fired up the engine, and eased onto the lake.

Ram had been to the old Victorian house many times. He'd helped modify the huge basement, a rarity on the isles, then worked at making it look even more decrepit and deserted.

As he approached, he wished he hadn't done such a good job with the dock. But he finally managed to get the thing tied off.

Making sure his machine pistol was loaded and ready, the extra magazine accessible in his pocket, he stepped from the rotting wood onto the weed-infested grass.

"Hey, mon," a voice came from an olive-skinned man who revealed himself at the side of the house. Like Ram he wore casual clothing, but his was far more expensive—formfitting, flashier. "Day say you wan' to see the operation," he said. "I don' know why. You been here enough."

"They just want to know the possibilities here," Ram said. He knew the guy only as LaCosta.

And now LaCosta reached out a hand. "Well, then, let's go down and take a look."

Ram remained a couple of steps behind the Colombian, sizing him up. He wasn't as beefy as Ram—his shoulders and torso were thinner, his arms wiry. He walked so lithely and gracefully that Ram wondered if he had feet or paws in those five-hundred-dollar shoes.

LaCosta walked to the storm cellar door and opened it. Stairs leading into the shadows.

They negotiated the steps, LaCosta going first to turn on the single bulb.

Standing at the foot of the stairs, Ram scanned the huge room: cement floor, four cinder block walls, worktables, heavy-duty scales and small lift trucks. Along one wall were large drums. *Ephedrine*—the cutting compound—was written on the side of some of them. The setup looked good. But there was no time to be impressed. He had a job to do.

"We can do it all here," LaCosta said, apparently enjoying his role. "Usually we just weigh it to make sure it all got through and then pass it on. But we can also cut it here; we can step on it how ever many times we want." His back to Ram, LaCosta moved farther into the room.

Seizing the opportunity, Ram planted a heavy hand on LaCosta's right shoulder and spun him around. "I got a mess—"

"Got what, gringo?"

Ram was looking at the sharp point of a stiletto, its blade glistening even in the dim light, the point an inch from his nose, poised to go right into his brain.

"Well," said Ram, his rigid stance relaxing as if about to defuse the situation.

He didn't. He brought his right hand up and grabbed LaCosta's arm. Counting on his superior strength, Ram pushed the arm and knife away, then brought up his left fist and slammed it into LaCosta's jaw. Or at least that's what he wanted to do.

Before he connected, though, LaCosta drove his right fist into Ram's midsection. His fist was small, like a ballpeen hammer, and the blow was well placed. Ram felt his lungs deflate and a spike of nausea drive into his stomach. He bent forward involuntarily. Grabbing for air, he got less than a mouthful when LaCosta jammed the same fist into Ram's kidneys, then again, this time up under his rib cage. A volcanic pain gushed through him, the lava burning to his backbone. Through a growing haze, Ram felt LaCosta wrench his knife hand free. Knowing his life depended on a quick, dramatic response, he struck out with his left fist, but LaCosta wasn't there. He'd spun and now kicked Ram with those five-hundred-dollar shoes in the spine. Ram heard himself scream, the pain like a hot poker just above his tailbone. He fell against the cellar wall, the unforgiving rock boring into his back. He had to recover or it was over. Another kick, this time in the kidney. Unable to maintain any control of his legs, he felt himself collapse to his knees. Arms folded in front of him trying to keep his insides from falling out, he remained there, weaving back and forth, pain surging through him, a debilitating tide.

If he didn't get to his weapon, he'd be a dead man.

Ignoring the fiery pain as best he could, Ram grabbed for his pistol but before his hand could get to it, one of those five-hundred-dollar shoes planted itself on his hand, pinning it to his chest, pinning his back against the wall. The knifepoint was a hair from his eye.

"Enough, amigo?"

Ram grunted. The stinking little fighter had gotten the better of him, and any second he'd feel the stiletto burn through his eye. Would he feel anything when it reached the brain? Or would it be over so quickly it wouldn't matter? This was the fate of his business. It was payback time.

"Tell your boss that he's to keep his hands off Señor Perez's people. We don't like it."

To emphasize the point, LaCosta planted his toe deeply into Ram's ribs. Ram couldn't help but cry out, the force of the blow toppling him on his side. He lay on the cold floor wanting to cry.

"Well, gringo—I hope you enjoyed the tour. I'll be going now." Ram felt the guy grabbing his machine pistol, then cutting the holster off his shoulder. He heard him slip the gun into it. "I like these—good choice." A moment later, eyes watery so that he only saw distorted shadows, Ram perceived he was alone—and still alive.

The pain seemed to invigorate his hearing. He heard himself groan, heard his labored breathing, heard himself curse and curse again as he tried to work himself up into a sitting position. "He'll regret leaving me alive," he gasped, the mere act of breathing sending out hot tendrils of pain. He leaned against the cinder blocks and tried to relax his muscles, testing the expansion and contraction of his lungs against his ribs. Only after he had rested for several minutes did the pain begin to lessen. But could he move? "You'll regret this," he called out. But not too loud.

He wasn't sure when he actually moved. It seemed like he'd lain there only a minute or two, but it was possible that he'd passed out. The pain excruciating, Ram worked his way to his feet. Then, stumbling forward, he took the stairs one painful step at a time. Outside he staggered, fell, then staggered again as he made it to the boat.

Balancing on each plank, he made it to the spot above his boat, then all but fell into it. He tried to tell himself that it was only pain, that if he just ignored it, he could do anything he wanted. But it wasn't true. The pain was unignorable.

Working as if life depended on it, he unhooked the tie line and fired up the engine. A moment later he was on his way home.

But he didn't quite make it.

Mary Seymour had walked halfway across the United States in the last couple of weeks, and only now did her feet hurt. They didn't actually hurt. They were defeated; she was defeated.

She'd gone out to look for a job and hadn't even gotten to where the jobs were. She must have been thinking of looking for work in L.A. where jobs were counted by the square foot. Here it was hard to count them by the square mile.

She'd passed a cottage or two and actually stopped at one to see if there might be a domestic job available. But after seeing the pudgy little lady in the housedress who answered the door, she didn't even ask.

But defeated or not, she had to earn some money. There was nothing free to eat out here but roots and apples, and after the first couple of apples, the roots started looking pretty good. But the God of escaping girls had provided for her before and had now given her a sheltered place to stay; surely he would provide her with a job—and a way to get to it.

Before she could think about it further, she heard the guttural growl of an engine. Just the sound of it told her that something was wrong. It growled just above an idle and coughed occasionally as if strangled for gas. A moment later it came into view. A good-sized boat, sixteen or seventeen feet long, sleek, capable of incredible speeds. But it was realizing none of them today. It chugged along maybe ten yards off-shore.

There was someone at the helm, but he looked drained, maybe unconscious. Was it a heart attack or something? She couldn't tell.

She thought of leaping into the water and swimming out to it. But even at an idle it was moving faster than she could swim. Then she realized that she didn't have to catch up with it. The boat was heading for her boathouse, the guy at the wheel steering it as best he could.

She saw his eyes widen as he saw her. He was probably just trying to find a spot to dock and rest. Instead he'd found her.

The bow pointed right for the boathouse door. Although the guy was obviously injured, he was able to steer it. But then, just as the tip of the bow crossed into the boathouse shadows, the pilot seemed to be seized by whatever had afflicted him. He grabbed his side, bucked backward, then forward.

Mary Seymour gasped but acted quickly. Knowing the boat was about to slam into the rear of the boathouse, she leaped aboard, grabbed the throttle away from the guy, and eased it into reverse. The boat stopped. She then turned off the ignition and tied the boat off. A moment later she stood over him.

"Are you okay?" she asked, wrapping nursing arms carefully around his muscular shoulders.

Surprised, Ram looked up into the caring blue eyes. "Where'd you come from?"

"What happened? Did you have a heart attack? Here, rest. Just a second, let me be your pillow." She sat in the seat next to him and tried as best she could to cradle him. It was awkward at best, but she did feel like she was helping. "What happened? Can you remember?"

"I fell," he finally said. "Down stairs. Deserted house."

"Oh, you poor man." She patted him on his shoulders. His hair was so black. Usually black hair had highlights of some kind, she thought. But his was raven black. Dark as his eyes. They opened and looked up at her.

"Can you make it to the back of the boat where you can lie down?" she finally asked. "If I can get your shirt off, maybe I can help bandage you up or something."

Without a reply, Ram struggled to a sitting position, then planted a firm hand on the back of his seat and pushed himself up. She pulled herself out of the way and watched as he stepped behind the seat to the padded side benches. Falling onto one of those, he sat there for a moment.

After he was seated, she took up a position beside him. "Lean on me for a moment," she said. "Can you breathe okay?"

"Some. It's my insides."

She slowly moved out of the way so he could lie down on the padded bench. Now on his back, he peered up at her with eyes dull with pain. "I'm going to remove your shirt," she said, then mused to herself, *Not an unpleasant thought.*

Hovering over him, she delicately unbuttoned his shirt. He was in remarkable shape, probably from working out. But now his firm stomach and side were stained by deep blue and yellow bruises. Each stair must have left its own individual mark.

"Can you breathe better lying down?"

"My insides hurt. I thought I'd be okay once I got into the boat, but the rocking and slapping made it hurt more."

"Let's get your shirt off. We can wet it—then it'll probably feel good against those bruises."

What an upper body—muscular, defined, firm—when the bruises fade, he'll be dynamite. She dipped the shirt over the side, wet it thoroughly, then eased the shirt around him and tied it gently in front. She then lifted his head and laid it in her lap. "Rest a while," she told him.

He only nodded. Now the rocking didn't seem so bad. He must have slept for a moment or two because he suddenly had the feeling of waking. Eyes fluttering open he saw her again. *Sometimes even plain can appear beautiful,* he thought. She was a little above plain, her short blonde hair rustled by a growing breeze, her eyes worried and blue.

"Do you live here?" he asked after a while, his voice little more than air, his insides aching mush. "This place looked deserted from the water."

"Sightseeing," she told him. "I've lost count of the states I've gone through. I'm staying here 'til I find a job and my own place."

"You're too pretty to be hitchhiking," he croaked.

"Pretty? Me?" She blushed. "I didn't—well—hitchhike. People gave me rides."

"What did you give in return?" he asked. There was an innuendo in his voice that she resented.

She frowned. "They were nice people. I like it here. If I find a job, I'm staying. I was on the West Coast for a while but just got restless. You probably know how that is," she said, surprised at how fetchingly she said it. Then she said in a tentative tone, "You got a nice boat."

"I borrowed it," he said. Trying to sound like what he wasn't, he added, "My daughter likes it—she likes the lake."

"Daughter? How old is she?"

A stab of pain caused him to tighten his facial muscles and grab his side.

"You okay?" Mary asked, alarmed.

The spasm passed. "She's ten," he said.

"Ten," she repeated, feeling a lie coming on. "I took care of a ten-year-old for a while. Worked as a nanny. A rich couple in Newport Beach, California."

"My wife's gone, so it's just the two of us."

"I'm sorry," she said, not sorry at all. This was a good-looking single guy. How could she possibly be sorry? "You feeling any better?"

"A little. Maybe you could wet that shirt again."

This time he watched her as she bent over the side of the boat. She had a great little figure and moved smoothly. He'd hire her as a nanny if he could. But he could see the boss's face when he showed up with her. The ice he'd be skating on would be awfully thin.

When she had wrapped the shirt around him again and his head lay in her lap, she found herself massaging his temples. "That feel good?"

"Great," he managed, sounding a little worse than he really was. "Magic fingers."

She smiled. "What's your name?"

"Ram Lucha."

"Italian?"

He nodded. "How 'bout you?"

She thought. "Mary Seymour."

"Not Italian," he commented. Although movement still brought stabs of pain, the constant ache inside had dulled. He could easily make it to Sorrell's now—but not yet.

"Tell me about your daughter," she said, her warm fingers still massaging his temples, then his neck.

"She's a little older than her years," was all he said.

He couldn't take her back to the inn, but maybe he could come up to visit. It'd be nice to have someone to visit again. In New York there was always someone.

"It must be hard being father and mother both."

"Mother? Not me. First female thing her body does and I get her a book. Do the temples again. That's good."

She'd drifted to the back of his neck but returned to the temples. He'd be getting up soon, firing up the boat, and she'd never see him again. She couldn't believe herself. It was always like this. She'd meet a good-looking guy, and after fifteen minutes she was planning her whole life with him. That approach had never worked in the past and probably had something to do with her being hunted now. And yet his eyes were deep and dark, and that stomach was like a washboard.

"You don't mean that?"

"What?"

"That you'd just get her a book. Your daughter needs a woman around sometimes."

Wincing with pain, but managing just the same, he got himself to a sitting position. "I really have to get going. You gonna be here for a while?"

"I guess. I don't know."

"Well, if you're not, it'll be my loss. I really do have to get going."

He sounded stronger than she thought possible. Had he been sandbagging her—having fun with her? Well, if he had, even that wouldn't be so bad.

He moved to the main chair and fired up the engine.

"Untie it, will you?"

She did, then leaped to the walkway. "I hope you get home okay."

"I will," Ram said. "I can't thank you enough."

"Anytime," she said, wondering what to say next.

He deftly backed the boat out into the sunlight, then grimaced as a stab of pain struck him in the side, but when it passed, he eased the throttle forward. As the engine intensified and he gained speed, he waved good-bye.

She did the same.

"Why do all the good ones end up leaving?" she said to herself. A few minutes later she was back on her sleeping bag, but she wasn't napping; she was dreaming—dark eyes, broad shoulders, and a washboard tummy. Not bad.

The boss, resting on the edge of a pool table, looked up at Ram as he stepped into the room. "How'd your shirt get wet like that?" he asked.

"It was hot out there. I dipped it to cool off."

"Yer walkin' funny. You deliver the message?"

"Yes—as ordered."

"Really?"

"Really."

"Word has it that LaCosta beat you up pretty good," the boss said, then waited for the reply.

"What do you expect him to say?"

"Said you laid a hand on him and that was the last hand you laid on him."

"Not true."

The boss's eyes became narrow and they bored right into his man. Suddenly he jabbed Ram in the appendix with his fist. To his surprise, Ram didn't flinch.

"Like a rock, isn't it?" Ram said.

"Go up and get some rest. You'll be up all night."

Upstairs, before rapping on Gatlin's door, Ram succumbed. He grabbed his stomach and swallowed a cry. Like the first time with LaCosta, the pain was volcanic. The boss had a fist like the end of a broom handle—or a hot poker. He leaned against the wall for several minutes while he regained himself. Then he knocked lightly on Gatlin's door. It instantly opened. "Daddy, you made it back okay."

"Piece of cake," he said.

"Can you go with me to the beach?"

"I need to get some sleep, sweetie. I've got a late night ahead." Then a thought struck him. "Is that Sorrell guy around? Why don't you find him?"

"But I want to go swimming. He doesn't do that."

"It'll at least get you out of your room."

Disappointed, Gatlin sagged, but she said okay and went to find Sorrell.

Her disappointment ended when she found him in the basement. Before she had the opportunity to say hello, he presented her with a brand-new doll just like the one that had been broken. "Melissa," she gasped when he held it up.

"I got it while I was shopping. I got Waco to stop at a toy store."

"I'm the one on crutches," Ginger said, "but you're the unhappy camper. What's wrong with this picture?"

"I guess I'm still in recovery."

"It must have been a horrible thing to see."

Win had stopped by Ginger's after work. The late afternoon breezes were blowing off the lake, bringing waves that seemed a little more in earnest. "Where's Chad?" he asked.

"Sitting on a rock out there with his fishing pole."

"I wish I liked fishing more."

162   WILLIAM KRITLOW

"He likes it for you. You can see him in a minute. Want a Coke?"

"I'll get it. Are you getting around any better?"

"Some. I was hobbling without the crutches this afternoon but then twisted it again. You didn't hear me scream? Funny."

"I spent the afternoon sewing up the tear in the side of the tent. Canvas is hard to sew. I went to a sail maker to get the thread. You ought to see the thimble. It's like a dog dish." He sipped the Coke and took a place on the arm of the sofa. Ginger sat down, her injured leg up on the coffee table on a pillow. "Bray thinks the bad guys are still around," he said.

"He's paid to think that."

"He thinks that note to Phillips was a fraud."

"It wasn't sent by people with impeccable credentials."

"Phillips said that too."

Ginger liked the idea that she was in Phillips's company.

"If that wasn't an accident last night, they might make another try for you."

"I don't know anything. The key wasn't significant. I can't identify anyone—at least I don't think I can. It was an accident."

"Well, then, I'll get dinner. Want me to barbecue some chicken?"

Chad had every hope in the world that the little girl would return as she said she would. He even posted himself on the rock starting in late afternoon. The only time he left it was to have dinner with his mom and Win. Then he remained there until nearly ten, although he was asked to come inside several times. "Mom, this is really fun, and I'm right where you can see me," he argued.

But the girl didn't come.

She couldn't.

It wasn't for lack of trying. At about eight-thirty, when the sun was all but a crimson memory, she did as she had done the previous night. She stood by the back door for a while, then, when the other visitors were used to her being there, she just slipped outside.

But this time, as she crossed the backyard no-man's-land, the lookout saw her. Seconds later she was scooped up by two guys and a few seconds after that, Ram and his daughter stood before the boss.

"I am *not* disobeyed," the boss said, his voice much like a snarling dog's.

"She's only a kid," Ram said.

"She's got to be locked up."

Ram sighed. The boss could be stubborn. "What if I found someone to take care of her? Like a nanny or something."

"Here?"

"Why not?"

"You do know what we're doing here?"

"She'll never find out, and if she does, we'll get rid of her."

"Just lock the kid up."

"You can't lock a kid up. She'll go nuts. Or escape first and then you don't know what might happen."

Suddenly the boss's gun was out of its holster and placed right against Gatlin's head. Ram's breath caught. Gatlin's eyes strained to see it. She dared not move. This man was perfectly capable of dispatching her right there without blinking an eye. But he didn't. The gun came down.

"She's not the enemy, boss. Really. And we don't talk about anything around her anyway. Nobody does. It'll work. Really."

The boss's brows dipped as he thought.

"Get the nanny. If she learns anything—kill the nanny. And do it tomorrow. You got work tonight. Lock her in her room tonight. Understood?"

"All of it."

"If this doesn't work, she's off to Benny's Academy for Young Girls. Is that understood?"

"Right."

Chapter 11

Todd Breckenridge knew that tonight was the night. He didn't know how he knew, but he did—maybe it was the powerboats easing along the lake late at night, maybe something inside him went off when something wild was about to happen. It didn't matter what told him; the fact that it did was what mattered. And since it had told him the first time a couple of weeks ago, he'd collected a good supply of the stuff they shipped—that coke stuff. Although he didn't know all the ins and outs of it, Todd knew he was putting together a small fortune just a little at a time.

Working his way up the coast, he positioned himself where the boat would be the closest to land and waited. While he did, he practiced with the "tosser-thing." He was getting good at it; he only resented the fact that he couldn't show his ability to anyone.

But that didn't matter either. As a ten-year-old boy, he was on his way to becoming rich. And he didn't resent at all not being forced to share that with anyone.

The boat would be coming along soon. It would appear like a black ghost on the river, its side wheel churning at about half speed—*whoosh, whoosh*. A steady pulse of paddles dipping into and leaving the water. It would move with the barest light, pinpoints that glistened and ringed the upper deck, and two headlights on either side of the bow.

It moved steadily. Silently.

It was like this the first time he'd snuck aboard. But the second time had been last Friday night during the party. He'd found the stuff in a different place that night, but he'd still found it.

Moving like a cat, Todd had eluded detection by slipping down this corridor and that, into this room and that. Finally he stopped sneaking around and began working as a busboy. He was mistaken a couple of times for a member of the crew—albeit a little member. He liked that best.

Now he waited as silently as he'd waited before.

He checked his pockets. He had his knife, the tape, the Ziploc baggie, the "tosser-thing" because now he never went anywhere without it. He had a lot of other stuff too. He always did. The things in his pockets were his. Everything else he was borrowing from someone else. It was important to have the things that were his with him.

There it was.

He saw the headlights first, the tunnels of light reaching out in front of it, igniting the mist that blanketed this part of the lake.

Then the bow appeared, followed by the rest of it—a huge, black silhouette.

This was a particularly narrow part of the lake, where the side-wheeler eased close to shore as it slipped around a bend. As he had before, Todd walked out into the water until he was waist deep, then he began swimming. There were ropes that surrounded the lower deck. He grabbed one of them and swung himself aboard.

He could hardly contain his excitement. Todd Breckenridge lived for freedom, lived for adventure, and climbing onto a side-wheeler in the middle of the night among smugglers was both—it was being a pirate and an outlaw. It was being just about everything he'd ever hoped for.

Wet and cold, he slipped along the lower deck, past a cabin where he heard men's voices, to the room where they always hid it. He loved this. No one ever guarded it, because they probably thought there was no one to guard it from. He opened the door just wide enough to slip inside. It was a neat room. A lot of stuff was on the walls—pictures, brass plates, statues, and big mugs. On a table in the corner were some supplies. Todd grabbed a plastic stick they used to stir their drinks and stuffed it in his pocket. He remembered the stick from when he was there on Friday. Now he had one. He turned. There it was. A pile of the stuff. It was wrapped in heavy plastic in three-foot-by-two-foot bundles. Stacks two and three deep.

As he did before to keep anyone from knowing he'd been there until it was too late, he found a place where there was a small space between the bales. Opening his knife and taking the baggie from his pocket, he wedged himself between the bales and slowly, methodically, began to cut away at the plastic cover.

He never finished.

A hand as big as eternity grabbed his leg and pulled him out. As if it could actually make a difference, Todd lashed out with his knife at the man who stood over him. The man pulled away quickly enough to only be nicked.

Whatever chance Todd had before he cut Ram Lucha's arm evaporated afterward.

Win's phone rang at about five in the morning. "Huh," he said, his consciousness breaking through the haze.

"It's Mel. I just got a call from the Breckenridge family. Todd's dead."

Win cleared his throat and worked himself to a sitting position. "What? How?"

"Drowned. The police found his body near one of the bridges. I'm going meet his parents at the morgue. You wanna come along?"

"Of course. Was there any violence?"

"Don't know. Why would there be?"

"I guess it's just the way I'm thinking these days."

The morgue sat in a wing of the Fletcher Allen Med Center. At five-thirty in the morning there were only a couple of cars in the lot.

Frank and Lois Breckenridge sat in the waiting room just outside the morgue, a coroner's assistant was with them when Mel and Win arrived. The instant Mel stepped through the door, he inserted himself between the family and the assistant. Taking the parents' hands, he began to talk to them. Mel was good at this, he cared—cared deeply. Their loss was his loss. Soon they were talking about their son, relating stories about him from birth. The coroner's assistant finally had to break in to finish asking his questions. When done he stood and began to walk away. Win buttonholed him. "Where'd they find him?"

"The bridge to North Hero. Face down."

"Where'd he go in?"

"We may never know."

"Any evidence of violence?"

"Some—but it's hard to determine whether it's relevant until after the autopsy."

"That'll be tomorrow."

"Or the next day."

"There's no doubt it's him?"

"They identified him."

"He always carried a lot of stuff in his pockets. One of those things might have been mine. Did you find a thing—it was a barrel on a string connected to a stick. You toss the barrel . . ."

As Win spoke, the assistant thumbed through several sheets of paper on a clipboard. "There wasn't anything in his pockets," he said.

"You sure?"

The assistant showed him the clipboard and pointed to a section marked "Found on Body"; the two lines below it were empty except for Todd's clothing. "Maybe he left the stuff at home. Or maybe he took it all out of his pockets before he went wading. Whatever the reason—those pockets were empty," the assistant said.

"Thanks," Win said and returned to Todd's parents.

Mel was praying with them. As he did, a natural warmth radiated from him.

At the amen, Mel looked up at his colleague. "Mr. and Mrs. Breckenridge asked if you'd seen Todd recently."

"No. He and I chatted about a toy I owned, but that was all. I haven't seen him since Sunday. My fiancée's son knew him pretty well. I wish I knew him better."

"I don't think we ever knew him, really," Todd's mother said. "He always seemed to be somewhere else—body and mind."

"He carried a lot of stuff in his pockets," Win said.

"That he did," his father said, his voice betraying a deep

fondness for his son. "All kinds of stuff. He once said it was everything he owned—his stuff."

"He didn't leave any of that stuff home when he went out last night?"

"He never would," said his mother.

"It didn't come out of his pockets unless he was going to use it," his father affirmed.

"I'm leaving now," Win said. "But I want you to know that I'll miss having your son to talk to."

"Thank you so very much," his mother gushed, tears beginning.

"We've never really been church people," the father began. "But maybe we'll see you next week."

"We would be happy to hold a memorial service for Todd," Mel told them. "I'll call you."

Out in the parking lot Mel stepped up to Win, who leaned against the Chevy's driver's side door. "You okay?"

"Not really."

"God appoints our deaths. He's in charge of all that."

"Kids are supposed to be my thing. I didn't do very well with that one."

"We only plant the seeds; God produces the crop."

"I guess it's all been said. There's nothing left but clichés."

"What was all that about his empty pockets? What's that mean?"

Win shrugged. "I don't know, but I bet it means something."

Ginger was awake and dressed in a very loose-fitting blouse and shorts when Win arrived to make her breakfast. "I didn't expect you so early," she greeted, swinging cautiously on her crutches from the hall heading toward the kitchen.

Seeing the bandages on her legs and arms and the dressing on her cheek wound, Win forgot everything else for a moment. "How's the pain?"

"Pain is never good," she said, "but it's getting a little better. It's easier to move. My back still stings like crazy. I guess I've got some real holes back there."

Careful not to bring more distress than comfort, he hugged her. Pulling back and returning to the kitchen, he finally said slowly, "Todd Breckenridge drowned last night."

"Todd?" It was Chad's voice. He stood in his bedroom door in his pj's.

"How did it happen?" Ginger asked.

"No one knows." Win walked toward Chad. "A cop on patrol found him floating near the North Hero bridge. His pockets were empty."

"Then something's wrong," Chad injected firmly. "He always carried stuff in his pockets."

Win began making coffee.

"You think somebody killed him?" Ginger asked incredulously.

"But why?" Chad asked, in deep confusion. "He's a ten-year-old kid." He gasped. "Somebody might kill me!"

"Only if you don't clean your room," Ginger told him—then smiled.

"But we have to do something," Chad said.

"It's a police matter," Win said, clearly stepping away from the question's implications.

"Mom's the police."

"The detectives will look into it."

"But people drown all the time in the lake," Chad said. "It'll just be another drowning. No one will care."

"His parents do," Win said. "They were genuinely touched by the loss."

"Well," said Chad, slipping from the stool. "I'm touched too." He stomped off toward his room. "And I'm going to do something about it."

"Chad Glasgow," Ginger barked. "Stop in your tracks."

Chad did.

"Face me."

He did, his expression chiseled but not rebellious, mostly concerned with a touch of puppy-dog submission.

"This is a police matter. They'll handle it. Now I know this has to be hard on you, and when things like this happen we want to fix them. But the Lord's in control of these things."

"It's the plan, right, Win?" Chad said, but this time there was sharp sarcasm in what he said.

"It is, Chad," Win replied, his tone soft and serious. "And just like you, there are times when I don't like the plan. But

God's working things out for our good. Sometimes it's hard to see that."

"Like he worked it out for Todd's good."

"Todd wasn't his, Chad. You are. We can't do anything about Todd's condition now, but we can do everything about ours—or at least most things. Right now our job is to go on living as godly people."

Chad softened a little. "Okay," he muttered and went to his room.

"You handled that pretty good, pastor," Ginger said, placing a consoling hand on Win's shoulder.

Win planted frustrated hands on the counter. "But Chad's right. The plan just doesn't make sense. I feel like we're being taunted. Nothing's concrete. We have keys that don't mean anything, yet you get run off the road. We have a kid who is drowned with empty pockets that should be full of stuff—including my 'tosser-thing.' But why would you kill a kid then empty his pockets?"

"You know what I think?" Ginger said.

Win poured her a cup coffee, then one for himself. "What do you think?"

"I think you're feeling guilty. Todd's dead, and you were his only spiritual connection."

"I keep telling myself that God's the one who completes it, not me. He just didn't do it this time. But the words ring so hollow."

Chad reappeared. He was fully dressed and carried his fishing pole. "I'm going to go catch a big one. For Todd."

It was mid-morning when Ram Lucha pulled the boat up to the once deserted boathouse. He and the others hadn't finished loading the shipment onto the trucks until nearly dawn. When he returned to the inn, he'd hoped to sleep most of the day, but the boss met him at the door and reminded him of his promise to make sure Gatlin was taken care of. After a few hours' sleep and a quick breakfast, he climbed into the boat and headed north. Now as he approached the boathouse he called out, "Mary Seymour, you there?"

A head peeked around the corner of the open door.

"It's you!" she exclaimed happily. "Why are *you* here?"

"Got a proposition for you."

Her face soured slightly. "Proposition?"

"I need a nanny."

"For your daughter?"

The boat was slipping into the berth now. He handed her a rope to tie it off, and he leaped onto the wooden dock. "I was thinking last night. You're right. Girls need a woman around, and if you're willing . . ."

"Sure. I was just wondering how I was going to find a job. Finding jobs has never come easy for me. I'm not the most forceful person in the world. Me being a little shy won't change your mind, will it? Because I am a little shy."

"That actually might work for you in this case. Go ahead and gather up your things."

Bubbling with the overwhelming feeling that there was a God of some kind looking out for her, Betty Harmon, who now had forgotten completely that her name wasn't truly Mary Seymour, began quickly tossing her toiletries and other things into her Barbie knapsack. The last thing she placed in it was her clown. He got a huge, grateful kiss on the top of the head before she buried him next to her makeup. She quickly rolled the sleeping bag and tied it off.

While she did all that, Ram Lucha told her, "We've leased out this inn south of here, and the people there all work with us. Some are on little vacations and things, but they all work with us. And what we do no one is to know about. I'll tell you this, it has to do with international mining. Gems, gold, other precious metals. The only way I was able to get my boss to let you come is to get you to promise to mingle with no one but my daughter and me. And certainly to say nothing to anyone outside the inn. If you go along with that, it'll be like being on a permanent vacation. You'll like the place."

She did.

The instant she saw it, she knew she'd love it. The green, tightly manicured lawn, the white buildings, the rich, dark woods in contrast. The guests relaxing in the late morning sun, the rusty rocks on the left, the beach next to the boathouse on the right, the trees. It was wonderful.

"We'll get you settled, then you're going shopping. We have to get you some clothes."

"Clothes?" She squealed with delight. "Oh, thank you, thank you, thank you."

"Now wait here on the patio for a minute—just at one of the tables. I'll find out where the boss wants you to stay."

Ram didn't have to go far to find out. The boss, his eyes hard as little black stones, stood just inside the patio door to the game room.

"I don't want her in the inn," the boss said. "I want her away from people. The old gardener's shack over there." He pointed to a boxy shed that sat near the water's edge beneath a canopy of oaks. "Fix that place up. You told her to keep away from everyone?"

"Sure."

Ram turned to go, but the boss added, "They found the kid."

"I knew they would. There wasn't time to do much else. But he just drowned. Kids drown."

"For your sake I hope that's true." The boss returned to the pool table. "Now get her settled."

"Right." Ram stepped back through the French doors.

Stepping up to Mary, he smiled. "Come on," he said, "let's put your stuff in your room." He led the way. "It's the old gardener's shack. You're probably going to gag at this place, but it's the only room we have available, and you look like some one who's handy."

When the door to the place opened she did gag but just a little. Although it was a mess, it had definite potential. And right now potential was good enough.

Surrounded by trees, it looked every bit like a shack from outside. That was true on the inside too. Sparsely furnished, there was a small kitchen consisting of a sink, counter, and a two-burner butane stove. Before it was a small table with two wooden chairs. On the table was a dirty cereal bowl and a carton of milk—the sour odor hit them the instant they entered. Obviously, when the gardener was let go, he'd made no effort to straighten things up. The sofa bed was folded out and unmade, three pillows scattered on top. Newspapers and magazines were strewn everywhere, and dust covered it all. There was another door on the far side of the building. As if giving a tour, Ram crossed to the door and opened it—a toolshed—a room lined and filled with gardening equipment. There was another door beyond the connecting door, probably to the outside. The equipment room was far neater than the living quarters.

"Just drop your stuff on the sofa there, and we'll go meet Gatlin."

Doing as she was told, Mary followed him into the main building.

"Nice place," Mary commented as they entered the inn through the French doors. She drank in the rich mahoganies and maple, the luxurious rugs and furniture. She followed Ram upstairs to Gatlin's room. He knocked lightly. A moment later Gatlin opened the door.

"Daddy, you're back!" She threw her arms around his neck and gave him a relieved hug. "I thought you were on another job."

His side still hurting, he winced as he wrapped his arms around his daughter and hugged her back. "Gat, I got someone I want you to meet."

"I'm Mary Seymour." Mary extended a hand. Gatlin took it suspiciously.

"She's going to be your nanny," said Ram.

Gatlin looked up at Mary. Gatlin's eyes revealed little. Both remained silent.

Ram entered his daughter's room while Mary stayed near the door. He spoke to Gatlin. "You're getting older, and you need someone like Mary to talk to."

"But I'll talk to you," Gatlin said, sounding a little betrayed.

"You're not losing your dad," Mary explained. "I'm just here for you. I wish I had someone for me when I was growing up. We'll be friends. I know it."

"On that note," said Ram, "I'll leave you two to get acquainted.

A moment later, Mary and Gatlin were alone, each eyeing the other tentatively. After a moment of this, Mary sensed that thoughts were beginning to swirl around in Gatlin's head. Finally Gatlin said, "I want to show you something."

Without waiting for a reply, Gatlin stepped directly across the hall. Rummaging in her pocket she found a key and unlocked room eight. The door opened, and Gatlin stepped inside.

Mary followed, and her mouth dropped in wonder. "Dolls. It's wonderful. I wish I had dolls like this when I was growing up. Do you play in here? Oh, I wish I had a room like this growing up."

"It's neat, huh?" Gatlin whispered, and when she did, to Mary's surprise, she slipped her hand into Mary's.

"Neat," Mary echoed. "I guess the only thing left is to know what I should call you. Your dad calls you Gat, but I think maybe Gatlin would be better. I think I like Gatlin better than Gat. I mean your dad can call you that. But girl to girl, Gatlin seems better. What do you think?"

Gatlin liked that rattling quality of Mary's speaking. There was a nervous energy about it. And energy meant fun. And it would be wonderful to not be cooped up when her dad was away. This was going to be great—having her own grown-up.

"Wanna help me with my room?" Mary asked.

"Sure."

The gardener's shack hadn't changed at all in the ten minutes Mary had been away, and yet with the two of them standing at the door, Mary sensed an even greater potential than before.

All Gatlin saw was the mess. "At least there's no chickens."

"Are there clean sheets?"

"In a closet near my room. They send them out once a week."

"When I get this cleaned up, will you come down and visit me?"

"You'll be too busy visiting me," Gatlin told her. "You're *my* nanny, remember?" Fortunately there was a twinkle in Gatlin's eye.

"Well, would you be willing to get the bedding, while I start cleaning things up? I think I'm going to like it here."

"I'm gonna love it," said Gatlin, stating fact.

"You want to investigate the kid's drowning too?" Breed asked, looking up at Grogan from a desk covered with paper. "Don't you think you're taking on a little much?"

"Maybe, but something's going on. The guy Glasgow had the fight with, her accident, now this. Maybe they're all related to what the DEA was investigating."

"Okay. But there are twelve other guys on the force when the load gets too much for you."

"I'll either connect 'em or not."

Breed nodded vacantly.

Grogan saw a paper on Breed's desk and read it, upside down. The heading was: "Recommendation for Commander's Replacement." The time had come. Bray Sanderson had to go.

Win stepped from the elevator, saw that Bray's guard was gone, then stepped over to the nurse's station. "Can I see him?"

"He's got a friend in there now. The guy really knows how to pull our chain. Fortunately, this friend calms him down."

"Pam?"

"His blood pressure stabilizes the instant she walks in the room. With you it skyrockets. Of course it goes even higher when he wants you, and you're not around. What's going on between you two?"

"It's a kind of love-hate thing. I love him, and he hates me. But he likes ordering me around."

Pam emerged smiling broadly. "Hi," she cooed to Win. "He's doing so much better. So much."

"You're a tonic to him."

"He's one to me too. There's no sub-clause in the unequally yoked thing we're not considering, is there?"

"None that I'm aware of."

"Well, I keep praying."

"Sounds like it's working. He'll likely live."

"The doctors are probably going to upgrade him to serious and remove him from ICU sometime today."

"Good. Well, into the lion's den I go."

Bray was cooler to Win than Win expected. There were no smiles, and smiles were certainly possible now. There were no warm words, only a rocky stare.

"I didn't send for you," he said.

"I wanted to talk for a minute."

"I send for you when I want you."

"I didn't know there were rules."

"There are. What's up?"

"There's been another death on the lake."

Bray's bed had been cranked up a little, so Win could see his face. His brows dipped. "Who?"

"A ten-year-old kid."

"A drowning?" Bray asked.

"Yes, but there's something strange. This kid normally had a bunch of things in his pockets—a knife, string, tape, just about anything you could imagine a kid might like. When they found him, his pockets were empty."

"A robbery?"

"No. Nothing was that good—anyway, who'd know what was in there? I don't think it was robbery."

"Then he saw something," Bray decided.

"That's possible. But why would they empty his pockets?"

"Maybe they were looking for something. Maybe the kid took something, and they caught him. Maybe they didn't like him taking something and they killed him. Or maybe they didn't kill him but left him to fend for himself, and he drowned trying."

"They all boil down to the kid being killed."

"Ten years old." Bray pondered that for a moment. "Maybe I've gotten you into something that won't do you any good," he mused, his voice still weak, but there was a fatherly concern that touched Win. "Maybe you should back off. I've been a little paranoid and have been making you do things that you're not ready for."

"There's not much I can do anyway. I'll just keep my ear to the ground like I did the last time. I'm sure you'll want any information I might get."

"But don't get too involved. Sounds like these guys have no

problem with offing just about anybody. As much as I can't stand the sight of you, I don't want you offed."

"Why don't people just say 'killed' anymore? But thanks for at least that much. Are you ever going to let me back in—to your life, I mean?"

"I trust you for things like this—to a point, of course. But meddling in my life—no. You and your religion have cost me too dearly."

"Well," said Win, his heart in sudden tatters. "I'll see you later. I'll be praying for you."

"I'm not sure why you think that makes me feel better."

Win returned to the tent and got to work.

Mary began cleaning as soon as Gatlin left for the main house. Over her thirty years she'd cleaned many places for many different reasons—most of them far more elegant than this little shack. But there was something hugely different about this place.

This was the jumping-off spot for her second chance.

The God of escaping women had brought her here. There was no doubt of that, and he was throwing a door wide open for her. A door that revealed a fresh new world with abundant opportunity. The door had opened even wider when a guy, who introduced himself as Waco, took her to a Burlington mall. He had handed her five one-hundred-dollar bills and told her to go shopping. She did.

Cleaning and straightening this little shack—turning it into a little home—became the most exciting thing Mary had ever done. And she did it under the watchful eye of her little clown. Soon after Gatlin left, Mary had placed the clown at the center of her little dining room table after giving its head a kiss.

At sunset, as the western sky out over New York washed in a strange, yet breathtaking, orange and fuchsia, she sat in her newly cleaned breakfast nook with a cup of coffee she'd brewed herself. Coffee was beginning to keep her awake at night, but she didn't care. This was an extremely important cup of coffee, and she was going to drink every drop of it.

As she sat, she drank in the room. So much promise lay in

the little place that she kept thinking of it as far more elegant and comfortable than it was. Beside the door was a window with tan curtains the texture of burlap; the sofa bed was worn and needed a good cleaning; there was an end table and lamp, but the end table was scratched and the lamp shade dented. There were pictures on the walls, but they were faded and charmless. The walls themselves were painted a sort of green. The kitchen was little more than a dent in the wall where a sink and counter were placed. The stove was a double-burner butane thing that looked like it might have been used by Custer at the Little Big Horn.

But none of that mattered.

To Mary, the room sparkled.

Martin Sorrell first saw Mary early in the day from the basement window as she stood outside waiting to be summoned inside. *She is lovely,* he thought. Rose lovely—delicate, innocent, sweet. And as she stood for a few moments looking out over the lake, Martin's heart began fluttering.

This frightened him.

It felt so good, so liberating, like a drug—great now but debilitating later. He had to keep from acting on it. After his first glimpse of her, that seemed a realistic goal. But after the second . . .

He saw her again when she appeared outside her front door, shaking the dust from a rug or something, then he heard Gatlin refer to her as her nanny. There was a moment when he reflected on how bizarre things were getting—murderers, kids, nannies.

But then he noticed that blasted heart of his again—fluttering like a whole swarm of butterflies in need of Prozac. It fluttered even more vigorously when he heard she'd be staying for a while. Maybe it was her eyes—sea green, hauntingly full, wide with innocence—eyes that would never hurt or ridicule anyone intentionally. These he saw through a small pair of opera glasses he found near the window.

Later, from his upstairs window, he watched her clean some more—her shadow through the window and door, her loveliness as she shook the dust mop outside or carried armfuls of paper to the trash bin near the main house. These, of course, were the best times. He saw more than shadows. She worked so hard, was so dedicated and industrious.

Making a home.

Martin liked that about her the best of all.

Then, when there was nothing left to watch but the yellow light glowing through the window, he watched that for a while, his heart fluttering all the more.

He had to approach her.

But how could he?

She was outside the inn. There was no way for him to go outside the inn without an escort—usually Waco. And having Waco standing there while he spoke to this lovely rose-petal of a woman would be—well, impossible.

But he just wanted to meet her. Say hello.

Surely Waco could see that.

He'd be gentlemanly, cordial. He'd measure his words like Cary Grant might. Nothing elaborate. He'd be cool.

A few moments later, the rest of the inn all but empty for some reason, he rapped quietly but firmly on Waco's door behind the reception desk. He heard a grunt from inside, then some scurrying sounds as if Waco were suddenly running around the room knocking things over. He opened the door and pushed his face out—red nose and redder ears.

Booze. The odor steamed up from him. His eyes were vacant, his mouth in an "all's-right-with-the-world-and-I'm-doing-everything-I'm-supposed-to" grin. "Huh?" he said.

"I'm going outside to meet the new young lady," said Martin boldly.

"You?" He opened his mouth wide and gave out a single "Hah."

Martin gagged. "I promise not to run away."

"You think I'm drunk, don't you?"

"I'll not tell anyone about it."

"That's all I wanted to hear. Go ahead." The head was pulled back, the door closed; a body hit the floor.

Well, now. That was unexpected. Martin could make more of this visit than originally planned. But what? It was like his credit limit had just been raised, and he wasn't sure what to buy.

Roses.

Of course. He had roses in the basement, and since he was able to roam his grounds freely for once, he could even select something particularly beautiful from his garden.

But how many roses were appropriate. He didn't want to send the wrong message. He wanted to get to know her, but he didn't want to marry her.

One rose seemed too intimate, ten too extravagant, five might be close—three seemed a little sparse. Four. It was a noncommittal number but a good number. Four. Good.

He found two in his basement and the other two in his garden. Two white hybrid teas, a pink floribunda and a blushing old English—they made a nice, simple bunch—lovely.

Back in his basement, he found a plain glass vase. After placing the roses and some water from a hose in his garden in it, he took a deep breath and then his first step. Before his second, he began to recite to himself what he was going to say—that Cary Grant cool thing.

Mary was sipping her second cup of coffee when she heard a gentle rap on her door. Gatlin? Ram Lucha?

Setting her cup aside, she stepped hurriedly to the front door and opened it.

"Huh," said the man who stood there, his eyes on her for only a moment, then they dropped to her shoes.

"Yes?"

"I—uh—" he seemed to be struggling for words. Then he extended his hand. In it was a vase of four lovely roses.

"Thank you," Mary said, taking the vase and pushing an appreciative nose into the blush rose.

"I—uh—just th—thought—" There was another moment of struggle before he grunted something in frustration, turned, and slunk away.

Mary thought for a moment of calling him back. But this was her evening, and though the roses were a welcome punctuation to it, she didn't want to share it with anyone. She closed the door and placed the roses on her kitchen counter. They brightened the room even more.

Martin felt pretty good. Admittedly, he could have been more lucid—he *had* stumbled with his words a little—but at least he'd done it. He wasn't *exactly* cool—but cool wasn't everything. He actually whistled softly as he stepped brusquely down the basement steps.

Win and Ginger began to worry about Chad when he missed dinner. That was not like Chad. He'd been out in his twelve-foot aluminum craft since early that morning. There were times when he'd get tied up with a friend and have lunch away. Normally he'd call, but sometimes he didn't. There was no real trouble he could get into on the lake that he couldn't get into right in front of the cottage. But when dinner came and went, that was something else again. Particularly after what had happened to Todd. Ginger called her friends on the force but got nothing more than they'd keep an eye out.

"It's like that night before the storm when you had to go out and pull his sorry fanny out of the lake," Ginger moaned.

"He'll be fine," Win said confidently. "Why don't we go out and have our coffee on the dock? At least we'll see him sooner that way."

But they didn't have to do that. As they were pouring their cups, Chad burst through the back door. The instant he was visible, Win's heart leaped to his throat. In Chad's hand, swinging freely, was Win's "tosser-thing."

"Where'd you get that?" Win asked.

"I know where Todd was killed," Chad said with a choking note of triumph.

Chapter 12

Where?" Win asked, crossing to his son-to-be with quick steps.

"About ten miles from here."

"You went ten miles in that boat?"

"I went all over the place—you know, Win . . . I don't like calling you Win . . . I want to start calling you 'Dad.'"

It was a surprise—and completely out of the blue—yet Win found himself warmed by that thought. "Okay, son. But go on."

"I was going to say that there is a God. And he's somehow involved in all this."

"I'm sure he is, Chad, but . . . ten miles in that little boat of yours?"

Chad nodded. "I know I shouldn't have. But I kept heading up the coast. I felt like I had to do something for Todd. I didn't do anything for him when he was alive."

"Been there," Win whispered to himself.

"So I kept looking around, I figured that maybe I'd see something, anything that might give me a clue. About an hour ago I was feeling a little like jumping overboard myself when I prayed. I said, 'Jesus, this is a big lake, but you know where I should go in it.'"

"And you saw something?" Win exclaimed.

"Sitting on this rock was a kid a little younger than me, and he was playing with this." Chad now handed the "tosser-thing" to Win.

The paint was chipped in just the right places, so Win recognized it right off.

"Where?"

"A cove up on North Hero."

"Could we drive there?"

"I guess. I know it from the water. The kid said he found the toy on the ground in that cove. It looked like someone had thrown it there."

"Like someone tossed it right out of Todd's pockets." Win was already walking toward the car.

"I guess. He also found this." Chad pulled out Todd's bone-handled knife. "The rest of the stuff is probably there too."

Ginger hobbled over to the phone.

"Who are you calling?" Win asked.

"Breed. He'll want to know this."

"Let's wait on that," Win cautioned.

"Should we?"

"Let's take a look around ourselves."

Ginger's brows rose. She kind of liked the idea.

To everyone's amazement, Chad remembered a motel sign that he'd seen and found the place easily from the road.

The cove wasn't much different from the one they'd battled that guy in. It wasn't much different from a thousand other coves. And yet this one could be the place where a little boy had met his end less than twenty-four hours ago.

"Fan out. Look everywhere, but don't touch anything you find," Win said.

They did. Fortunately, it wasn't a large cove, and they were able to give it a thorough going-over pretty quickly. When they finished, they'd found string, tape, water-soaked baseball cards, small puzzles. "Recognize any of it?" Win asked Chad after all three walked carefully from discovery to discovery.

"This beebee puzzle—he'd do that around me—roll 'em in the little holes."

"Is that it?" Win asked them.

"There was some junk," Ginger said. "Picnic stuff. It's not easy picking things up with the crutches."

"Where?"

Ginger pointed with a crutch toward a notch in the surrounding shale. "There. It's all yucky stuff."

Win crossed to it quickly and found the remains of a camp

fire. It had been covered once, but time had uncovered it. Time had also uncovered a pile of trash—paper and old food. Bugs made the pile even less appetizing.

But something caught Win's eye. Something plastic, brown, and lying off to the side. It could have been with the rest of the stuff, but it seemed unlikely. It was a swizzle stick—the kind used in bars to mix drinks—with nothing written on the upside. He carefully turned it over, making sure he left no fingerprints. "The *St. Albans*" circled a small representation of the boat.

Win knew that plastic didn't rot. It could have been brought here with the garbage or by someone who'd been on the party boat recently. In any case, it seemed unlikely that it was part of Todd's stash.

Win left it there and returned to Ginger.

The sky was now turning into a gray dusk. There seemed to be a storm coming in. Clouds were billowing and black, and as Win watched, a distant bloom of lightning detonated inside, the flash muted by the clouds surrounding it. Before he spoke to Ginger, as if to get closer to the storm, he stepped toward the water and allowed the lapping waves to touch his shoes.

"What are you doing?" Ginger asked.

He didn't answer. He couldn't.

As if suddenly walking into a room—into the bell tower again—he was aware of the presence. Oppressive, pervasive, all around him, all through him. He shuddered. But unlike before, there was more beyond the feeling of it merely being there, being a part of him. It seemed to be communicating. Not in words but in the sense of things. And what it communicated caused Win's anger to boil—an instant boil—it became more than anger. It became rage. But then he went beyond rage to resolve—iron resolve—like none he'd ever known before.

Before he knew he was doing it, Win's eyes were cast skyward—off toward the towering black clouds, off to the war of lightning within them. He cried in an exploding voice, "You'll never win again. Never."

His cry echoed across the lake, but before it died, Ginger and Chad were beside him, their hands clinging to his arms.

"Win, you okay?"

Win was shaking.

"Dad . . . you okay?"

He was. It was gone. Maybe at the moment their hands touched him. Maybe at the sound of their voices. But it was gone. The memory lingered, though, and he took a long moment to recover completely. He stood at the water's edge then was led to a place to sit. Only then did his breathing return to normal.

"What happened?" Ginger asked. "Was it one of those spooky things?"

Chad's mouth dropped. "Were you possessed or something?"

"There's something going on with me sometimes," Win said. "But this one was stranger than any of them. Whatever it was had something to say."

"It spoke to you?"

"Not in words, but I knew what it meant. This is too weird. I don't believe in any of this. I don't. But it's happening."

"What did it—say?"

"Todd was killed here. Maybe drowned in the water right here. And it was laughing. Ridiculing me. Like it had won with Todd—and I'd lost. God had lost."

Chad frowned. "God can't lose."

"The moment I—sensed—it, my blood boiled."

"I guess," said Ginger. "You sounded like a kettle going off."

"We just can't escape the spiritual warfare. It might look like we're fighting drugs or killers or whatever, but it's all spiritual warfare. Satan trying to thwart God and God bringing in his people."

"So what now?"

Win looked about. "We'll call Breed. This is a crime scene."

"I guess I have to give up the knife." Chad frowned.

"When the police arrive."

"What then?" Ginger asked.

"I can't let them win again," he said to Ginger with iron resolve. "It's time to do something rash. There's something happening on this lake, and I think the Lord is telling both of us that it's time to get involved."

Less than an hour later, Mike Grogan and the crime scene unit stretched the yellow police tape about the whole cove and set up flood lights. That done, they went to work combing the area. Grogan questioned Win, Ginger, and Chad, but not all that vigorously. They told him about everything except Win's feeling.

When they finished, Grogan smiled with uncharacteristic warmth. "If I need anything else, I know where I can find you."

It was getting late, but Chad could sleep late in the morning, and Ginger, being on sick leave, didn't have to go to work at all, so when they left, they knew there was more to come.

"Let's go see Bray," Ginger said. "He might be out of ICU."

He was.

It took all of an hour to get to the Medical Center, and although visiting hours were over and the hospital seemed bedded down for the night, they found Bray. The instant they spoke to the night nurse, they heard his weak but persistent voice coming from a room down the hall. "Let 'em in."

After they told him what they'd found, Bray thought for a moment, then said, "He saw something." He spoke with finality, his breathing erratic and loud. "After they found him, they looked for something in his pockets and threw things around helter-skelter."

"Todd was on the east side of North Hero," Ginger told Bray.

"I'd look all along there. The kid saw something. Maybe you'll see it too."

"This is the second time I've violated one of Grogan's crime scenes, and he hasn't been too concerned about it," Win said.

"He must be mellowing in his old age." Bray suddenly looked incredibly tired. "Why'd you guys come?" he asked.

"We're working on this together," Ginger told him. "I'm thinking about becoming a detective."

"You're kidding," he taunted.

"I think I'd be a good detective."

"Do yourself a favor—get married and have kids. Being a detective's hard work. You end up hurting more when you're alone—unless you find a great woman. But then your friends might come along and tear the two of you apart."

"You're just a bitter old man," Win jabbed. "We'll take a look around in the morning. In the meantime, you get better."

"If you think I'm not mad at you anymore, you're wrong."

"You'll get over it," Win said, suddenly feeling very close to the old guy.

On the way out, Ginger asked Win, "Have you sent that invitation to your dad, yet?"

"What made you think of that?"

"I have no idea."

Win and Ginger sat in the front room, the lights low, listening to Ginger's favorite jazz station. She rested her head on his shoulder and cuddled his arm with gentle hands. Every now and then she'd wince when one of her wounds acted up. "They seem to be on random firings," she finally said. After another moment or two she said, "We're working together."

"I know."

"Who'd a thunk it, huh? Me a cop and you a preacher."

"I like it."

"Do you really? You don't think you've been seeing too much of me in the past few days?"

"I never see enough of you."

"Really?" There was a surprised little squeal in her voice. She kissed him on the cheek.

"Do you think I need to know how to protect myself?" Win asked.

"Like with a gun?"

"Well, yeah."

"We're only going to look around," she said.

"I guess. It's just that if there is trouble, I don't want to protect myself by hiding behind my wife."

"So a wife should hide behind her husband?"

"Of course."

She snuggled up to him again. "I think you're getting more settings," she muttered.

"What?"

"More settings. You're more than Einstein and Goofy now. You've got a dash of Rambo thrown in. I'm finding that very sexy."

He kissed her lightly on the top of the head. "Rambo. That's good."

The morning paper reported that Bray had been moved from ICU with an upgraded condition of serious. Mike Grogan also heard it on the radio. Somehow the radio gave it more validity. He could wait no longer. Breed would be recommending Bray for the commander's job for sure. Grogan was a planner, and it was time for the execution.

Grogan called the inn from a gas station phone booth. Ram answered the phone, and Grogan said, "Let's meet."

"Why?"

"Believe me, you want to."

Ram hesitated. Grogan wasn't a "made man" yet—wasn't part of the family—but someday he would be. Plus he was pretty straight. If he said it was important to meet, it probably was.

"Where?"

"Take the boat north fifteen minutes, and you'll see a small island with a chimney on it—the house burned down. I'll meet you there. About ten."

"We need that much privacy?"

"Yes."

"Whatever," Ram said, staring at the receiver for several seconds before hanging up.

Poking his head into the game room, he called to the boss, "I'm gonna take the boat out in a couple of hours."

"What do I care?" Then the boss remembered something. "You might have solved that skimming problem. The latest shipment looks good. I'll send an apology to LaCosta."

"I'm still gonna fix his clock one day. I don't like him."

"I can imagine," the boss said, his tone clearly hearkening back to the vicious rumor that LaCosta had bested him.

Ram only gave him a weary look that gave the boss something to laugh about.

Gatlin had never had a nanny before. She'd seen them on television, but that couldn't be reality. But what *was* reality? This one seemed nice enough. A little talkative, but that was okay as long as she didn't get on her nerves.

And she liked dolls.

This was going to be all right. Now, if something happened to her dad on one of his nights out, at least there'd be someone to take care of her.

No. That's not true. Mary wasn't her mother. She was an employee. Someone who worked for her dad, so if something happened to him, the employee would be fired and Gatlin would still be on her own.

That was something to think about.

The morning was already beginning to heat up. *Thank goodness for the lake,* she thought. *At least there's a cool breeze sometimes. And swimming!* It being midweek, there weren't many of the old guys and their girlfriends around, but there were still a few left. They lay out on the grass on big blankets or sat at the patio tables with coffee or big red drinks—Bloody Marys she heard one called.

Mary wasn't anywhere to be seen. Could she still be asleep?

Cutting through the dewy grass, Gatlin reached the shed and knocked on the door. But she didn't wait to be asked in. Turning the knob, she pushed the door open. Friends and nannies could be popped in on. This nanny was still asleep, curled up in a ball, both hands together sweetly under her cheek.

Gatlin leaned down next to her ear. "Hey!"

Eyes and mouth popped open, the body jackknifed into a rigid sitting position, the cotton nightgown that had been bought for her the day before pushed down, exposing her shoulder. Covers flew everywhere. "Oh. My goodness. You scared me."

"It's nearly nine. Time you were up. You have nannying to do."

"I overslept. But with coffee and all the excitement—"

"Nannying starts early around here," Gatlin said, a certain twinkle in her eye.

"I'll do better," Mary said, easing herself out of bed. Glancing toward the suddenly inadequate kitchen area she said feebly, "I'll make us some breakfast—"

"My dad fixes me breakfast," Gatlin said with a certain pride. "Neat clown." She observed the little guy on the counter. "Cute."

"He seems like a very special guy."

"The clown?"

"Your dad."

"All dads are."

"Mine wasn't—or I can't imagine he was."

"After breakfast I want to go swimming. Can we do that?"

"I don't see why not."

Gatlin saw a vase of roses sitting on the kitchen counter. "I bet I know where those came from."

"From a very nervous guy—tall—kind of a Barney Fife-ish—but cuter."

"Barney who?"

"The old *Andy Griffith Show*—you're probably too young. But this guy seemed nice—bringing me flowers was thoughtful."

"At first I thought he was a little weird."

"But?"

"I don't think so anymore. He's nice. Weird—but nice. We've got a Monopoly game going."

"Where?"

"In the basement. He's mostly there with his roses."

"Who is he?"

"Martin—Sorrell. I think he might own this place, but I'm not sure."

"Well, about swimming," Mary said. "I don't have a bathing suit. I got a few things yesterday but forgot a bathing suit—"

"You didn't bring your clothes?"

"It's a long story—one a nanny shouldn't burden her boss with."

Put that way, Gatlin was hard-pressed to ask anything else, but she did have her wants. "Okay, but you got shorts and a top or something, don't you?"

"Several. There was a sale."

"You can get those wet, then."

"Okay." Mary smiled. For having grown up with her dad on the road—as Mary assumed to be the case—Gatlin was surprisingly well-adjusted. She, Mary—Betty Harmon—should be so well-adjusted. But what about Gatlin's mother? There was probably a story in there somewhere, and maybe she, Mary, could help. "Well, let me get dressed, and I'll see you in a little while."

Ram clocked himself. He'd been growling north on Sorrell's boat for ten minutes. At that point he started scanning the forward horizon for Grogan's chimney island. Spotting it a few minutes later, he eased his boat over to it. Grogan's boat was a larger, more bloated version of Ram's, and it rested in a natural inlet. Grogan was pacing expectantly on the bridge.

"Ram," he called out when the boats were about ten yards apart, "good to see you."

"In a bar with a scotch straight up—that's good. None of that out here."

"You've been making me work overtime."

"The pay must be good then. That where the boat came from? Overtime?"

Grogan laughed. It was all he could think to do. Ram was a powerfully built man, a man without conscience. Even being this close to him was disconcerting.

"I've got a proposition for you."

"The boss handles all my propositions," Ram replied.

"Not this one."

By now Ram was sliding up beside Grogan's cruiser. He manipulated the steering and throttle to stop before he bumped, then he killed the engine. Tossing Grogan a line, he watched as Grogan lashed the two boats together. "Okay, why am I here?"

"I want you to do me a favor."

"What?"

"Kill Bray Sanderson."

"The guy I made a hero? Seems a little ironic. But why would I want to do that?"

"Because I'm the one who needs him dead, and I need an alibi."

"You can hire some jerk off the street."

"This has to be done right. It can't look like a hit."

"How's it supposed to look?"

"Like he just died. Like his heart gave out. Like that."

"And how do we manage that?"

"Inject him with an air bubble. His heart won't be able to take it. No heart would. And he's dead. He's got so many holes in him now no one will notice."

Ram shook his head. "Something like that would have to come from the big boss. We're supposed to lay low."

"I'm a little surprised that's coming from you. In fact, how would you like to be known as the guy who blew this whole deal here?" Grogan countered.

Ram didn't like the sound of that.

"When you hit the kid, you left something lying around," Grogan continued.

"What?"

"Evidence that he'd been on the *St. Albans.*"

"What evidence?"

"Doesn't matter. But that evidence might fall into the wrong hands. It wouldn't take much at all for that cop and her boyfriend—your sparring partners on the beach—to put it all together. If the *St. Albans* is fingered, everything goes. The transportation chain is broken. Then there's the key you lost. I've buried that, but it could be resurrected. If either happens, I don't think I'd want to be you."

Grogan saw Ram's hand flinch as if he were thinking about killing Grogan where he stood. "I've written all this down, and it's in my desk for someone to find if I don't come back," Grogan continued quickly. "But there's no reason to be mad.

I want something, and you want something. I want Bray Sanderson dead, and you want to remain a living part of the family. Why don't we work together and accomplish both? You take care of Bray and all the evidence gets buried—real deep."

Ram took a deep breath and stared out on the lake—maybe the answer to his dilemma was out there somewhere.

"When?"

"You need to scout the hospital first. He's out of ICU on the fourth floor. You can dress as a doctor, get a needle, do those kinds of things. How about within thirty-six hours? Tonight you can check things out. Give me a call when you do. Tomorrow you can do the deed. How's that sound?"

"Like a death knell. But I've heard 'em before." Ram returned to his own boat and released the tie. "Don't ever turn your back, Grogan."

"This is strictly business. If Bray comes back, he'll get the job the family wants me to have. I'll be dispatched if I don't get it. It's life and death for both of us."

"It's more death for you." Ram's eyes remained leveled on Grogan, much like a snake stalking its prey, as he fired up the boat and pulled it away from the island.

Grogan watched him roar away. Ram would be a man to watch. But first things first—he had to survive now in order to watch him later.

After filling his sixteen-foot Bayliner with fuel, Win picked up Ginger and Chad. Giving the throttle a punch, the craft's nose lifted, and they began their coastal search.

Ginger hated boats—not the boats themselves, but that they went on water and could sink. Chad, on the other hand, loved boats and loved Win's boat in particular. While Win and Ginger took the two seats, Chad stood behind Win, holding on to his chair.

"Where do you think we ought to start looking?" Ginger asked.

"North of where Todd was killed," Win said. "We know the drugs are coming down from Canada, so they have to be coming down from the north."

Next to Sorrell's boathouse was a small, sandy beach that provided Gatlin with a launching pad. Mary was surprised at the fun Gatlin had—she was a true free spirit when it came to the lake. Skipping stones, playing catch with a half-inflated beach ball Mary had spotted in the gardening shed, racing, hopping, swimming, running, splashing—Gatlin was a wild competitor. All her activities were punctuated by uninhibited laughter and screams.

Now draped across the underinflated beach ball, Gatlin kicked madly and made pretty good time moving toward the boathouse.

"Don't go out too far," Mary called to her. "It's deep." She actually only assumed it was, but she figured better safe than sorry.

Balancing precariously, Gatlin waved.

Although Mary sat facing the water, she could see the back of the inn out of the corner of her eye. The French doors opened, and she saw a man standing there. He stood in the shadows, but she was certain he was the one who'd brought her the flowers. After a moment, he returned indoors and sat at a restaurant-type table just inside.

Wanting to thank him for the flowers, Mary got to her feet, smoothed the long pullover T-shirt she wore, and walked over to him. Making sure she could adequately see Gatlin, she sat down in the chair opposite him.

"Hi," she greeted.

He'd been deep in thought and was actually surprised to see her sitting there. He gasped but then regathered his thoughts. "Uh—hi," he said, straightening in his chair and clearing his throat.

"Thank you for the roses last night," she said.

"I—" he cleared his throat. "I—well, I thought you'd—" He made some kind of grunting noise as if clearing his throat again but had nothing to clear.

She interrupted by extending a hand. "I'm Mary Seymour, and I don't bite. Say anything. It's okay. Say it wrong, and I'll let you say it again."

Martin Sorrell had never been confronted so sweetly before, nor had any words been more welcome. He took her warm hand and gave it a pump. "Thank you," he managed.

"What's your name?" she asked.

"Martin Sorrell," he said, clearing his throat again, his nervousness returning.

"Anybody ever call you Marty before? There was a movie out a long time ago. I saw it on TV once. I liked the name. Could I call you Marty? That's probably a little forward. Gatlin says you own this place. It's probably a little forward for someone who owns this place."

Martin only smiled. "Marty's okay." Actually, he couldn't imagine it. But she was so cute.

"Those flowers were very sweet. No one's given me flowers in years. I mean *years*. I was a nanny in a wealthy person's house for a couple of years, and although there were flowers all over the place, none of them were ever mine."

"I grow them downstairs—and in my garden."

"Your garden?"

"Out back, by the boathouse."

"So this *is* your place?"

Martin noticed the boss enter the dining area. He took a cup of coffee from the pot near the door then sat facing them, his eyes hawk narrow. Martin could not mistake his reason for being there. This woman wasn't one of them—Martin could easily see that. She was too sweet to be one of these thugs. Martin was to keep his mouth shut.

"I've—well—sort of subleased—yeah, subleased—uh, my inn to some—well, some other people."

"Subleased?"

"Right—subleased. Subleased—yes."

Mary was about to ask another question when she heard Gatlin calling to someone over the growl of an approaching boat. Turning, she saw Gatlin's dad powering up in Sorrell's seventeen-footer.

"Having a good time?" he called to his daughter.

Gatlin bobbed underwater, and when she surfaced she smiled broadly and whipped the water from her hair. "Great, Dad!" she cried, diving toward the boat and swimming with remarkably firm strokes. Ram, seeing her heading his way, eased the boat over to her.

Noting that all was well, Mary said, "She's quite a gal."

"I didn't like her at first. I like her now."

"How could you not like her?"

"A misunderstanding."

"She says you have a Monopoly game going."

"We've hit one of those boring parts. Maybe you could— uh—join us sometime."

"Sure." Mary smiled. "Well . . . I'd better go out and make sure all is okay with them."

"Of course," said Martin Sorrell. He watched her walk toward the boathouse. She was so lovely. And the way she babbled on was so endearing. *Oh, no.* His heart was fluttering again. That miserable heart. Why didn't it behave?

Win's Bayliner grumbled up the coast. The weather was beautiful—warm and the air still. The humidity even seemed a little lighter. The storm that had threatened last night had never materialized. Because it was so calm, Ginger began to relax a little, and by the time they'd gotten to the cove where Todd had met his end, she was sitting calmly.

The moment they rounded a finger of land that jutted out into the lake just beyond Todd's cove, they moved in closer to shore. Now it was as if all three of them were one person. Their eyes were glued to the shore, watching every tree, every rock, every house. And there were a lot of houses in this area. Backed up by a thick fir forest, the cottages seemed stacked side by side. Being the middle of the week, many were vacant, but there were a few with boats bobbing at their docks. An older gentleman was repairing his dock as they passed. Seizing the opportunity, Win pulled the boat over. "Hi," he called out.

"Hi, yourself," the guy answered.

"You see anything out of the ordinary two nights ago? Probably late?"

"No," the guy called back. "Nothing like that. You working on the investigation into that kid's death?"

"Yes," Ginger replied, feeling her reply would sound a little more official than Win's.

"Terrible thing. But I didn't see anything out of the ordinary at all. Nothing."

They went on. They saw another couple of guys along the way who replied the same way to the question. They also added that on the lake most people retired early and got up early. "Things are quiet out here. If there's someone making noise we usually just shoot 'em. The kid wasn't shot, was he? I've threatened a few of 'em in my life."

"No, he drowned."

"Ten years old. Where were his parents?"

"Home, asleep."

"Then that's where he should have been."

Win only nodded.

The complexion of the shore changed. The deep fir forest ended, and scattered oak and maples began. The shoreline became more irregular, bubbling with brush then cleared and manicured. The cottages were fewer, homes more abundant. Now and then there was a deserted one, a weathered-looking thing probably locked in some probate court somewhere.

Although interesting, there was nothing unusual that caught their eye.

"It might be easier to find needles in haystacks," Win finally said. "At least you know you're looking for a needle."

"There's an old boathouse over there," Ginger pointed. "The house must have been blown down. The door's open. That's weird . . . you'd think it would be closed or battened down."

"Might as well take a look."

"You know, guys," Chad said, "I've been really good about not asking when we're going home. But when are we going home?"

"Right after this," Win said. "So far, our first outing as detectives has been a bust."

"Go on inside, it'll get us out of the sun for a little while anyway," Ginger said.

Win eased his Bayliner into the shadows. Ginger was right.

He didn't realize how intense the sun was until he was in the shade.

"Pretty exciting place," Chad said, leaping onto the walkway.

"Nothing much here, my sweet," Win said, preparing to leave.

"Wait. There's something over there." Ginger pointed to something shiny that lay off in the corner. "Get that, Chad."

Chad looked around for a moment, found what his mother was referring to, and returned with it. "A lighter," he said.

"I'll be," Ginger said, marveling at it.

"You'll be what?"

"Well now. I'm flabbergasted. I helped a woman a couple of nights ago. She was running from a violent husband, and I bought her some toiletries. And this lighter. I remember the rose." She handed it to Win. "She must have spent the night here. I wonder how she's doing."

"I'll tell you how she's probably doing. While you, who helped her out, are stuck with some no-money preacher, she's probably found herself a rich millionaire with whom to share eternity. How's that for irony?"

"Yeah, right," Chad said. "Hey, what's that?"

The two of them turned to see the *St. Albans* emerging from a large inlet. The last time Win and Ginger had seen it, the boat was draped with lights and charged with terrified revelers. Now it appeared lifeless, and it churned north, probably returning to its mooring at the city of St. Albans.

"Well," Win said, "time to head home. If we've seen anything that has to do with Todd's murder, we obviously didn't recognize it."

Chapter 13

Gatlin and her father spent most of the day together. There wasn't much for Mary to do, but that was okay. No one believed more than she did that a daughter should have a good relationship with her father.

Mary spent her day reading. There was a small library in the game room, and she found an old copy of *Dr. Jekyll and Mr. Hyde*. She'd never read it, but the idea fascinated her—to be in a dangerous situation that appeared harmless. Finding a place outside in the building's shade, she read a little of it, then put it down. She found a *People* magazine. Even though it was several months old, it was still more enjoyable than the book.

Although she sat by herself, a minute later a woman of about thirty-five with a gray streak sweeping through shoulder-length auburn hair, sat down beside her. She, too, was reading a magazine, but Mary sensed there was something else on her mind.

"You're taking care of Ram's kid," the woman stated.

"Gatlin. Yes."

"She's got to be a mixed-up kid."

"Why's that?"

"All that's happened to her."

"Like what?"

"No one told you?"

"About what?" Mary was uncomfortable now.

"About her mamma."

"What about her mamma?"

"Of course, she wouldn't tell you; she was too young. She was, what? Two. I bet there's some memories but little else."

"What happened to her mamma? She run away with someone or something?"

The woman's eyebrows rose, and her expression darkened.

Mary turned to see what the woman saw. A skinny man stood there. He had hollow eyes that were gray as gravestones. He stared down at the woman for a moment, then turned and walked away.

As the woman watched him leave, her expression remained concerned, maybe frightened. But she had a story to finish, and no one could scare her into total silence. She pressed a hand on Mary's forearm and whispered, "He killed her."

Then she got up and scurried away.

Brows raised incredulously, Mary instantly thought the woman had a screw loose. If it was common knowledge that Ram Lucha had killed his wife, why wasn't he in jail? Maybe he had killed her accidentally—or had gotten in an argument with her, and she'd run off and gotten hit by a truck. Most likely the woman just had a screw loose.

Ram left the inn soon after dinner, which was Mary's cue to resume her nannying assignment. She found Gatlin in her room on her bed reading. "Hi. Thought I'd just check in and see how you're doing."

"He's leaving again. I get worried sometimes when he leaves."

"Why?"

Gatlin couldn't say anything. She couldn't tell Mary that she worried because her father might not come back, and she would be sent off to some horrible life somewhere. "I just worry," she said.

Mary glanced around at the posters on the walls: heavy metal bands—Metallica, The Cure, others. They covered a beautiful country decor. "When I was a nanny for that rich family, the ten-year-old gave up on these posters. The groups weren't cool anymore. Heavy metal was out. Replaced them with Precious Moments."

"Dad would croak. Hey, wanna play Monopoly?"

A few minutes later, excited for reasons she didn't completely understand, Gatlin threw the basement door open and called down, "Clear the board, Martin, we're starting over."

Martin looked up from his roses and saw Mary stepping down behind Gatlin. For a moment Martin remembered when his father told him he'd be going to Vermont. It had sounded like music. Now he sat near his precious roses ready to meet the woman who made his heart flutter. She was truly a symphony to him.

"Good," Martin said, screwing up his courage. "It's always better with more people."

"I hope we're not interrupting anything," Mary said.

"Interrupting? You? Not possible." He was surprised at how smooth he sounded.

Gatlin was already at the board. With quick fingers she assembled a new game, counted all the money out, reassembled all the property cards, and gathered up all the houses and hotels. "What's everybody want? I like the little car."

"High die goes first," Mary said.

"You've played this before," Martin noted.

"I'm a champion. You people are in trouble. Since I walked through that door upstairs, I was hoping someone would ask me to play Monopoly. I am a Monopoly-tiger."

Gatlin won the toss. And the game began.

Fletcher Allen Medical Center was a seven-story brown brick fortress on the University of Vermont campus; its parking structure was right in front. Now sparsely lit, for Ram it possessed the necessary sense of seclusion, and he slid from behind the wheel, slammed the door, and stood by the car for a long moment. There were a couple of things about this gig he didn't like. Doing business in large, enclosed areas, particularly with the victim near the center, made him uncomfortable. Exits could be quickly closed, escape routes severed, the noose tightened too easily. He also preferred to use a heavier hand—sneak in, blast away, and get out in the confusion. It was easier. Witnesses, if there were any, tended to give conflicting stories, and they could always be convinced not to testify. But he was willing to live with the setup. The pay was right—real right—and he'd continue breathing. Grogan might not. But he would.

What followed in the next fifteen minutes was a curious odyssey. When he looked back on it as he stood beside Bray Sanderson's bed, he felt like he'd moved about the hospital innards with the indifference of a pinball.

He found a costume—green scrubs—on a back dock where they were being delivered. He not only found one to wear now but took another to wear the next night. After changing into the scrubs in a bathroom, he began a search for an ID, name tag, and one of those stethoscope things. The IDs had the employee pictures, but that shouldn't matter. No one looked at them, anyway.

That search ended when he rounded a corner and slammed into a chubby doctor in a white smock. When the guy regained focus, he was not only minus name tag, ID, and stethoscope, but his white smock had disappeared too.

Getting into Bray Sanderson's room was easier than he had hoped. After he stepped from the elevator on the fourth floor, the nurse hardly looked up as he grabbed a clipboard and read it. "How's it going?" he asked casually.

"How does it ever go?" Now she looked up. "You're new."

"I'm here for a couple of days—a replacement." He turned toward the patients. "I'll be in the back," he said and stepped toward the rooms. Sanderson's was the second one he entered. After standing for a moment over the sleeping form, he looked in on another couple of patients, thanked the nurse, said he would probably see her tomorrow, and said good-bye.

Stopping at a pay phone, he called Grogan.

"I'll do it tomorrow night," he said when Grogan answered. "Just remember, this won't come free."

"You going to tell Bray we were a zero today?" Ginger asked, sipping an iced herbal tea.

"Have to. I went by and saw the Breckenridges this afternoon. She makes great apple juice—crushes and presses her own. As good as that place in Stowe."

"Well," Ginger began, "I hope I never go through what they did. But all that's looking back. This time last night we were ready to set the world on fire."

"When we found where Todd died, I thought we were on to something. Went nowhere."

Ginger took another sip. "I wonder if Grogan's found anything."

"I doubt it—we're talking Grogan here."

"Do you think we really could chase bad guys?" Ginger asked cautiously. "As a profession together?"

"I love you, Ginger. You know that. I could work with you eight days a week. But that's not my calling."

Ginger sighed. "It must be nice to have a calling. I mean something you know God wants you to do. What's that like?"

"I thought you had one."

"I think I was just confused. I thought being scared to death while climbing out of a car in a tree before it fell on me was a calling."

"Today we took a long shot and found nothing. Sometimes detectives take months to find what they need, going house to house through a whole city. You ready for that?"

"I don't know. I guess I just want to make a difference. All my life I've been doing things because they were the thing to do, because I had no other choice, or because I was too dumb to realize I did. Now I want to do something because I *want* to do it, and I'm having second thoughts. You ever have second thoughts? Sure, you do. Sometimes those are the only thoughts you do have."

Win laughed.

"I'm serious. You think about something, and when it doesn't go the way you want, you think about it again. But this isn't about you. It's about me. I want to be a good wife to you, a good mother to Chad—and a good something for me. But I'm not sure what that something is. Anyway, if the Lord wants me to be a detective, he's going to have to do more than toss me into a tree."

Win glanced at the crutches leaning against the wall. "More than that? Are you sure you realize what you're asking for?"

"Positive."

"Well, if I'm going to be up to that rescue effort, I'd better start working out more often."

She poked him in the side with a hard fist.

The game had started innocently enough. Martin moved his piece silently; he was having a hard time looking up. Mary, on the other hand, was talking most of the time. She had a voice that sounded a little like chimes so Gatlin didn't mind. Martin didn't seem to mind either.

"You know, I've always had a feeling that no other game so imitates life as Monopoly. Don't you think so?" She didn't wait for anyone to nod. "It does. Everyone's competing, and that's how it is in real life. Of course, you compete in volleyball, and volleyball's not like real life at all. Except when someone spikes it right in your teeth. That happens in real life a lot. But Monopoly has good things happen to you and bad, too, with those Chance cards. Life's like that sometimes. You roll the dice and pick a card, and suddenly you're in jail, or getting out of jail free, or in the hospital not able to pay your bill or getting a bunch of money from somewhere just because you're walking and breathing. Life's like that. And you buy and sell—oh, my turn again." She'd roll and then move, buy something, then start talking again. "And you're moving along all alone. That's like life too."

"Are you alone?" Martin finally asked.

The question just came out of the blue. Gatlin hadn't expected it. She was half listening to Mary and counting her money. She'd bought Illinois and Indiana and had her heart set on Kentucky, all of them red, and she'd already collected rent on them. Eighteen or twenty bucks wasn't going to win the game though. So she wasn't expecting Martin to ask anything, particularly the way he was having trouble looking at Mary. But he must have gotten the courage, for out came the question. Another surprise was the answer. Where Mary had been babbling on about nothing in particular, certainly nothing that interested Gatlin—Gatlin had a game to win—Mary stopped and considered the question, or at least thought about what it meant before answering.

"Sometimes," Mary began, studying Martin a little, "we're taking the world on all by ourselves. Maybe more than sometimes."

Gatlin saw Martin straighten. His shyness was still there, but he seemed bolder somehow. "We're all alone. In the final analysis, we're all we have."

Mary looked like she wanted to say more but hesitated. It

looked to Gatlin like she was looking for just the right words. "I've never liked it," she finally said, her eyes looking at Martin rather strangely, Gatlin thought.

"Why would you? No one . . . uh . . . likes being alone. I don't. But we are, aren't we?"

"It's safest," she said.

"Sometimes. In some respects."

"We tend not to hurt ourselves."

"Depends on . . . uh . . . who we are, I guess. Some people . . . all they do is hurt themselves," Martin said. "Sometimes we dig holes for ourselves that we know we can't crawl out of. Or sometimes we stay places when we should leave," he said carefully.

Gatlin's ears burned. Martin had voiced what she'd been afraid to think. She liked Mary. But Mary didn't really belong here. Her dad had brought her, but her dad did bad things sometimes. If she really liked Mary, why would she want her here in this situation? And yet to say something would betray her father, and deep down inside, somewhere at the very core of her heart, Gatlin knew the price for doing that.

"Leave?" Mary sounded shocked. "Who would want to leave here? Why, it's beautiful here!"

Gatlin saw Martin draw back within himself. He'd said too much. Gatlin knew that. "I wasn't talking about here, really. Just in general," he said quickly.

"Okay, you guys," Gatlin interjected, hoping to get the game moving again. "It's Martin's turn and then me, so no more talking for a while."

Mary took her literally. She was quiet for the first time since she had sat down. But that didn't mean there wasn't communication going on.

But now it was Martin who was doing it all.

By means of the game.

Gatlin became aware of it when Mary landed on purple St. Charles Place on her next turn. She, of course, bought it. But then Martin landed a little while later on purple Virginia Ave., and he didn't buy it. In fact, he'd looked right at her when he declined. Gatlin, of course, couldn't allow someone to get two of the same properties this early in the game, so she outbid

Mary for it and ended up nearly broke. After Martin bought a couple of the utilities, he did the same thing with the yellows. Mary landed on Ventnor Ave. and bought it. Martin then landed on Marvin Gardens and didn't. This time Gatlin didn't have enough money to bid at all, and Mary got the property. Gatlin just couldn't understand.

"You guys are working together, aren't you? That's no fair."

"No," Martin protested—too fervently, Gatlin thought. He'd been caught, and he and she both knew it. "No. I just didn't want it. I like the railroads and the utilities and save my money for the expensive side of the board: Boardwalk, Park Place, and the greens."

But that didn't hold true either.

He landed on one of the greens and didn't buy it either.

"You're helping her win," Gatlin said.

He caved. Martin might be able to keep a good lie going but only for a while. "You're right. Forgive me. It's just that—" suddenly Gatlin saw him look into Mary's eyes, like he'd fallen into a well or something, "she's so beautiful."

"This isn't a game about—"

But Gatlin stopped as she saw Mary blush. It was a deep blush too. It seemed to cover her whole face, then her eyes dipped away as if she was suddenly not able to look at Martin. Gatlin was about to inquire as to her health, when Martin spoke again. "I'm sorry. I didn't mean to be so forward. I'm really not trying to come on to you or anything. Really. It's just a fact, I'm afraid."

"A fact?" That almost made Mary blush more.

"Something's going on here," Gatlin said.

"No. Nothing, really," Martin said. He looked at Mary quickly. "Please, I've embarrassed you, and that's the last thing I ever wanted to do. You're so sweet to come down here and spend time with me. Both of you. These roses are all I have sometimes, and it's so sweet of you."

"You didn't embarrass me," Mary said. "Come on, let's play the game. And no helping anyone win. Let's play this game like life is—we go after each other's throats."

"Right!" Gatlin exclaimed. "Throats."

"Now wait a minute," Martin said, his hand suddenly across

the table on Mary's. Now that was something to see. The instant his hand touched hers, Gatlin was aware that everything about Martin changed. If there was something he'd wanted to say, it was gone. Suddenly he was transfixed on the hand that was resting on hers. He looked like he wanted to leave it there, but he also looked like he'd touched a hot stove. The hot stove won. He pulled it away.

"What were you going to say?" Mary asked.

"Nothing—well, yes, there was something." His eyes came up, and Gatlin saw him take a deep breath. Gatlin could see he was about to become completely truthful. Adults had a hard time becoming truthful, and completely truthful was always really hard for them. Martin was working on the hardest of the two. "I don't want to be at your throats."

"Then why play Monopoly?" Gatlin fired. "That's the game. Run everybody out of business. It's a great game. Like Mary says: it's life. Take your turn."

"But it's not *my* life."

"What is your life, Marty?"

"Marty? He's Martin. He even looks like a Martin," Gatlin fired at her.

"I don't know. Maybe I'll figure it out someday. But I know it's not trying to tear out your throat. Caressing your throat maybe—oh, my word. Did I say that? I'm so sorry. What you must think of me. Please forgive me "

"It was sweet. There's—"

To everyone's surprise the door up the long wooden staircase opened, and Gatlin's father stood there. "Gat, you down here?"

"I'm playing Monopoly with Mary and Mr. Sorrell."

"Sorrell?"

"I'm right here," Martin called back up.

"It's time for bed," Ram said, his voice disapproving.

"Can she play just a little bit longer, Ram?" Mary asked.

They heard his footsteps as he descended the stairs. When he got far enough down, he poked his head into view. He didn't look happy. Mary actually thought she saw some jealousy. She thought it strange, but then reconsidered. Good-looking men were often jealous.

"It's time for bed. It's nearly eleven," he said.

"Have we been playing that long?" Martin quipped, hoping to keep things as light as possible.

"Upstairs," Ram stated flatly.

Reluctantly, Gatlin stood and went to the bottom of the stairs. Then she turned. "Thanks for the game."

"Mary," Ram said with equal disapproval, as if he had the right to send her to bed as well, "you need to come up too. Remember what I told you."

That she did. She was to speak with no one. That must include Martin Sorrell. "I'll be right up."

"Now," Ram said as if ordering a child.

Mary didn't like it, but there was no mistaking the menace in the voice. Ram was used to getting what he wanted, and right now he wanted her upstairs.

"Okay," she submitted. "Thank you for the game, Martin. You've been a perfect gentleman."

Martin noticed she didn't call him Marty. She probably didn't want to appear too familiar.

"I hope we can continue it sometime," Martin said.

"Unlikely," Ram said, this time his eyes were on Martin, and they were menacing—like a prowler or a beast of prey. Ram waited for Gatlin and Mary to climb past him, then he turned and went up himself.

Martin watched the empty staircase for several minutes before he finally moved. His heart was both devastated and joyful. Devastated that she had to leave, maybe never to return. Joyful that he had made a connection with her. Their eyes had met and spoken.

His heart fluttered again. But this time it wasn't the hopeless fluttering of when he first saw her. Now it fluttered with promise—so much promise.

Betty Harmon, now Mary Seymour, had a real stubborn streak. She'd never really labeled it as such until now, but looking back, she could see it at work. Mary Seymour, a woman who'd had pretty much everything she wanted as she worked among the rich in Newport Beach, would probably have just chalked up Ram's rough authoritarianism to a foible of the rich and accepted it.

But Betty Harmon, used to knocking around the not so rich and working for, or talking people out of, everything she needed, viewed Ram's behavior differently.

Ram was challenging her right to live her own life.

She'd scrambled all the way across the country to secure that right.

And no man, no matter how good looking, was going to snatch it away from her.

Of course, she needed to be discreet.

After about a half hour in her shack, she eased out the side door through the connecting toolshed. She took a wide circle along the trees and shrubs—out of sight of the lookout—to the side of the main building. She moved stealthily along the perimeter to the main house, saw that the place was deserted, and crossed by the game room to the basement door.

Since Gatlin's and Mary's departure, Martin had not been idle.

He was not a drinking man.

There was a time fifteen years ago in France when he'd gotten a bottle of fine Beaujolais. He'd overindulged—four generous glasses—and after he had struggled back to his bed, the world had swirled about him like an unbalanced kaleidoscope. He remembered it now because that night, even as the alcohol was marauding his senses, he had felt so free—frighteningly so.

Now, surrounded by the prison of his roses and the basement they commanded, he needed to feel free again, free of the profound ache, free of the knowledge that a woman hidden away in his gardener's shack would never love him, free from knowing that he was aiding men to commit unspeakable horrors simply out of fear. Alcohol was definitely the magic carpet out of this place.

When the evil men had arrived, they'd decimated his wine cellar in just a couple of days. Before they'd finished it off, however, he'd managed to spirit away three bottles of his finest. He'd hidden them in his basement, behind the rose trellis against the stone wall.

He grabbed one of them.

A Californian cabernet, Groth Vineyards, six years old, velvety smooth. He'd had a glass about a year before at a private party at the inn, and it was all he could do not to have another. Ahh—that party. He'd been in a black tie, gracious in the beginning, bubbly toward the end. Would there ever be private parties at the inn again? If there were, would he be alive to enjoy them?

He glanced at his watch. Nearly midnight. Excellent. He had all night.

But there were still preparations to be made. Drinking a whole bottle of wine, or as much as he could, couldn't be done while standing at his workbench. The floor was too hard. He'd have to be sitting. Over the weeks he'd made his cot a comfortable place—a down sleeping bag as a mattress, several soft pillows for support, one with a white satin pillowcase. Now he positioned it all into a tight, horseshoe-shaped sitting area. He could drink until he toppled and, as long as he kept from toppling forward, he'd be okay.

What about a corkscrew? He'd forgotten to grab one when he'd pilfered the bottles—his own bottles—in his own inn. And now he couldn't just go up and get one. Corkscrews meant wine bottles—full wine bottles—and nothing would get their attention more than a full wine bottle.

Caught in mid-frustration, he heard the squeal of the basement door. Grabbing the bottle, he hid it behind himself before turning to see who it was.

"Hi," Mary greeted softly from the top of the stairs. She wore black shorts and a black top—perfect for sneaking around at night on those wonderful willowy legs.

Martin's grip relaxed on the bottle. He let it rest on the workbench, shielding it with his body. "Hello," he returned stiffly.

"Couldn't sleep. Too hot. The house I nannied in overlooked the Pacific Ocean. Even on the hottest days there was always a cool breeze at night."

"It can get hot here."

"I wanted to thank you again for the game. And the roses. Thank you. Really."

"I thought Mr. Lucha didn't want you down here."

"I thought he was a little rude. We were having a nice time, and he ruined it. So I thought we could have that nice time again. Your roses are so beautiful." She pushed her nose into a delicately cupped pink bloom and breathed in, savoring its fragrance. "Wonderful," she sighed.

"It's—well—sort of named after you."

"Me? Really?"

"It's called the Mary Rose. It's English—blooms all year."

"It's gorgeous. And what's this one?" She pointed to another tightly cupped pink.

"Heritage. I keep those down here because I love them so much."

"You don't love them all?"

"Some I'm working with. These dark ones over here." He pointed to a wall of roses several feet wide, their trunks sprouting from several small wooden casks. "They're all from the Prince Charles. It began as a deep purple rose, and I'm slowly weaning it of color. There's still some red in it—"

"Why would you not want color?"

"I want a black rose."

"Black? But the pink ones are so beautiful. My nanny home had wonderful roses all over it."

"Many rosarians want to create the black rose. I'd be the first."

"You'd really *be* someone, then. Of course, you're someone now. At least *I* think so."

"Someone—yes. You do?"

She let her eyes come to rest on his. "There was a time when I wanted that too. Now I'm content just to be here. Just me."

"This place is not what you think," he said, eyes darting around as if to see if the boss might be listening.

"I don't care. It doesn't matter. I'm safe here and have a job, and I'm helping Gatlin." Then she became aware that he was consciously hiding something behind him. "What's back there?"

He blushed uneasily. "Wine." He stepped aside.

"Groth. From Napa, California," she read on the label. "I spent a month or so in Napa. My boss was thinking about buying a vineyard there. He took his whole family up there just to see how it would go. It didn't go all that well. I never heard of Groth, but Napa's beautiful. Met what turned out to be my roommates there. Then I went back with them in the fall. Brrrr, cold, wet—and so green. I'd just stand out in the rain. I felt so clean. I wasn't, but I felt clean. That matters, doesn't it, that you feel clean?"

"I don't know—I guess."

"Well, let's open it—" she said excitedly, but then drew back. "I'm sorry. I assumed you'd want—"

"No, no. Join me, please. But I can't get it open. No corkscrew."

"Isn't that the way," she said, collapsing against the workbench. "Good things always seem both close and unreachable." She straightened. "And I can't just run upstairs and get one. I'm sort of sneaking around."

"Then what should we do?"

Up to the challenge, Mary looked around the basement. Spotting a small toolbox beneath the stairs, she said, "There. We'll drive the cork into the bottle. My old roommates and I would do that sometimes. We never did have a corkscrew. We bought screw tops usually. But sometimes we splurged."

"After nannying with all that wealth, you'd think you'd learn to appreciate fine wine," Martin said.

Mary thought quickly. "There was no drinking. But my roommates liked wine now and then. We just never thought ahead and got a corkscrew."

"This is good wine," Martin protested. "But what the heck."

Finding a thick-necked Phillips screwdriver in the box, Mary removed the foil wrapper from the top of the bottle, placed its pointed head in the center of the cork, then tapped it lightly until the cork gave way and floated on the crest of the ruby liquid. "There," she said, holding the bottle up. "Got glasses?"

"A couple of mugs," he offered, pointing to four coffee-stained mugs, each with the same painting of the inn on the side. "I used to sell these."

"A mug of wine—how great is that! Got something to clean them with?"

Getting into the spirit of the occasion, Martin pulled out his shirttail and gave two mugs a swift brush on the inside with it. "All set."

The first mug of wine went down quickly. The second was half gone before either spoke.

"I think I could get used to this," Mary said, the wine sending warm tendrils through her. "My roommates and I used to grab a night now and then and just get bombed. We'd laugh like there was no tomorrow." She became grave. "There wasn't," she said, to herself.

"What did you do when you lived with your roommates?" Martin asked.

"Waitressed a little," she said, tossing her answer aside. She finished the second mug. Finally, two weeks after eluding her would-be executioner, the tension, as tight as a headband, began to loosen. It felt magnificently welcome.

"What brought you here?" Martin asked.

"Some nice people, and a few jerks," she said, pouring herself another mug. This time, though, the bottle ran out before the mug did. "I wanted to see the country," Mary said, the words tumbling out casually as if the truth.

"Vermont's the country to see," Martin said, his words beginning to slow, still only on his second mug. "I liked it, loved it, actually, the first time I saw it. A little cool in the winter—my nostrils freeze. Ever have frozen nostrils?"

"When I drink a slushy margarita real fast." She laughed, the laughter coming easier. But realizing that someone might hear, she popped an uncertain hand over her mouth and quieted. But then she laughed again behind it. "We're out of wine." After a deep breath, she placed a hand on his forearm. "I really do need this. Just tonight. And I can tell you're a *real* gentleman." Her movements were comically exaggerated; when she said "real," she pushed her face toward his with an expression crammed with sincerity. Nose brushed nose.

"Gentleman? No—just scared," he said, getting to his feet and moving unsteadily to the workbench and grabbing another bottle from the wastebasket. "My wine cellar's small but effective." He tapped the cork into the second bottle and refilled her mug.

She took a small sip this time. "So you like it here," she ventured, settling into a conversation.

"My father exiled me. He's rich, very rich—beyond rich—and he didn't want a son; he wanted a clone. I guess I wasn't clone enough or smart enough. But I love this place—or used to." He was about to tell her that this place he loved had been stolen from him by a band of killers. But his eyes darted toward the stairs as if he expected a dark intruder to float down any moment, guns blazing. "Not so much anymore," he added, the wine accentuating his despair.

"I think you're smart and sweet," she said, taking another sip. Her head was beginning to float somewhere above her shoulders. "So you and your father don't get along?"

"I was like one of those talk show victims. Verbally abused. Never measured up. I failed at everything. He finally gave up on me, gave me a bunch of money, then tied me to a bunch of accountants who won't let me spend any of it." Actually that wasn't true, but it was the story he told. It had worked with his houseguests and had probably protected him from blackmail or extortion—so far, anyway.

"I didn't have a father," she said. "And you know something else?"

"What?"

"I'm a liar." She sighed. "I lie to everybody. I've even lied to you."

"I know."

"You know? How would you know?"

"Because you said the guy you nannied for wanted to buy a wine vineyard but didn't allow drinking."

"What if they'd been table grapes?"

"Table grapes come from Fresno—that area. Napa, Sonoma, and Mendocino counties are wine grapes. Good ones too. I had to investigate it for my dad once. This wine is really good, isn't it? Goes down real smooooooth."

"Smooooooth." She smacked her lips. "Good. Then I can tell you the truth. I want to tell you the truth. You're so sweet. You were so sweet during the Monopoly game. See, I'm not even drunk. I can say Monp—Monolipy—there."

"But I'm happy with the lie," he said.

"Happy? With a lie?"

"It's a good lie. It doesn't threaten me. It makes sense. What if the truth makes me have to do something, maybe lose you?"

"Oh," Mary said gravely, her eyes drinking in his, her lips as near to his as her heart. "I don't ever want to lose you. Never. But I want us to like each other, the real each other, and the truth lets you know who this—" she poked a finger in her own chest, "—who each other is. Gosh, I like this wine."

He topped off their mugs again, and they both took long drinks. The world was so wonderfully mellow.

"I didn't have a father," Mary said, her eyes downcast. She took another drink, a long, full one. She was beginning to breathe heavily, her eyelids fell to half-mast, and it was all she could do to keep them open. Just talking about these things sapped her energy "Or a mother," she said. "Well, that's not true. I guess everybody's got a mother. You have to come from somewhere. After mine had me, she wrapped me in an old, baby blue blanket and dropped me in the trash." Another drink.

"Trash? Not you."

"Oh, you're so sweet. It was in the back of a liquor store." She smacked her lips and toasted with the mug. "Coming back to my roots tonight, huh?"

"At least you're vintage."

"I read the police reports when I was a teen. They said I was near death when they found me. Which isn't surprising because the rest of my life has been a near-death experience. It's like I've lived in this tunnel with a light at the end somewhere out there."

Martin found his hand on her arm.

It felt warm to her. Hands on her before had always been threatening. This one wasn't. "What happened? Were you adopted? Did they find your mother?" he asked.

"As a little baby, I was in demand for adoption. Or at least that's what they told me. But for some reason the couple who took me changed their minds or had problems. Before long I wasn't a baby anymore. I ended up being shuffled from foster home to foster home. I never even had a real name until I was three. They tell me the court gave it to me."

"Is Mary Seymour it?"

"Now." She turned toward him and placed a loving finger on his lips. "I'm going to tell you my real name but I hate it. I really hate it. I like Mary Seymour much better. Maybe I'll change it permanently. Are you ready for my real name? Betty Harmon. Don't you hate it too?"

"How could I possibly hate your name?"

Her fifth mug was half gone now, and she realized how maudlin all this must sound. "But I made it—sort of."

"Life must have been tough."

"I guess. I don't remember a lot of it."

"Were people . . . mean?"

"No. There were a couple who were a little quirky. And one guy enjoyed me a little more than he should have. I hated that—hated myself for taking it as long as I did. But I've learned to take care of myself." Another long drink. "It's just hard sometimes not even knowing who you are, knowing there's a family out there, grandparents, maybe some jolly old uncle that I've never met. Never will." She licked her lips and took another sip. "This is good stuff; it's not Groth anymore?"

"Robert Mondavi," he said, his words coming even more slowly. He'd finished his mug and had poured another. "I only have a couple of glasses of this a year. I'm getting drunk."

"Why'd I tell you all that stuff?" she asked him. She looked at him with longing eyes. "It's scary to trust someone."

"I'll let you down. I let everyone down sooner or later. It's a gift."

"Not on purpose, I bet."

Martin winced inside. A real friend would tell her to leave as soon as she could get her things together. Why didn't he? Because he'd be found out and shot, that's why. And she'd be gone. He didn't want her gone. He wanted her right here. "Is it true about your roommates?"

"It is. I let it slip out and then had to adjust the story. This lying gets complicated."

"Where'd you and your roommates go after Napa?"

"L.A. We had dreams of the movies. But trash-babies don't make it in the movies. The closest we got was buying a ticket."

"Sounds hard."

Realizing she'd slipped down on the cot now and her legs

were stretched far, far out, she straightened. It turned into a monumental effort. "I don't want to talk about this anymore. My mug's empty."

"Should you have any more?"

"Of course I should." She snatched the bottle from his hand and poured. The first splash missed the mug and stained his cot. "You men always want control, don't you?"

"Me? I can't control a light switch."

"L.A. was nothing but palm trees and Mickey Mouse and people killing other people or making them do what they don't want to do. Not my favorite place."

"Your roommates must have missed you when you left."

"No," she said, her head shaking in exaggerated swings. "Nope, they didn't."

"How come?"

"I better go," she suddenly said, placing rubbery hands beneath her and trying desperately to launch herself. "I don't want to talk about this anymore."

"Maybe you need to talk," Martin said, eyes focusing as best they could on her. "Maybe that's why you want the wine. To give yourself an excuse for telling me everything."

"Excuse? I don't need an excuse." Anger. "This *is not* fun—like with my roommates." She choked slightly on a tear. "I loved them," she said, her voice straining with emotion being carried forward on waves of numbing alcohol.

"If there was so much love, why do you say they didn't miss you?"

Mary tried again to get to her feet. Bending forward, her head just above her knees, she gave the cot a massive push. Nothing happened. "I think I'm getting sick."

Martin took her hand. "Maybe all this truth isn't what it's cracked up to be." He thought for a moment—an effort equal to Mary trying to stand. "Maybe I should lie too. I bet living a lie could really work. Who cares about reality anyway? I bet I could think up a real pip about all my needs, my desires."

"Desires?" she asked, turning toward him, immensely interested.

"Well, I'm a man. Men have desires. Mine is, well, that I don't want you to leave."

"Leave this whole compound . . . or the basement?"

"I haven't got that far in my thinking. I really don't think I'm capable of thinking right now. Are you capable of thinking?"

"Yes. That's actually a problem." There was something immensely trustworthy about Martin. She liked the name Martin again. It was stronger than Marty, and he was being strong right now. She could say "I love you" to him right now. Of course, it had to be the wine. She always loved everyone when she'd had too much wine. But this was different. He was a man who'd been through a lot, who'd been beaten down most of his life, whose only confidence was in his ability to work with flowers—people defied his understanding. But not all people. He was understanding her. No mean feat there. "I'll tell you why they don't miss me, but you can't ask me anything else," she pleaded, "please."

"Sure. Why not?"

She gulped some air. "They're dead," she said, her eyes dim, but firmly anchored on Martin's gentle face. "Isn't it your turn now?"

"For what?"

"To tell me something you don't want to tell."

"Me?"

"Yes, you. You sit here holding my hand making me tell you things."

"There's nothing. I've told you everything."

"Not about me."

"What about you?"

"Your desires. What are your desires?" she asked with a rubbery coyness.

"I told you already."

"That wasn't a desire; that was just a want. What about your desires? Real desires."

Martin could do nothing but look at her. His mind was both moving in slow motion and racing. He knew exactly what he wanted to say, but it was not within him to say it. He couldn't tell her that from the moment he'd seen her, his heart had been churning. Nor that simply being close like this was nearly more than his heart could take. The wine seemed the only thing keeping it from exploding. As it turned out he simply said, "You're wonderful."

She didn't hear him. Her eyes had closed, but she remained upright. But then, as he watched her, she fell back, hitting her head against the stone wall. "Ooo," she groaned. But she didn't wake. Not for nearly an hour, and in all that time Martin didn't move for fear of waking her. Instead, he held her hand lovingly.

When Mary did wake, she looked at him as if wondering who he was. Finally she smiled as if giving up trying to remember. With a gentle pat on his hand, she removed her own. She staggered to her feet and, surprisingly, made it all the way up the stairs to the door. After fumbling a bit, she opened it and even closed it quietly behind her.

Martin regretted letting her leave more than he'd regretted anything in many years—maybe in his whole life.

Taking the half-empty bottle, he covered it with a bit of foil and returned it to the wastebasket. He then rearranged his cot and nestled himself into it. Although he expected to remain awake thinking wonderful thoughts of her, the wine had other ideas. He fell asleep and woke well after dawn.

Though there was no way for her to know it, Mary woke about the same time, her pounding headache reminding her of her evening with Martin. It also reminded her that she'd talked too much. She'd made herself vulnerable, and her survival depended on her not doing that. That day she avoided Martin.

Mel visited Frank Breckenridge at the apple orchard and made final arrangements for Todd's memorial service. It would be held Saturday morning. He was working on his message back at the tent when Win arrived.

"This is going to be delicate. We've got to think of the living now—tell the truth without offending or driving them away. Delicate," Mel mused.

"Or maybe a different focus," Win said casually.

"Like what?"

"The dead are gone. We the living have a responsibility to

God. That's the message of death. It's the finish line; how we run the race is all we have control over. Actually, we have little control over any of it, but we have to run the race like we do."

Mel liked that. "Good," he said, taking a note or two. Then he had a thought. "Maybe you'd like to deliver the message."

"Me?"

"Sure. You're the youth pastor in this little enterprise."

"I'd say something stupid. I'm really no good in these situations."

"I bet you're very good, but you just don't loosen up and let yourself be. This'll be good for you. The risks aren't that high."

"Just two parents' souls."

"Well, there's that, yes." Then Mel commanded, pushing out the note paper for him to take, "Do it!"

"Okay. But I've warned you." Win put the notepad down and also laid the "tosser-thing" on his desk. "Could you get ahold of that woodworker? I still want to get some more of these." Then he saw the invitation to the wedding lying there. "I promised Ginger," he muttered. Slapping it against his hand for a moment, he decided the time had come. In the next second or two he signed it, addressed it, and sealed the envelope. "You going to the post office? No. That's okay. I've got to visit Bray and take Ginger to the hospital to have her wounds checked. I'll do it."

Ginger's wounds were doing fine. The doctor changed her dressing, took out a few stitches on the minor ones, and studied the major ones. "No infection. Still hurt?"

"Some—a lot."

"They will for a while. The fact that there's no infection is the big thing. We cleaned them out, but we're never sure we got everything. And sometimes the antibiotics need help." He then examined her finger. "It's healing well. Your ankle sore?"

"I've started to limp on it."

"Just don't reinjure it. I'm keeping you off duty for another week. It'll give everything a chance to heal."

That done, they went up to the fourth floor. The nurse at the station said that Bray had had a slight setback during the night. "With all the internal injuries we watch his blood pressure pretty carefully. He had to go in last night and get some patchwork done. Your visits do him some good, so I'll let you in but just for a few minutes, okay?"

They nodded.

Bray was as weak as he'd ever been. His eyes remained mostly closed, and his words were strained. He couldn't help giving Ginger a jab though.

"A detective? You couldn't even find your socks."

"At least I know where they go when I find 'em. People keep telling you to stuff 'em in your mouth."

"Good one," he groaned.

They left his room and bumped into Larin Breed on his way off the elevator. "He's weak. They had to cut into him again last night," Ginger told him.

"He okay, though?"

"Just weak," Win told him.

"Well," he said, eyeing Ginger, "if you have a minute, I'd like to talk to you."

"Me?"

"You told your sergeant you wanted to be a detective. I'm the commander. I'd be the one to hire you. Let's get a coffee."

In the downstairs cafeteria Breed bought them coffee, and they sat at one of the Formica tables.

"You know how this process works?"

"No," said Ginger. She had a good idea. Others had done it. But seeing things work from the outside was sometimes different from going through them personally.

"You're in the uniform division and you want to cross over to the detective division. There are thirteen of us now. No women. And frankly I'd like to have a woman over there. The language does get a little rough sometimes. Can you handle that?"

"I guess—sure."

"You're religious, right?"

"I'm a Christian."

"You're not going to bring in placards or anything?"

"No."

"Good." He took a long drink of the scalding liquid. It didn't seem to bother him a bit. Win and Ginger were both carefully sipping theirs. "I choose my people based on experience in crime scene work, evidence gathering and handling, interview techniques—you have to be a good listener. You listen good? She listen good?" he asked Win.

"Wonderfully."

"Yeah, right." Breed took another drink. "You've got to have common sense. I'm sure there's at least one woman somewhere with common sense—maybe it's you. You got common sense?"

"The commonest."

Breed laughed. "What are you now? A senior patrolman?"

"Senior, right."

Breed nodded. "Good. Well, there is an interview process, with the other detectives and me. Then an oral exam—we go through all those things I just mentioned. Then a list goes up that's ranked. As the positions open, they're filled from the list. I'm probably going to be the next opening when I retire in six months or so. You think Bray will be recovered by then?"

"You're giving it to Bray?" Win asked. "Last time I looked, he thought you didn't like him. Thought you liked Grogan more."

"Well, Grogan did have the inside track. He's young, good. But when Bray did what he did, I realized what was important. Bray's a good man, and good men can get other good men to follow them. That's what I want."

"How's Grogan taking that news?" Ginger asked, remembering Grogan's temper, particularly a moment when it was directed at Win.

"He knows. The last couple of days I've made it clear to him. I might lose him. But those're the breaks. I'll fill his position from the list."

"How many people are on the list?" Ginger asked.

"About two or three years' worth."

Ginger winced. "That long?"

"I'm a popular guy," Breed smiled. "I gotta get going. If you hear anything about Bray let me know. I try to call but sometimes I get too busy."

"Two or three years? Can I wait that long?" Ginger asked when Breed had left.

"If God wants it, it'll happen," Win answered.

"But two or three years . . . Chad'll be in high school. That's forever."

While Gatlin and her father played in the water, Mary sat by herself in her room. She'd picked up *Jekyll and Hyde* again. For some reason, it was beginning to make more sense.

After reading for about a half hour, she set it down and went into the kitchen to get a Coke. She was returning when the door to her shack opened and a woman spun in, closing the door quickly behind her. But she didn't close it all the way. She stood, her back to Mary, peering out the sliver that remained. "Good," she finally said, turning. "No one saw me."

It was the woman with the gray streak in her hair. The one who had told Mary that Ram had killed his wife.

Chapter 14

The woman stood there for a moment just looking at Mary. It was as if she were finalizing something she'd come to say. Or deciding whether she wanted to say it all.

A half hour later the woman left.

Mary was devastated.

It was as if nitroglycerin had gone off in her stomach.

The woman had spoken quickly. Nonstop really. She had no time for questions. She had something to say, and she had to say it. The other five women at the Inn knew Mary wasn't one of them. They'd compared notes, and they knew. The other four didn't want to say anything. It wasn't their problem. But it was hers, the woman with the gray streak—no names, please.

She, Mary, had to leave. "You have to escape right now before you either become one of us—or die. All the men here are part of a crime family—no names, please—they kill people, they deal in drugs and prostitution and whatever else turns a buck. They have wives and lovers and girlfriends. I've been all three at one time or another, and I don't want any of that for you.

"From the moment you walked in here I've been trying to get up the nerve to warn you. You have to get out. Now. Maybe wait 'til dark. But no longer. And don't cross over the grass, there's a lookout. Go through that window right there. But go."

The woman left Mary mute—and shocked.

It was all true. She knew it was. The dark skinny guy with the hollow eyes, Ram's gruff authority. It was like back in L.A.

How could she have been so wrong? Everything looked so safe, yet all the while she was back in the fire—a hotter fire than before.

She'd been betrayed. Martin could have warned her. He could have given her all the details when they were down in his basement. He could have laid it all out. Well, he had, but indirectly—those references to her leaving—that was a poor attempt. Of course, he might have been in terrible danger too. Had she left, they might have blamed him.

Then she'd nearly fallen for a killer—Ram Lucha. She had mistaken cunning for charm and swallowed his lies whole. *Mining! What a crock!*

But how could she have known beforehand? It was the lake. Its beauty, the water, the cool breezes—even the hot nights were tempered by the endless water. It had seduced her, lulled her. And she'd let it. She'd failed to be vigilant. There was only one person taking care of her—herself—and that's who she had to watch out for now.

Escape was her only out.

The woman had suggested the window above the kitchen sink. She'd be shielded from view, but what happened after that? She couldn't swim across the lake. She was a recreational swimmer, not an Olympian. She might be able to sneak around the edge of the inn and make it to the road, but they'd be looking along the road and people would see her.

But even if she could get away, where would she go? As soon as she left here, she'd be wanted on both coasts by people who would kill her on sight. She'd have to make her way to middle America—a farm in Iowa or Kansas. Or maybe a remote sheep ranch in Idaho. She suddenly hoped she wasn't allergic to wool.

What if she worked her way along the water and used the road only when absolutely necessary? That might work. There was still a half-moon to navigate by and lots of trees and rocks to hide behind. Okay, that's what she'd do.

What about Gatlin?

Did she know her dad was a hired killer? Why would Ram tell her? Some of these guys actually have family lives. She saw it on PBS. Their wives think they go to the office every day and tell office jokes and worry about deadlines and getting raises. But these guys weren't the ones PBS was talking about. There were no families here.

No, Gatlin was on her own. She'd been okay so far. She'd survive—just as Betty had.

What about the police? Nope. No police. She didn't know anything to tell them, nothing but the rantings of a woman with a gray streak in her hair.

Choices depleted, heart thundering, breath coming in quickly labored gasps, she waited for sunset. Then, when the brush of red had faded to gray, she turned her radio and all the lights on. Making sure her jacket was visible through a break in the curtain, she stuffed her knapsack with everything she came with, plus some of her new clothing. Then after kissing her little clown on the top of the head, she placed it gently on top and zipped it up. She opened the back window above the sink and with great difficulty climbed out and dropped to the narrow ledge of shale below.

"I sure didn't like the way Bray looked today," Win said at dinner.

"You want to go visit him again?" Ginger asked, limping sans crutches to the refrigerator. Win had been doing all the cooking, and now that she could get around, she insisted on helping.

"After dinner."

"What are you going to say at Todd's service?" Chad asked, a white milk mustache on his face.

"I'm working on it. As Mel says, it's delicate."

"I sure wouldn't know what to say," Chad said.

Ginger returned to the table with another lemonade. "It's a tough one," she said to Chad.

"I'll let you know as soon as I do," Win said. "In the meantime, help me with the dishes. I'm feeling incredibly guilty watching your mother hobble around like that."

"Why do you think I do it?" Ginger pointed out.

Mike Grogan sat at the bar—his favorite bar. The bartender knew him there, had served him many times. The regulars knew him, too, and though there were only a couple there now, that would be enough. They'd be his witnesses, attesting, if need be, that he'd been sitting there all night. After about fifteen minutes and a couple of beers, he began joking with the bartender before settling in to watching the Red Sox game on the television that hung above the bar. Grogan laughed inside. Sometime tonight a little air bubble would flow into Bray's heart, and the heart would gag on it. The thought alone was better than . . . well, a lot of things. *So long, Bray.*

Ram had hidden the hospital scrubs, name tag, and stethoscope under the Chevy's driver's side front seat. He retrieved them and changed in a wooded area along the way. A few minutes later he crossed the final bridge to the Vermont shore and headed south toward Burlington.

With Win gone to the hospital and his mother doing housestuff, Chad decided to sit on his rock and fish. Maybe his friend would come back. Gosh, she was cute. But maybe her visit to the lake was over, and she had gone back home. Anyway, he did want to try his hand at night fishing again.

The air was balmy, the lake sparkling. *What a great place to grow up,* he thought. "Thank God," he said, his eyes studying the line, his hands sensing any movement. He liked being a predator. It suited him.

After about ten minutes, he'd caught nothing, and the balmy breeze was growing into a chilly wind. He began to think night fishing had some fundamental flaws. He was about to reel in his line when he heard movement just north of him.

Something or someone was coming. Slithering along the shoreline, pushing the leaves and brush aside, it was splashing into the water. At first, Chad's excitement grew. His cute little friend was returning. But the feeling quickly died when the someone lost her footing and swore.

Silently Chad slid from the boulder and crouched behind it. Still holding his fishing pole, he listened.

He didn't have to listen long.

The secret advance of whomever abruptly ended with another, more pronounced splash then a groan of pain and more cursing.

Leaving the pole, Chad worked his way toward the injured person. "Don't worry," he said just above a whisper. "I'm coming." A moment later he tripped over her. Catching himself before he fell, he saw her in the sparse moonlight. She sat on one hip, her injured leg pulled up. She massaged the ankle feverishly.

She spoke frantically. "Go. Leave me alone. Forget you ever saw me."

"You're hurt."

"I'll be okay."

But Chad didn't think so. "Is it broken?"

"Oh, no. I hope not."

"You need to get it fixed. Don't go anywhere."

As she watched the boy run off, Mary knew she had no other choice but to remain. She couldn't walk on the ankle. She'd already tried and collapsed. She needed help.

Ginger reacted quickly to Chad's concern. Limping on her own injured ankle, she carried the crutches with her toward the lake. Standing over the injured woman, Ginger exclaimed, "I know you. You're the woman with the violent husband."

"You're the cop," Mary said, concerned that she'd be slowed down by the weight of the coming questions.

"Use these." Ginger offered the crutches.

"You came prepared."

"Always," Ginger said, as she and Chad helped the woman to stand. "Come on, we'll get you fixed up."

Win spent about five minutes talking to the nurse. Bray had started the day pretty low but had steadily improved. By late afternoon he'd had a good chat with Pam. Now, exhausted, he slept comfortably.

Win thought first about just returning to Ginger's. But then he remembered the little chapel down one floor. Things had been going so quickly that he hadn't had time to commune with his Lord.

Finding the chapel again, Win knelt in prayer.

There had been so many parts of the Lord's plan Win hadn't understood, still didn't understand—why he'd afflicted Bray as he had, why so severely and persistently? Why had he not turned Bray's heart toward the gospel message even though it seemed like a prime opportunity? Why was Todd killed before Win was able to present the gospel coherently to him? So many whys and no answers.

Mel probably hit it on the head when he said that Win was mourning the loss of a friend—the Lord.

In seminary that's how he saw the Lord. As his friend. The Lord was always there for him, and Win was always learning about or praying to him. They were special friends. But now the Lord wasn't taking him into his confidence.

And yet Win knew he existed. The three "spiritual" episodes confirmed it, if there were a need for confirming it. How strange that he'd be touched in those ways—touched by God himself, and then twice by the other guy. Why him? Was he to somehow nurture this gift—or run from it? He certainly didn't want to expand Satan's ability to talk to him. He'd just as soon cut that off altogether. But it was nice to feel the Lord's presence—in any form. So nice.

Win's prayer covered all of that and more.

It ended with a fervent appeal for Bray's salvation and for wisdom to say the right thing at Todd's memorial service.

When his prayer ended, Win sat in the pew for a long moment just wondering where he fit in God's grand mosaic.

Hoping Bray was now awake, Win left the chapel and took the elevator back to Bray's floor.

Win didn't have a lot of faith in his own instincts. He'd never been praised for them by his parents, and, except with Ginger and Chad, had never been served particularly well by them. So there was no good explanation for his relying on them so completely in the next few minutes. Yet had he not, Bray Sanderson would have been murdered.

After stepping from his own elevator, Win saw a doctor step from another. Win instantly thought the man looked familiar. But not from the hospital. He was from a different setting. But where?

The doctor carried the regulation stethoscope around his

neck, had a name tag, and carried something large in his hand, something long, in a case like one might carry—cigars.

The guy from the cove! Sure. It was him. The angle from which Win was looking at him now was the same angle from which he'd approached him on the beach. It had to be him. No one else. And he was going to the nurse's station. But could it really be the same guy? If it were him, why was he here?

The guy nodded to the nurse and continued back toward the patients' rooms.

The nurse seemed to think he was a doctor. But what was in the black case? A gun?

Win stepped up to the nurse's station. "Who was that?" he asked, keeping his voice low.

"A Doctor Williams. He was here the other day. I think he said he was a replacement."

She doesn't know him, he thought.

He'd gone into Bray's room, hadn't he? Without a moment's hesitation, Win stepped around the nurse's station and moved quickly toward Bray's room.

"What's going on?" the nurse called after him.

But Win wasn't listening. Within seconds he stood at Bray's door. The "doctor" had the black case open and a large, wicked-looking syringe in his right hand. There was nothing in the tube. "What are you doing?" Win demanded.

Ram looked up, surprised. This was the worst-case scenario. To be discovered before the deed was done. He's given it a lot of thought on his way up there. When he'd grabbed the needle from an open office, he'd been thinking about it. He decided then that if he were found out, his first priority was to get away. He couldn't be caught. If he were caught, the family would kill him—if the cops didn't. But he hadn't been found out quite yet. This was some street bozo—no—oh, man, it was the guy from the beach, the guy who'd found the key. Why in heaven's name was he here?

"Get away from him," Win demanded. His eyes were on the needle.

Now the nurse was beside Win. "You have to leave," she commanded Win sternly. But then she glanced at Ram and saw what he was about to do. "What are you doing with *that?* That's a spinal needle."

That did it. It was over. Ram knew it. With catlike agility, he turned, faced Win and the nurse, waving the syringe as a weapon. "Out of my way," he said.

The nurse stepped back.

But Win didn't. The syringe was so big it looked like a rapier, but he'd had needles stuck in him before, and he wasn't about to let his guy go just because he might be stuck again.

Knowing that his life depended on his getting away, Ram was not about to be stopped. Certain that security would be on its way, his only hope was to get to the stairs and out of the building in the next few seconds. He charged. The needle extended in front of him, targeted at the bozo's chest.

Sensing his own doom, Win saw the needle being thrust at him. Instinctively he brought his hand up. The needle plunged into his palm, the point of it protruding from the back of his hand. A searing pain burned up his arm. The guy shoved him out of the way, and as Win fell against the wall, the guy headed toward the corridor.

His hand burning, the needle still firmly buried in his palm, Win steadied himself and ran after the guy who was headed for the stairs. Win was only ten yards behind him as the guy slammed into the doorway, pushing it open. He slowed down slightly, bringing Win a few critical steps closer. The guy was on the fourth step down when Win burst through the doorway. Without hesitating he launched himself from the landing. His solid two hundred pounds struck the fleeing man in the back at about the shoulders and drove him forward down the stairs. Win heard a *whoomf* as the guy lost all air. When they both slammed against the cement stairwell wall, he heard a sound like a melon hitting the pavement.

Atop a silent, still body, Win collapsed against the wall, his hand, forgotten during the chase, throbbed again.

The door opened above, and the nurse stood there. Seeing Win, his chest heaving, she asked, "How is he?"

That's when Win saw the blood on the wall, a splashed circle of crimson, like a hurled tomato might leave.

"Oh," said the nurse.

Energy sapped, the realization still working its way through his skull, Win groaned, "I think I killed him." Then he held up his injured hand, the huge syringe firmly planted there. "Can you help me with this?"

"It doesn't seem broken," Ginger said, her voice a little less concerned than before. Mary sat on the sofa, her tennis shoe off, her bare foot and swollen ankle resting on a pillow on the coffee table. Chad sat on the arm of the sofa, his eyes never leaving her foot. "But it looks sprained," Ginger continued. "You should stay off of it for a few days."

"I haven't got a few days," Mary said impatiently.

Ginger sighed, sensing the woman's anguish. "At least relax for a few minutes. Let me get you something."

Mary tried to lift the foot, but her ankle cried in pain. She allowed it to sink back into the pillow.

"You could spend the night here."

"I can't stay. I'll rest a minute, then get going."

Ginger sighed. "Have you thought that maybe God's trying to tell you something?"

"What God?"

"I didn't believe in God for a while," Chad said, continuing to study the foot. It was growing red, and the ankle was continuing to swell, the skin shining. "But then I did. I was nearly drowned."

"I feel like I'm drowning too," Mary groaned. "Anyway, God wouldn't do this to me—he wouldn't do this to anybody."

"Sprained ankle? People get sprained ankles all the time," Ginger said.

"Not just a sprained ankle."

"What then?"

"Nothing," Mary said abruptly.

"God sometimes brings trials so that we call on him. He could be telling you to stop—find him."

"I can't stop. My ex found me."

"Jesus will take care of you," Chad interrupted.

"I take care of me." Mary looked around agitatedly. "Where

are those crutches? I'm leaving. You got an ace bandage? Something to wrap and support it?"

"If you make it only a little ways, then fall . . . there are wild dogs out there," Chad stated.

"They're already after me. Please." Mary grabbed the crutches leaning against the couch and attempted to get to her feet.

"Help her, Chad. I'll put some things together for her," Ginger ordered.

Returning to the kitchen, Ginger gathered together some cookies and a pack of gum, along with some other things that might make a dismal journey a little brighter. On the hutch by the dining room table, she found her old New Testament and Psalms. She'd gotten it from her Uncle Joel, the one who'd introduced her to Christ. Maybe it would help Mary. "I'll put all of this in your knapsack."

Chad had turned the television on. "She wants to know the weather report," he explained to Ginger.

The news was on and what they heard made them forget the weather. In the next few seconds they learned that someone had tried to kill Bray Sanderson, that the would-be murderer had been killed himself as he attempted escape. "A civilian interrupted the murder attempt, and in the process of tackling the assailant, slammed his head against the stairwell, killing him instantly."

Ginger gasped as Win's driver's license picture appeared at the upper corner of the screen. "A Mr. Winsome Brady—" the newscaster continued.

"Win?" Ginger gasped in shock. "He killed him?"

"Way to go, Win—Dad."

"Now how's he going to take this?" Ginger asked herself. "Win's my fiancée," she explained to Mary.

Another picture replaced Win's, and now it was Mary's turn to gasp. It was Ram's picture. "We've been given the name of the assailant, a Ramero Lucha from New York City. Reports are coming in that he . . ."

Mary straightened. "Ram?" she whispered.

Ram was dead. At least partial justice had been dealt. Although she hadn't asked for revenge, she'd gotten it. But had anything changed? It would be the skinny boss who'd sic the dogs on her when he discovered she was gone—Ram's death meant there was only one less "dog" to pursue her.

The television showed Larin Breed stepping into a press room, followed by Win. The instant Win came into view, flashbulbs started popping. Win turned his head away to defend his eyes. "Poor Win," Ginger sighed. "This has to be torture."

"I've got to get going," Mary said, reaching for the crutches. While Mary struggled to her feet, Ginger grabbed her knapsack. Unzipping it, she stuffed in the food and the Bible. Feeling the hard figurine, she pulled out the little clown. "Cute," she said and replaced it right on top. "I've put a Bible in here. Read it the first chance you get. I know that Jesus is in there waiting for you."

"They're interviewing Win," Chad said.

Before she had fully zipped the knapsack, Ginger turned all her attention to the television.

With desperate eyes, Win stood before the camera, the mike against his lips. "You're a hero. How's that feel?" someone asked.

Win looked like he was about to say something, but then he stopped. He eyed the newsman as if caught in a moment of extreme disbelief. Then he said, "I can't talk right now. I can't." He walked away while the newsman tried to call him back.

Drawn to the torture her beloved was experiencing, Ginger hardly noticed the woman making her way to the back door, the knapsack slung over one shoulder, the crutches planted cruelly under her arms.

Chad opened the door for her.

"Oh, you'll at least need a flashlight or something." Ginger ran to the hutch and pulled out a drawer. Grabbing a little penlight, she thrust it into Mary's hand, then, with one eye still on the television, Ginger and Chad watched as Mary Seymour worked legs and crutches to steal away into the night.

Win couldn't remember driving home. Nor could he remember walking to the boathouse. Memory returned as he fired up his sixteen-foot Bayliner but then lapsed again until he found himself out on the black water. Feeling a sudden surge of rage, he punched the throttle with his injured hand, a move that sent a lance of pain up his arm. The engine roared, and the boat's nose leaped out of the water, the wake parting behind. But after only a few minutes reason returned, and with it a strange, almost imperceptible idea. The idea was coupled with a memory. A scrap of a memory among much larger, more ponderous ones. He found it hard to believe it would have the *umph* to come to mind. But it did. It had happened months ago, in a moment of extreme duress, yet it rang out in his mind as clearly as if it had happened only minutes before. Suddenly his role in the man's death was secondary to the notion beginning to bloom in the back of his head.

"Sure—that's the only thing that makes sense."

Easing the Bayliner around, he headed back to Ginger's.

Chapter 15

The boss hung up the phone and grabbed his cue stick. But only for support. He hated talking to Grogan—it was like talking to meringue—all sweet and no substance. But at least he was on top of that thing with Ram.

Why would Ram do that? He was always a rogue, but he usually followed orders. Why? Well, whatever the reason, he had to keep the inn out of it.

One way to do that was to just let it lie. Family honor required that Ram be avenged, but the success of this billion-dollar operation meant they couldn't do anything now. Maybe in a few months that preacher would end up sleeping with the lake perch but not now.

If the truth were known, what really preyed on his mind was telling the girl. He glanced toward the gardener's shed. The windows were dark. The nanny was asleep. He'd wait 'til the morning to tell Gatlin—and he'd give that job to the nanny. Then he'd figure out what to do with the kid.

Worried beyond worry, Ginger busied herself cleaning while Chad stood on the dock waiting for Win. He'd called earlier and said he was going out on the boat and that he'd be gone for a while. The way his mother was talking, Chad expected Win to be depressed. A pastor, having just killed someone, no matter what the circumstances, would probably be depressed. But Win wasn't. The way he piloted the boat indicated that. He came barreling out of the night like he was being chased. Then when he was only a few yards from the dock, he powered back and eased the boat up beside Chad. Tossing the boy the line, Win leaped onto the dock before Chad had tied it off.

Hearing Chad announce Win's arrival, Ginger hobbled into

the front room holding a pair of jeans she had found under Chad's bed while she was cleaning. Win was already through the back door. Not wanting to wait for Ginger to hobble over to him, Win unceremoniously scooped her up in his arms and deposited her on the kitchen stool near the telephone.

"What's going on?" she asked incredulously. "I thought you'd be dragging your chin on the floor."

"I probably should be, but I don't have time. We have to go back, just for a second, to those thrilling days of yesteryear before you and I were an item. Actually the day we became an item. When I had that fight with Grogan."

That had been a strange day. Win had come upon Ginger and Grogan kissing in Ginger's house. Because he'd just faced a trauma of his own, he'd exploded and attacked Grogan.

"Remember when he had me on the floor and was pointing his gun at me? Remember that? Then you said something, and he suddenly realized he wasn't alone. Remember what he said?"

"Something about him and me having a good time? I hated him for saying that. As if that's all I was to him."

"Gee, I'd almost forgotten that. How close were you two, anyway?" Win seemed distracted for a moment.

"Oh, shut up, and get on with this."

"I don't remember the exact words, but he looked at you then said something like, 'What's going down is too important,' and he put the gun away and left."

"What's that mean?"

"What was the name of that hotel that burned down? The one he said the key belonged to?"

"I'm supposed to remember that?"

"Sure, you're the wanna-be detective. What did you hear?"

Ginger groaned, but then she put her brain to work. "Okay—Remington—no—Beaverton—Bremerton—the Bremerton Inn."

"Very good. Now if it burned down only three months ago, it would probably still be in the phone book," Win said.

Chad found one in a drawer and handed it to Win.

"If it burned down, they won't have a phone," Ginger pointed out.

"But they would have an address. And we can locate other hotels around it."

Win quickly found at least two on the same street. He called the first one, but they said they were across town from the old Bremerton. The next one he called had been just down the block. "Is there anyone working at your place right now who used to work at the Bremerton?"

"Sure. Me. Good old place."

"Would you describe the room keys for me?"

"This one of the radio contests or something? Do I get a prize for this?"

"Please."

"Well, okay. There weren't any actual keys. We used those little cards with holes in 'em. They worked pretty good. Why?"

"Thanks for your help." Win hung up. He repeated the information to Ginger.

Ginger's mouth dropped and when it did, something else did, too, right from the pocket of the jeans she held in her hand. Even more flabbergasted, Ginger picked up a brass key with italicized numbers. "That's the key! Chad, where'd you get this?"

"Oh, wow. I forgot I even had that. There was a girl I met a few days ago. Out back. Where we saw that woman tonight. We used her key to scrape some prize cards. I guess I didn't give it back."

"Where was she from?" Ginger asked.

"I don't know. She didn't say."

"What woman tonight?" Win asked.

"I'll tell you later. But what are we going to do with this information?" Ginger asked. "The key I found is not from the Bremerton—and it must be from a place that's still operating."

"It's hard to know who to trust," Win said.

"What about Breed? Is he with us?"

"Let me think about it for a minute. We're dealing with some high-powered killers here."

"You're not thinking alone," Ginger said with finality. "Come on, let's go to the sofa, and we'll think together."

Mary struggled. She struggled harder than she ever had before. The penlight held in her teeth, her underarms painfully chafed, the knapsack heavier than ever, her ankle torturously inflamed, she moved with slow, agonizing steps. One at a time around boulders, through groves of trees, often stumbling, more often bumping into unseen obstacles. Each step harder than the last. Each firing a salvo of pain from her ankle to her heart.

But she couldn't stop.

Continued life depended on it. She knew that as surely as she knew whatever energy she had was nearly tapped. That fact terrified her.

Then she fell.

She'd been battling through a grove of maples, down what she thought was a narrow path, the feeble cone of light giving her little more than a hint of what lay ahead. Planting her crutches on firm ground, she swung her legs ahead, but her injured foot struck something—a rock or log. A volcanic pain shot up her leg, all but paralyzing her entire side. She stifled a scream but couldn't keep the tear dam intact. It broke, and they gushed down her cheeks. Standing there, hoping the pain would subside, she still thought she might recover. But one of the crutches must have been on soft ground for it began to sink, throwing her off balance. Instinctively she planted her injured foot on the ground. But it came down on the side of the obstruction she'd just struck, and she twisted it again. No recovery would be possible now. She collapsed, the penlight and some of the contents of her unzipped knapsack spilling onto the ground.

She'd come to the end.

She knew it.

She'd never experienced anything like this before. Her entire life had been one of movement—usually forward. Of escape. Of learning. There was always something coming, something sought, something over the horizon. Even during her darkest moments, there was always hope—a dawn to struggle toward, a better day somewhere out there.

But no longer.

If her life was a path, she'd come to the end of it. If a full glass, the last drop had just dribbled away. If a day, the sun had just set on it. There wasn't another step left in her. If there were a happier day out there somewhere, it belonged to someone else.

It was over.

Her heart felt flat, void of anything that could be remotely perceived as hope. Sobbing, moist earth grinding into her cheek, she lay motionless, as if dead, the pain in her ankle a persistent, merciless throb. Several minutes passed. The pain lessened slightly, the throbbing now a sharp ache. She tried to rise up, her heart pounding, her eyes burning. Through the blur of tears, she saw the penlight lying a few feet ahead of her, its light illuminating a strange scene, one that caused her eyes to narrow and for the first time caused her to drop the thought of pain to second place. It lit a small book, and sitting atop its open pages was the clown, its open arms welcoming her to it. Mary managed a sitting position and leaned against a nearby tree. She looked at the book and the clown sitting upon it. "Home's in there, isn't it?" she whispered. "Did you drop him from the sky for me?" she asked the One dwelling in the book. "Jesus," she whispered, hearing the cop's voice in her inner ear. "You around here someplace?" she asked, her whisper void of sarcasm.

The pages of the book rustled, a breeze having blown up from the lake, the heavy statuette keeping them down.

A curious coincidence the way they fell out of the sack like that, Mary thought, suddenly remembering that her name was no longer Mary, remembering that no name was truly her own.

"Do you know who I am?" she muttered, a little above a whisper this time—the haunting feeling that someone was there to hear.

The pages rustled again; this time the breeze that caused it was too faint to feel.

The pain in her leg was now a swollen, burning ache—the skin felt as though it might burst. Ignoring it, Mary crawled awkwardly to the book, lifted the heavy clown, and cradled it in her arms for a moment. She then grabbed both the book and light in one hand and worked her way back to the tree. Holding the penlight in her teeth and directing it toward the book, she read.

Awareness is a light being snapped on in a dark room. But sometimes the contrast is subtle, for often darkness is perceived as light.

She read several things before the light went on. But the words began to live in her—strange words, words about a shepherd leading his sheep and sheep knowing his voice and hearing when he calls.

Calls.

The word possessed a special meaning. In her mind's eye she could see and hear this shepherd calling, his voice the authoritative essence of love and understanding.

She read further. Jesus was telling the story. Jesus. When the cop said the name it was more sound than substance. Now the opposite was true. A tear broke from the corner of her eye. She wasn't sure where it came from. With all the tears of pain she'd shed, this one was as different from those as water from oil, as pain from joy. It was a tear of longing, of a child grieving for her mother, her father.

Then she read, "I am the gate; whoever enters through me will be saved. He will come in and go out, and find pasture."

The words cut to her heart like no words had ever done before. She wasn't sure why, but they seemed to have a life and purpose of their own. There was no denying the result. Her heart filled. Less than five minutes before, she had lain in the mud, her heart void. Now it was like she had a new heart altogether.

Hope.

Undirected hope. A hope that existed of itself. A hope for nothing in particular. But a hope that seemed to spill over the brim of her heart and surge through the rest of her.

She read more and more.

Through the rest of John, into Acts, through it and on to Romans. She read every word, quickly, drinking the words in thirstily, in great gulps. "And we know that in all things God works for the good of those who love him, who have been called according to his purpose. For those God foreknew he also predestined to be conformed to the likeness of his Son, that he might be the firstborn among many brothers."

"Called" again.

But now there was something else. He foreknew her. She wasn't sure exactly what that meant, but it meant something very important to her. He knew who she was—knew her before she even existed. Not only had he known her, but he'd predestined her to be part of his family. A family. A royal family. There were so many times she longed to be part of a family, one that cared about her, one that would work to make sure all was right for her, that taught her and nurtured her. Now she was not only known by the king, but she was part of his family.

Or was she?

These words referred only to those who called upon Jesus for salvation. She hadn't done that yet. What did it mean?

She thumbed back to Acts. She remembered reading something early in that book. Yes, chapter two. Peter's sermon. It was all there. And there was that word again, "*Repent* and be baptized, every one of you, in the name of Jesus Christ for the forgiveness of your sins. And you will receive the gift of the Holy Spirit. The promise is for you and your children and for all who are far off—for all whom the Lord our God will call." Repent. Call.

She was being called—called to repent. Called to be his.

There was no doubt in her heart.

"I've lived my life lost—like in a desert or something. I lie—all the time—to get what I want. I didn't think you'd get it for me. I'm sorry, Jesus. I'm so sorry. Forgive me. Please. You know me. You know all my wrinkles. Can I know you too? My heart is so full." She began to weep, and tears rolled freely down her cheeks and neck, her throbbing leg forgotten. "I need you. I want to be in your family. I truly do. My heart feels so full. I want to know you—all about you. Love me, Lord. Please love me."

She spoke to the night, the trees, the lake beyond, eyes open, unashamed, knowing she was being heard.

Things were different now. She wasn't sure how different. But she knew she believed. Believed in God—Father, Son, and

Holy Spirit. She also believed that even though she didn't know what was in it, everything in the book she held was true.

And because it was true and because she needed to know, she continued to read. She stopped reading when she came to 1 Corinthians 13. She read it three times, and at the end of the third, she knew what she had to do. As she read, she thought of only one person—Gatlin. Love "bears all things, believes all things, hopes all things, endures all things."

She had to go back. She couldn't leave Gatlin in that "family's" hands. To end up desperate like that woman's life had been. *But they'll kill you. What good will you be to Gatlin then? Or anyone else for that matter. Keep running. God will use you somewhere else.*

It was nearly an audible voice, the words popping in her brain like a string of firecrackers. They probably *would* kill her. But maybe they didn't even know she was gone yet.

Sure they know. Keep running. God didn't reveal himself to you to just have you slaughtered.

Keep running. The words played again and again, and each time they cemented her resolve to return. The people of God she'd already read about in these pages never ran. Peter faced death a number of times, Paul more times than she could count.

But she was still frightened. Fear descended from the darkness like tendrils of moss from the trees, seeking her out. It found her. In near panic she began reading again. This time, firmly believing her strength came from the words written there and that she was being guided, she thumbed ahead scanning for passages. She found several, but her terror only melted before the fire of faith when she got to Philippians 4. "Be anxious for nothing—"

Prayer. She had to lay it before her new God, before Jesus.

When she had, her resolve had hardened to steel, its edge sharp and glistening.

Gatlin needed her. She was a child among wolves. But more important than her circumstance was the fact that just as Mary knew she'd been called into God's family, she was now being called to Gatlin's side.

Slipping the small Bible and the clown back in her knapsack

and zipping it up, she worked herself back onto her crutches. "Okay, let's put all this to the test. Ready, Lord?"

She took her first step back toward the inn, then she took another and another. A few minutes later she was moving with assured agony.

"Commander Breed, it's Ginger Glasgow," Ginger said into the phone, trying to sound as official as she could.

"Listen Ginger, I don't make any decisions about detectives until—"

"No. It's not about that. It's about Win and that guy he detoured tonight."

"I'm sorry, I didn't even think about that. I just left Grogan at the hospital. He's heading up that investigation. Working like a beaver since I told him Bray—well, that's not important. What about Win?"

"I think we have some important information."

"What?"

"Meet us down at the Winooski station in about fifteen minutes."

"Morning's not good enough?"

"Not good enough. And once we verify a suspicion, you'll agree with us."

Twenty minutes later, Win and Ginger pulled up to the blue checkered building. Breed was already there. "You're late."

"Chief," Win began, sounding a little more familiar than Breed liked, but he shrugged it off. This preacher had saved Bray. "I need to see Grogan's report on what was found at Todd Breckenridge's murder site."

"Grogan's? Why?"

"I'll tell you after I read it."

Breed went to the files and, after fingering through it, produced a typed report several pages long. Win didn't read it all but turned immediately to the list. After reading it once, he read it again. He straightened and sighed. "It didn't work."

"What do you mean, it didn't work?" Breed said.

"I can't find anything missing. I mean it might be there, but it doesn't come to mind."

"What's this all about? You been drinking or something?"

That did it. Win grabbed the page again. A moment later he exclaimed, "I was wrong! It did work. There's something missing."

"What?"

"Let us lay a little foundation for you," Ginger began.

She then told Breed about the key and how Grogan had misled them. "But we thought maybe it was just a mistake someone else had made. We know the key is from around here, but maybe it was mislabeled in your box of keys."

"What box of keys? We don't have a box of keys."

Win continued, "Then we thought that if Todd was murdered by someone Grogan was trying to protect, Grogan might try to conceal some piece of evidence. That evidence wouldn't show up on the list. He did, and it didn't."

"What?"

"The swizzle stick. There was a swizzle stick from the *St. Albans*—that party boat. If it didn't matter to Todd's death, Grogan would have included it. Everything else near it was—look—all the trash is listed. So it has to do with the murder."

"You think Todd was murdered on the *St. Albans?* The autopsy came back that he was drowned." Breed was clearly puzzled—and growing impatient.

Ginger leaned over Breed's desk. "I think Todd Breckenridge got aboard the *St. Albans,* took the swizzle stick as a souvenir, saw the drugs it was hauling, and was killed because of it."

"That's why the DEA didn't find any drugs in those power boats. The drugs were on the party boat," Win added.

"The boat that Bray saved," Ginger concluded triumphantly.

Breed looked at the two of them for a fleeting moment, then picked up the phone. After punching in a number he knew by heart he waited for the answer. "Raif, this is Larin. The *St. Albans* docked there tonight? Got any idea how I can get on and off there undetected?"

Mary's windows were dark. She'd left her lights on to give herself more time. Now they were out. That meant they knew she was gone. The boss or one of the others must have wanted her to take care of Gatlin and found her missing. She thought for a moment. She could say she'd taken a walk, hurt herself, and took a long time to get back. Why not? After all, if she wanted to escape, why would she return?

"Okay, Lord, here we go."

Her underarms raw, she balanced on the crutches while opening the door. She acted just casually enough to show whoever might be waiting that nothing was out of the ordinary. She forced herself to make some noise so she couldn't be accused of sneaking back.

Her breath caught. The noise evoked a groan from the darkness.

"Who's there?" she asked, forgetting where the light switch was.

Another groan, then a snoring, gagging sound. Then, "Mary? That you?"

"Martin? Why are you here?"

She heard the sofa bed creak and in the dim shadows saw a lump beneath the thin blanket turn over and work itself into a sitting position.

"No lights," Martin warned. "They'd alert the house. Hey, you're hurt. Where'd you get the crutches?"

"Sprained an ankle. Someone helped me. But that doesn't matter. You'll never guess what happened to me," she said excitedly. "Never in a million years." But then she sobered. "But why are you here?"

"Pretending I'm you. I came to apologize for last night. I shouldn't have let you get so drunk. I've felt horrible about that. Like I took advantage."

"You didn't, did you?"

"No—certainly not. Though you were—are—cute."

"But you're in my bed."

"I found you gone. I was glad—at first—well, almost glad. I knew I'd miss you. But I'd rather miss you than mourn you. I wanted to make sure that if anyone came looking for you they'd find you. I was going to disguise my voice." He forced a woman's falsetto, "I'm just a little sick—nausea." His voice went normal. "If the visitor were drunk, hard of hearing, or just plain stupid, I knew I'd pull it off."

"They would have killed you when they found out."

"But you would have gotten that much farther."

Mary's heart filled. Martin had offered his life to save hers. Unselfishly—more than unselfishly, nobly. Like Jesus.

"That was a very loving thing to do," she said, her voice tearful.

"Loving?"

"Very. And now I'm going to do something loving for you."

Martin yanked the covers to his chin. "You are?"

"Something happened to me tonight, and I want to share it with you. Something wonderful."

"Wonderful?"

"I've never had a family. And from what you've told me, your family wasn't the greatest."

"At best."

"Well—I became part of a family tonight."

"In the woods?"

"Jesus' family. I met him out there." Her heart pounded with the anticipation of telling him. And tell him she did, excitedly, passionately. When she finished, she was sitting on the edge of the bed, the crutches set aside. "And there's more."

"How could there be more?"

"I just have to tell you the rest about me."

"It's not important. Truly. Your past doesn't matter."

"You love me, don't you?" she said, her voice betraying the wonder of what she was asking.

The question should have stopped Martin in his emotional tracks. It didn't. "My heart aches when you're gone," he said, "and it aches more when you're near. I want you safe more than anything . . ."

"But you didn't tell me they were killers."

"You found out."

"I found out," she repeated.

"I couldn't tell you before. They would have killed me. But after the other night, I couldn't let them get you."

"I've got to finish the story I started the other night."

"I told you, I don't care."

"I don't care that you don't care. You have to know all about me."

"Why? What's wrong with mystery?"

"It's important to me—now—so be quiet and listen." She took a deep breath. "I'll pick up from when we were in L.A. My three roommates and I tried halfheartedly to get into the movies. But it was more of a lark than a passion. We didn't get very far. Then Sandy, one of the girls, got mixed up with drugs—crack mostly. She hooked one of the others, Tanya. Billie and I fought hard to get them clean, but before we knew it we were visited by this truly creepy-looking guy. He had this scar that ran from his left eye to his neck. I hated him. He was Sandy's supplier. He told all of us that either we joined his merry band of prostitutes or we'd be dead. Sandy and Tanya needed lots of money for their habit, so they signed on right away. Billie and I, well, we hesitated—but suddenly this guy was beating us up. I'd been knocked around all my life, but nothing like that had ever happened to me. I had no one to turn to."

"How long before you left?"

"About a month. Sandy and Tanya died. It was a suicide pact or a murder suicide. It doesn't matter—they were found in an alley. Billie and I knew we had to get out after that. We put this plan together, but Scarface must have had our place bugged or something because just as we were about to escape, he showed up. I was late getting back to the apartment. When I arrived I saw his car out front. I knew what had happened, and I started running."

"Were you right?"

"The newspapers said she was beaten to death." Mary shuddered, reliving the moment she had read about it. "I knew he was after me. I could finger him. I even saw him once in some small town—he got that close. After that I kept to back roads and lied my way across the country. I used every name and story I thought would get me somewhere. And finally I ended up here. I couldn't believe it. I thought I was safe, but I was right back where I started from. I had to get away again. But this time I ran right into the arms of God—of Jesus. My only hope."

"I have no hope, but you." Martin looked straight into Mary's eyes. "I've been kidding myself. They're not going to let me live. Why would they? I know too much. I knew you were important to me, but I didn't know how much until you'd gone."

"Martin. You need Jesus too."

"He's only been a name to me," Martin said thoughtfully.

"Out there in the woods I started reading the Bible, and I couldn't stop. The words leaped off the page, bloomed in my head like your roses. It's all real, Martin. All of it. And he's real—alive. Everything in the Bible's true. Every word. Finally I just couldn't hold back. I prayed. I called upon the Lord. It says that everyone who calls upon the name of the Lord will be saved."

"Were things different?"

"My heart felt like it was going to burst. But there was something more subtle. It was like I'd been living my life looking in just one direction, then I turned around and there was a whole, big world out there—the real world. The one with God in it. Things were all the same, yet they were never more different. God's here now—with me." She looked firmly at Martin, his features little more than shadows. "I'd like him to be here with *us*."

She pulled the small testament from her knapsack.

"Read to me," he said.

"Read it yourself."

In the pages of a little three-by-five-inch book, no more than three quarters of an inch thick, Martin Sorrell met an infinite God. After no more than five minutes of reading John, Martin was in tears. By the end of it, he and Mary were praying.

She kissed him lightly on the cheek. "So much has happened to us."

"Yet physically not much has changed. We're still right in the middle of some very dangerous people."

"I have to protect Gatlin," Mary stated. "Out there in the woods I knew God wanted me to. I couldn't leave her. She's me twenty years ago."

"Since Ram's dead, things will change. We'll have to keep our eyes open."

"What do you think they're doing?" she asked, her eyes cast toward the inn.

"Drugs—maybe gambling, hijacking trucks, whatever those evil little minds can dream up—drugs most likely."

"We should find out," she said. "Gosh, I feel so strong. I'm a gimp in the middle of a hive of killers, and I feel so strong. Maybe we can prove something, we can get the cops in here—"

"What would happen to Gatlin then?" Martin asked.

Mary ran a weary hand through her short blonde hair. "Foster homes."

"It may be that way anyway. We're not going to be here 'til she's twenty-one."

"I can't leave her. My being here's what the Lord wants. I know that."

"We don't have much choice but to stay anyway. If we left, they'd hunt us down like dogs." They fell silent, and after a moment, Martin gave Mary's hand a squeeze. "Could your ankle use some ice?"

"It aches. Not as bad as before. I'll be okay."

"Why don't you climb in bed here, and I'll get back to the house? It's nearly dawn anyway."

She yawned. It was the first time she had allowed herself to feel tired.

Martin slid from the bed and helped Mary get into it. After he kissed her lightly, he walked to the door. He didn't open it right away but stood for a moment thinking. Then he said to her, "This isn't going to be easy."

"We'll make it. We've got the Lord on our side now."

"Well, then," he said with a forced smile. "I guess all three of us are walking into a meat grinder."

Jason Pipps had been the guard on the *St. Albans* for nearly a year, ever since it had been renovated and put back into service. Although he didn't travel with it when it went on its excursions, he was on board when it rested at its mooring at the village of St. Albans.

Both boat and village lay at the end of a long, irregularly shaped finger of water in the lake's northern regions.

Jason had just finished his 2:00 A.M. rounds, a five-minute walk around the lower deck, and he returned to his place on a padded bench on the bow. He was about to set his wristwatch to wake him up in a couple of hours for another round when he suddenly heard squealing breaks and tearing, popping metal. On the road just above the mooring, two cars slammed together.

The sound was doubly a surprise because there were usually no cars at all in St. Albans on a weeknight at 2:00 A.M., let alone two trying to occupy the same spot at the same time. Mildly curious, he got wearily to his feet and moved to the bow's tip.

There they were. Two old junks. One was buried into the rear section of the other. Two people, a man and a woman, both sounding a little drunk, stood on his side of the cars staring at the wreck.

"Staring at it ain't gonna fix it," Jason laughed to himself.

Suddenly the woman's voice exploded. "Nice shot, ace."

"You turned right in front of me."

"Yeah right. Where was I going—into the lake?"

"Possibly—you sure got the brains of a fish."

"Better fish brains than fish breath."

"At least I don't look like I'm hanging from a hook."

"What's that mean?"

"Doesn't matter what it means."

That's when the woman's car exploded. A geyser of flames erupted from near the gas tank.

The woman started screaming. "My babies! My babies are in there."

Making no attempt to help, the guy stepped away from the car and looked befuddled.

"Please, help me! My little girls!"

Jason Pipps had to act. He wasn't a brave man, but he was a man. He leaped to the dock and ran up the long incline to the accident. The moment he reached the burning car, four shadowy figures darted from the bushes and leaped aboard the *St. Albans*. When Jason got there the woman began screaming at him to do something. The flames were intense; they enveloped the whole backseat.

"My babies, my babies," the woman was crying.

Suddenly another car appeared, and a guy bounded from it with a fire extinguisher. He aimed it at the flames and overwhelmed them with the frosty spray.

While the new guy fought the flames, the woman danced all around Jason, crying and screaming. Finally, when the flames were nearly out, the woman could take no more. She fell into Jason's arms. He hadn't expected it, so he nearly missed her, but he was able to get his arms up and catch her.

"Can you help me, please?" he asked the driver of the other car, the woman hanging from him like a limp rag.

"You seem to be doing fine," the driver said.

"Well, the flames are out," said the guy with the fire extinguisher.

"She said her kids were in there," Jason told him. "Her babies, she said."

"Don't see no babies," the guy with the fire extinguisher said. "I guess I'll be going."

"You're leaving?" Jason asked. "But you can't. You have to help me with her."

She was still unconscious, her bottom hanging near his feet.

"Sorry, pal. I was supposed to be home an hour ago." The guy with the fire extinguisher got back into his car and drove off.

Jason could hold her no longer. She slipped out of his hands and landed on the ground leaning against his legs.

"Well," said the other driver. "I think my car can still run. I don't have all night. I guess I'll be seeing you too."

"You can't leave. You're involved. You can't leave the scene."

"Sure I can. Watch me."

A moment later Jason Pipps stood in the middle of the road, the unconscious woman sitting at his feet, leaning against his legs. Exasperated, he eased himself down to a sitting position so that she didn't fall over and managed to cradle her against his chest.

"Help," he cried to the darkness. "Raif Johnson," he called to the village constable who had to be somewhere. "You need to help me now. Help."

A voice cried from a house about a hundred yards down a dark street, "Keep that up, and I'll be gettin' my moose gun."

Jason Pipps called out a couple more times, but finally gave up. The woman was beautiful, and she smelled good. He didn't mind her leaning up against him. Then, after what seemed like a half hour but was probably only half that, the woman began to stir, and just as she did, an ambulance and a flatbed tow truck showed up.

"Who are you?" the woman asked, eyes popping. "Why are we sitting in the middle of the road?"

While she struggled to her feet, the tow truck driver attached chains to her injured vehicle and started cranking it onto the inclined flatbed.

"I was helping you," Jason protested.

"Sure. Right. What did you do to me while I was asleep?"

"I didn't do anything."

The ambulance attendant grabbed her by the arms and pulled her over to the open doors. They all but threw her inside but before the doors could close, the woman shouted, "You'll hear from my lawyers, you pervert."

"I was only trying to help."

Inside the ambulance sat Win and Larin Breed.

"Did you find anything?" Ginger asked.

Breed held up a Ziploc baggie, in the corner of which was some white powder. "Found it between the boards. They should vacuum." Then he pulled something from his inside jacket pocket. "Ever seen one of these?"

"What's that?" Ginger asked.

"I thought you said you saw this," Breed said.

"I saw it," said Win, taking it in his fingers carefully. "That's the swizzle stick—that's it."

Chapter 16

A knock at her door. Eyes burning from lack of sleep, Mary forgot her injured ankle and swung it from the bed and planted it on the floor. It painfully reminded her it was there. "Yes?" she called.

It was Waco. "The boss wants to see you in the game room."

"I'm just waking. It'll be a while."

"He's anxious."

If that was supposed to make her move more quickly, it didn't. She read the next couple of chapters in her New Testament, then prayed before hobbling to the shower. The morning sparkled with a sense of newness, and for the first time she awoke clean and with regal purpose—a family purpose—one to which she belonged. In spite of her ankle, she emerged from the shower invigorated.

After struggling into a pair of shorts and a sweatshirt, she grabbed her crutches and left the shed.

"What happened to you?" the boss asked.

"Sprained ankle, I think. I fell over a chair, twisted it. I found these crutches in the closet."

The boss waved her silent, impatient to get it over with. "Ram was killed last night. Tell Gatlin."

"Mr. Lucha? Really? How? She'll want to know."

"Why should she care how?"

"Will she be able to go to the funeral?"

"It won't be around here. Probably New York. Tell her we'll send her. You can go too."

"She loved her dad."

"We all did," he said dryly. "He was a peach." His knuckles went white around the pool cue. "Now do it."

Mary nodded and swung toward the stairs.

Negotiating them while using crutches was difficult, but not as difficult as knocking on Gatlin's door. Mary had never done anything like this before—the only good part about being an orphan.

But she did want to be there for Gatlin. She knocked.

"I'm still asleep," came the voice from inside.

"It's Mary. I've got something to tell you."

Silence greeted her—a long, disquieting silence. Finally the door opened. Gatlin stood in the narrow opening. She'd never looked smaller to Mary, her large eyes never more vulnerable.

"Can I come in?" Mary asked gently.

Without reply, Gatlin opened the door for her. Mary hobbled in.

"You sprain it? Trying to get away from Martin?"

Mary blushed, but then sobered as she remembered why she was there. "It hurts."

"Bad?"

"Not as much as telling you this."

"He's dead, isn't he? Dad's dead."

Mary's eyes were near tears as she studied Gatlin's face, then she nodded slowly.

Gatlin's expression remained still, eyes fixed—like one of the dolls in the other room. "Was he on a job?" she asked.

"I don't know."

"What's going to happen to me now?" she asked Mary.

"I don't know. No one's saying anything."

Gatlin suddenly wrapped longing arms around Mary's waist. "I'm scared. I mean, really scared."

"It'll be all right. We've got God on our side now."

"It hasn't helped much, has it?" Gatlin fired back.

"We're still alive. We'll be okay. We just have to take it one day at a time."

Gatlin straightened. "I'll be in my dad's room for a while if you need me." She left Mary standing there.

Win slept like a baby. The problem was he didn't start sleeping 'til after three. And he woke at six, his usual time. He hated that about himself. And why didn't he feel guilt? He'd punched a guy's ticket to hell, and yet he felt exhilarated, like he'd dispensed justice.

After his shower and an unusually long prayer, he heard a knock at the front door. Donning his terry cloth robe, his hair in disarray, he answered it. He was taken aback.

His father, Walter Brady, stood there. In his early fifties, a few inches taller than Win, dressed uncharacteristically in sports shirt, no tie, and slacks, he stood there with what might be a smile. "You're not easy to find," he said.

"I didn't expect you," Win said, immediately tense. Years of failing to measure up grabbed at his heart. Years of having to measure up angered him—almost involuntarily.

"Can I come in?"

"Sure. Coffee?"

"Any decaf? I've been dealing with gout. The doctor doesn't want me to have caffeine."

"I drink decaf anyway." With an expression that was unenthusiastic at best, Win led his father into the kitchen. "Grab a stool."

Walter Brady perched himself on one of them and planted his elbows on the counter. "You had some excitement last night."

"More than you know," Win said, scooping the coffee into the filter.

"What happened?"

Win found it hard to start. He shrugged at one point, but then finally found some words somewhere to use. "I'd seen the guy before. I challenged him. He ran. I slammed his head against a wall."

"Then you're a hero."

Win flipped the switch, and the coffeepot started groaning. "I don't think so."

"You should. You did something brave. I read that you were hurt."

"Just a needle." Win held up his bandaged hand. "It went through."

"Well, I came to see how you were doing."

"I'm okay. Great actually." He was.

The black liquid was beginning to fill the pot.

"The story said something about a fiancée," Walter ventured.

"I sent you an invitation."

"To the wedding? I didn't get it."

"I sent it yesterday."

"Who is she?"

"Ginger Glasgow."

"I mean *who* is she? Is she rich, poor, beautiful, not so beautiful? *Who?*"

"She's great—wonderful. I love her."

"Good," Walter said. "That's good."

The pot was full so Win poured two mugs of coffee. He set one mug before his father and they each took a sip.

"Well, then, I want to help you out with the cost of the wedding."

"We'll do all right," Win said, taking another sip. Writing a check on an anonymous account was one thing; taking money right from his hand was quite another.

"Just a couple thousand. I know you're not making much."

"I make enough." Win lied.

"Take some of it and buy her a nice ring."

Win paused. Ginger deserved a ring, and yet . . . "We've talked about that," Win said. "She knows we're just getting this church going. When it gets large enough, this ox'll start eating."

"I know there's still a position open in St. Louis."

"I like it here."

Walter Brady gave a knowing grunt. After he took a long slurp of coffee, he asked, "What do you feel about last night?"

"How'd you get up here so fast?" Win countered.

"I heard about you on TV. Read an early edition on the way up. I was in Boston and came up on a friend's corporate jet. I'm rich. I do things like that. So how do you feel about it?"

"I'm okay. Surprisingly okay."

"You prayed about it?" Walter downed the last of his coffee.

"That's like asking if I brushed my teeth this morning."

"What's God saying to you in your prayers?"

"God talks to me through his Word."

"But when you pray, don't verses come to mind?"

"No. When I pray, I pray—there's no two-way conversation."

"What about the money for the wedding? I have millions. A couple thousand means nothing to me, and it could make things a lot easier for you."

"I'll talk to Ginger."

"No. This is your thing. I want you to decide."

"I'm not going to take money from you without talking to Ginger first."

"It's just between you and me. She doesn't have to know I'm bailing you out."

"Bailing me out?"

"I know you're broke. Small churches keep you broke. Do you want it or not?"

"Bailing me out? What's that mean?"

"Last call. Yes or no."

"No."

"Well." Walter took another sip of coffee, then set the mug down. "Looks to me like you're coping." He paused. "I'll be coming to the wedding."

"So by flying up here you saved a stamp?"

"You're saying I'm penny-wise and pound-foolish?" Walter Brady walked to the front door and rested his hand on the doorknob. "Call sometime."

"You're leaving already? Don't you want to meet Ginger while you're here? She's a bigger fan of yours than I am."

"That describes just about anyone. Maybe I'll just make the money a pre-wedding gift."

"I don't want your money."

"Sure you do. Everybody wants my money." He glanced at his watch. "They want me back."

"Well, I'll see you at the wedding then."

"You take care." Walter Brady left.

Win stared at the door for several seconds wondering if it truly had been him. Or just a bad dream.

He didn't have time to wonder long. The phone rang. Still feeling like he'd been hit in the stomach by his father's surprise visit, he answered it. It was Larin Breed. Bray wanted to see him.

The woman with the gray streak eyed her in disbelief, and Mary hopped down the stairs on one foot carrying her crutches. Reaching the main floor, she swung along on her crutches, going directly to the basement door. Safely on the other side of it, she faced a choice: get Martin to carry her down or slide down the stairs on her nose.

"Martin, I need your help here."

"Just a sec," he called back, waving her to silence. He was near one of his mini-hothouses.

She dipped her head below the ceiling and watched him. He was listening to something coming from the heating ducts. After another few minutes he straightened.

"What is it?" she asked.

Martin spoke in whispers. "There's a shipment coming through tonight. About 2:00 A.M.," his voice apprehensive. "They mentioned a boat—it's coming down the lake."

"A shipment of what?"

"Whatever they ship."

"Help me down from here, and let's talk about it."

"Oh, I'm sorry." Martin leaped up to her two steps at a time. When they were safely down, after a sweet, lingering kiss, they sat on the cot. "What are we going to do?"

"When's it coming?"

"They said after 2:00."

"That's a pretty good heating duct you've got. Better than some telephone links."

"I wish we knew which boat, but, then, how many boats will be on the lake at 2:00 A.M.?"

Martin eyed her with concern. "Should we tell the police?"

"Would your houseguests know it was us who told?" Mary asked.

Martin took a deep breath. "I don't think we have a choice. It's the right thing to do."

Mary nodded. "It's funny how there's a right and wrong now."

"If it is drugs, which it probably is, people could die if it gets through."

Mary straightened. "I know who we can tell."

"Who?"

"The policewoman who helped me," she said. "She lives about a half hour south along the shore. Has this white wrought-iron furniture in the backyard. You can't miss it. I'd go, but not with this ankle."

Martin pursed his lips inquisitively. "But how do we get me out of here? I just can't walk outside. They'd shoot me the moment they saw me."

"Could you fit through there?" Mary pointed to the window.

Without reply, Martin stepped quickly to the oblong opening. Unlatching it, he pushed it open. It allowed only six inches—clearly not enough room to squeeze through. But after a quick evaluation, Martin concluded, "If I unscrew this latch bar, it might open wide enough. It's a Phillips head—" He smiled broadly back to her. "Our corkscrew."

Finding the screwdriver they'd used to open the wine, Martin quickly undid the latch. As he'd hoped, the window now opened at least eighteen inches. "I think I could make it."

Mary frowned. "It'll be so dangerous for you. I couldn't bear to lose you after I've just found you. Can we pray about all this, please?"

After closing the window again, Martin took Mary's hand. "We'd better. Boy, had we better."

Win approached the nurse's station and found Larin Breed there as well.

"He's still weak," the nurse told him.

Bray was weak. But he wasn't down. The bed was raised slightly, and when Win stepped in, he smiled. Breed took up a position opposite Win.

"How you doing?" Win asked, placing a hand on Bray's. Bray wrapped his hand around Win's. "You've called it right every time. Has Breed told you the latest?"

"Tell me later," Bray said. "Breed says you had a busy night last night."

"Very."

"You saved my life."

"Anybody would have."

"Anybody didn't. You did."

"I was here. I recognized him. He was the pilot of the boat you went after."

"Breed told me. It took courage."

"It took more to do what you did."

Bray coughed. There was something inside that rumbled. He winced from pain. "Now they say I'm fighting pneumonia. It's not a fair fight."

"I've been praying for you."

Bray nodded. "Thank you. Keep it up."

"You believe in prayer now?"

"You saved my life. Pray all you want."

"I will."

Bray took a deep breath, and Win heard the congestion. "This is the second brave thing I've seen you do. Saving the kid—Chad—and now saving me."

"I do what I have to do," Win said slowly.

"What your God gives you to do."

"Right," Win said, thrilled at hearing Bray say it that way. Now if Bray would only believe.

"You live your faith. You believe it, and you do it," Bray said.

"It's all I can do."

"There's more," Bray said, cutting Win off. "Your faith's been true to you too. Your God says 'be brave' and then he comes through."

"He can be your God too," Win said hopefully.

"I just want you to know, I still think it's all poppycock. But I'm not going to hold it against you."

"About Pam?"

"You saved my life. I owe you my life."

"I've missed the coffee and Danish with you."

Bray's head turned, his eyes seemed to fog. "I need to rest."

"I'll come by later."

Win all but floated from the room. It wasn't seeing his friend saved, but it was a good second best.

Chapter 17

Nightfall.

The sunset only a darkening of hovering summer clouds, the light was extinguished, leaving a black and foreboding earth.

"It's just about time," Martin said, eyeing the window and taking a deep breath, his billowing lungs charging the rest of him, particularly his courage. He turned to Mary. "I love you," he said. "Have I said that yet?"

"I'm not sure. But it sounds like the first time."

"I know I've dreamed of saying it to someone like you."

Mary swallowed hard. "I'm terrified. Do you know how many times in my life the things I've really wanted haven't worked? And now two wonderful things have happened to me in twenty-four hours—Jesus and you. I'm on a very tall emotional ladder and I know I'm going to fall off—and *splat!*"

"But we'll splat together. I'm up there too. Maybe higher. Look at me. I'm a real nerd, and someone wonderful like you says she loves me. I'm on the Mt. Everest of emotions, and the snow on that peak is pretty slippery. But—" he found his hands resting warmly on both her shoulders "—I'm willing to trust in a Father for the first time in my life."

It was Mary's turn for a deep breath. "You have to be really careful; scoot along the house, then get to those trees as fast as possible. I know there's a lookout. That woman told me."

They had already pushed a stool to the window, and now Martin climbed onto it and pushed his head through the opening. "I should be back in about an hour," he said.

"I'll be praying every minute of it."

Martin nodded. He launched himself into the opening. When his legs started struggling, Mary helped by giving him a shove. Was she actually helping the man she loved commit suicide? "God forbid," she whispered.

But Mary didn't begin praying right away. After watching Martin fade into the shadows, she decided there was something she needed to do first.

Ankle still aflame, she managed to climb up the stairs to the second floor carrying her crutches.

She knocked lightly on Gatlin's door. No answer. Then she remembered that Gatlin said she'd be in her father's room. Mary knocked there. A tentative, weak voice told her to go away, but Mary persisted.

The door opened and as it swung open on its own, Mary saw Gatlin return to a place on the edge of her father's bed. Mary made out something in Gatlin's hands that terrified Mary, something Gatlin studied as if deciding to make it a part of her—deciding to devour it.

"That's a gun, isn't it?" Mary asked rhetorically.

"A Walther PPK/S," she said. "Dad liked James Bond sometimes."

"Why do you have it?"

"I think I need it. Nothing else will protect me now."

"I'll protect you."

Gatlin looked up with hopeless, desperate eyes. "You're kidding, right?"

"Jesus will protect you."

"You're more likely," Gatlin said, ignoring Mary's words, "and you don't stand a chance against the boss. No. I need to protect myself. Daddy always said that—I'd have to be tough."

"Gat, I know you've been on your own most of your life. That's true of me too. But I'm not alone anymore. The Lord's with me now. He's stronger than any crime family."

"I'm going to join them," she said. "I can't fight them. So I'm going to join them. Which means you can't be my nanny anymore. I have to tell the boss I'm joining him; then he won't hurt me. He'll have to protect me."

"Join them? How?"

"I don't know. But with a gun I'm equal to them. So you'll have to leave. I have to think about things. I have to figure out what to do. Daddy would have wanted it that way. I have to keep myself from being hurt by them." Gatlin's eyes came up, the gun now a part of her hand, its barrel pointed casually, but in Mary's direction, nonetheless.

Heart leadened by an immense feeling of impotence, Mary could only nod. She then hobbled down the hallway toward the stairs. Prayer—for Martin, for Gatlin, for herself. In that order.

"I can't believe it, with all this other stuff happening, he shows up now. Are you sure he didn't want to stay for dinner? To meet me? That's really a slap." Ginger asked, putting the last of the dishes away.

Win had stewed about even telling Ginger about his father's visit and had finally relented at dinner. Even though his problems with his father were not something he wanted to share, Ginger *was* going to be family. She had a right to know about the rest of the family's comings and goings. Win folded the towel and hung it on the refrigerator handle. "That's him, though—control by surprise."

"Breed said he had something special planned for Grogan. What could it be?" Ginger asked, changing the subject.

"It'll be good, whatever it is."

"And he said our work on this would help my chances at making detective? I like that."

Ginger's arms were around Win's neck now, even though lifting her arms caused her wounds to sting a bit. "I've mostly got you to thank for that."

"We worked together."

"I like that most of all."

And they kissed—a real kiss.

"You guys still doin' that stuff?" Chad injected, standing by the breakfast counter. "I can hardly wait 'til you get married and all that kissing stops."

"It better not," Ginger said.

They heard a noise on the back windows.

"Hmmm." Win grunted. "Stay here," he said and stepped to the back French doors. The other two ignored his order and followed right behind. They all peered out into the unusually black night.

A moment later, a handful of pebbles clattered against the glass then danced onto the cement patio. "I'll go take a look," Win said.

"I'll get my piece," said Ginger, "just in case."

She grabbed the leather braided belt that hung by her front door. From it she extracted her Glock, rehung the belt, and joined Win at the back window. Eyeing Chad, she told him to stay put, then she and Win stepped into the backyard.

"Who's there?" Win called out.

A voice rose up from the rocks that lay between Mrs. Sherman's property and the lake. "The policewoman there?" The voice was a man's, softly strained, a forced whisper.

"I'm here." Ginger took another few steps, her weapon pressed against her leg. "Come out, and we'll talk."

"Can't. And don't come too close. Frankly, I don't want you to know who I am."

"Okay," Ginger agreed. "What can I do for you?"

"I have news."

"What kind of news?"

"Of a shipment. Drugs, we think. It's coming down the lake on a boat of some kind at about 2:00 A.M."

Win whispered, "The *St. Albans.*"

"How do you know this?" Ginger pressed.

"I can't tell you," the voice said. "But there's one thing that's very important—life and death, really—make sure the interception looks like an accident. They must not know you've been told about it. Please—will you assure that?"

"Then you're in danger?"

"More than you know. Will you assure it'll look like an accident?"

"Yes, I'll make sure."

"Good," said the voice, greatly relieved. "I have to go."

"I'm sure we can protect you."

"I'm sure you can't. Just do it the way I ask."

"Okay," Ginger affirmed.

Then Win and Ginger heard footsteps beyond the rocks

fading to silence, replaced by the deceptively peaceful lapping of the waves.

Ginger glanced at Win. "What do you think?" she queried.

"His voice is familiar," Win said.

"Who was it?"

"I don't know. But I've heard it before."

"Well, you rack your brain while I call Breed. He can figure out what to do from here on."

When Ginger hung up she joined Win, who still stood on the back patio. "Remember yet?"

"My mind's a blank. I wish that were unusual."

Ginger smiled. "Keep at it. Breed's alerting his people. And Grogan's going to be in the middle of it."

Larin Breed called his people. The plan was simple. With permission from the local constabularies, Breed's people, backed up by some uniforms, would follow the *St. Albans* in silent, battery-powered boats. There didn't need to be many of them. They'd follow it to where it loaded the stuff and to where it let it off. When Breed had that information, he would decide what to do next.

He wasn't anxious to apprehend anyone tonight—or at least any of the unknowns—but he was anxious to know as much as he could. These people were heavily armed, and there was no need to put any of his men at risk without a good, foolproof plan.

At about nine-thirty, just after getting the call from Ginger, Breed made the necessary contacts. The one he especially enjoyed, he made in person. Knocking on Grogan's door, he waited patiently while Grogan fumbled around inside for a minute then opened it. "Larin, what are you doing here?"

"Come on. We got a problem. I would have called, but I was close by when I got the call myself."

"What's shaking?"

"It has to do with all that work you've been doing. I want you to work with me on this one alone. High security stuff."

"I'll get my gear."

Grogan crossed quickly to his bedroom. Whenever a shipment was coming down, his job was to let the boss know if there was any unusual police activity. Not only was his gear in his bedroom, but so was the phone. The instant he went into his bedroom, he grabbed the phone. He was about to punch in the numbers when he sensed someone in the room.

"Who are you calling?" Breed asked.

"Oh, a date. I was to pick her up in about fifteen minutes."

"No time for that. She'll understand. A cop's life and all."

"Right."

Feeling corralled, Grogan did as was expected of him. Breed followed him out the door and locked up after him.

At the police dock south of the isles, Breed, Grogan, and two from the uniformed division, Officers Blake and Sallow, posted themselves in a small guard shack and waited for a call. Blake and Sallow were in dark gear, the word "police" covered by a Velcro flap on their backs.

"What's going on?" Grogan asked.

"It's about that kid's death. We got an anonymous call saying that the killers were going to be on the lake tonight. All they said was that it was going to be late, and in a strange boat. We've got spotters out there looking for a strange boat right now."

"What kind of boat?"

Breed shrugged. "I guess we tap all strange boats on the shoulder."

Grogan nodded. After sitting there for about five minutes, he said. "I need to go to the rest room."

"Me too," Officer Blake said. "This night work plays havoc with my bladder. All the coffee."

"Blake," admonished Breed, "that's already more than I want to know about you."

"Sure, chief," Blake managed.

It was after ten when Martin got back. Seeing Mary's room light on, he slipped through the side door to the toolshed, then to the connecting door. She opened it the instant he knocked. Wrapping arms around him, she gave him an earnest kiss.

"I guess we've done all we can do," Martin said.

"Well—please be careful crossing the grass."

"We'll be okay," Martin said to her. Kissing her lightly on the forehead, he slipped out the side door.

A few moments later, he shimmied through the window and dropped to the floor. Before he could close the window, the upstairs door to the basement opened. Looking up, trying to appear nonchalant, he saw Waco's beefy head pushing through the open doorway. "Just checkin'," he said.

"I'm coming up," Martin said. "I need a Coke or something. I'm close to a breakthrough. I'll be at this all night."

"Roses. What you fairies come up with." Waco's head disappeared.

Martin only smiled, but when Waco left, Martin quickly fixed the window and fell onto his cot, exhausted.

Grogan couldn't believe what he was seeing. In a boat with Breed and the two cops, he was watching the *St. Albans* slide around a small horn into view. They knew. The cops knew. How? What had he done wrong? Did someone turn informant?

As soon as the boom was lowered, the family would suspect him—that he'd cut a deal. His life wouldn't be worth the cost of the chemicals they could squeeze out of it.

He had to warn them somehow. He knew that there was a cellular phone on board the *St. Albans*. It was part of the early warning mechanism, and he knew the number by heart, for he *was* the early warning mechanism. But how to get space enough to use his own cell phone?

Fortunately, he and Breed were not bobbing in the middle of the lake but were at a private dock across the narrows from where he knew the boat was going.

"I really got to go to the bathroom," Grogan said to Breed. "This bouncing around all night's done some terrible things to my intestines."

Breed sighed. "This is technically your case. Don't you want to see the conclusion? It won't be long now."

"I'll be back. Believe me, this won't take long."

Breed nodded and Grogan slipped off into the night. When

he was out of sight, Breed nodded to Blake and Sallow. Less than a minute later the two cops returned dragging Grogan between them. Blake tossed the pocket-size cell phone to Breed. "He was using this."

Breed nodded. "We didn't know what you'd do, so we had a number of different plans in place. We did capture your signal at the cell, recording, and changing the number to divert it. I'm sure the number you called will have something to do with tonight's operation. Won't it, Detective Grogan?"

"I'm not saying anything."

"You don't have to," Breed said, returning his attention to the operation at hand.

A few minutes later, in a clearing a little north of Sorrell's Inn, Breed watched as a flat launch appeared from the shore and began accepting large bales from the *St. Albans*. "It's right out in the open!" Breed exclaimed. "I guess like any cargo. No one would care."

Blake peered through binoculars, watching every detail of the operation. After a few more minutes, after Grogan had been cuffed and dragged to a nearby police car, he turned to Breed. "They're loading it into a couple of pretty distinctive trucks, Chief. I bet we could have it intercepted down the line without jeopardizing continued surveillance here."

"What kind of truck?"

"Flatbed—chickens—cages of chickens around a cocaine core."

Breed smiled. "Have 'em stopped to make sure none of them chickens got three legs—that'll work."

Martin had no idea how long he'd slept, but however long, sleeping was over. Suddenly hands grabbed him by the arms and neck; they wrenched his clothing and ripped it. Voices growled and barked at him. At first he thought it a terribly violent dream, but it was all too real. Hands grabbed a leg and dragged him from his cot, the cot overturning as his bedding followed. His head hit the cement floor—hard. He found his voice and cried a shocked protest, but the only reply he got were more hands tearing at his neck, pulling him roughly to his feet.

"What's going—"

"Shut up," someone barked.

His eyes struggled open and he saw blurred visions. Men—one he thought was the boss, but he wasn't sure. His head was whipped around as they forced him upright. "What are you—"

A thick hand slapped him against the temple. A sharp pain shot through his head.

"Tie him to the beam," someone barked.

Rope was wrapped savagely around his hands, then thrown over a wooden beam. He was hoisted up so his feet dangled above the floor. Someone struck him again, this time in the side. He cried out in pain but then realized how wimpy he sounded. He stiffened his resolve. Whatever was going to happen, he was going to take it like a man—certainly keeping Mary out of it.

But suddenly there was no way to do that. The door at the top of the basement stairs flew open, and Mary appeared. Both arms were pinned behind her back, and some guy pushed her violently, several steps at a time. When she reached the floor, she was thrown roughly to a chair. "Oh, Martin," she cried, "what's happening?"

"Shut up," a voice barked—it was the boss. He stood between them, looking at each as he spoke. "We lost a shipment last night. Two tons. A hundred and sixty million dollars." Pointing at Mary, he said, "You're going to tell us what you had to do with that. Or he's going to be a lot shorter."

At that instant one of the men opened a yellow case he'd been carrying. He pulled out a chain saw, and fired it up. The growl filled the basement like the cry of a hungry animal.

Win bolted upright. He remembered. Somewhere in his sleep, down some hidden corridor his mind had taken, he'd come in contact with the memory. He'd heard the voice only a couple of times at Sugar Steeple—no wonder he couldn't remember it.

Grabbing the phone on his bed fender, he dialed Breed at

home. He didn't find him there so he dialed 911. They found him.

"It's Martin Sorrell. The guy at the lake. They must be at the Sorrell place. It all fits. The drop-off was near the inn. Everything's changed there. And you'd better go quickly. I'm afraid they're not going to let him get away with what he did."

Breed, still tired from a night of making sure Grogan remained someplace airtight while they tried to figure out what to do next, welcomed the news. He didn't welcome having to move quickly. All that was beat out of him. But he did. Within seconds, several cars were on their way to Martin Sorrell's Inn.

"Please," Mary cried. "We didn't do anything."

"Tell that to the angels," the boss growled. "Show them we mean business."

The guy with the chain saw nodded and brought the grinding blade closer to Martin's calf. He still wore jeans and the material tore as the teeth devoured it. Then blood was thrown everywhere as the blade ate into his flesh. The guy withdrew it, leaving an inch-long gash.

Martin began breathing again, the pain excruciating.

Mary sobbed. "This isn't happening," she kept crying. "Lord, please, this isn't happening. Don't do this to us, please."

"Shut up, and tell me."

"We didn't do anything," Martin gasped.

"Okay, fifty million or not, that's it. Take his legs."

Martin saw an evil smile spread across the guy with the chain saw's face.

Mary screamed, "No, please. No."

"Shut up. You're next."

Martin's eyes widened. "No. Not to her. Please. I'll tell you everything."

Now it was the boss's turn to smile. His skinny face glowed, and his yellow teeth shone like a shark's. "You just did. Do him."

At that instant the door at the top of the stairs flew open. "Cops," the lookout yelled. "All over the place."

Instantly knowing half a Sorrell would do them no good in court, the chain saw went dead. "Stay or go," the boss babbled.

"Better let the lawyers handle it," someone said.

"Cut 'im down. It'll just be his word against ours."

Martin heard sirens, then a moment later the front door exploded open. But for all that, it took more than an hour for his heart to calm.

Chapter 18

Todd's memorial service went well and became an opportunity to witness that Win would have only dreamed about. Not only did the church members show up in good numbers, but so did many others. Including the press. As the news was reported about the Corelli family's activities and that Todd had been murdered when he found out too much, there was a public outpouring of affection for him and his family.

Although he softened his rhetoric a little, Win didn't soften his message. When done, he felt he'd accomplished all the Lord wanted him to accomplish. And he could ask no more of himself than that.

After the service Win, Ginger, and Chad went to see Bray.

"Cheese Danish and coffee—that's progress," he greeted, eyeing the greasy white bag Win set on his movable counter. "I also want the comics next time. But none of that's important now. Tell me everything—particularly about Grogan. Tell me that part twice. And I find two things very hard to understand. Where did Sorrell and that girl get all that backbone?"

"I know you don't want to hear it," Win said, "but the same place I did. The Lord. He brought them both in, and when you've got the Holy Spirit in your heart—well, you do what you gotta do."

Bray nodded thoughtfully. "I have to admit there's something going on. But I'll think about that later. The other thing is how you remembered Grogan making that comment over two months ago—three months ago—whenever? There has to be more to it."

"It stuck with me. After all, 'I can't because what's coming down is too big,' is a weird thing to say. But there was something else. Grogan was the only person who would profit from your death. The assassin just did as he was told. The question was, who told him?"

"But Grogan was a cop," Bray asked, coughing slightly. "Why would you think he'd do something like that?"

"Because he nearly did it to me."

Bray nodded.

"Grogan's singing like a canary too. He'll probably end up in a witness program somewhere," Ginger added.

"Or dead," Bray injected. "You know which one I'm hoping for."

"And I'm going to be a detective. When you take over from Commander Breed, I'll be working for you," she continued.

"We'll see," Bray said, not giving an inch.

"Well, we need to go," Ginger said. "Sorrell's in the hospital here. He got his leg cut up, and he's suffering a little from exposure or something. I just think he wanted out of the inn for a while."

"Win, can I talk to you for a sec?" Bray asked.

Ginger nodded. "Chad and I will meet you at Sorrell's room, Win. Number 230."

When Win and Bray were alone, Bray said, "You did a bang-up job. Saved my life, nailed Grogan. I'm impressed. Better than I could have done."

"When are you going to learn that God is watching out for me? He's real, Bray."

"I'm actually beginning to believe that."

Win couldn't believe his ears.

"Relax. I was speaking philosophically. I got a letter this morning."

"From whom?"

"I might not be going back to the force after all."

"Really? Why? What kind of letter was it?"

"I'm rich—well, comfortable."

"How?"

"My uncle died. I hated the guy, but I guess he liked me more than I liked him. He put an insurance policy in place that pays me interest on a million bucks for as long as I live. That's a hundred grand a year forever."

"Wow—you're kidding! Such a deal. And when you die you can will me the million. How's that?"

"No. That goes to someone else if I die. Someone my uncle already designated. But what do I care anyway? I'm on my way to Florida."

"Florida? I don't like Florida. I like it here."

"And I'm supposed to care that you don't like Florida?"

"I thought we were a team."

Bray grinned. "I guess we are, sort of."

"You certainly used me while you were flat on your back in here."

"Yeah. I did. But staying here with you and suffering through another fifty-degree-below-zero winter versus going to Florida and sitting on a beach all year around . . . which sounds best to you?"

"Here. Be a man." Win laughed. "One thing about that policy. Someone's going to want you dead awfully bad. Who gets the money when you go?"

Bray groaned. "Thank you very much. I hadn't thought of it that way. Boy, have you made my day."

"Well, find out. Maybe you ought to split what you get with him right up front."

"Great. You're just sunshine all over."

Ginger and Chad stood at the foot of Martin Sorrell's bed. His leg was bandaged and lay outside the sheet. Other than that, he looked pretty good.

"I can't thank you guys enough," he said. "And I don't want to be rude at all, but have you seen Mary?" he asked.

"I'm sure she'll be here soon," Ginger answered. Soon after the police had invaded Sorrell's Inn and Martin and Mary were brought to the hospital to be checked out, Win and Ginger had arrived. Of course, Ginger was surprised to see who Sorrell's love was and even more surprised, gratified, and thrilled when Mary told her of their conversion. "It was the Bible you gave me," she'd said. "And your kindness. Can you believe Martin and I are brother and sister in the Lord? If I have my way, we'll be more than that, very soon."

Now Martin pressed Ginger, "You sure you didn't see her?"

"Positive."

Suddenly a distinguished-looking man in a shark gray Armani suit stepped into the doorway. "Martin," the man said.

Ginger instantly saw Martin's eyes pop. "Dad? Why are you here? You buy this place or something?"

"The hospital business can be too erratic. No. Just read about what happened and came to see that you're okay."

"I'm okay. Hurt my leg. A chain saw fell on me." Martin indicated Ginger and Chad. "These are some of the people who rescued Mary and me. Ginger and Chad—this is my dad, Carl Sorrell."

"Nice to meet you," Ginger said, pushing a hand out to him. He shook Ginger's and Chad's.

"You were quite brave," Carl Sorrell continued. "I was impressed."

"With me?" Martin was incredulous.

"You used to run away from things like that."

"Not any more. I've changed."

"How?"

"I know Jesus, Dad."

Carl Sorrell grunted. "Did Jesus put a contract out on you?"

Martin's brows knit. "I got one of those?"

"Word's out."

"There's a word?"

"I'm a billionaire. I hear words. Now we talk your safety."

"I'm okay, Dad, really."

"Not the way I see it."

Carl Sorrell turned toward the door and whistled. Four guys in black jumpsuits with Uzi's stepped in and took positions in the four corners of the room. They looked quite formidable.

Before Martin could comment, Mary followed them into the room. Dressed in a pert, brightly colored summer dress, she looked like only good things had ever happened to her. In one hand was her gilded clown. Tied to each hand, each stem in a small vase, were two roses. Without a word to anyone in the room, she slipped up to Martin and pushed the roses in front of him. His mouth dropped and his eyes grew. He gasped, "A white rose—and the black one?"

Setting the clown and roses on his tray, she squealed, "You did it," she exclaimed happily. "You were so sweet to bring me flowers that first day we met, I thought I'd go back to the inn and get some for you. When I went downstairs, there they were. Side by side. Like the white one was presenting the black one to you."

"God's so good," Martin said, his voice glowing. "I don't deserve him."

"Who does?" Win inserted, stepping into the room.

"I sure don't deserve you," Martin said, squeezing Mary's hand.

"I got another one here nobody deserves," a man's voice came from the door. Larin Breed stood there, Gatlin beside him, eyes wide with excitement. She held her doll, Melissa, tightly in her arms.

"You're the girl with the key," Chad exclaimed.

"It's you," she said. "Wait a sec." She rummaged in her pocket. "I still have these," she announced, pulling out the games cards they found by the lake. "We can share the winnings now."

"I get the Quarter Pounder."

"But their breakfasts are like cardboard."

"Good." Win laughed. "There's a real relationship forming here." Win tousled Chad's hair.

Without hesitating, Mary ran to Gatlin and wrapped relieved arms around her. "Gatlin, you're okay," she exclaimed.

"We didn't even know she was on the second floor at first," Breed said. "We only found her when we did a second search."

"I was so scared," she said, some of the terror in her voice returning. "But then the police came."

"She's going to be a ward of the court," Breed told them, "and I know they'll be looking for a place for her to stay. She might even be available for adoption."

Mary eyed Martin. "She can stay with me. But now that all the 'guests' are gone, I don't think I should be at the inn."

Martin turned to his dad. "Get her a cottage, Dad."

"Get her one yourself. You've got money."

"You know," Martin said to his father, "Mary's probably in danger too."

"You take on the mob and you fall in love. This religious stuff sure works on you." Carl Sorrell then looked at one of the bodyguards. "Protect her too." The man pulled out a cellular phone and punched in some numbers.

Sorrell turned to Win and Ginger. "Ever since I stopped going to Sugar Steeple—for reasons known by everybody in the world—I've wanted to redeem myself. Win, that church of yours will never get through the winter in that tent. All I have to do is knock some walls down and there'd be plenty of room at the inn. When I do, you're welcome to meet there."

"Really? What a wonderful gesture. And it'll save you gas—you won't have to drive to church."

The rest of the day flashed by swiftly as days do when there are few troubles to slow the minutes down. There was a sense of summing things up, of taking stock. Mel couldn't have been happier about Martin Sorrell's offer and went to see him as soon as he heard. Then, for the rest of the day, he helped Mary and Gatlin on their cottage quest. They found one not too far from the inn but far enough away for propriety's sake.

Night fell like most summer nights on the lake—warm, crystalline, with a horizon painted with great brushes of orange and red, splashed with gold highlights, all of it igniting the occasional cloud in a magical fire. Ginger, Win, and Chad sat on white wrought iron furniture silently watching the sunset, sipping fresh lemonade, and batting away the more than occasional mosquito.

"Sorrell's a hero. Who'd a thunk it?" Ginger mused, taking a sip.

"I went through a lot of grief second-guessing the Lord and trying to figure out what he was doing. I can even remember thinking I'd lost him as a friend," Win said.

"So what do you think now?" Ginger asked.

"God doesn't forget his people. And his people all play a role in his plan."

"What about tapping into the warfare like you seem to do?"

"I don't know about that," Win said with consideration. "It's spooky. But it served a purpose. It got me thinking, got me going, got me back on track. It's very eerie though, and I still don't know what to make of it." Win took a long sip of lemonade. "What about you?"

"The only way to get you to do something you don't want to do is nag you 'til you do it. I learned that."

Win nodded. "You're my kind of woman."

"And it got me thinking about my calling. I really do want to try being a detective. And I love working with you. And I love you very much. All good."

"You sure we have to wait three more months?"

"Just three."

Win was now nibbling on her little finger, kissing it from tip to knuckle.

"You guys make me puke," Chad said. "If I ever do that kind of stuff, I hope somebody shoots me."

"Oh, Chad," came a little girl's voice. Gatlin appeared at the side gate. "Can I come in?"

"Sure. Wanna go fishing?" he called to her, getting to his feet and running to let her in.

"Well, maybe. But what's that smell coming through this little window up here?" She pointed to the high, bathroom window.

Ginger's brows dipped inquisitively.

Win turned nearly around. "There is one thing, Ginger, that I've really missed about myself. That kinda impish—"

That's all Ginger needed to hear. She leaped to her feet and ran into the house. Less than a minute later she returned. Hands on hips, she exclaimed, "Winsome Brady, you get that goat out of my bathtub this instant!"

Gatlin, now standing near the table, gasped. "Now I know I've come to the right house!"

"Well," said Chad, "if not fishing, how 'bout a ride on our goat?"

About the Author

Bill Kritlow was born in Gary, Indiana, and moved to northern California when he was nine. He now resides in southern California with his wife, Patricia. They have three daughters and five grandchildren. Bill is also a deacon at his church.

After spending twenty years in large-scale computing, Bill recently changed occupations so that he could spend most of the day writing—his first love. His hobbies include writing, golf, writing, traveling, and taking long walks to think about writing. *Fire on the Lake* is the sequel to *Crimson Snow*. Bill has also written *Driving Lessons* and the three-book Virtual Reality series: *A Race Against Time*, *The Deadly Maze*, and *Backfire*.

Don't Miss

Book Three
in the Lake Champlain Mysteries

Coming in Winter 1997